PRAISE FOR CHRISTOPHER GOLDEN

"A new book by Chris Golden means only one thing: the reader is in for a treat. His books are rich with texture and character, always inventive, and totally addictive."
—Charles de Lint, author of *Someplace to Be Flying*

THE MYTH HUNTERS

"Stoker-winner Golden launches a promising new dark fantasy series with this chiller.... Fast pacing, superior characterization and sound folklore yield a winner."
—*Publishers Weekly*

"Vivid action and snappy dialogue ... A fun and creepy adventure story."
—*Kirkus Reviews*

"The colorful, vividly imagined world and unresolved major plot line of Golden's thrilling yarn make a sequel a sure thing."
—*Booklist*

"A chillingly suspenseful tale of nightmares and childhood legends come to life."
—*Library Journal*

"One of those novels that started off good and got even better as it went along ... a fantasy that didn't feel like it was merely reusing all of the existing clichés in the same old tired manner that has been done myriad times before ... a true classic."
—*Green Man Review*

"In the world of speculative fiction, writers cross the line every day. But when Christopher Golden crosses over, it's time to get on board. . . . Golden's now going about rebuilding everyone's notions of the OtherWorld, the land of Faerie, of Legends. But he's not just reinventing the wheel, Golden is also writing a throat-gripping monster adventure. . . . What's really great about Golden is that he manages to straddle nicely between two worlds himself. Those would be the world of page-turning surreal adventure and the world of page-turning mainstream adventure. Golden manages to snag the most appealing aspects of both worlds and combine them in his novels to make the best parts of each seem new when juxtaposed within his work. Thus, his novels seem consistently exciting and surprising."
—*Agony Column*

"A fast-paced, energetic romp filled with a wide variety of enthralling characters and a history that could take several books on its own detail . . . Golden has succeeded in crafting a story that is at times adventure, mystery, horror, and fantasy, and fills it with believable characters and relationships that make you care for each and every one of them. His gift for getting in the heads of his creations is in top form in *The Myth Hunters* and I found myself coming back to reading this at every opportunity I had. . . . If you're looking for something that's out of the ordinary on almost every level, but somehow manages to also be compelling and familiar, seek out *The Myth Hunters*. You'll thank me later."
—*Horror Channel*

"A dynamite read . . . Golden gives himself a big sandbox to play in here, using the cultural melting pot of the Veil to bring in creatures from many mythologies and religions. He handles these creatures with skill and confidence, and seems to find artistic freedom in breaking free of the 'elves, dwarves and hobbits' or the 'Greek myth' dichotomy set down by Tolkien and Lewis. It's a refreshing change of pace in a genre that often relies on a handful of well-used mythological creations. . . . A journey that many readers may wish to share . . . Recommended."
—*sfrevu.com*

"Pathos is one of the hardest emotions to sustain in a novel of the supernatural, yet Christopher Golden manages it very well in *Wildwood Road*. This is a story bathed in wan November moonlight, a little lost girl by the side of the road, the fey touch of a Ray Bradbury in the haunting.... What I found most rewarding about his style was that he develops his story through his characters.... Subtle is the storytelling of this author."
—cosmik.com

"Christopher Golden has taken what would appear to anyone who has read a lot of horror, a very overused tale of the spooky house on the hill with voices and children doing odd things and blatantly run with it and his own imaginings. It should be cliché and bland, but his style with the pen is just spot-on. His characters are real and palpable. Even his reflections of life within marriage hit the nail on the proverbial head. This kind of horror has a fusion of normalcy and suspense that cannot be quantified by most writers in the horror genre. It just works.... It all makes for the best horror I have read in some time. Modern contemporary horror, fused in a counterpoint with the classic horror elements that will always thrill and unnerve us. A truly great, fast-paced read that hits all the buttons and gate-crashes the reader's composure with wild abandon. Just brilliant."
—*SF Crow's Nest*

"Golden latches on to a very intimate situation that's thoroughly understandable, and makes the fear all the more chilling because of it.... The novel's internal logic is, perhaps, its greatest strength.... Golden is becoming more assured in his plotting and pacing ... and it has only made him a more effective, readable author."
—*Fangoria*

"I'm going to go out on a crazy limb and say that, in my humble opinion, Christopher Golden is the newest Horror/Supernatural master.... The most important thing that Christopher Golden does with his horror is to always go for the truth of the moment.... It is in these truths that Golden excels—the fears of the real world. Never mind the fact that his pure horror knocks the wind out of you just as well. *Wildwood Road,* like every other Christopher Golden novel I've read, will knock your socks off with its brilliant dialogue, truthful characters, and its plot—which always leads you exactly where you would never think you were headed. It's a good read and I promise you, I didn't feel too comfortable turning off the lights at night when I was reading this one—a true sign of a new horror classic!"
—g-pop.net

THE BOYS ARE BACK IN TOWN
One of *Booklist*'s Top Ten SF/Fantasy

"Christopher Golden collides the ordinary and the supernatural with wonderfully unsettling results. *The Boys Are Back in Town* is a wicked little thriller. Rod Serling would have loved it."
—Max Allan Collins, author of *Road to Perdition*

"Christopher Golden is one of the most hard-working, smartest, and talented writers of his generation, and his books are so good and so involving that they really ought to sell in huge numbers. Everything he writes glows with imagination."
—Peter Straub

"Well-crafted ... a nostalgic, unsentimental portrait of adolescence [with a] suspenseful plot and strong atmosphere."
—*Publishers Weekly*

"Captivated me from the first page and did not let go until the last. Mr. Golden is so talented that the reader believes anything and everything is possible.... Chilling. I loved it."
—*Rendezvous*

"Christopher Golden continues to stake his claim as a modern master of horror with *The Boys Are Back in Town* ... a rip-roaring story reminiscent of early Stephen King."
—*Romantic Times*

"Golden takes a truly creepy fantastic premise and delivers in spades; this gripping story is not to be missed."
—*Booklist*

"Rod Serling territory ... Golden takes another step toward becoming a major player in horror fiction."
—*San Francisco Chronicle*

"*The Boys Are Back in Town* is a winner. It is a smart, thoughtful, and delightfully unpredictable novel that does not disappoint. For fans of the fantastic, these Boys should be near the top of the to-be-read list."
—*Surreal Magazine*

"Time travel is usually the stuff of science fiction, but Christopher Golden proves it has a place in the realms of horror/dark fantasy as well. His talent for suspense is razor sharp. *The Boys Are Back in Town* is a winner. It is a smart, thoughtful, and delightfully unpredictable novel that stays with the reader for weeks after it's read. An immensely talented writer who just keeps getting better."
—*Hellnotes*

"Upon completing the final page of *The Boys Are Back in Town*, I believe my heart just shivered a little.... A master of horror and suspense, Christopher Golden does no less than leave you perched on the edge of your seat.... Golden creates characters that sing with reality and make us remember our high school days.... An interesting and complex read, well-written and truthful to its core. Well worth the price of admission."
—*g-pop.net*

ALSO BY CHRISTOPHER GOLDEN

THE MYTH HUNTERS: BOOK ONE OF THE VEIL

WILDWOOD ROAD

THE BOYS ARE BACK IN TOWN

THE FERRYMAN

STRAIGHT ON 'TIL MORNING

STRANGEWOOD

The Shadow Saga

OF SAINTS AND SHADOWS

ANGEL SOULS AND DEVIL HEARTS

OF MASQUES AND MARTYRS

THE GATHERING DARK

THE
BORDERKIND

BOOK TWO OF THE VEIL

▼

CHRISTOPHER GOLDEN

BANTAM BOOKS

THE BORDERKIND
A Bantam Spectra Book / April 2007

Published by Bantam Dell
A Division of Random House, Inc.
New York, New York

This is a work of fiction. Names, characters, places, and incidents
either are the product of the author's imagination or are used
fictitiously. Any resemblance to actual persons, living or dead,
events, or locales is entirely coincidental.

Bantam Books, the rooster colophon, Spectra, and the portrayal
of a boxed "s" are trademarks of Random House, Inc.

Library of Congress Cataloging-in-Publication Data

Golden, Christopher.
The borderkind / Christopher Golden.
p.   cm. — (The Veil ; bk. 2)
ISBN: 978-0-553-38327-0 (trade pbk. : alk. paper)
I. Title.

PS3557.O35927B67 2007
813'.54—dc22   2006024177

Printed in the United States of America
Published simultaneously in Canada

www.bantamdell.com

BVG 10 9 8 7 6 5 4 3 2

For Tim Lebbon, gentleman, scholar, and friend

ACKNOWLEDGMENTS

As always, my deepest thanks to Anne Groell, for finding Oliver's heart and putting it where it belonged, and for all of her inspiration and enthusiasm. Thanks to the entire Bantam team, especially Josh Pasternak and Loren Noveck.

My eternal gratitude to my wife, Connie, and our mad brood, Nicholas, Daniel, and Lily Grace. Thanks also to my entire clan, and to Tom Sniegoski, Jose Nieto & Lisa Delissio, Mike Mignola, Amber Benson, Rick Hautala, Allie Costa, Deena Warner, Kathy Hein, Ross Richie, and Wendy Schapiro, and to all of the members of the cabal and the Vicious Circle, whose support and camaraderie are invaluable. Finally, a special thanks to Peter Donaldson and Jay Sanders for their hard work, friendship, and determination.

THE
BORDERKIND

ire engulfed the church, radiating such heat that the snow falling around it was vaporized instantly. Julianna Whitney stood a moment and stared at the flames eating their way through the roof and licking fiery tongues from the shattered remnants of stained glass windows. Four inches of fresh snow had fallen since the storm had begun, but this close to the fire it was melting away. The dusting of flakes on her hair turned to beads of moisture as she glanced around the little island village.

The church was not the only building on fire. There was another large structure that might once have been an office or shop, whose elegantly detailed front porch had now been burned black, embers glowing in the wood. A couple of small cottages were also ablaze.

A handful of people—no more than a dozen—had gathered in the center of the village to watch the conflagration. They hung back as though afraid the fire would engulf them. None of them so much as looked at Julianna, but she frowned as she studied them. She had seen dozens of small houses and cottages. Admittedly, some of them had looked abandoned, but could there really be so few people living on this island?

The gray sky hung low and heavy, and with the blanket of snow muffling all sounds, the whole island had a claustrophobic feel. When the sound of cracking wood split the sky, Julianna jumped as though it had been a gunshot.

But it was only the roof of the church buckling. Red embers sprayed into the sky.

A strong hand grabbed her arm and pulled her backward, and she turned to glare at the man who'd taken hold of her. It was Halliwell, his sad eyes dark with confusion.

Julianna shook herself free. "Don't do that, okay?"

Halliwell gave her a look as cold as the storm. "You were too close."

Before she could respond there came another crack of wood and then a splintering noise, accompanied by the hiss of the fire. Julianna spun to see the church roof give way and the steeple start to fall. It snapped in two, part of it crashing down inside the blazing ruin. But the top of the steeple struck the ground only a few feet from where she had been standing, the fire sending up tendrils of steam as it hit the snow.

For a moment she could only stare at the ground, then she let out a shuddering breath and glanced at Halliwell. "Thank you."

The detective replied with an almost imperceptible shrug, then turned to survey the village, as though he was back in Maine and this was just another case. Halliwell was thus far doing an excellent job of pretending he was undisturbed by what they had seen as they arrived at Canna Island. They'd come halfway around the world in search of Oliver Bascombe on a journey financed by the law firm of Bascombe & Cox. Halliwell was a homicide detective, moonlighting for the firm because Oliver was wanted for questioning in connection with the murder of his father. Julianna was an attorney working full time as a case investigator for the firm.

Oliver Bascombe was her fiancé.

He had disappeared shortly before his father's murder—gone missing in the middle of the night, in a snowstorm far worse than the one currently assailing Canna Island. Then, on the night of Max

Bascombe's murder, Oliver's sister, Collette, had gone missing as well. There was so much more—theories that Halliwell had, imagined connections to the mutilation murders of dozens of children around the world—but there could be no answers to any of those questions until Oliver was found. The murder of one of its founders had been ugly enough; if there was to be more bad publicity, the firm wanted to be in a position to do some spin control.

Julianna and Halliwell had tracked Oliver here and paid a local man an absurd sum of money to take them out to the island in the midst of the storm. On their arrival, they had been rewarded with a brief glimpse of Oliver as he strode toward them—toward the dock—with the fires beginning to burn in the village behind him. But Oliver had not been alone. He had been accompanied by a man with blue feathers in his hair, an Asian woman wearing a copper-red fur cloak, and a man made entirely of ice.

She and Halliwell had not discussed that particular topic, but she was not prone to hallucination. She knew precisely what she had seen, and that man had not been a mirage.

Then the ice man had stretched out a hand and drawn a kind of oval; the air there had begun to shimmer, and Oliver and his companions had simply stepped out of this world, disappearing one after the other.

Halliwell spoke her name. The man was a curmudgeon by nature, gruff and distant. But somehow the events of the previous few minutes had created a connection between them that had not existed before. For when he spoke to her now, Halliwell seemed almost gentle.

"Focus," he said.

Julianna did. "What happened here?"

The detective glanced at the islanders who had gathered. "No idea." He turned to face them. "My name is Ted Halliwell. I'm a police detective from the U.S. Anyone have any idea how these fires began?"

Blank faces stared back at him. Several people began to whisper to one another. Others started to walk away, eyes averted, as though the last thing they wanted was for Halliwell to talk to them.

Halliwell shook his head as he turned back to her. "Had a feeling that was going to be useless. I know from back home that islanders are xenophobic as hell, but this is different. I think they saw something, all right, and it isn't just that they don't want to talk to outsiders about it. They don't want to talk about it at all."

Julianna glanced at the people. Some of them were no more than gray shapes in the storm. More had begun to drift away, going back to their lives. She wondered if any of them had had their homes destroyed, and what they would do about it. No one was coming from the mainland in this storm.

Embers floated and danced with the falling snow.

"Let's keep looking," Halliwell said. He stared at Julianna, waiting for her reply. When she nodded, the detective started around the church, moving toward the large building whose beautifully carved porch was little more than charred kindling now.

"Wait!" a voice called.

A lone woman strode toward them even as the other islanders retreated into the storm. Her grim features were cast into even sharper angles by the firelight.

"Do you know what happened here?" Halliwell asked her.

The woman ignored him, focusing on Julianna. "You'd be looking for them what came before. The young man and his friends—the fox girl and the others."

Julianna shivered and hugged herself, the thick coat suddenly not enough to protect her from the cold. Or perhaps this chill came from within.

"That's right," she said.

"Ma'am, could you tell us what you saw?" Halliwell urged. "It's not a difficult question."

But the woman only narrowed her eyes and gazed at Julianna. "They've gone. Came to see the professor, and this is what comes of it. Maybe that's the end, though. No more strangers on the island. Better for everyone if you just let us clean up the mess. Turn round and go back to the mainland. Those you seek have gone."

Halliwell sighed and gestured to indicate that since the woman was ignoring him, Julianna should ask the questions.

She narrowed her eyes and gazed at the woman. "What professor? Where is he?"

The woman scowled and pointed. "Continue on the way you're going if you must, but you won't like what you find."

Then she turned and strode away without a single backward glance. Julianna watched until she had left the main square, then turned to find Halliwell watching her expectantly. She took a breath and let it out slowly.

"Let's go," she said.

Halliwell nodded and together they continued on toward the building whose porch was now crumbling in flames. Bits of the ornate woodwork had burned away completely. Railings had fallen, withering in the fire. The flames glowed within the gutted structure, its windows like the eyes of some gigantic jack o' lantern.

The burning church was behind them now, along with the two other houses of worship and a number of cottages. Julianna felt the chill of the storm, the snow whipping around her face as the wind picked up, but as they neared this other fire, its heat made her feel as though the skin on her face was stretched too tight.

"What is that?" Halliwell said, his voice barely audible over the hungry roar of the blaze.

Julianna picked up her pace. Her boots slid in the slushy melting snow. To the left of the burning building was an old rock wall that ran out of the village square, the stones piled up decades—or perhaps centuries—earlier as some sort of boundary. It lined a path. In the firelight they could clearly see a cottage at the end. The little house had been destroyed recently enough that there was only a dusting of snowfall on the shattered interior, now exposed to the elements.

Fire had not been the culprit here. At first glance she thought an explosion had taken place, but then realized that much of the debris had caved inward rather than blowing outward.

Yet she spared only a moment's thought for the cottage.

It was the carnage that drew her attention. In the diffuse daylight that filtered through the storm and the bright glare of the fire, they could easily make out motionless figures scattered on the ground, shrouded in a thin layer of fresh snowfall. Dark stains spread out from the corpses, and already a frost was beginning to form on the puddles of blood. There was something odd about the corpses, but Julianna could not focus on them long enough to determine what it was that unsettled her.

Because there was another corpse in their midst that made her breath catch in her throat. She could only stare at the creature—for she could not think of it as a man—impaled upon jagged stalagmites of ice that jutted from the ground. Thin, frozen blades punctured the creature's leg and side, shot up through its chest and belly and skull . . . and wings.

Julianna could only stare. Though it had the shape of a man, its upper body and head were that of some giant bird of prey, and its wings were enormous, dark-feathered things.

"My God," Halliwell rasped beside her. "This can't be real. None of it."

He started forward and knelt by the nearest corpse, brushed away the snow to find orange-and-black fur beneath, and a snout full of deadly fangs. The dead man was not a man at all, but some kind of tiger that walked like a man.

"You mean like the ice man we saw with Oliver? And the way he and the others just disappeared, like they were stepping right out of the world?" Julianna asked, staring at him. After a moment she glanced at the tiger-man again, and then at the bird-thing impaled on the ice. "You said we'd follow, wherever they went, Ted. You've got a whole lot of mysteries on your hands, not just with Max Bascombe's murder and the little girl in Cottingsley, but with the other children you think are connected to this killer who's removing their eyes. I'm having just as hard a time with this as you are, but you can't turn back now."

Halliwell's expression darkened. "Who said anything about turning back? I'm not going anywhere. I just . . . the world isn't supposed to be like this."

Julianna swallowed. Her throat was dry and tight and she didn't think it was from the fire's heat.

"Let's go inside," she said.

The detective nodded and they started for the ruined cottage. As she passed the dead things scattered around her, she tried not to look too closely, but could not help herself. Some were missing limbs, at least one figure beneath that thin blanket of snow had no head, and one of the things on the ground had horns. There was even a creature that was no larger than a dog, with wings folded against its back.

Julianna hurried on.

She reached the front of the cottage. Where the door had been there was a hole, with no sign remaining of the frame. For a long moment she studied the wreckage, trying to determine how she might safely enter. In the midst of the ruined home, she saw snow-dusted legs poking out from beneath a portion of collapsed roof. Jagged, broken beams jutted out of the ruin, and Julianna thought that perhaps they had come as far as possible. Whatever they could learn about what happened to that cottage, they would have to determine from outside.

"Julianna," Halliwell said.

She turned to see him crouched a short way back along the path and off to the left. The snow there had been disturbed, and as she walked over to join him, she saw that in addition to a small pool of frosted blood on the ground, there was a spattering that seemed more recent, even fresh.

Halliwell touched the spots of blood and lifted his fingers to show that they were smeared with red.

Since they had arrived on Canna Island she had been nearly numb. Wonder and confusion and horror had swirled in her mind, but this was the first time she had been afraid.

"One of those things . . ."

Halliwell nodded. He gestured to the ground and she saw that the path of broken snow—where one of these things had crawled or dragged itself on the ground—went around the side of the ruined cottage, past one of the walls that was still standing. Halliwell started to follow the trail.

"Wait. Ted, please. I don't think we should—"

He shot her a dark look. "What did you just tell me about finding answers?"

Julianna moistened her lips. Her pulse was pounding in her temples as she nodded. "All right."

Halliwell went around the corner of the house. Julianna followed warily, peering into the ruin of the house and looking carefully at the stone boundary wall to make certain there was nowhere for anyone to hide. But the trail continued, the broken snow sprinkled and streaked with fresh blood.

The wall went on perhaps fifty yards past the house, where it intersected with another at a tiny structure built of the same stone, with a roof of cracked and faded tiles. The little building might once have been an outhouse or some kind of storage—perhaps even a workshop—but its two small windows were cracked and covered with grime.

The heavy wooden door hung open. The trail ended there.

"Ted," Julianna whispered.

Halliwell did not even hesitate. He went to the door, tensed as though he might jump aside if an attack was forthcoming, and flung it open. The hinges creaked loudly. Inside there was nothing but dust and shadows.

"What the hell?" Halliwell muttered, and stepped inside, glancing around to be sure there was nowhere for the wounded creature to hide.

Julianna watched him for a moment and then followed. As she stepped into the little building, she peered into each corner and then up at the ceiling. There was a third window at the back, opposite the door, and Halliwell went over to it and examined the frame and the lock.

"Whatever came in here, it didn't get out this way," the detective said.

"But it didn't go out the door," Julianna said. "So where is it?"

Halliwell looked at her, frowning. Then he inclined his head and pointed past her, to the deep shadows hidden behind the open door. Julianna held her breath. If something was back there, she had been only inches from it a moment ago.

The detective came up beside her. The two of them stood a moment and just listened. If something was in here with them, wounded and enraged, surely they would hear it breathing. But there was no sound at all.

Halliwell swung the door closed. The latch clicked shut. If the storm had turned the afternoon dark and gray, inside that little stone house, behind those grime-smeared windows, it was like midnight. It was a mistake on Halliwell's part. If something had been there in the corner, it could have killed them both in the seconds it took their eyes to adjust.

But the corner was empty.

Julianna breathed a sigh of relief. "Let's get out of here."

"Agreed."

She went to the door. It seemed to stick a moment, and then the latch gave and Julianna hauled it open, hinges creaking again.

Outside the door, the world had changed.

The storm was gone, and so was Canna Island. A blast of warm air rushed in to greet them. A light summer rain fell from a sky striped with low clouds, speckled with clear spaces where the blue sky showed through.

Julianna could not breathe.

Shaking, she stepped out of the little stone hut. It stood now at the top of a long, sloping hill of rock, striated with colors like thousands of years of volcanic eruption. At the base of the hill, far below, a river rolled gently past. Some small brush and greenery grew on the banks of the river, but on the other side, once again, there was nothing but rock. She turned in a complete circle. Around her there were only mountains, though far to what ought to have been the south she saw the tops of trees in the river valley.

A short way along the rocky slope was the still, lifeless form of the tiger-man, who had escaped the carnage of Canna Island only to die here, alone on the craggy hillside.

"This . . . can't be," Halliwell rasped.

Julianna studied his face. Tentatively, she reached out a hand to touch him. The moment her fingers confirmed that he was real and solid, she felt foolish. Of course he was real. But in that moment, she had been uncertain of everything.

"Go back," she said. "Go back through."

Halliwell looked stricken, but he nodded and quickly reentered the stone hut. She followed him in. Even the warmth of the day and the gentle rain made her skin crawl, simply because it was wrong. Unnatural.

They exchanged a silent look. Trembling, Julianna reached out and closed the door, casting them once more in the grim gray darkness within those stone walls, behind those filthy windows. She expected to feel cold almost immediately, but the warmth remained.

A terrible weight settled upon her and Julianna bit her lip as she opened the door. But beyond it, nothing had changed. There was the barren hillside and the river below, the summer rain pattering the rocks. Whatever sort of door they had just traveled through, it only swung in one direction.

After a moment's hesitation, she stepped back out into the impossible world. Her heavy jacket was too warm and she unzipped it, then slid it off and dropped it on the ground beside the open door.

She wouldn't be needing it here.

Julianna turned and glanced at Halliwell. She was surprised to find not fear or confusion, but determination etched upon his face.

He stepped out after her, treading heavily upon the rocky terrain.

"All right, then," Halliwell said. "Let's go."

"Go?" She knew they had no choice, but had no idea how to begin, which direction to take. "Where are we going?"

"The job hasn't changed. We're going to find Oliver. And we're going to find some goddamned answers."

Grim silence embraced Oliver and his companions as they made their way along the bank of the Sorrowful River. When they had crossed through the Veil from Canna Island, they had emerged on a rocky slope not far from the water. Blue Jay had transformed himself into a bird and taken to the air to survey their surroundings. He had returned with the news that not only did the river valley become fertile and wooded to the south, but that he knew the area and believed they were not far from a place called Twillig's Gorge.

Kitsune had balked at this. She believed Twillig's Gorge was only a story, a legend amongst legends, but Blue Jay insisted it was real. So they had set out, following the river as it ran through the valley and then into a forest of whispering leaves and cool shade.

The longer Oliver spent in the forest, the more troubled he became. It was peaceful here, even pleasant, but it simply felt wrong to him. It was jarringly discordant, moving from the carnage of the battle they'd fought in his world to the gentle respite provided here, beyond the Veil. He knew that it could not last, that there would be fear and blood to spare in the days to come. But to experience the calm beauty of this wood and the rushing river was unsettling.

They all felt it. He knew that they did. But none of them would speak of it. Blue Jay led the way, the wind making the feathers tied in his hair dance, and he rarely looked back to see that they were following. Oliver and Kitsune were side by side—though as close as she was, still she seemed far away from him. Frost trailed them all, sometimes falling back so far that he was nearly out of sight. The winter man's face was a frozen mask. Icy mist trailed from his eyes, but he said nothing.

Amongst the four of them, fewer than a hundred words had been spoken since they had arrived here. Oliver understood. Jenny Greenteeth had betrayed them, and Kitsune had been forced to kill her friend. Gong Gong, the Black Dragon of Storms, was dead. Professor Koenig, the man they had gone to Canna Island to meet, had been murdered by the traitorous Jenny. Oliver blamed himself for the professor's death. If he had never tracked him down, the old man would still be alive.

But what choice did he have? He was under a death warrant, an Intruder on this side of the Veil. If he could not do as Koenig had done, and persuade the monarchs of the Two Kingdoms to spare his life, he would soon be dead.

Yet Oliver felt certain that the future weighed even more heavily upon his friends than the past. There was a conspiracy afoot in the Two Kingdoms, a clandestine effort by forces unknown to eradicate all Borderkind from the world. The Myth Hunters had been pursuing any creature that could still freely move back and forth through the Veil—from the world of legend to the human realm—and many had already lost their lives. Others had gone into hiding. The Borderkind could not count on aid from the legitimate authorities of either kingdom, neither could they know who was trustworthy.

An underground resistance had begun to form, but those with whom Frost, Oliver, and Kitsune had contact had already been captured or killed. All save Blue Jay. The time had come for the surviving Borderkind to take action. Frost had fulfilled his obligations to Oliver. He would be determined now to discover who was responsible for the slaughter of his fellow Borderkind, to stop the killings and take vengeance. Oliver had to assume that Kitsune and Blue Jay would accompany Frost.

And he would be alone.

In his own world, back home in Kitteridge, Maine, Oliver's father had been murdered by the Sandman, who had then abducted his sister, Collette. But why had he not simply killed her? What the Sandman wanted with her and what had driven the monster to kill their father in the first place, he had no idea. But Oliver had no choice except to find Collette. And that did not even begin to address the question of how he would get near enough to the monarchs of Euphrasia and Yucatazca to prove he was worthy of their trust. Finding Collette had to come first.

Oliver had not yet inquired about the origin of the name of the Sorrowful River, but he found it apt. As beautiful and calming as their surroundings were, he was not soothed. There was room for little else but sorrow in his heart, though he managed to find space for dread.

Soon enough, they would reach Twillig's Gorge and they would rest. And after that their paths would diverge, and Oliver would be forced to make his way alone.

The Sword of Hunyadi hung heavily at his side. Though he had acquitted himself well with it back on Canna Island, he felt foolish carrying the thing. He was no warrior. No hero. He was just a smartass New England lawyer who wished he was an actor.

He wanted to scream, just to break the silence of his companions . . . the friends who would soon abandon him. But how could he blame them? They were in just as much danger as he was; they and all their kind.

There was nothing for Oliver to do but keep walking and enjoy their company until their paths diverged.

Oliver had tied his jacket around his waist. Even with the cool breeze and the shade of the trees, he felt warm, but he would not leave the jacket behind. Experience had taught him that the world beyond the Veil was impossible to predict. He ran a hand over the stubble on his cheeks and rubbed at the corners of his eyes. It had been long enough that he could no longer recall what it felt like to get a decent night's sleep. He would have given almost anything to be able to lie down there on the riverbank, use his coat as a pillow, and sleep with the gentle shushing of the wind in the branches as his lullaby. But there was to be no respite for him. Not yet. Perhaps not ever.

His boots pressed into the damp soil on the bank of the river. He dropped his gaze and watched the water while he walked, wondering again at its name. The river washed over rocks, the current picking up as it ran almost imperceptibly downward, with only the occasional small drop-off or waterfall.

When Kitsune touched his hand, he flinched away.

The sting of his reaction showed in her eyes.

"Sorry, you startled me."

Kitsune gave him a melancholy smile. "You were very far away."

"I've been far away for a long time. Feels like I'll be far away forever."

She nodded. Her red fur cloak swayed around her as she walked. The hood lay against her back, draped in her silken black hair. Her green eyes were like smooth jade. Kitsune reached out to take his hand again, and this time Oliver did not flinch away. They continued like that along the riverbank for several minutes. Oliver took some comfort in the contact, but did not fool himself into thinking that all would be well. Kitsune had other allegiances, and he understood that.

But after a while he began to enjoy her touch and remembered the way she sometimes looked at him, recalled the sight of her at the inn in Perinthia, when he had seen her coming out of the shower, and broke the contact again.

Kitsune did not look up, only kept walking close beside him. She was perhaps the most desirable woman he had ever met—though woman was not entirely accurate—but he was engaged to be married, and instead of shaking his love for Julianna, the wildness and terror of recent days had only crystallized those feelings.

He wanted to say something to Kitsune, to express those thoughts, no matter how foolish she might think him. But even as he opened his mouth, he saw that Blue Jay had paused on the riverbank just ahead.

The Native American shapeshifter turned toward them with a satisfied grin. The mischief had disappeared briefly from his eyes, but it was back now.

"Twillig's Gorge," he said.

Oliver and Kitsune caught up to him and the three of them stood, awaiting Frost. The river turned slightly eastward ahead, and the quiet forest ended in the shadow of a sheer mountain cliff hundreds of feet high.

The river flowed right into the cliff face. Somehow it had carved a cave into the rock, or else the river went underground.

"I don't get it," Oliver said.

"The gorge is further along. Gods and legends, Borderkind and Lost Ones—all sorts of people live there. Creatures who want to hide away from the rest of the world, who don't want to have anything to do with the Two Kingdoms," Blue Jay explained. "There are a few places I can think of that would be safer havens for us right now, but nothing else within easy distance. It's as good a place as any."

Oliver stared at the cave where the river entered the mountainside. Frost could have gotten over the top easily enough, and Blue Jay could fly, but he would never be able to climb that sheer cliff. There seemed only one way to get to Twillig's Gorge for an ordinary man.

As he contemplated this, Frost joined them. Oliver glanced at the winter man, at the blue-white ice of his eyes, but Frost was not looking at him at all. With a toss of his head that made the jagged ice strands of his hair jangle together, he turned to Kitsune.

"You're aware that we're being followed?"

Kitsune nodded gravely. "A Jaculus. It has paced us since the moment we made the border crossing."

Oliver began to glance around, looking first across the river and then up toward the branches above them. "What the hell's a—"

But Frost ignored him, focusing only on Kitsune.

"Kill it," said the winter man.

Coiled around the branch of a massive oak tree, Lucan could not hear the whispered words of the Borderkind below. But he saw the Intruder—the Bascombe—go rigid and begin to look around, and he knew that his quarry were aware of his presence.

His instinct was to attack. His eyes were excellent and he could see the way the veins pulsed in the throat of the Bascombe. He could smell the femaleness of the fox, Kitsune. What Lucan desired more than anything was to launch himself from the tree and plunge straight down on one of them, fangs bared. They would underestimate him because of his diminutive size, and that would be his advantage. He felt certain that he could use his venom to paralyze them, and then twist his serpentine body around their throats, cracking neck bones even as he drew their life out of their veins. He would have dearly loved to put his confidence—and his speed—to the test.

But Lucan had his orders.

The moment the fox raced toward the tree in which he was hiding, he loosed his grip upon the branch. As she leaped for the lower branches, he spread his wings and sprang upward, bursting up through rustling leaves of the oak and taking to the sky.

There were shouts from below, threats hurled skyward, but the Jaculus did not slow down. If the trickster shifted into bird-shape and followed, Lucan could kill him easily. And the winter man was weakened now, and too slow. In moments, the winged serpent was over the top of the mountain and soaring toward the southern horizon.

The Strigae were excellent spies, but Ty'Lis and Hinque had asked Lucan to come himself to be sure that there were no mistakes, that someone was there to report the outcome of the Myth Hunters' attack. Now they and the others would be waiting for word. The Bascombe was supposed to be dead many days ago, and the Borderkind who had allied themselves with him as well. These were simple measures, precautions to be taken before the rest of the plan could be put into action.

But it was too late now. The whispers had begun, the violence would follow shortly, and then there would be war. And in the midst of that, the Bascombes and the Borderkind would be little more than an afterthought.

Yet Lucan knew that, to Ty'Lis, nothing would be as important as the death of these most dangerous enemies. The rest of the Borderkind had to be exterminated, no matter how many Hunters had to die with them. And Oliver Bascombe along with the filthy *myths* he had befriended.

The Veil itself depended upon their deaths.

And an empire would be forged upon their graves.

CHAPTER 2

n the darkness, surrounded by the whisper of the shifting sands, Collette could see nothing except the glowing sphere of white light that waxed and waned and danced in her cell in the Sandman's castle. Sometimes it disappeared entirely, but it always came back. From time to time it would speak to her in hushed tones about her impending demise. The Vittora was a death spirit, forged of all the luck she had accumulated during her life, now preparing to abandon her because it sensed she would soon die.

It had become her only friend.

Collette needed a friend now, in the madness of this impossible world, for she lived in terror, and her dreams were screaming nightmares.

Most of the time she sat with her back against the rounded wall of the chamber of sand, wiping grit from her eyes and spitting it from her mouth. Her scalp itched like mad, but no matter how she tried she could not get all the sand from her hair. Her captor brought her barely enough water to drink, and trying to use it for personal hygiene would have been idiotic. But still, the itch was maddening. Her body had begun to itch as well and the stale smell that came from her every pore made her nostrils flare in revulsion. Collette often took more than one shower in a day. She hated being unclean.

But it was amazing to her how easily she could get used to certain things if it meant staying alive.

Pissing in the corner of the chamber, for instance. At first she had held on so long that the need had brought her to tears. Then, when she could not hold off any longer, she took off her pajama pants—for she was still in her pajamas from the night of her abduction—and simply went where she stood.

She camped elsewhere in the chamber from then on, and that spot had become *the* spot. For a couple of days she had tried to eat as little as possible of the fruit and cheese and bread the Sandman brought to her, knowing that it would eventually mean defecating in the same spot. But again, need overcame dignity. What unsettled her even more was that after she had relieved herself, the sand always shifted and the offending waste disappeared, disposed of somehow.

In a part of her mind that had begun to fray, she had begun to think of the spot as "the litter box."

When she slept, curled into fetal position, the sand felt as though it crept across her bare flesh. At night, the sand was still warm, retaining some of the heat of the day. When the sun was up, however, the heat was terrible. The round chamber was wide and airy, with no doors but a dozen tall, arched windows set at intervals all around her. There was no glass, the opening to the outside world tantalizing to her, but they were twenty-five feet from the soft sand beneath her, and the walls were hard-packed sand like granite. Even in her few hopeful moments, she never imagined being able to climb up there to escape.

The days seemed to last an eternity, and the nights even longer, so that she knew her impression of how long she had been imprisoned could not possibly be accurate. Her body, though, told her the only thing that mattered … it had been too long. The muscles in her neck and back and shoulders were knotted from sleeping on the sand and the rest of her was stiff just from sitting against the wall.

Now, every few hours, she spent twenty minutes walking the

perimeter of her prison, during the day moving from one shadow to another. At midday she always rested. There was no hiding from the sun when it was directly above and it was best not to exert herself then.

After dark, the walking continued.

The sand shifted beneath her feet as she marched on, sometimes stumbling as it gave way. Her arches were bands of pain, but she ignored them. The light of the Vittora accompanied her, hovering up near the windows now as though watching her, and it spurred her on. The walking kept her from withering, from just curling up and waiting to die. She would not surrender that easily. It was both a tiny bit of madness and the thing that staved off the deeper madness that awaited.

Step after step, she followed the circular wall, somehow always aware of the spot she had made her litter box. No matter that the sand drew the shit and piss down into itself, leaving no trace; she still circumvented that spot on her walks.

When she had first awoken to find herself captive, she had found comfort in her memories of her favorite films. Movies were a vital part of her life, so often she lost herself in them, and time and again now, her mind went back to those worlds, to *Casablanca* and *Notting Hill,* to *L.A. Confidential* and *Rear Window,* to *The Philadelphia Story* and *The Godfather.* But the Vittora was inside her mind and heart. It could see her thoughts and sometimes taunted her for her fantasizing about those films.

Love and tragedy: those were the things she appreciated most in the movies. Some of them had monsters, but all of the monsters were human. She'd never had an interest in the other sort ... could not invest any real fear in them, because she did not believe.

But Collette believed in monsters now.

One of them had murdered her father and torn his eyes out, and kept her captive even now. From time to time she would look up and see the Sandman looking down at her from one of the windows with those filthy lemon-yellow eyes, face all sharp angles and fingers like daggers. Sometimes his fingers were covered with blood. He had spoken to her shortly after he had first captured her, but never since.

Now only the Vittora spoke.

"*Put one foot in front of the other,*" it said in a singsong voice that scraped off of the sound all around the chamber, "*and soon you'll be walking out the door.*"

Collette shuddered, eyes moistening. It had plucked the song from her mind, some snippet from one of the Christmas specials she'd loved to watch on television as a little girl. The edge in its voice might have been irony or comfort or mockery, or some combination of all three. Clearly, the Vittora did not think she would be walking out the door, or it would not have appeared. It was the harbinger of her death, and though most of what it said was a nonsense echo of her own thoughts, there was a morbid amusement in its tone that made her want to scream.

But she would not scream.

The Vittora was light in the darkness and meant her no harm. It was not tragedy, but the observation of tragedy. It was the ringing phone in the middle of the night, resonating with dread, but still only the messenger.

Left foot, right foot, she moved in that dreadful circle. Soon she would sleep, but for the moment, she walked just to feel alive.

As much as possible, Collette tried not to think of home, but her thoughts were often untamable. She missed the glory that was New York City: the corner delis and the busy sidewalks, the fountains and the parks. It was winter at home, must be nearly Christmas now, or Christmas might already have passed. She had wanted to skate at Rockefeller Center on the outdoor ice rink there and smell the roasted chestnuts sold by sidewalk vendors and see her breath in front of her and all of the decorations. Christmas in New York could lift any heart.

She missed her friends. Terri Ehrlich would be grieving by now, presuming the worst. She missed her job at *Billboard* magazine and the people there—Lydia and Jane and Elissa and the funny guys in the mailroom. She wondered how long she would have to be gone before they would hire someone to replace her at work, and how long before the people who loved her would begin to lose hope that she might still be alive. She'd gone up to Maine for her brother's wedding, but by now they must all know of her father's murder, and that someone had taken her.

How long before most of them simply forgot about her?

Oliver, Collette thought. *Oliver will never lose hope.* If the Sandman was to be believed, her brother was still alive, and somewhere here, in this nightmare world.

That was half the reason she was here, after all, and the reason he had not killed her yet. The Sandman was using her as bait. They thought there was something different about her and Oliver, something special. Whoever *they* were was a mystery for another day. For now, all that mattered to Collette was that whoever had enlisted the Sandman to murder her father and kidnap her from their family home had done so in order to draw Oliver in, and that if Oliver did eventually come for her, they would likely both be executed.

God, how she wanted him to come and take her away, to save her from this! The idea of seeing him, talking to him, was almost enough to make her weep. But, of course, she could not stand the thought of anything happening to him, and so the other part of her hoped that no matter what they did to her, Oliver would stay away.

Hear that, little brother? she thought. *Stay away!*

The flannel pajamas were all she had to wear—not even panties beneath them—and they were far too hot during the day, though necessary to protect her from the sun. But at night, as now, they were vital. The chamber grew cold after dark, and colder still as night wore on.

Collette shivered and crossed her arms over her breasts as she continued to walk, staggering a bit as a pile of sand gave way.

"*Start spreading the news,*" the Vittora sang, knowing, mocking, and yet somehow sorry as well. "*I'm leaving today.*"

"Shut up!" she snapped, twisting in the sand and glaring up at it.

The light flickered and diminished, the sphere shrinking a bit, as it often did. It even disappeared from time to time, though she could sense its presence. When the time came that it was really gone, she was sure she would know that as well. But by then it would be too late. Her life would be slipping away like a fistful of sand.

Heart hammering with frustration, skin prickling with the cold and with grief for her own fate, she began to walk again, determined to dedicate another fifteen minutes to staying alive.

Then she heard his voice . . . the voice of the Sandman.

"*You see. A Bascombe. Just as promised,*" it rasped, voice grating and cold, words clipped and alien.

Collette halted and it took her a moment before she could glance upward in search of her captor. Her breath caught in her throat. The monster was little more than a shape framed by one of the windows high above, a deeper darkness silhouetted against the night sky beyond. Those hideous lemon-yellow eyes gleamed, reflecting back the light of the Vittora.

For the first time, the Sandman was not alone.

Beside him was a thing whose appearance made her gasp. It was crouched, like a gargoyle perched on a building's ledge, and large, feathered wings jutted from its back. In the illumination cast by the spirit of her impending death, she thought the feathers looked green. It wore shapeless, dark garments that only partially covered its long, bony limbs. Yet what unnerved her most was that it had the head of a stag, with wickedly sharp antlers. Some ancient dread welled up within her at the sight, as though in the primitive part of her brain she knew that this thing was a predator. Beneath its gaze, she felt like a field mouse fleeing from a screech owl.

And there were others.

They shifted in the dark, moving to other windows with a rustle of feathers. There were at least three more that she could see, staring down at her as if she were an animal at the zoo.

What did it mean, A Bascombe?

And what were they, these things that the Sandman had brought to observe her?

The Vittora, shrunken now to a size no larger than a baseball, descended in a gliding, drifting pattern until it hovered nearby, and she heard it whisper. Words. Answers to the questions in her mind.

"*Perytons,*" it said. "*Hunters.*"

A shudder went through her and for a time selfishness triumphed over her love for Oliver in her mind. She knew that if he came for her, it would mean his death, but now that she knew the Sandman was not alone, that he had allies, she felt certain they would eventually find him anyway.

"Come on, Ollie. Find me," she whispered, in a voice that was lost in the murmur of the shifting sands.

If they were both going to die, she would rather face the end with her brother. Nothing terrified her more than the thought of dying alone.

Oliver stared up through the trees as Blue Jay darted down toward them, an astonishingly small figure against the breadth of the sky. The bird opened his wings and glided between branches, not disturbing a single leaf. As he reached the ground, he beat his wings to pause in midair, but for a moment, to Oliver's eyes, he seemed to continue descending. It was an optical illusion, however. The bird was not descending, but growing, transforming into a man. His wings suddenly spread out behind him, enormous, and then they were barely visible, just a trace of an image in the air.

And then gone.

Where the bird had been, there was now only the man. Blue Jay tossed back his hair, the feathers tied in it whipping in the breeze, and thrust his hands into the pockets of his blue jeans.

"Well, that's shit luck," he said.

Oliver might have laughed were it not for the utter gravity with which the words had been spoken. He glanced at Kitsune, who paid him no attention at all. She was scenting the air and studying the branches above, searching for any sign that there might be some other spy about.

Oliver turned to Frost, only to find the winter man studying him as though he were a riddle that Frost could not sort out. Oliver didn't much like the feeling.

"So what now?" he asked.

Frost glanced at Blue Jay. "We'd hoped that Twillig's Gorge might be a refuge for us, at least for a time. Now, at best, we can rest there briefly before moving on. We've no idea who the Jaculus calls master, but the way it lit out of here upon being discovered, we can be sure it means us ill."

"Time to go, then," Oliver said.

Blue Jay frowned, glaring at the sky. "If Gong Gong had been here, the thing would have been dead, and its master none the wiser."

Kitsune lifted her hood, though they were deep in the shade of the woods. She hung her head slightly so that only her perfect mouth was visible beneath the fold of fur.

"Yet Gong Gong *is* dead. And so shall we be, I think, if we don't move now. I am putting my trust in you, Blue Jay, that this Gorge truly exists. And trust is hard to come by today."

"Isn't it always?" the bird-man said, and then turned toward the river.

Just ahead, the woods ended at a sheer cliff face and the Sorrowful River continued right through it, a stake through the heart, into a natural tunnel, perhaps some ancient cave system. The light of the sun extended only so far into the tunnel and then all was darkness. The idea of wading into that river and letting the current take him into the dark was not at all pleasant, but neither was the thought of remaining here and waiting for the Jaculus to return with more formidable associates.

Still, Oliver stood and watched as Blue Jay went to the riverbank and stepped in without hesitation, water soaking into denim, making the legs of his jeans a darker blue. Oliver smiled wistfully. Trickster he might be, but Blue Jay was all right. He could easily have transformed back into a bird and flown through the tunnel, above the water.

When he had waded in up to his hips, the river flowing around his waist, he paused and looked back, waiting in silence. Oliver glanced at Frost, saw that the winter man was watching Kitsune, and looked at her.

She was still preoccupied with the trees, and he understood that she was faulting herself somehow for not having caught the Jaculus. It was not that she suspected the presence of other spies, but that she wished there were more, so that she might redeem herself.

"It wasn't your fault," Oliver said.

Kitsune glanced darkly at him and bared her tiny, sharp teeth. "Go on."

He was about to argue, but Frost touched his arm with icy fingers that sent a shock of cold through him, making his muscles ache. Oliver pulled away, but nodded and started for the water. At the edge he sat and removed his boots, tied the laces together and hung them around his neck, with his socks tucked inside. He debated the wisdom of this for a moment, knowing that the river bottom would likely be quite rocky, but even if he didn't mind soaking-wet boots, they would actually make it difficult to walk, weighted down with water. Using the same logic, he untied the jacket from around his waist, wrapped the Sword of Hunyadi in it, and carried them over his shoulder as he stepped into the river.

Oliver hesitated a moment. He slipped his hand into his pocket and felt for the single, large seed that the gods of the Harvest had given him. Konigen had said it might be helpful to him one day, when he needed it most. The last thing he wanted to do was to lose it or, worse, ruin it now. But he chose to leave it where it was. Better a damp seed in his pocket than a lost seed if he risked trying to stash it in his boots or hold it in his hand.

Frost was right beside him. As the winter man put his foot in, the water on the surface of the river just around his calf formed a thin layer of ice, which broke off and floated away, dissolving almost immediately. Then Frost and Oliver were moving toward Blue Jay. The water turned frigid, the current cold where it had flowed past Frost, and Oliver shivered and let him get ahead a few paces.

Back on the bank, Kitsune spared a final regretful glance at the trees and then slipped into the river. He expected the fur cloak to weigh her down, but the water seemed to run off of it. The cloak began to float, spreading across the river as she waded deeper, and then pooling around her as the current quickened.

"Let's try not to get too deep," Oliver said. "I'd rather stay on my feet if possible."

Blue Jay reached the opening in the cliff and braced a hand on the rock. "I'm with you. The Gorge is on the other side of the tunnel, where it opens up again to the sky, but there's no telling what's between here and there."

Oliver grimaced. "Wonderful."

Then Blue Jay ducked his head and disappeared into the darkness, river and cave both seeming to swallow him. Frost followed suit a moment later without a backward glance. Though Oliver knew that the winter man had a great deal on his mind, still it made him feel more alone.

The water was mid-chest high by the time he reached the opening in the cliff face. The darkness beckoned. Despite his fear, something about it was inviting. The little boy in him, the explorer and believer in all things magical, relished the idea of the place. Sounds of dripping came from within, and echoes of tiny splashes—hopefully made by Blue Jay and Frost and not anything else.

Oliver stepped inside, though still within reach of the daylight.

As he moved out of the sun and into the darkness, the world shook around him, once, twice, a third time. Oliver shouted, his panic echoing back at him. In the diminishing light he could see a shower of dust and small rocks slide down the walls of the cave and into the water.

"Kit, tell me that's not an earthquake," he said, reaching his right hand out to touch the rock wall.

Her voice, when she replied, was hushed. "Worse."

Oliver turned. She had thrown her hood back and her face and body were outlined against the sunlight at the mouth of the cave. Kitsune had turned and was staring upriver.

Perhaps half a mile north stood a creature as tall as the tallest tree—a towering, grotesque, albino giant. Its back was to them and he could see that its spine was a column of jagged spurs that jutted out through the flesh.

"What is it?" he said, only loud enough for her to hear him over the ripple of the river passing around them.

"Kinder-fresser." Kitsune glanced back at him. "Child-guzzler, they call it. According to legend, of course. I've heard the tale, but never seen the thing. The story says that the river is made of the tears of all the mothers whose children it has eaten."

"The Sorrowful River," Oliver said, a tight knot in his gut.

"Must have come down from the hills. Just be glad it's going the other way."

"Why? If it eats children—"

"A flesh-eating giant might have preferences, Oliver, but hungry is hungry," she said, and when she glanced at him there was a lean sort of desire in her eyes that was not at all sensual. He wondered, as a fox, what Kitsune had eaten, then wished the question had never occurred to him.

"Shall we go?" she said.

Oliver nodded and turned, moving into the darkness. Whatever lay ahead, it could not be worse than the gargantuan abomination they had only narrowly avoided. He pitied whatever creature it came upon next.

He waded deeper into the tunnel, comforted by the presence of Kitsune behind him. The echoes in the cave were like ghosts flitting about, whispering in his ears. Distance was impossible to gauge, sounds coming from everywhere and nowhere at once. Oliver rapped his elbow twice on the tunnel wall to his right and so moved the other direction.

The bottom sloped steeply, and he dropped a foot with a single step. The current tugged at him, propelling him forward so that he had to struggle just to keep from being swept away. He swore as he realized that his boots and jacket had gotten wet, even as he moved into shallower water.

The tunnel roof was higher here—he could no longer feel it above him—but he kept his head ducked just in case that should change. Soon enough he had a painful crick in his neck, but still did not stand to his full height. Walking slightly bent was better than giving in to the current and being dashed against some enormous rock or down an underground waterfall.

These were his silent fears as they made their way deeper into the tunnel. Indeed, there was a downward grade to the river, but no dramatic drop-off. There was also very little sediment on the bottom as they went deeper into the tunnel. Over the ages, the water had worn it nearly smooth, and the walls as well. Perhaps at certain times of the year the river rose nearly to the ceiling, he thought. That would explain the smoothness of the walls above the waterline. He was grateful this was not one of them.

One of his fears proved true enough, however. Blue Jay called back several times to warn them of large rocks in their path.

"Do you think these are pieces of the tunnel, caved in?" he asked Kitsune.

"Perhaps. I'm even happier that the Kinder-fresser was going the other way, now."

There was a lightness to her tone. Oliver thought she was trying to alleviate his fear, but it didn't help. His throat was tight and his pulse raced with every moment in the darkness. His eyes had adjusted, and he had them wide open to take in any trace of available light, but after a while, there was none. In all his life he had never known a darkness so complete—save for one Halloween when Collette had taken him to the windowless back room of their basement to tell him scary stories by candlelight, and then blown out the candle, plunging them into utter darkness.

Oliver had screamed that night. A shriek to wake the dead.

But he would not scream now. *You will not,* he said to himself, again and again, as he held the jacket-wrapped sword over his shoulder with one hand and searched the darkness in front of him with the other like a blind man.

The sound of the river was not a comfort. Here, across the Veil, it seemed just another predator, ready to swallow him at a moment's notice.

They came to a place at last where the river did drop significantly, and the bottom was strewn with rocks that had accumulated there from cave-ins past. A fault in the mountain above them, probably.

He held his breath as he descended.

"We're going to be all right," Kitsune assured him, and it sounded as though her voice was right at his ear, an acoustic trick the tunnel played upon him.

With a deep breath, he mustered his will and pressed on, working with the power of the river rushing around him and pushing him onward, instead of struggling against it.

He blinked.

For just a moment, he thought he could see again. It looked as though the walls of the tunnel encircled him, and there were windows cut into the walls, high above. Beyond, he could see the night sky. It lasted only an instant, and then he heard another voice in his ear, this one barely a whisper, far more distant.

"*Come on, Ollie. Find me.*"

The voice was Collette's. She smelled faintly of her favorite shampoo, coconut-scented stuff from Australia.

Stunned, Oliver stopped walking. In an instant he realized his error. The river knocked him down, plunged him under. The laces of his boots wrapped around his throat and began to strangle him. He rolled along the river bottom, across the rocks that lay there. Desperate, he clutched the sword to him—still wrapped in his soaked jacket—and clawed at his neck to loosen the laces of his boots. But they were filled with water, the weight tightening the cords even more.

Then, Oliver struck an enormous rock that jutted from the river bottom. He expelled the last of his air and began to drown. Still, his mind was working. Twisting around, he used the rock to brace himself, found the bottom with his feet, and forced himself upward. With his free hand, he reached upward and found a grip.

The water turned cold around him. Then a strong hand closed on his wrist and helped to pull him up onto the rock. He coughed up the water he'd swallowed even as other hands slipped the laces of his boots from around his neck.

He wiped at his eyes and saw his friends around him. Frost stood just upstream, gaze set with concern. Blue Jay had helped haul him out of the water, and Kitsune had his boots in her hands. They were at a place where the river had leveled off somewhat, the current slackening.

"Are you all right?" Frost asked.

Oliver blinked. "I can see."

"That's a good sign," Blue Jay told him, a smirk on his trickster's face.

The light in the tunnel flickered and Oliver looked around to see that there were torches set in sconces high on the walls, the fire burning bright and hungry. Whatever was burning, it was no ordinary flame. He stood, still trying to catch his breath, neck sore from the chafing, and throat raw from choking on the water. But he was all right.

He'd live.

"It might have been simpler if you'd dropped the sword," Kitsune said, head tilted with the fox's curiosity.

"True," Oliver replied, a bit sheepish. "But it's the king's sword. I'm counting on it to buy me a few seconds to beg for my life, when the time comes."

"You might want to think about using it to cut off the head of whoever's trying to kill you," Blue Jay said helpfully.

Oliver laughed, then winced at the pain in his throat.

"We have company," Frost said, his voice low and dark.

The river grew colder as it swept past them. The winter man was summoning his power. Oliver tensed, hoping Frost would not need it.

"Nagas," Kitsune said.

Oliver looked. In the torchlight that flickered through the tunnel, he saw several people coming toward them, armed with long bows, each with a quiver of arrows slung across their backs. They looked ordinary enough, though they had long, sharp talons that likely made weapons unnecessary.

Then he saw the way they moved and realized they were not ordinary at all. From the waist down, they were serpentine, and their bodies moved swiftly under the water as they came upriver.

Beyond them, Oliver could see the end of the tunnel, where it opened into sunlight, and he gritted his teeth and shook the sword free, ignoring the jacket as the current carried it away. All that mattered now was living long enough to wish he'd held on to it.

Halliwell had never felt so old. It hurt him to think about it. Here he was in a place that should not exist, having seen more fantastic things in a single day than most people would see in their entire lives. Some dim part of his mind told him he ought to feel more alive, feel some thrill that there was truly such a thing as magic. Instead, he felt tired and hopeless and lost. Of course, he *was* all of those things.

The only direction he had now was to find Bascombe, but not because it had been his assignment—to hell with that. The only way to make sense of anything was to find the one person who might have some idea how to get him home.

Once he had Bascombe, of course, he still wanted answers. The mystery of the murdered children and their missing eyes and the connection to the Bascombe family was a riddle he needed solved. But getting back to the world was even more important. Untethered from everything he'd ever known, he had no touchstone for what mattered. What did it mean to be a policeman if there was no one to recognize his authority?

His service weapon was clipped to his belt at the small of his back. He'd worn it under his jacket, but now the jacket was abandoned. Halliwell felt no need to hide the weapon, but he had seen Julianna looking at it warily. She had been astonished that her firm, Bascombe & Cox, had arranged for him to have a permit to carry the gun in the United Kingdom. Halliwell had not.

Money greased the wheels of the world.

His world, at least.

He had no clue how *this* one worked.

But Oliver would. And Oliver was in love with Julianna. Having her along for the ride had at first been troubling to Halliwell. Now it had turned out to be vital. For if Bascombe got wind of her presence here, then he would come find them, and they wouldn't have to search for him anymore.

For now, though, the hunt was on.

Julianna had caught up with him as they walked down the craggy, rocky slope to the river. Halliwell had taken a look to the north and seen only more of the same, unwelcoming landscape, so he had turned south instead, toward the forest. They'd been walking alongside the river ever since, and been in the shade of the trees for a while now.

"You seem awfully certain of your direction," she said.

Halliwell kept his focus on the bend in the valley ahead, where the river turned and disappeared in the woods. "I am."

"How do you know Oliver went this way?"

"I don't."

Julianna faltered and fell behind. But when Halliwell didn't wait for her, she caught up to him quickly and moved around in front of him, forcing him to stop.

"I thought we'd established a pretty decent rapport, Ted," she said, searching his eyes.

Halliwell let out a breath and nodded. He reached up and scratched at his stubbled chin. "We have. I'm sorry. Maybe I'm not handling this as well as you are."

"Funny, I thought you were handling it better. I'm feeling pretty brittle at the moment. One little thing and I might shatter."

He smiled wearily. "At least you're young. I'm an old bastard and pretty sure I'm in shock, and not in the best shape for a cross-country hike."

"Bullshit," Julianna said, eyes narrowing sharply. "You're in better physical condition than I am. And you're fiftysomething, not eightysomething. If you're freaked, that's fine. Me, too. But we're here together. Talk to me."

Halliwell nodded, thinking how beautiful she was, how fortunate Bascombe was to have a smart, pretty girl like this in love with him. How tragic it would be if anything happened to her here.

"Can we walk?" he asked.

Julianna got out of his way and fell in beside him as he started downriver again.

"Water is life, kid," Halliwell said. "If we follow the river, we're likely to find a settlement somewhere along the way. The other direction wasn't exactly inviting terrain, you know? So I'm following my instincts, and a little logic. That doesn't mean Oliver went this way, but if we have any chance of finding him, we've got to find *people,* to learn something about this place, figure out how to track him."

"Logical enough," she replied. "But you could've said—"

"Did you feel that?" Halliwell interrupted. He stopped and glanced around, staring at the ground.

"Feel what?"

Halliwell didn't have to answer her. A moment later he felt it again, and saw in her eyes that she had felt it, too. A small tremor in the earth beneath their feet. It came a third time, more quickly, and he saw the leaves shaking on the trees.

"What the hell is that?" Julianna asked in a whisper.

He had no answer for her. The tremors continued, but this was not an earthquake. It was too regular, too rhythmic, to be anything of the sort. It was more like he imagined a battlefield would be, the impact of mortar shells or bombs not too far away.

"Let's keep going," he said.

They walked more quickly now, moving along the river's edge beneath the shade of branches of the trees along the bank. The tremors continued at a slow, steady march, but they were growing in intensity.

"It's getting closer," Julianna said. "Ted, maybe we should go a different way."

Halliwell shook his head, not in disagreement but simply in confusion. He had no idea what to do. Again, they faltered and came to a halt. Now the branches and leaves all shook with each tremor. The shaking of the earth was not strong enough to throw them off of their feet, but if it kept growing, it soon would be.

"Maybe," he said at last. "Through the woods. West, I guess it is."

Julianna turned to go into the trees, away from the river. Halliwell went to follow her but took one last look downstream. As he did, he saw the albino giant come around the bend in the river, towering as high as the trees.

The giant was hideous, the bones in its bleached white face jutting through taut leathery skin, eyes gleaming pink like a fresh scar, the bones of its ribs so sharply defined that they seemed about to tear through the flesh. It bent to snatch at something in the water and Halliwell saw jagged ridges of bones that protruded from the skin along its spine.

His hands shook, one going to his mouth as if to keep himself silent, the other to his chest, which tightened with a sharp, unfamiliar pain. Halliwell froze and stared at the thing, unable to breathe. He had never known terror before, and it engulfed him, unknown and unwelcome.

The thing had frozen as well. From a hundred yards downriver, it stared at him. Then it stood and cocked back its head. He was sure it was sniffing at the air, catching their scent on the wind.

"Weird," Julianna said, a few feet away in the trees. "The ground stopped..."

Her words trailed off. He glanced over and saw that she had seen the thing now. She screamed, the sound tearing the air like fabric. The wind died in that moment, as though it were composed of spirits who stopped to listen, to watch.

A breath burst from Halliwell's lips and then he was sucking another in, learning how to fill his lungs all over again.

The giant threw back its head and screamed in return, as if mimicking Julianna. Then it began to run toward them, a thunderous gait that was far swifter than Halliwell would have imagined. Its eyes were narrowed and its lips pulled back in a snarl that exposed a jagged mess of teeth.

He grabbed Julianna's wrist. "Go!"

The two of them fled into the trees together. Low branches scratched at him and he held up his free hand to ward them off. They plummeted through the woods on a roughly westward path. Julianna was shouting questions at him, clutching his hand with such terror that he thought his fingers would break.

The ground shook now with each pounce of the towering monster. Once. Twice. They made it half a dozen feet between each impact. On the third one, Halliwell heard the splintering of wood behind him and bits of the forest crashed down.

He was not a man prone to prayer. Now he whispered to God; thought of the daughter he had not seen in so very long, who had never really understood how much he loved her, and stopped. Julianna cursed loudly, madness in her eyes, hair wild, face scratched. She struggled to be free of him, but he held her fast.

"We can't—"

Its shadow fell upon them, swallowing the sun, and then it landed ten feet away, trees crushed to pulp beneath its mass. It stared down at them with those revolting pink eyes and snarled, baring its filth-encrusted, jagged, broken teeth. It slid its tongue out and a thick string of drool dripped to the ground.

It looked hungry.

Julianna staggered backward, still wild-eyed; there would be no reasoning with her. Halliwell was nearly beyond reason himself, but suddenly the pain and tightness in his chest gave way. This wasn't the death he'd imagined for himself. But if he was going to die, it wouldn't be screaming. He'd been a cop all his life.

"No," was all he said, as the thing reached down to scoop them up, one in each hand. Julianna tried to run and its fingers scurried after her, snatching her easily.

In the moment before it picked him up, Halliwell drew his gun.

He was cold inside. Like ice. Numb.

Maybe this is how it feels to be dead, he thought.

The giant carried them back to the river, walking now, in half a dozen strides. Halliwell hung limp in its grip, staring up at it, repulsed by the sickly white flesh and the way its bones jutted from the skin. It paused, standing in the water, and lifted Halliwell up to its face. He wondered dully if it would eat him. It sniffed at him, nostrils curling. A little voice in the back of his head urged him to fire, but he could only watch.

It lifted Julianna toward its mouth and then breathed in her scent as well. From deep in its throat came a sound of contentment and desire that was the single most unsettling noise he had ever heard. The grotesque perversity of it curdled his insides.

It studied her greedily for another moment, then opened its jaws and brought her toward its mouth.

Halliwell raised the gun and pulled the trigger, all in one motion. The first bullet burst one of its eyes, sending a shower of pustulent fluid down upon Julianna. The second bullet struck its temple, bringing a foul trickle of black ichor. He kept pulling the trigger as the giant staggered against the current, walking upriver, shaking its head like a wet dog.

On the fourth bullet, it dropped them.

Halliwell hit the water and the current took him. He was under for a moment and he tried to swim. He got his head above the water and looked around, saw Julianna surface nearby. She saw him, and the terror was still in her eyes. But they were free.

The river carried them southward. Halliwell hoped the giant had fallen, that it was dead, but then he saw that it was still standing and feared it would pursue them. As they swept along downstream he watched it stagger in the opposite direction, slapping the side of its head with an open hand as though trying to dislodge the bullets in its skull. Half-blind, perhaps brain-damaged, but it kept walking.

Then they were carried around the bend and out of sight.

Gun still clutched in his hand, Halliwell fought the river only enough to get nearer to Julianna. "We're all right," he told her. "We're okay."

She didn't argue, but the look in her eyes was enough to show him how ridiculous she thought his words were. And she was right. They were a whole world away from being all right.

Soon they came in sight of a cliff rising at treacherous angles ahead. Halliwell started toward shore, unsure where the river went from here. Julianna followed suit.

"It looks . . . can it go right into the mountainside?" she asked.

It did. The river plunged into a dark tunnel in the cliff face.

"We're not going in there," Julianna said, standing in the water as it rushed around her, moving for the bank.

"Damn right," Halliwell replied. After what they'd just been through, no way were they swimming some underground river, with God knew what waiting in the darkness for them.

On the bank, they followed the river until they reached the cliff.

Julianna looked up. "What now?"

Halliwell felt the exhaustion in his bones. But there was no rest yet. Not when all they had for a direction was a guess. He pointed westward, along the base of the cliff.

"We go up the side of the valley until we can cross over the top. The river's got to come out somewhere."

She hesitated. As a plan of action, it was shit. But they didn't have anything else.

"I hate being wet," she said, holding out her arms and looking down at her sodden clothes, nose wrinkled.

Then she started along the base of the cliff, westward, and Halliwell followed.

liver expected to die. Beyond the end of the tunnel he could see the sunlight streaming into the gorge, but he did not think they would ever get there. He had been battered and bruised by his collision with the rocks, his throat was raw from nearly drowning, and his companions seemed exhausted as well. There had been all too much of battle in these past hours, then the trek along the river had drained them further. Blue Jay and Kitsune were ragged and weakened. Frost was their only chance.

The Nagas swam at them, serpentine lower bodies gliding under the water, moving upriver slowly, watching them carefully as though searching for the precise moment to strike. From the waist up they were ordinary enough, men and women carrying bows, arrows at the ready. But below the waist they were enormous snakes, with all the deadly speed that would entail.

"What do we do?" Oliver whispered, his voice resounding eerily off the walls of the tunnel.

"Nothing," Frost said. "Do nothing."

He cocked his head, watching the serpent-people as they came nearer. His icicle hair made a familiar clinking noise and a white-blue mist rose from the corners of his diamond eyes.

Oliver nodded. If Frost had the strength, he could stop them. With a wave of his hand, he could turn the air so cold around their arrows that they would shatter. Perhaps, he might even momentarily freeze the river around them. But Frost looked just as drained as the rest of them, and Oliver did not share the certainty in the winter man's voice.

He raised the Sword of Hunyadi.

"Oliver, no!" Kitsune shouted.

Blue Jay burst from the river, spraying water across the rocks and his companions. In a blur of motion he became a bird, crying out as he darted forward, then he spun in the air, ready to block the arrows of the Nagas.

Not a single arrow flew.

Oliver frowned, staring, sword still at the ready as the Nagas turned to one another, whispering. Their serpentine lower halves undulated beneath the water, keeping them from drifting.

Frost and Kitsune exchanged a look of confusion, and then the winter man gestured for Oliver to lower his sword. Reluctantly, he did so.

"We are travelers in search of brief sanctuary," Frost announced. "We come openly and without pretense. I am Frost of the Borderkind. My companions and I need rest, and they need food as well. Legend says that Twillig's Gorge is a place of safe haven for travelers of any allegiance, so long as their intentions are peaceful. Is the legend false?"

The Nagas rose up from the water, swaying cobralike for a moment. They opened their mouths and hissed, but their arrows still did not fly.

"Time changes even legends," one of the females, perhaps the leader, said. "Perhaps legends most of all. You know that very well, Cailleach Bheur, just as I am certain you know that these are perilous times in the Two Kingdoms. Perilous for Borderkind most of all. There are others of your kind in the Gorge, but they have lived here for many years, and we protect our neighbors. We will fight for them. Risk all for them, just as they would for us.

"But you are not our neighbors," the Naga said, nodding her head first toward Frost, then toward Kitsune and Blue Jay. "None of you. The company of myths is a danger to us all, when so many want you dead. Why should we risk it for strangers?"

Kitsune growled at the use of the word *myth,* a term the Borderkind despised. She might have attacked them then, but this time it was Oliver who held her back.

"You'll turn us away out of cowardice, then?" Frost demanded.

Blue Jay landed atop the rock Oliver had crashed into, changing again into his human shape. He crouched there, glaring down at the Nagas.

"I never would have believed it," the trickster said. "The world really has changed."

"Better allies than strangers," Frost said, voice low. Mist drifted up from his mouth. The light from along the tunnel made the sharp angles of his icy body and face even more severe. "Better friends than enemies. Now more than ever. If you have Borderkind amongst you, the Hunters will come for them. We mean to stop them before they ever get here. That serves us all."

The Nagas watched them carefully for several long, tense moments, and then the leader raised her bow, let the pressure off of the string, and returned the arrow to its quiver. The others followed suit.

The leader bowed, then looked at Frost, her smile savage. "I ought to kill you just for calling us cowards. But this is not a time for those with no quarrel to slay one another. It may come to pass soon enough that we will all be short of friends. But you understand we must be wary. In these times, visitors to the Gorge are scarce and mostly unwelcome."

Kitsune squeezed Oliver's hand but stared at the Nagas. "But you will let us in?"

"To rest. To eat. You will be gone by dawn. And if others of your kin leave to join you on your quest, all the better."

Oliver felt the tension go out of him. He slid his sword back into his belt and then stretched, feeling every one of the bruises he'd gotten when he slammed into that rock.

He waded downriver toward the Nagas, not liking the way they watched him. Though he was the least dangerous of the group, the sentries of Twillig's Gorge seemed unduly focused on his movements. Blue Jay, Kitsune, and Frost joined him and the four of them strode to where the Nagas slithered in the water.

The leader, sleek and beautiful from the waist up, her hair cut short and ragged, gazed at him with wide, green eyes.

"That does not apply to you, brother. You are welcome to stay as long as you like. You have a home with Nagas, wherever you find us."

Oliver stared dumbly at her. She turned and swam away down the river, the other Naga sentries following her. With the undulating of their serpentine bodies, they rode the current, and were out of the tunnel and into the sunlight of the gorge in moments.

"What the hell was that all about?" Oliver asked, glancing around at his friends.

Kitsune frowned. Beneath her hood, her expression was as puzzled as Oliver's own. "I have no idea. 'Brother'? Who do they think you are?"

Oliver opened his mouth to repeat the question, but Frost and Blue Jay had already set off after the Nagas, wading toward the end of the tunnel, where the river flowed into the gorge. They must have heard the Naga's words, and his own reaction, but neither of them slowed or looked back.

"Could it be just that I'm not Borderkind? That I'm no danger to them?"

Kitsune smiled. "I suppose. If they only knew that having you here is even more dangerous than harboring us ... The Hunters stalking the Borderkind are working in secret. You've got the whole of the Two Kingdoms after you."

Oliver laughed softly and they set out together. But as they went, he watched Blue Jay and Frost, up ahead. They walked quickly and did not so much as glance at one another, as if neither one of them dared to speak.

It troubled him, though it seemed more strange than important. Idly, he slid his hand into his pocket and touched the seed given to him by the Harvest gods. Though it clung wetly to the damp fabric inside his pocket, he was strangely reassured that it was still there and seemed undamaged.

Then they emerged from the tunnel, and all other thoughts were banished instantly.

In his mind he had pictured Twillig's Gorge as a river canyon lined with caves, in which its residents would dwell. That much was true. But it was also far more than that. The walls of the gorge were several hundred feet high and as sheer as the cliff face on the ocean bluff behind his father's house. The village that had blossomed there in the gorge went on for a mile or more before the river disappeared into the face of another cliff. Twillig's Gorge was closed in on four sides. From what Oliver could see, the only way in was down one of those sheer cliff faces or through a river tunnel.

There were caves, as he'd imagined. Most of them had balconies built on the outside, some with beautiful awnings. The caves were connected by ladders and walkways fixed to the gorge walls, somehow bolted into the stone, and the gorge itself was spanned by arched, stone bridges of elegant, ancient construction, and by nearly primitive hanging bridges of wood and thick rope, strung at odd angles.

From the look of it, that was how Twillig's Gorge had started. But there had to be a limit to the number of cave dwellings, and so they had built out from the walls. Oliver gaped at the sight. He had seen homes on steep hillsides in his own world—some of them the product of sheer madness, in his opinion. Much of Southern California, or so it seemed, had been built with the front of a house on solid ground and the back on stilts. In comparison to the houses of Twillig's Gorge, those homes were on bedrock. Some of them spanned the whole gorge, right over the river, and those seemed the safest. Others, though, were so precarious as to defy gravity. They clung to the stone cliffs with only struts beneath them, braced at angles against the rock face.

It was impossible. But Oliver had grown used to the impossible.

Twillig's Gorge was alive with motion. People moved across bridges and up ladders. Fishermen cast their lines out of cave mouths and sat on balconies awaiting a bite. There were a great many humans of varying race and origin—Lost Ones who had passed through the Veil at a place and time where it had worn momentarily thin and been trapped here. Perhaps two-thirds of the population looked ordinary enough.

Then there were the legendary. A crew of dwarves was excavating a section of the eastern gorge wall. On the western wall, two others, seemingly ignored by the main crew, were carving an enormous tableau, an image of mermaids sitting upon a rocky outcropping in the midst of the ocean. There was something about the image that chilled Oliver. The mermaids were elegant, but looked cruel. Sailors flailed in the water not far away, and the fragments of a shattered sailing ship thrust from the waves.

That was what gave it away. They weren't mermaids at all. They were Sirens, luring men to their deaths. It was a warning, but he did not know if it had any significance beyond its artistic merit.

There were other legends as well. On either side of the river was rough terrain, perhaps thirty feet on the eastern bank but over one hundred on the western. Nothing should have grown there, but still there were crops, coming right up out of what seemed like gravel. A farmer drove an ox-drawn plow through solid rock, churning it up, ready to plant more seed. The ox was blue.

As Oliver and his companions waded past the field of wheat and corn and toward what appeared to be a boat landing up ahead, he scanned the bridges and ladders. A minotaur crossed a hanging rope bridge above and he flinched as it passed over them, the clop of its hooves making him feel certain the bridge would give way under its weight.

There were boggarts and sprites tossing one another about in what appeared to be a playful manner. Lithe figures that seemed made of water rose out of the river and watched them as they passed. Twillig's Gorge also had dozens of varieties of animal-people. Oliver had come to group them all together, though he was sure those legends would have been deeply offended. Some had the heads of birds or jungle beasts, others the heads of men with the bodies of horses or apes or alligators. And those were only the ones he saw.

Oliver tried not to stare at the griffin that sat curled upon a rocky ledge on the eastern wall. He ignored the strangely ephemeral people, tall and thin and clad in gauzy colors, who seemed almost invisible unless he stared directly at them. Fairies, or something like them, he was sure.

What he could not ignore were their kin, the tiny little figures that darted all through the gorge like butterflies and dragonflies. Whatever they were—pixies, or peries like the ones he'd seen in the Oldwood shortly after first crossing the Veil—they were beautiful. And there were hundreds of them, perhaps thousands. The pixies needed no caves or houses or bridges. They flitted through the air, alighting only for an eyeblink before setting off again, their colors like the petals of a million flowers cast into the air.

"Wow," Oliver whispered.

Kitsune laughed in delight beside him. For a few moments, as he took this all in, he had forgotten she was there. Now she looped her arm through his and leaned against him, and he liked the warmth of her there.

A pair of men sat together on a high balcony, a hundred feet or more above the river, but they had bodies and limbs as thin as sticks and faces like anteaters, and their legs hung all the way down to the water, their feet curved as though they might hook an enemy, or simply prey, and bring them up to their cave.

Of all the things he had seen thus far, they were the only ones that frightened him.

At the river landing they climbed a set of stone stairs out of the water. Frost and Blue Jay waited for them there, but the two Borderkind were alone. Lost Ones went by without sparing them a glance. Humans on this side of the Veil had lost any sense of awe. Some of them were dressed in strange garments that he thought might be Aztec or Mayan, for he knew that those ancient peoples had ended up on this side of the Veil long ago.

No one stopped. Legends averted their eyes as they passed, not wanting to get involved. The Nagas had presumably returned to their sentry duties, leaving them to fend for themselves. A woman whose body was knotted wood and gnarled, cracked bark, and who had tiny leaves sprouting from her flesh, paused and smiled.

"Welcome," she said, spreading her hands with their thin, spidery, branch fingers, and offering a small bow.

Frost and Blue Jay returned the bow.

"Our thanks," Blue Jay said. "You seem the only one willing to make us welcome."

"Strangers pass with the river. They'll pay little attention to you unless you stay." The woman, whose teeth were tiny thorns, smiled. "Are you staying, then?"

"No. Only passing through," Frost said.

"Pity. But you'll want the inn, then. Shouldn't be any trouble getting a room. Very few visitors, these days."

Oliver leaned in to whisper to Kitsune. "With their hospitality, it's no wonder."

Kitsune bumped him playfully. Frost thanked the tree-woman, some kind of forest spirit, Oliver assumed, and they started off along the landing, continuing southward. Oliver noticed that the cliff face on the eastern wall had been carefully carved, transformed so that it almost resembled the façades of old European rowhouses. It was not a city, but the illusion of one, and it chilled him.

There were shops in caves both natural and excavated, all along the landing. A butcher, a bakery, a market, and several little clothes boutiques. Of all the things he had seen in Twillig's Gorge, that seemed strangest to him. Almost too civilized.

Atop the shops, and below the dwellings that were higher up on the gorge walls, there were stone figures carved and standing sentinel above the river. Gargoyles. Not one of them looked alike, but they were hideous, terrifying to look at. The demonic stone figures had also been placed atop some of the bridges, and one of the homes that spanned the river. It made Oliver think of Venice, in Italy, and some of the beautiful architecture that went into arched passages above the canals.

But some of these were not merely bridges. They went under two homes that had been built across the gorge, and then came in sight of a third structure—a thing of stone and wood that cast a long shadow upon the river and the walls below, with a row of strange peaks across the top, and a small bell tower to cap it all.

"The inn," Blue Jay said.

To the right, a figure stepped away from the front of a little marionette shop, a wiry little man with matted brown hair, a long face, and crazy eyes.

"You always were pretty fast on the uptake, Jay," he said.

Blue Jay laughed and stepped forward, pulling the man into a tight embrace.

"Cousin, it's good to see you."

The wiry man laughed as well, but his was cold and cynical. "Good to see *you* alive, Jay."

Oliver glanced at Kitsune, whose jade eyes had hardened. Blue Jay began to introduce his cousin to Frost, but Oliver leaned in to Kitsune.

"What is it? Who is this guy?"

Kitsune spat on the ground that separated them from Blue Jay, Frost, and the other.

"Oliver Bascombe," she said, voice rippling with disgust, "meet Coyote."

The Jaculus flew low, skirting over treetops and the peaks of hills, never so low as to encounter travelers nor so high as to draw undue attention from other airborne predators. Or so he thought.

Hunger gnawed at Lucan, and as he slipped through the air, body undulating, wings propelling him, he nurtured a bitterness in his heart. He had done the right thing, followed his orders to the letter. Ty'Lis and Hinque had sent him north to spy for them, to follow Malla and the Falconer and to watch from this side of the Veil, just in case things went wrong.

And, oh, how things had gone wrong.

It seemed impossible to him that an ordinary man, an Intruder from the other side of the Veil, and a pitiful few Borderkind had defeated and killed not only Malla and the Falconer, but an entire cadre of Kirata, and others. He shivered with pleasure at the thought of what it would have been like if he had been able to attack them when they came through on the hill above the Sorrowful River. Frost might have presented a problem, but the others ... he would have loved to sink his fangs into Kitsune's throat, to wrap himself around her soft fur and tender flesh. And as for Blue Jay ...

The Jaculus sniffed as he flew, snorting mucus into his throat, amused at the thought of how easily he could have dispatched the trickster bird. He disliked eating birds. All feather and bone. But with Blue Jay he would have made an exception.

Frustration burned in him, but he pushed it away. He had his orders, and Lucan prided himself on loyalty. He had pledged himself to Ty'Lis and he would fulfill his vow to the edge of death and beyond. Thus was the nobility of the Jaculus.

His tiny wings beat so fiercely that they made a cricket buzz. It was a long way to Palenque, the capital of Yucatazca, but that was why Ty'Lis had sent Lucan. The Jaculi were amongst the fastest creatures in the air.

Lucan crested a hill so quickly that the details of the ground below were a blur. He zipped over tall grass on a long field, then shot through the upper branches of a small stretch of forest with such swiftness that leaves were torn off their branches by the vacuum of his passing.

A wide ribbon of blue crossed his path ahead. The Atlantic River. Off to the north he saw a battalion of Euphrasian soldiers on the march. What they were doing there he had no idea, but it was none of his concern.

His keen eye caught movement, a blur against the blur, down on the riverbank. The Jaculus twisted in the air, almost swimming down from the sky, zipping toward the ground. The vole that had been nibbling at some scattered seeds darted away, sensing Lucan's approach. It skittered toward a thick stretch of prickly shrubbery on the river's edge and nearly made it to cover before the Jaculus struck.

Lucan darted his tail downward like a scorpion striking, coiled around the vole, and swept it up toward his jaws in one swift motion. He snapped his fangs closed around its body, plunging venomous needles into its flesh, and it began to shudder, dying. The Jaculus opened his maw, jaw unhinging, and thrust the squirming vole into his throat.

As he beat his tiny wings harder, gliding through the air above the Atlantic River, he swallowed the creature whole. The Atlantic Bridge was just to the south and he swept by it in seconds, though the act of digesting slowed him down some.

A pleasurable shudder went through him. He was going to be

sleepy after eating the vole. If only he could have coiled himself into a shady tree for a rest. But it was not to be. He had his duty to fulfill.

In a blink, the river was no longer below him. He slashed across the sky, watching the Truce Road unfold ahead. The terrain was rough, but he could see woods off to the north where the hills rose and there were mountains in the far distance. That was not his course, however. Instead, Lucan turned south, cutting away from the Truce Road. Below, he saw a farm with hundreds of cattle grazing. Past that was a small village, and soon the Truce Road was far behind him.

As he flew south, the air grew warmer. He enjoyed the feel of it. The Jaculus relished heat, and cold made it sluggish. Lucan had embraced the role of spy, but hoped in the future his assignments kept him in Yucatazca.

His path took him through gray afternoon clouds. A light rain began to fall.

High in the eastern sky, something black flashed against the storm. Lucan might have ignored it, but a moment later another shape joined the first. Two birds, black and broad-winged, paced him a hundred feet above.

The Jaculus felt his stomach rumble, acid working on the vole. But he was slowed by the meal and could not digest it any faster.

With a single twist and a thrust of his wings, he switched direction, turning toward a copse of trees at the edge of a field below. Lucan dove, fangs bared, toward the uppermost branches. He shot his tail beneath him like a javelin, grabbed hold of a branch, and swung around, wrapping himself around the tree limb. As he glanced up, he saw the birds descend, their talons out, enormous wings beating the air.

Strigae. They were spies for Ty'Lis as well.

"What are you doing?" the Jaculus cried.

The smaller Strigae crashed through leaves, snapped a branch, and grabbed hold of Lucan, tearing him from his perch. The Jaculus hissed and bared his fangs. He lunged once, missed, and prepared to lunge again, but then the Strigae landed, battering him against the hard ground. The other alighted beside the first and shot out a talon, holding his head down, keeping him from striking. His wings beat uselessly against the dirt.

"Where are you going in such a hurry, sky-worm?" cawed the Strigae who stood upon his head. It bent down and stared into his face, tiny black eyes like stones.

"Returning to Palenque," Lucan muttered, the talon upon his head making it difficult to speak. "And you had best let me be on my way. I serve at the will of the sorcerer Ty'Lis, as I believe do you. I have vital information for—"

The Strigae pushed the Jaculus's head into the dirt and put his beak closer to Lucan's face. "What information?"

"Information I will only reveal to my master."

The Strigae cawed angrily, and the other followed suit. The two birds were so loud that Lucan's ears hurt. He twisted and coiled the lower part of his serpent body, but could do nothing. The vole weighed heavy in his gut.

From above came the sound of other wings, much larger, much heavier. The Strigae stopped their cawing and looked up. Lucan tried to see past them, but at first the drizzling rain spattered his eyes and the gray light that filtered through the storm made it difficult to make out the two creatures that flew down and landed heavily a few feet away.

Then Lucan blinked the rain away, and he stopped wriggling beneath his captors. There were few things in any world the Jaculus feared, but the Hunters that slunk across the dirt now, almost blending with the trees, were fear themselves.

Perytons. Their antlers glistened with the rain, wide eyes bright despite the gray storm clouds. The two Atlantean predators moved with a crawling stealth, green-feathered wings pinioned against their backs.

"Jaculus," said one of the Strigae, as though in answer to a question, though neither of the Perytons had spoken. Lucan was not sure the Hunters ever spoke.

The other Strigae cawed and bent his head in obeisance to the Perytons. "Says he serves Ty'Lis. Says he's got information for him."

One of the Perytons stepped back, a grotesque motion like the scuttling of a crab, wings pinned. It slid between two trees and dipped its head as though listening to a voice.

Only then did Lucan see that there was a figure in front of one of the trees. A crone, a terrible hag. She turned and smiled at him, and even from this distance, he could see that her teeth were stone. Her skin was blue, her nose hooked and bulbous.

Jezi-Baba, he thought.

The Jaculus knew he was as good as dead if he did not speak.

The Peryton with Jezi-Baba nodded to the Strigae. The huge black birds cawed loudly. The talon on his head pressed harder.

"I will tear off your head if you do not speak the truth, and now. If there is information for Ty'Lis, it may help us to locate our quarry. If you do not share it, and so thwart us, your master will flay you alive."

Lucan shuddered, the last trace of strength gone from him, and he told them all that he had seen.

As he spoke, the Perytons closed in around him. The Strigae withdrew, letting him up. He considered fleeing, but only for a moment. With the vole in his belly, they would surely overtake him quickly.

"You mean they saw you? The Borderkind and the Bascombe? They know that you were spying upon them?" the smaller Strigae demanded, ruffling its wings, black feathers gleaming wetly in the rain.

"It could not be helped," the Jaculus replied, coiled upon the ground, wings aquiver. He bent his head respectfully. "I would have attacked, would have slain those I could, but my instructions were specific. Watch, only, and return with word."

The Perytons snorted and pawed the ground with clawed, twisted, nearly human hands. They spread their wings with a sound like banners unfurling. Beneath the trees, Jezi-Baba sneered and ground her stone teeth.

"You are useless," the larger Strigae said, black eyes like buttons. "You were seen. And now you have freely told what you swore to keep secret."

Lucan could not breathe. "But … you compelled me. You serve Ty'Lis as well."

The Strigae cawed loudly and looked to the Perytons. First one, then the other, turned their backs, spread their wings, and took to the air.

"No," the Jaculus pleaded. "No, wait. I . . . I am loyal. I did as I was told."

"You are weak," a voice said, like the whisper of the leaves, and Lucan looked amongst the trees to see Jezi-Baba merging with the bark of a tall, twisted oak. Then she was gone.

The birds began to laugh.

The Jaculus screamed as they closed in around him, beating him with their wings and pecking him, beaks piercing his flesh.

Sleep. Just the thought of it had an allure that Oliver would never have imagined possible. In all his life he had never been so exhausted. His muscles ached as though he'd been pummeled by a prizefighter, arms and legs and back and abdomen all stiff and sore. His eyes burned and his head felt stuffed with cotton, like the worst hangover he'd ever had, except he hadn't taken a drink.

But he could have used one.

It was mid-afternoon on this side of the Veil. Twillig's Gorge had obviously not been hospitable to visitors of late, and so there were plenty of vacancies at the inn. Coyote was staying there, and had been for weeks. Apparently his idea of hiding from the Myth Hunters had been to hole up in a place they would inevitably look, but someplace they could not arrive unannounced. Very few beings could approach Twillig's Gorge without notice. According to Kitsune, Coyote was a master of vanishing when trouble began. Such was the way with troublemakers.

Frost had a quiet conversation with Coyote while the innkeeper— a voluminously fat man with a shaved head and a thick beard— supplied the rest of them with keys. Blue Jay, Kitsune, and Oliver were given rooms next to one another on the third floor, facing north. Frost asked only that he be allowed to rest in the inn's cold storage and the innkeeper was happy to oblige, for a fee.

At the bottom of the stairs, out of earshot of the innkeeper, Frost addressed them.

"There's a tavern here at the inn," he said. "Coyote tells me it's empty this time of day. Go upstairs and wash. Rest a while. Coyote has sent for clean, dry clothes for all of you. But I'm afraid we cannot sleep yet. We must leave here in the morning, and that means that our planning must begin now. We'll meet in the tavern in an hour, with any Borderkind in the Gorge who are willing to speak with us."

Oliver followed Blue Jay and Kitsune up the stairs without a word. He was too tired for questions and just the thought of a bed and a shower drove him on. The inn was stone and wood on the inside as well as out, like some ancient castle. The stairs wound up through the heart of the place. As he made his way up, admiring the tapestries on the walls, he thought of his father. The old man would have loved this place. It was just his style.

But the old man was dead.

Blue Jay had the nearest room, right at the top of the stairs. His clothes were soaked through, and at some point he'd torn the leg of his jeans. He nodded once before disappearing into his room, looking genuinely haggard.

The second room was Oliver's, while the third, at the end of the hall, had been given to Kitsune. As he stopped at his door, she smiled at him and wrinkled her nose.

"It appears we both could use a bath," she said lightly, jade eyes sparkling. Her hood was thrown back.

"Do I stink that much?"

Kitsune nodded gravely. "Oh, yes. Terribly." Then she leaned in toward him and kissed his temple. "Not to worry, Oliver. We'll sleep well tonight in soft beds with softer pillows. We deserve one pleasant night before we head into the lion's den."

The smell of her, so close, was intoxicating: cinnamon and mint, and something else he could not identify.

She held his gaze and one corner of her mouth lifted in mischief, then she turned and went to the door of her room, humming something under her breath, her fur cloak swaying around her.

Oliver watched her until she went inside.

Then he turned the key, and the door swung open, not quite straight in its frame. The room was simply appointed with a wide, sturdy bed upon which lay a thick, floral comforter and a pile of goose down pillows. There was a washbasin on a bureau beside the tall window, and at first he was disappointed, thinking that would be the closest he could come to a bath. But through a narrow door on the other side of the room he found a bathroom complete with claw-foot tub. There was no showerhead, but a bath would do fine. In fact, he thought a bath was just what he needed.

When he had peeled off his damp, filthy clothes, and at last slid down into the hot water and began to run the soap over his body, he could have wept.

He thought of Kitsune's mischievous grin and her marvelous scent, and a flash of guilt went through him. As alluring as she was, and as much as she flirted with him, he couldn't allow himself to become entranced by Kitsune. He had begun to cherish her companionship, but—more and more—his mind turned back to Julianna.

When he had first crossed through the Veil, his thoughts had been so overwhelmed with astonishment—and later, as the dangers became clear, with anxiety—that Julianna was just one part of the jumble of thoughts and emotions and fears swirling in his head. But with each passing day his longing for her grew. He felt the distance between them more keenly than ever now, here in this bizarre, hidden village.

What would Julianna have thought of the place?

Oliver thought she would have coped perfectly well. All her life, she had been the one who could adapt to her surroundings; the one without fear of change. How could he not have fallen in love with her, trapped as he was by his inability to escape his father's expectations?

He had no memory of their first meeting—which was really no surprise, considering they must have been toddlers at the time—but Oliver's recollection of the first time he had ever really *noticed* Julianna was incredibly vivid.

Every summer, Bascombe & Cox held a picnic at Beacon Point Park for all of their employees. From Max Bascombe, the most senior of senior partners, to Sam Small in the mailroom, every member of the law firm's staff would attend, with spouses and children in tow. Beacon Point Park overlooked the ocean, and several crumbling concrete staircases led down the breakwater to a private beach, where the picnickers would toss Frisbees or play volleyball, and the brave might take a brief dip in the cold northern waters.

At the end of a rocky promontory stood the lighthouse that gave the park its name. There was no prettier spot in all of Wessex County.

When not in the water, the kids would ramble across the green lawn of the park, playing soccer or Frisbee, while the grownups fired up half a dozen barbecue grills. The firm could have afforded to have the whole thing catered, but Max Bascombe liked to make a big show of the generals cooking for the troops. They ate at picnic tables under the shade trees that surrounded the open lawn. The children, in the moments when they paid any attention at all to the adults, were always greatly amused by the rare spectacle of their parents becoming pleasantly inebriated.

Oliver's memory of these summer picnics was idyllic. He was sure there had been incidents and arguments worthy of scandal, perhaps when some lawyer got a little too drunk for his own good, but he could not remember any of them. With his father playing host and chief cook, he and Collette had been free of his usual stern regard; free to simply be children, instead of *Max Bascombe's children.*

In retrospect, he knew that Julianna had always been pretty. But she had been quiet and serious, so that—even though they were in school together, and saw one another at the summer picnics, and perhaps even passed the ball to one another in those haphazard Beacon Point Park soccer games—to him she was just another girl.

In late July, the month before high school began, that changed.

In the midst of the ritual of the Bascombe & Cox summer picnic, Oliver and several of the other boys—many of whom he saw only once a year, as their families did not live in Kitteridge—were playing catch with a Nerf football in the ocean. They dove over waves, passing the sodden ball back and forth, salt water splashing in their faces.

Oliver had just tossed the blue-and-orange Nerf to Danny Hilliard, blinking salt from his eyes. He blinked hard and reached up to rub them, to clear his vision. A strong wave staggered him, and as he got his footing again he turned.

As he opened his eyes, he saw motion out on the jetty. Someone was out there, moving from rock to rock, out past the lighthouse. It took him a moment to recognize the long, wavy, auburn hair; to realize that it was Julianna Whitney out there on the promontory. In a purple bikini top and cutoff denim shorts, and barefoot, she leaped so lightly across the gaps in the rocks that she seemed to be dancing.

Captured by her grace, and by the aura of loneliness that seemed to encircle her, Oliver watched as the slender girl made her way all the way to the huge rock that thrust up at the end of the jetty. The waves crashed against it, sprayed up into the air, and rained down upon it.

Julianna threw her arms back as a crashing wave soaked her. The droplets of ocean water sparkled with prismatic color. Even from that distance, Oliver felt sure he could hear her laughing. For a moment he envied her, so unafraid to be out there on her own.

Then she stepped to the edge of the rock and dove in.

Oliver held his breath in fascination as the waves continued to roll in. He waited for her to come up, and when she did, pushing the damp curtain of her hair away from her eyes, he smiled to himself and started to wade out toward her. There was such abandon in this girl— the girl he'd barely noticed before—that he wanted to be a part of that.

He'd gotten three steps when the waterlogged Nerf struck him in the back of the head, then plopped into the ocean, bobbing on the waves. Laughter erupted, and Oliver turned and picked up the ball, trying to figure out which of the guys was responsible so that he could unleash watery vengeance.

He hadn't spoken to Julianna that day, or any other day that summer.

But he had never forgotten how she had looked, there on the very tip of the jetty, in the spray of the ocean, or the way he'd held his breath when she'd dived into the waves.

Even now, he held the memory—that image of the thirteen-year-old Julianna—close in his mind. Somehow, it felt to him like a tether to home—like no matter how far he roamed, as long as he could hold on to moments like that, he could still hope to return to Julianna one day.

With every day that passed, he regretted even more the hesitation he had felt on the night before they would have been married. When his father was still alive, he would have blamed the old man for making him so discontent with his life that he doubted even what he felt for Julianna. But, as much of a bastard as Max Bascombe had been, Oliver knew the blame lay with himself. He'd never had the courage that Julianna had.

Crossing the Veil had set him free. He felt different, here: more confident, more *himself*, than ever before.

But the last time he had spoken to Julianna, her voice had been filled with hurt and doubt and hesitation. His disappearance had given her reason to feel all of those things, and he longed, now, for the opportunity to make it up to her. He had to find Collette first, to get his sister back safely. And he had to convince the monarchs of the Two Kingdoms to grant him a reprieve, to let him prove himself. With every day, he was moving further away from Julianna.

But he felt closer to her than ever before.

For the first time in his life, he felt as if he might be worthy of her.

he tavern was on the first floor. When they'd arrived, Oliver had had other things to distract him, but as he descended the stairs he was extremely conscious of the fact that the whole building hung suspended above the river. The inn was old—a century at least from the look of it, and probably more—but if it had lasted this long, he told himself, it would survive another night.

Outside the windows, in the gorge, the shadows were growing long. Evening was not far off. After a bath, and clad in the new clothes Coyote had brought by only ten minutes ago, his exhaustion had subsided to a dull heaviness. He needed sleep, but he could propel himself forward another hour or two, however long it took for this meeting, and a meal.

The shirt was a rough tan cotton, long-sleeved and open at the collar, and the pants might have been denim, but dyed black. They were a bit long, so that when he put on the new boots Coyote had brought, they dragged underfoot, but Oliver was so impressed with the fit in general that he would not have complained, even if he dared.

The best thing about his new clothes was the thick, soft cotton socks and the light undershorts, which were woven from a fabric unfamiliar to him. Putting them on was almost as soothing as his bath.

His hunger, as he entered the tavern, was a ravenous beast, growling in his belly. The smells that wafted along the corridor only made it worse. But once inside, he forgot about food for several moments.

"Apparently, I'm the last to arrive."

Frost looked up from the gathering. Several dark wooden tables had been pushed together to make one long enough to rival the conference room at Bascombe & Cox. Blue Jay was beside him, dressed almost identically to Oliver, though his jeans were blue and he still wore feathers in his hair. Kitsune was next to him, her hood back, her fur cloak gleaming luxuriously in the fading afternoon light. Her raven-black hair framed her face severely, and when she glanced at him he expected a smile but found only a grimness of purpose.

It was the time for plans to be laid and companionship to be abandoned. Oliver felt strangely cold and isolated. This gathering had so very little to do with him now that he wondered if he ought to have been there at all. But there was food to be had—barbecued beef and poultry and boiled potatoes and vegetables, from what he could see— and he knew that he would need at least advice from this assemblage before they parted ways.

"Please, Oliver, come in. Sit down," said Coyote, standing up from the darkest corner of the table. He wore his thief's grin, as Oliver's father would have called it. Oliver would not have disagreed.

There were others there, of course. Coyote had gathered a group that seemed just as odd as Oliver's traveling companions. More so, in fact, given that one of them was an enormous frog-thing that sat on the ground instead of a chair, legs up beside it as though it might leap at any moment. Its bulbous eyes were a putrid yellow, its skin a pale greenish-brown, ridged, mottled, and slick.

"Oliver?" Frost said sharply.

The frog-thing muttered something in a guttural language he could not understand.

"Excuse me?" Oliver said.

Coyote leaned back in his chair, arms crossed. "Tlatecuhtli says it's not polite to stare."

"Ah, yeah. Right. I'm sorry about that," he said sheepishly, going over to take the empty seat beside Blue Jay. "Just takes some getting used to. All of this."

The frog spoke again, its voice vaguely disgusting, like a series of belches. Oliver looked to Coyote for help.

"He forgives you," Coyote said. "You're an outsider. You don't know any better."

Oliver smiled at the frog, whose name he could not even begin to pronounce. Cuhtli-something. "Thank you."

All of the Borderkind at the table were staring at him. Oliver wondered what would happen were he to remind them that it was not polite. He glanced at Kitsune, then at Frost.

The winter man raised his chin and shifted in his chair. His sharp, icy fingers scratched the table as he moved. This alone was enough to draw all of the attention in the room. Oliver was grateful. It was also clear that all of those gathered were willing to defer to Frost.

Mist steamed from his eyes. The afternoon light played a myriad of colors off of the angles of his frigid features. Frost gestured toward Coyote.

"Oliver, you already know Coyote."

"Yes. Thank you for the clothes."

Coyote touched two fingers to his forehead, almost as though he were tipping a hat, though he wasn't wearing one.

"You have just met Tlatecuhtli. He hails from Yucatazca, where he is still worshipped by some of the descendants of the original Aztec people."

The frog-thing let out a long, low noise and blinked once at Oliver.

The introductions continued. At the far end of the table, opposite Frost, was a monstrous, savage-looking creature from whom Oliver would have run screaming once upon a time. But his time in the world of the legendary had taught him not to judge so quickly.

The thing—called Chorti—was covered in shaggy gray-and-black hair. Though it was seated, Oliver figured it must have been nine feet tall at least, and it was twice as broad across as the table. Its hands were crossed over its chest as though it might be sleeping, and the long claws that jutted from its fingers were made of metal. Oliver had to look twice to confirm that.

Chorti smiled a mouthful of razors and offered him a little wave of greeting. A creature as frightening and imposing as this would make one hell of an ally in a fight. Oliver nodded to the beast and silently wished that it could come along with him to rescue Collette.

Beside Chorti, seated close enough to indicate that they were together, sat a coldly imperious woman with hair so white it looked almost silver. She wore a white dress, cotton and lace, and other than her hair she seemed entirely too proper and ordinary to be one of the Borderkind. Frost introduced her as Cheval Bayard, and Oliver took it from the accent in her quiet hello that she was of French origin.

Cheval leaned over to whisper something to Chorti and the beastman grunted in amusement, a soft, chuffing laughter coming from his chest. She stroked the thick fur at the back of his head. Apparently, she was not nearly as cold as he had imagined. He liked her better for her easy way with the beast-man.

Oliver studied them a moment out of the corner of his eye. The way Cheval had whispered to Chorti gave the pair the air of lovers, but as she stroked him, it was almost as though he were her pet. Yet, when he saw the way they looked at one another—the knowing humor there—neither of those theories seemed correct, and he was left wondering about the relationship between the strange pair.

The last of the gathering was a seven-foot, broad-shouldered man with a gray-streaked, rust-colored beard. When the man looked up from beneath a wide-brimmed hat with stone-gray eyes, Oliver knew he'd met him before.

"And this is—" Frost began when he came to the man, the last introduction.

"Wayland Smith," Oliver interrupted. "I remember you from Amelia's."

"Yes," Smith replied. "That was . . . regrettable."

The man was a weaponsmaster and forger, as well as a magician. And as far as Oliver was concerned, he could not be trusted. Smith toyed briefly with the fox-head of his cane, then rested it against the table.

After the introductions, that odd convocation began to eat. The beef had been marinated in some exotic spice, and Oliver thought it was among the most delicious things he had ever tasted. The boiled potatoes likewise surprised him. They had clearly been boiled as part of some other recipe, simmering with herbs and spices, and the flavor was rich, the potatoes creamy.

Several minutes passed in relative silence as the travelers began to sate their hunger. Low conversation went on amongst the local Borderkind. Frost was deep in thought and whispered several times to Blue Jay. Kitsune watched them, and Oliver thought she was irked to be left out of whatever scheme they were hatching.

His attention returned every few moments to Cheval Bayard and Chorti. The pair were such an unlikely duo—this beautiful, distant woman and her hirsute companion with his metal fangs and claws— that Oliver found himself unable to stop puzzling over them.

"Do you find her beautiful?" Kitsune whispered to him as the others continued their meal.

Oliver frowned and glanced at her, startled by the intensity of her eyes as she searched his own for the answer to that question.

"I suppose she is," he admitted, "but I was just curious. They make a strange pair."

Kitsune's expression softened. "Sometimes the most opposite people make the closest friends. That's true on both sides of the Veil."

Oliver nodded, unconvinced.

She leaned in and lowered her voice further. "Cheval and her husband were traveling in Yucatazca. They were set upon in the jungle by bandits. Chorti came to their aid. He saved Cheval's life but was too late to stop her husband from being murdered. The two of them fought the bandits together. None of the bandits survived. Cheval and Chorti have been inseparable since. Neither ever goes anywhere without the other."

Oliver glanced around the room as Kitsune told this story, not wishing to be caught staring at the beast-man and the silver-haired woman as they ate. The tragic story touched him, but it also reinforced the melancholy he was feeling at the prospect of setting off on his own to find Collette. Loyalty like that which Cheval Bayard and Chorti shared was precious.

"All right, my friends," Kitsune said when much of the meal had been consumed and the sharpest edge of their hunger blunted. She met Oliver's gaze across the table, then opened her hands to include them all. "Shall we get on with this? We are all, each of us at this table, in danger. But the stakes are much higher than our own lives."

She glared at Coyote, who only raised an eyebrow.

Frost tapped his fingers on the table again to get their attention. "Someone has set the Hunters after the Borderkind. *All* the Borderkind. Or nearly all. We have learned firsthand that some are collaborating with the Hunters, presumably to spare their own lives. Jenny Greenteeth was a traitor. She helped the Hunters track us, and for that, she died with them."

"Not Jenny," said Cheval Bayard. A tear slid down her cheek and she turned from them as she wiped it away.

"The bitch," Coyote said, his voice flat.

Oliver studied him, wondering if any of this was news. Coyote seemed to know much more than someone who had been in hiding ought to be privy to. Either that, or it was simply the arrogant air about him.

"We prevailed, but not without losses. Gong Gong is dead."

Chorti growled deep in his chest and his upper lip curled back from those razor-blade teeth. The frog-thing muttered something in his guttural tongue.

"He will be missed," Wayland Smith said. The old man reached up to tip his hat back, golden afternoon sunshine lighting his face. There was a kindness there that Oliver had not seen before. And now a sadness as well.

"This conspiracy against us must have been brewing for some time. First quietly, with a few killings scattered around the Two Kingdoms, and then more, until they had us all on guard or on the run," Frost continued. "If we had acted more swiftly, gathered together, we would have had a better chance of fighting back. But we are too solitary, all of us. Those who learned of the threat looked to their own safety without considering the danger to their kin."

At this, Frost glanced pointedly at Coyote.

Kitsune and Blue Jay nodded slowly.

Coyote slapped the table, sneering. His eyes were still crazy, twitchy, but now there was a bestial cast to his features that had not been there before.

"You'll watch your tone and insinuations, Frost. What could I have done to save Gong Gong and the others who've died? Me alone? The Hunters would have roasted me on a spit."

"Perhaps it's not too late," Kitsune snarled.

"Enough," Blue Jay said. His tone was quiet, but with an edge that calmed them all. "We are all kin, and there are many more of us who are in danger. The river flows, and we cannot concern ourselves with what is already past, only with what comes next."

Wayland Smith smoothed his unruly beard. "I expect Frost has a plan."

The winter man cocked his head slightly as though searching for some insult hidden in Smith's words. After a moment, he nodded.

"I do, though it isn't much of one, I'm afraid. The Falconer died by my hand. Before he did, he revealed the name of the one who had set the Hunters after the Borderkind. Our enemy is Ty'Lis, an Atlantean sorcerer who advises in the court of Yucatazca's king."

Chorti sat up abruptly and shook his shaggy head.

"I'm sorry, Chorti, but I speak truth. It would be dangerous to presume that Ty'Lis is acting on instructions from the king, but we must at least consider the possibility. The probability, really."

"He must be taking orders from the king," Coyote sniffed. "Atlanteans have been neutral since the creation of the Veil. That is why both kingdoms use them as advisors. Hell, it's the Atlanteans who created the truce to begin with. Without them, there'd be no Two Kingdoms at all."

Blue Jay glanced at Frost and Kitsune. "He's right, you know."

"I only mean that we must consider both possibilities," Frost replied.

Kitsune pushed a curtain of silken black hair away from her face and scanned the Borderkind around the table. She barely seemed to notice Oliver at all, and he wondered if he had somehow upset her.

"Whoever it is, they are powerful. The Hunters have used Doors through the Veil with unrestrained freedom. The sentries at the Doors have either been disposed of and replaced, paid for their cooperation, or are following orders. Influence is the key here. We could question the sentries, trace the influence back to the snake giving orders.

"But, really, king or sorcerer, what does it matter?" the fox-woman asked. "What we need to discover is what our enemy hopes to gain by destroying the Borderkind."

Cheval Bayard raised her chin. She inclined her head respectfully toward Kitsune. "I would like the answer to that question as well. But is it really vital? The enemy must be stopped. It would be difficult to combat the Hunters, but if we directly attack the one who commands them, surely that will end the threat?"

"I agree," Frost said. "With time against us, and more of our number dying by the day, the swiftest course is our only choice. We must travel back through Euphrasia and into Yucatazca, gathering as many Borderkind as we can along the way, find Ty'Lis, and force the truth from him. When he is dead, the Hunters will stop."

"You hope," Oliver said, surprised at the sound of his own voice.

All of the Borderkind turned to look at him.

"What do you mean?" Blue Jay asked.

Oliver shrugged. "Just that you'd better be sure he's the only one giving orders before you kill him. And even with him dead, if the Hunters have agreed to do the job, who's to say if they'll be willing to quit?"

Wayland Smith waved a hand. "Regardless, the task is the same. The only sensible course is to reach Ty'Lis, find the truth, and if he is our enemy, destroy him. But I won't be coming with you, I'm afraid."

Frost frowned, icy brow crinkling. "Why not?"

"You will gather only a handful of Borderkind on your journey. Someone must try to get the word out to others, bring them together, so better to defend ourselves."

"Where will you bring them?" asked Cheval.

"Why, here, of course," Smith said. He lowered his gaze and the brim of his hat cast his face in shadow. "The people of the Gorge may not like it, but this is the safest place. The Hunters will come eventually, as has already been stated, but if ever there was a place to stand and fight, this is it."

Coyote uttered a dry laugh. "In that case, I'll be leaving."

Kitsune sniffed. "Coward."

"I prefer the term 'survivor,' if you don't mind."

"But I do mind," she said.

"Nevertheless, I'll be taking my leave. My path is not with you. With any of you."

For a moment they all looked at him. Even Blue Jay seemed disgusted by Coyote's cowardice, and he had been quick to embrace his cousin before.

"So be it," Frost said, glancing around. "What of the rest of you? Will you join us?"

Chorti sat up straighter, his spine popping loudly. He glanced at Cheval Bayard, who nodded, and then both of them faced the winter man again. Chorti's black eyes gleamed as he uncrossed his arms and placed his massive hands on the table, knife-claws clicking on the wood.

"I stand with you, Frost," he said, his voice a slow rumble.

Oliver flinched. He hadn't thought the beast-man capable of speech.

"As do I," Cheval agreed. She touched two fingers to her forehead, dipping her chin. "The bond is forged, my friends. The Borderkind will live or die, but we are with you until fate decides."

Tlatecuhtli shifted wetly and a loud croak issued from his mouth. It sounded nothing like either English or the tongue he'd spoken before, but Frost only nodded his head in understanding.

"Your aid would be most welcome," the winter man told him, before surveying the others gathered round the table again. "It will be the six of us, then."

A tremor went through Oliver. Here it was, the end of things.

Kitsune raised an eyebrow. "Five, actually."

Frost turned to her, his confusion evident.

"What are you saying, Kit?" Blue Jay asked.

"I'm going with Oliver."

They all stared at her, none more so than Oliver. All through the conversation, Kitsune had worn a grave expression. She had barely looked at him. Now she smiled at him across the table and gave a tiny shrug, as if she had no real explanation for her actions. He felt absurdly grateful.

Coyote laughed. "You mean you're committing suicide."

With surprising speed, Cheval Bayard slipped from her chair and kicked Coyote with such force that he spilled from his seat onto the ground, his bastard's grin gone.

"You embarrass us all with your infantile behavior," Cheval said, the softness gone from her voice and face, a terrible wrath in their place. "Keep quiet, now, or you may find yourself bait for the Hunters."

Coyote rose, staring at Cheval with death in his eyes.

Blue Jay sighed at his cousin's behavior and then turned to Kitsune, his wild eyes warm with affection. "You're certain?"

"I can't let him go alone."

Oliver put his palm against his forehead. "Listen, Kit, you've done enough. I appreciate it, really, but Frost said he'd get me to Professor Koenig. You guys did that. I know you've got more important things to worry about now ..."

Kitsune gave a gentle laugh. "If you go back to the Sandman's castle alone, you'll die."

"Don't have a lot of faith in me, do you?" he said, the jest in his voice strained. *What are you doing, trying to talk her out of coming along?* he thought. *Don't be an idiot.*

Her expression turned uncertain. "I don't want you to die, Oliver."

"That makes two of us."

In the moment of silence that followed, he realized it had been decided. Kitsune would stay with him. He glanced at Cheval and Chorti, feeling as though he now understood them perfectly well.

Wayland Smith cleared his throat. "Still suicide. Coyote's a fool and a coward, but that doesn't make him wrong. The two of you haven't a chance of defeating the Sandman on your own. You're going to need help."

Oliver opened his hands, at a loss. "Any suggestions?"

"I have one," Frost said.

Once again, he claimed all of the attention in the room simply with the tone of his voice. All eyes upon him, Frost turned to Oliver.

"You know some of us have many aspects, different legends from around the world. We are separate beings, and yet aspects of the same legend. Kin in far more than blood."

Blue Jay snapped his fingers. As he shifted in his chair, the air around him blurred blue and there came the sound of rustling feathers. "I see where you're going."

"As do I," Cheval said, delicate fingers playing with the lace collar of her dress. "The Dustman."

Oliver frowned. "I've never heard of him."

"Nor I," Kitsune said.

Frost nodded, his enthusiasm for the idea increasing. "The legend is English, I believe. Not as well known in modern times as the Sandman. But the Dustman is Borderkind as well, and just as powerful."

"But he doesn't go around murdering children and ripping out their eyes?" Oliver ventured.

"No, he doesn't." Wayland Smith smiled. "That's an excellent idea, Frost. If the Dustman could be convinced to help—"

"Yeah," Oliver interrupted, "but how do I do that? How do I even find him?"

Blue Jay put his hand on Oliver's shoulder. "You sleep, my friend."

"It can't be that simple."

"According to the legend, the Dustman is a nursery spirit. Which means you'd need to be in a nursery, with a child," Wayland Smith said.

Cheval Bayard seemed to notice Oliver for the very first time. There was something odd about her long face, almost equine.

"You might want to be in England at the time," she suggested.

"Why not?" Oliver said. "It's on the way. I just wish there was a quicker way to get to Collette. It's a long trip back to the Truce Road."

Wayland Smith leaned over the table, staring at them intently. "But of course there's a quicker way. The Sandman's castle doesn't exist in only one location. It's in many places at once, all of the time. In Euphrasia, both east and west, in Yucatazca, and beyond the Two Kingdoms as well. There is a nearer Sandcastle, to the east, and a Winding Way that will take you there even more swiftly than an ordinary road."

Kitsune shifted in her chair, studying Smith. "Lost Ones can't travel the Winding Way. Ordinary men—"

Wayland Smith arched an eyebrow. "You've seen this with your own eyes, little cousin?"

"No. But I have heard—"

"It is your best and fastest course, whether the Winding Way will take you there or not. You know how to reach it, from the Orient Road?"

Kitsune nodded, brow furrowed thoughtfully.

"Well, then," Smith said, as though the matter was settled. And apparently it was, for Kitsune did not argue further.

Oliver sat back and glanced around, pleased to have a plan, and to know that he was not going to be traveling alone after all. He could not recall ever feeling as grateful to anyone as he did to Kitsune at that moment. Yet when he looked at Blue Jay, and then at Frost, he felt a terrible loss.

Frost had brought him into this, but purely by accident. They had relied upon one another, entrusted each other with their lives. They had become, Oliver believed, friends. It was going to be difficult to say good-bye.

"I just wanted to say—" he began.

Coyote shouted and leaped onto the table. The Borderkind were all in motion at once. Chairs crashed over as they stood, ready to defend themselves. Oliver pushed himself away from the table, chair legs scraping the floor, and he reached to his waist, only to find that he'd left the sword in his room.

At the end of the table, Chorti threw his arms up and bared his razor-blade teeth in a snarl as he flashed his claws, ready.

But it wasn't the wild man that Coyote was after. The only one of them who had barely moved was Tlatecuhtli. The frog-thing began to chatter in his terrible, guttural tongue. The rangy Coyote dove at the frog, fur growing on the back of his neck, bristling along his arms. His jaw elongated, bones cracking as it became a snout filled with wicked teeth.

The frog-thing tensed as though it was about to leap.

Coyote struck it with his body, drove it down to the floor, and then thrust his snout into its fleshy neck. He tore Tlatecuhtli's throat out, spilling bright green ichor onto the floor, spraying his muzzle with the swamp-stinking stuff.

"What are you doing?" Blue Jay cried.

"Take him!" Frost snapped.

Chorti was already moving. The massive beast-man grabbed Coyote by the arms in an iron grip. Coyote thrashed but could not free himself.

"You idiots! Don't you pay attention?" Coyote howled. "The frogs. Stop them!"

Oliver moved toward Cheval, thinking to pull her away from danger. As he darted forward, he saw the slit in the frog-thing's sickly pale belly—vertical lips that disgorged a small frog, no larger than his hand. And then another. And a third.

They were headed for the door, others for the windows. Several hopped toward the darkening corners of the room, searching for an exit that way.

"It's a spy!" Oliver shouted. "Don't you understand? You can't let them get away! He heard everything!"

It was chaos. Utter, disgusting chaos.

In the end, they thought they had managed to destroy all of the traitorous Borderkind's spawn, but they were not certain. Not certain at all. Even if the Nagas had not ordered them to leave in the morning, they would not have been able to risk remaining in Twillig's Gorge longer.

At dawn, they had to leave.

Though he had slain Tlatecuhtli for them, and in doing might well have spared them a confrontation with the Hunters, the rest of the Borderkind shunned Coyote as the meeting drew to a close. He bid a somber farewell to Blue Jay, ignoring the others, and was the first to leave the tavern.

Chorti and Cheval agreed to meet Frost and Blue Jay in the foyer of the inn at sunup, then departed. Wayland Smith promised Kitsune and Oliver that he would return an hour before dawn to see them off, and then he also took his leave.

At the bottom of the stairs, Oliver and his companions gathered, perhaps for the last time.

"I want to thank you all," he began.

Frost tilted his head, a smile on his sharply angled features. Outside, dusk had arrived, and it was a fading light that gleamed on his icy form now.

"I believe we're beyond debt or gratitude now, Oliver," Frost said, and his blue-white, frozen diamond eyes narrowed. "We are comrades now, aren't we? After all we've been through. Comrades, come what may. We will be parted for a time, but wherever we may go, we are brothers in arms."

Oliver could not speak. The winter man was not one for sentiment, and he found himself absurdly touched by Frost's words.

Blue Jay clapped him on the shoulder. "Until dawn, Oliver. Sleep well."

"You, too."

"Blue Jay, a word, if you will," Frost said.

"About our recruits, I assume," the trickster said.

Frost nodded and the two of them drifted back toward the tavern. Others had begun to enter the inn and head in that direction. There might not be many visitors in Twillig's Gorge, but that did not translate into a shortage of patrons for the tavern.

"Shall we?" Kitsune said, gesturing toward the stairs.

"Absolutely," Oliver said. "I'm tired enough to just go to sleep right on the steps."

"I think that might be frowned upon."

They smiled at one another and started up the stairs. As they reached the landing on the third floor, Oliver reached out to take her hand.

"Kit, wait."

One eyebrow raised, she turned to face him, jade eyes flashing with curiosity. Her cloak swayed around her, soft copper fur brushing his arm.

"I just wanted to say ... I mean, you don't know how much it means—"

Kitsune reached up to touch his face, then darted her head in and kissed him once, quickly, on the mouth. He'd never felt lips so soft, never smelled anything as wonderful as her scent.

She pulled back and watched him, one corner of her mouth lifted.

For several seconds, he only stood there stupidly. Then he shook his head. "Kit, you know ... when this is all over, I'm going home. This isn't my world. Julianna's waiting for me. She *is* home, for me."

A glimpse of sadness flashed in her eyes, but her smile never wavered.

"Go to bed, Oliver," she said.

Kitsune walked down the hall and disappeared into her room, leaving him standing by himself in the corridor.

His skin prickled as though he was surrounded by static electricity. When she had kissed him, and stood so near, the temptation had been powerful. Oliver could not deny that Kitsune stirred desire in him. She would have had such an effect on any man. Everything about her was magical; but, in the world of the legendary, *everything* was magical. He reminded himself of that now.

All his life, Oliver had believed in magic, in things beyond the scope of human understanding. No matter what peril it had brought him, he reveled in the discovery that he had been right all along. And yet the more he saw of magical creatures and enchanted lands, the more he longed for the simpler magics of the mundane world.

A small smile touched his lips as his mind flooded with memories and images of Julianna: the music of her laughter; the knowing, indulgent look in her eyes; the way her fingers slid into his on sheer instinct; and how perfectly their bodies molded together as they curled together, whether on the sofa to watch a movie or in bed after making love.

Simple magic.

They both loved the ocean best in winter, and at night. They shared a hatred of bars and a passion for bad Chinese food, and they were endlessly amused by each other's taste in music. One of the few times they had found themselves in musical agreement was a Saturday afternoon in September, their senior year in high school, when they'd driven down to Portland to see James Taylor at an outdoor music festival. Julianna rarely enjoyed older music, but had fallen under the sway of Taylor's sweet voice and acoustic guitar.

Sitting on a blanket on the grass, she had leaned in close to him, Oliver's arm around her, and they had just soaked it all in—four generations sprawled around the park with their picnic baskets and beach chairs, the beer and wine flowing, dancing and singing along.

Oliver had kissed her head, breathing in the scent of her.

"They're all about you, Jules."

She had looked up at him, confused. "What?"

"The songs. They're all about you."

James Taylor had launched into "Something in the Way She Moves" right then, and Julianna—eyes wide open, shivering just a little—had kissed him like he had never been kissed before.

That was magic.

Kitsune stirred something primal in Oliver; he could not deny that. But he could never have the intimacy with her that he shared with Julianna, and he would never sacrifice that simple magic.

Jules, he thought. *You'd hardly recognize me now.*

The night was long for Kitsune. The legend of Twillig's Gorge established it as a safe haven, a sanctuary for anyone who wished to escape the rest of the world and live peacefully. Yet there were enemies here. Worse, though there might well be spies amongst the Lost Ones and the legendary, they had found treachery amongst the Borderkind. It was appalling enough that some, like Coyote, were too frightened and selfish to stand with their kin and fight, but the idea that there were turncoats among the Borderkind was especially difficult to bear.

Jenny Greenteeth had been her friend. But now it had become distinctly clear that Kitsune could trust only herself, Oliver, Blue Jay, and

Frost. They had fought side by side and would have given their lives for one another.

How much simpler it would have been never to have left the Oldwood, to have just waited for the Hunters to come after her. Yet she pushed such thoughts away. This conspiracy against the Borderkind could not be allowed to go without reprisal.

Until then, however ... she would take care, and watch her back.

That night, she slept as a fox, curled up beneath the bed in her room at the inn. Anyone who entered thinking to do her harm would find rumpled blankets but no one in bed. Yet though Kitsune had slept through storms and blizzards, in bramble patches and underground dens, and despite her exhaustion, she did not sleep well.

At night, the inn was cold, and she wound more tightly in upon herself. Voices in the corridor or from out the window, down in the gorge below, carried to her and her ears pricked. Kitsune knew she had made the right choice, going with Oliver. Frost had promised only to see him safely to Professor Koenig, but to let him go off on his own now ... Well, they might as well kill him themselves. He'd proven surprisingly courageous and resilient for an ordinary man, but he was still just human. Not that she blamed Frost. The threat to the Borderkind far outweighed the potential loss of one human life.

But she had spoken truly. She did not want Oliver to die. Her pulse raced at the nearness of him. The fox in her *desired* him. It confused Kitsune horribly. How could she have such yearning for a fragile, mundane man?

Yet there was no denying it.

He was promised to another, and loved her. But Kitsune hungered for him, and she would see him safely on his journey or die herself.

All through the night she drifted in and out of sleep. It lasted an eternity, and each time she peeked out from beneath the bed to see that the sky beyond her window was still the rich black velvet of night, she was newly astonished. It seemed morning would never come.

When, at last, she opened her eyes to see that the darkness had taken on a golden glow, the first hint of impending sunrise, she was still exhausted, but she could not close her eyes again. Dawn approached, and they were to leave.

She stretched, tail twitching behind her. The floor was dusty and her eyes began to water. The fox sneezed, then shook her whole body before slipping out from beneath the bed. Kitsune glanced around the room, still anxious, and at last she began to stretch again. This time the motion did not stop, and her muscles lengthened, smooth as liquid, bones shifting.

In the midst of her room, she reached up and pulled back her hood. She had bathed before retiring the night before. Now she went into the bathroom, splashed water on her face, and ran her fingers through her long hair to straighten it.

Kitsune yawned and met the gaze of her reflection. She ought to go and wake Oliver, but somewhere in the inn, there was breakfast cooking. Her stomach grumbled. Greasy bacon would be wonderful. Eggs as well. Raw if she could find them. She wondered if there would be coffee. If she hurried, she could bring breakfast up to Oliver and they could be gone within an hour after sunup. That ought to be near enough to dawn to satisfy the sentries.

She left the room, locking the door behind her. Her tread silent upon the stairs, she descended to the first floor. In the foyer, the smell of breakfast cooking was powerful and merely inhaling it filled her with renewed vigor.

But there was another scent there, one that she recognized.

Wayland Smith had said he would be there to see them off at dawn, but his scent lingered. He had already arrived. Kitsune sniffed again, nostrils flaring, to be certain she was not mistaken. No, he was here. Had passed by only moments before.

Breakfast was served in a small room at the front of the inn, almost diagonally opposite the tavern where they had met the previous evening. The tavern would be closed now, the stink of stale ale remaining no matter how many times the tables had been scrubbed. It would be dark, and empty.

Or it ought to have been. But this morning, the tavern was not entirely unoccupied.

This early in the morning, she saw only the innkeeper as she walked noiselessly toward the tavern. Soon the few other guests at the inn would begin to rise to make their way down for breakfast, at least if the aroma of food was any indication. It occurred to her that the innkeeper and his wife might be feeding themselves now so that they could attend to their handful of guests when they rose. That was sensible.

But even as such thoughts crossed her mind, she was following Wayland Smith's scent and listening to the low drone of voices coming from the tavern. Kitsune narrowed her eyes and raised her hood, resisting the urge to transform. She did not need to be in the form of a fox to have a fox's hearing. Even before she reached the open arched entrance to the tavern, she could make out the voices well enough, and knew to whom they belonged.

Wayland Smith and Frost.

At first this set her at ease. She had been growing more and more distrustful, and was suspicious of Smith to begin with. He had been there at Amelia's the night they were betrayed, after all. But if he was with Frost, that was to be expected. They would be discussing the Borderkind, what message Smith ought to be conveying, and which of their kin Frost and his coterie might be likely to encounter on their way to Yucatazca.

But that was not the subject of their conversation.

"You're taking a great risk with the Bascombes," Smith said.

Kitsune froze, then slipped into the shadows just outside the entrance to the room. Frost and Smith both had keen senses, but nothing like a fox. They would not notice her as long as she did nothing foolish.

"It cannot be helped," Frost replied. "Whoever is behind the Hunters—whether it be Ty'Lis or some unknown enemy—they must be destroyed. I do not wish Oliver and his sister ill, but the needs of the Borderkind take precedence."

Wayland Smith laughed softly, bitterly. "When it comes to the Bascombes, how can you know what the Borderkind need?"

"I do not claim to. I only know that attacking our enemies directly will at least mean the deadliest creatures in the Two Kingdoms are too busy to chase them."

Kitsune frowned. All of this was gibberish to her. It did not seem that they meant Oliver harm, but there were secrets here, most certainly.

"You hope," Smith replied. "Why not just trumpet his presence, then? The Lost Ones would rush to his aid if they understood who he was. He and his sister."

"Oh, yes, excellent plan," Frost said. "At the moment, only a very few know who the Bascombes are, and what their presence could mean. If everyone knew, there would be far more who would try to kill them than protect them. Oliver is in enough danger as an Intruder, but he has a small chance of gaining a reprieve if he is clever. Why have every legend in the Two Kingdoms after his blood?

"No, there's nothing more that can be done. I must see to my kin first. His fate is in his own hands. And Kitsune's. Much as we could use her, I'm glad she is going with him. He stands a chance, with her."

From within the tavern came the sound of a match being lit, and then the smell of Smith's pipe, the tobacco rich and earthy. He spoke between puffs.

"You've really made a mess of this, haven't you, Frost?" he said grimly.

There was a moment of pause. From within the tavern came the tinkling sound of ice crystals as Frost moved.

"You'd do well to watch your tone with me, sir."

"Of course," Wayland Smith replied.

The fear in his voice made Kitsune shiver.

"It was bad enough when I began to hear of Hunters preying upon Borderkind, murdering our cousins. I knew right away something had to be done, that some dark power saw us as a threat and wanted to eradicate us. But when I heard whispers that they had been sent after the Bascombes, I knew I had to protect them. Had I time, I would have brought others. It would have been so much simpler. But the Falconer surprised me. He was faster than I expected. I was wounded."

Smith puffed on his pipe, and when he spoke again, his voice was rough from smoke. "You had no choice."

"None. I was too weak to spirit them away. Oliver helped me get to a place where I could cross through the Veil. The only way to save him was to take him through with me."

"Putting a death warrant on his head for trespassing?"

"It couldn't be helped," Frost said, his tone as crisp and cold as his skin. "Just as I had no choice but to leave Collette behind. I couldn't take them both—"

"But you only needed one to survive. So you sacrificed the sister."

"No," Frost snapped. "I was . . . fairly sure that the Falconer would pursue us. He could have found the sister at any time in the mundane world. But with Oliver in our world, that was trickier. It was a risk, I admit. But even now, they haven't killed Collette."

"They're keeping her as bait," Smith said darkly.

"But she's alive."

Kitsune shuddered. Once again she had misjudged who she could and could not trust. How many secrets was Frost keeping from her? From Oliver? There was more to this, and she would have answers, but this concerned Oliver more than it did her and he ought to be with her when she confronted Frost.

In swift silence she raced into the foyer. As she went up the stairs she caught new scents. Chorti and Cheval Bayard were about to arrive, ready to ally themselves with Frost. That was fine with Kitsune. It was time that secrets were exposed and true loyalties revealed.

No matter the consequences.

ith the dawn light peering over the upper ridge of the plateau where they had camped the night before, Julianna sat with her legs pulled up beneath her and stared at the breathtaking beauty of sunrise. Halliwell lay on the ground fifteen feet away, arms akimbo, snoring lightly. From the ache in her own bones, she knew that he would be a wreck when he woke. Every hour of sleep he had managed to steal on the hard-packed earth of the plateau would be another knotted muscle, but she could not bring herself to wake him.

She was not sure what to make of Halliwell now.

When he had first been saddled with bringing her along in pursuit of Oliver, the man had been distant and arrogant. No more so than many men she had known, of course, but it had been tiresome. As they had traveled from the States to the U.K., things had warmed between them. Julianna had decided that she liked him. Curmudgeon that he was, Halliwell was an intelligent man and good at his job. She had also begun to believe that her newfound respect for him was reciprocated. And perhaps it had been.

But here, the rules had changed.

Halliwell wanted answers to the mysteries that his investigation had presented, but they needed to find Oliver for a different reason entirely now. If they had any hope of getting out of here, of waking from the nightmare of this impossible place, it lay in Oliver's hands.

Whatever had happened to Oliver—and the surreality of their surroundings made it appear that there was no simple explanation for that—it was clear now to Julianna than he probably had not abandoned her without reason. If he had an explanation, she wanted to hear it.

She had loved him for so long that he was a part of her, under her skin and in her every breath. When she had thought that he had abandoned her at the altar, she had been crushed. But what she could never have explained to anyone was that what had shattered her heart was not the idea that he had decided not to marry her; it had been the thought that he did not trust her love for him enough to come and talk to her about it.

As horrifying as Max Bascombe's murder—and Collette's disappearance—had been, they had made her doubt the version of events that everyone she knew had been so quick to embrace; that Oliver had simply gotten cold feet and vanished. Julianna hated the fact that she had initially embraced this as truth.

She ought to have known better. Julianna was not a fool; she had sensed his hesitation, and she understood it. How could she not? No one in the world knew him the way she did. But if Oliver had changed his mind about getting married, he would never have let her find out at the altar.

They'd known each other most of their lives, but had only become friends during freshman year of high school, when they'd been partnered up in biology lab. Julianna had always thought Oliver was cute, but he was such a boy, and she didn't have time for the foolishness of boys when she was younger. Older guys intrigued her then, because she had been such a serious girl, a brooding poetess, scribbling her heart's every yearning and ache by candlelight in her bedroom. She had always been close to her father and their conversations around the dinner table had made her a thoughtful, opinionated child with a deep appreciation for a good debate.

Her poetry was private and full of all of the parts of her that her father would not have understood, never having been an adolescent girl. Her mother had tried to nurture her relationship with her daughter through "girls only" shopping trips and special dinners for just the two of them when Julianna's father was out of town, but the bond between father and daughter had been different. They'd always been at ease in one another's company.

When she and Oliver had become friends, that first year of high school, Julianna knew she had found the only other person in the world she had ever felt that way around. He understood how private her poetry was and never pressed her to read it, but whenever she allowed him to, he would look at her as though she'd given him some kind of gift. She had admired his closeness with his sister, who was off at college but came home to visit frequently.

Oliver had been one of the cutest boys in their class and friendly to everyone, but he and Julianna had become a clique all their own. But their friendship had not grown into anything more, which astonished everyone they knew. Instead, they advised each other on every crush and flirtation through the first two years of high school. She liked that Oliver never seemed to want the girls who wanted him. He preferred interesting to pretty, and focused on juniors and seniors, the same way Julianna herself did with the boys.

It was only much later that she came to wonder if they had both been concentrating on people who were beyond their reach in order to avoid falling in love with anyone else.

At the end of sophomore year, Oliver had appeared in his first play. He had always loved drama and music and Julianna had encouraged him to audition. His father had dismissed his interest in theater as an unnecessary distraction. Football would have been fine, but theater, somehow, did not fit Max Bascombe's image of the young man he wanted his son to become.

Oliver might have auditioned to spite him, or because Julianna would not leave him alone about it, but once he was cast in the play—

a production of *42nd Street*—his motives became pure. He had simply loved the magic of the stage, the freedom of transforming into someone else.

Julianna understood. Her poetry provided her a similar freedom.

The show was performed half a dozen times. Collette came all the way home from Boston College to see her little brother on stage, but Oliver's father never managed to attend.

After the last performance, Julianna had gone backstage and found Oliver standing in the wings by himself. He did not mention his father's absence, but she saw the hurt in his eyes.

She'd held him then.

Nothing was the same after that night.

They spent their junior and senior years lost in each other, physically and emotionally, happy to make their classmates' predictions come true. Somehow, rather than suffering from the intensity of their relationship, their grades actually improved. The future was important to both of them.

And it had almost ruined them.

The summer after their graduation from high school had been the saddest time of Julianna's life. She and Oliver had stayed together, but their every kiss and touch had been bittersweet. They had agreed that they had to pursue their own paths, that they would be doing a disservice to themselves and each other if they did not reach for their dreams.

Oliver had gone to Yale, in Connecticut. Julianna had attended Stanford, all the way across the country, in California. Surrendering to logic, they had promised one another that if, when college was through, they were both single, they would be together again, but that there would be no promises in the meanwhile. It was only practical.

At Yale, Oliver had followed the pre-law curriculum and spent all four years in the Drama Club, fulfilling his father's plan for him while still following his own heart. At Stanford, Julianna had fallen for a California guy two years older than she was. All of the anguish and drama of her poetry came alive in that relationship. He turned out to be shallow and callous, and forced her to wonder how she could be so wrong about someone.

The asshole went to Stanford Law. Julianna refused to follow him there. When she learned Oliver would be attending Yale Law School, she knew that she had to go as well. Older and wiser, she knew that the intimacy she'd shared with Oliver was a rare thing. To have such passion with someone, combined with an abiding trust, was so precious that only a fool would surrender it willingly.

They had a chance to make up for a terrible mistake they had made four years earlier. Julianna had never been much of a believer in destiny, but could not deny that it felt as though they had always been meant to be together.

She still felt that way.

Ted Halliwell needed to find Oliver because he wanted answers, and he wanted to go home. Julianna wanted those things as well, but what Halliwell did not understand was that, to her, finding Oliver *was* going home. The lunacy and horror that had intruded upon their lives had made her question her faith in Oliver, but she was beyond that now. She still had questions, but no longer had doubts.

All she really wanted was to be reunited with him. Everything else was secondary.

Halliwell had different priorities.

But to find Oliver, to survive in this place, she and the detective were going to have to work together. At first that had seemed obvious and natural, but now she had begun to grow concerned. Halliwell had cooled to her. She felt it. The truth was, they had been fellow travelers before, working together. Not friends. And Julianna was no fool. Halliwell knew where her loyalties were, and whose side she would be on if he had any conflict with Oliver when they caught up to him.

Yet they *had* to travel together. They had only each other to rely on.

Julianna shuddered and hugged herself tightly. The night had grown cold with the wind whipping across the top of the plateau, but there had been nothing they could do about it. She wished she had not left her jacket behind. That had been foolish.

She watched the golden light of the sun spread across the sky. Soon it would reach her, warm her, and the air would begin to heat up. Halliwell would stir.

During the night, she had woken several times and felt a rising spark of hope that she would find herself back in her world, in a place that made sense and followed the rules that she understood.

Now, with the sunrise, she realized that it had been a dangerous moment. She might have gone mad, fighting the need to accept the reality of the world around her. To accept magic and giants and rivers that spoke with human voices, and the dead things they had seen back in the real world on Canna Island.

"Real world," she whispered. "Can't think like that."

This place, this world, *was* real. Accepting that was the only way to survive. Yet from the look in Halliwell's eyes last night, she was not sure if he had quite accepted it. The detective was numb, moving from one place to another with the single-minded determination of an angry drunk.

Maybe he has to be that way. Maybe that's how he needs to survive, she thought. That made sense to her. Finding Oliver was all that mattered to Halliwell. Slowing down for a moment to look too closely at the world they were traveling through would only confuse and distract him.

The more she thought about it, the more Julianna thought that was a good strategy. Full speed ahead. Don't look too closely. And whatever you do, don't stop to smell the roses. No telling what they might really be.

They had spent all the long afternoon of the previous day making their way up the ridgeline to the top of the cliff, following a switchback for a while and then a steep hill. In the end, they had found themselves miles from where they had begun, but on top of the plateau, looking down into the valley as night fell.

This morning, they would strike back toward the spot where the river went into the cliff face, then follow what they hoped was the path of the river until they reached the other side of the mountain, the far end of the plateau, and then descend to the valley or basin or whatever they found there, and follow the water again.

If the river did not disappear underground forever.

In that case, they would not have a clue where to begin.

Julianna ran her fingers through her hair. Her bladder felt full and she got up, muscles popping in protest, her whole body aching, and stumbled off behind a stand of shrubbery to pee.

When she came back, the sun had just touched the edge of the plateau, nowhere near Halliwell, but the lightening of the sky must have been enough to rouse him, for he was stirring. Julianna had never asked Halliwell his age, but pegged it at early fifties. Not old, but a long way down the road from young. He was at least her father's age, but there was something she found attractive about the detective with his gruff features and piercing blue eyes, his somber expression and more-salt-than-pepper hair in need of a cut. Halliwell could have been an actor. Not a star, perhaps, but one of those character players that people recognized right off but whose names they could never remember.

She slipped her hands into her pockets and stood a few feet away as he slowly woke. A groan escaped his lips and he opened his eyes, reaching up to scrape the remnants of sleep away.

In his age and in his eyes there was the weight of something that haunted him. Halliwell was what people called a soulful man, and she realized suddenly that this was what she liked about him.

It reminded her of Oliver.

He grunted as he sat up, then slowly climbed to his feet. Halliwell stretched his back and arms and neck with a groan of protest; his bones popped loudly as he moved. He took a deep breath and gazed at the sunrise, rubbing the back of his neck. All of this was done without a single glance at Julianna, as though he had forgotten she was there.

"I feel a hundred years old," he said, without turning to her.

"You look it," she replied.

Brows knitted, he turned and stared at her. Then his mouth twisted up into a smile and he chuckled softly. Some of the weight seemed to lift from him.

"I'll bet I do."

Julianna walked over and stood beside Halliwell, staring at the eastern horizon with him. "We're really here."

Halliwell paused, exhaled, and then nodded. "Yeah."

"I have a weird question for you. I wouldn't even ask it, but you seem a little less . . . freaked out . . . than you were yesterday."

"Appearances are deceiving—" The detective turned to look at her and she saw the years in his blue eyes. "But what's your question?"

"Like I said, it's weird. But . . . okay, look, something has happened to us. We're lost, somewhere so far from what we know that we might as well be stranded on the moon. For me, the urge to find Oliver is even more powerful than the need to get home; he's the only man I've ever really loved."

She thrust her hands deeper in her pockets, shifting her weight awkwardly. "I want to go home, Ted. Desperately. But not as desperately as you do. I can't help thinking there's more to it than just going home for you."

Halliwell crossed his arms. "So what's your question?"

Julianna shrugged. "Just what it is, I guess. What's back there that's got you frayed so badly? I've got my parents, my work, my friends, everything. My whole life. What is it that's waiting for you back there that makes the thought of not getting home so terrifying for you?"

His blue eyes were cold. His nostrils flared in anger.

"We're wasting daylight," he said, staring at her, daring her to push it or contradict him. "If we have any hope of catching up to Oliver, we've got to move, find that river."

Her throat dry, Julianna almost asked him again. The thought that they might not get home panicked her, but it was obvious that it affected Halliwell far more, fraying at his spirit.

But all she did was nod.

Halliwell turned his back on her, studying the sky. "Give me a minute? I've just got to—"

Gruff as he was, he didn't want to talk about the need to relieve his bladder in front of her. The guy was an enigma. Julianna smiled and let out a breath.

"Sure. I'll start walking. You can catch up. Due west, right?"

"No. We've lost too much time. I think we need to go northwest, try to gauge where we might intersect with the river, and then turn north until we come to the other side of the plateau. If we haven't hit another valley first."

Julianna pushed her fingers through her hair again. "All right."

She started walking. Her feet ached from all the walking that they had done the previous day, but that was just the beginning. Somehow she doubted there would be a bus to carry them to their destination. Her shoes were comfortable, hiking boots that doubled for her as winter footwear. But this was no ordinary hike.

The sun had spread across the plateau, and as she set out, it began to warm her at last.

After several minutes, Halliwell caught up, not even winded. For his age, he was in pretty good shape. That was good. If he had been out of shape, they'd likely be dead by now.

In silence—the space of words unspoken between them—they walked across the plateau. Halliwell had been a Boy Scout as a child, which came as no surprise to Julianna. She herself had been forced into the Brownies, the junior Girl Scouts, but by the time she could have joined the older girls, she refused to have anything further to do with it. Hallie Terheune had by then become queen bitch of all Brownies, and she'd be going into Girl Scouts as well. But even now, Julianna remembered well enough how to navigate by the sun, and Halliwell had not forgotten much of his childhood love of the woods either. Growing up in midcoastal Maine, it was just the sort of thing children learned.

Time had passed, of course, and scouting wasn't exactly like riding a bike. Some things did fade. Yet Julianna felt sure they were on the right track.

The landscape reminded her of Arizona: dry and rocky with stretches of scrub grass. Not desert, certainly, but not exactly lush. Small ridges of rock jutted up from the earth as though carved out by ancient glaciers, and there were small, thin trees here and there—wiry things that resembled nothing at all familiar.

Within a quarter of an hour after setting out, Julianna was wetting her lips with her tongue, mouth parched. It was warm, but not uncomfortably so, and there was a breeze that brought a dry, sweet smell, like pressed flowers. But she was thirsty. Hunger had not begun to rumble her belly yet, but she was certain it would begin soon enough. She could do without the food for a while, but the water was going to be a problem. The river was important to them for more reasons than one.

The stale smell of her own body and the unpleasant way her dirty clothes clung to her reminded Julianna of mornings in college when she had woken after long, regrettable nights. But despite it all, she had none of the dullness of a hangover. The scent on the breeze, the feel of the sun, the colors of this world were all too vibrant to allow it.

Halliwell limped a bit as he walked. She was not even sure he noticed it, but he favored his left leg. A selfish twinge went through her when she noticed, and she hoped it was just sleeping out on the ground that had given him a kink, not something permanent. Something that was going to be a problem down the line.

Her shoelace came loose.

"Hang on," she said, as she knelt to retie it.

Halliwell paused and stood above her. As she finished, he spoke in a voice that was barely a rasp.

"We're not alone."

Outside Oliver's window, dawn's light was reaching down into Twillig's Gorge. Morning came later in the Gorge, the sunlight creeping down along the western wall as it rose. The Nagas had given them specific instructions to be gone by dawn, but Oliver could not move. He sat on the edge of the bed in his room at the inn and stared at Kitsune.

"That's insane."

Kitsune's eyes were always so wild, but not now. In this moment, they were rock steady. She leaned forward, silken hair hanging in black curtains on either side of her face.

"You think I don't know how it sounds?" she asked, an edge in her voice. Kitsune glanced around the room, hands fluttering, as though trying to search for some explanation for the inexplicable. "I am used to being on my own, Oliver. Solitary. Tricksters nearly always are. But when I learned that the Borderkind were being killed, I thought perhaps it would be best not to be alone for a while."

"And then you met Frost and me in the Oldwood," Oliver said.

The fox-woman nodded. Her hood was thrown back, the fur soft. Vulnerable. Oliver had never thought of her that way before.

"I thought I had found trustworthy companions whose goals were my own. To survive. To uncover terrible secrets. But there were more secrets than I ever imagined—"

Oliver held up a hand. "Wait. Just . . . just stop, okay? I get that you were just as much in the dark as I was, so can we focus for a minute? Does any of what Frost and Smith were saying sound familiar to you? Do you have any idea what he was talking about?"

Kitsune took a breath. "Not at all. It was clear he believes that you and your sister are somehow important to this world, that if the truth about you were to come out, it would be even more dangerous to you than the death warrant."

"How can that be?" Oliver shot to his feet. "What is more danger-ous than someone ordering your execution?"

He searched her eyes for answers but found only confusion that mirrored his own, and sympathy. Oliver put a hand over his eyes and sighed. Could it be that Frost was not his friend, that the winter man had been lying to him all along?

"Jesus," he whispered, dropping his hand. "All right. So the Falconer . . . wasn't hunting Frost. He was sent after me and Collette, and Frost was wounded trying to stop him. That's what you're saying?"

Kitsune opened her hands. "I have told you what I heard."

"Why us? What is it about us?"

"This is not the first time we've asked that question, Oliver. The Sandman wants your life so badly that he is holding your sister as bait. It is you he wants, not Frost. Not any Borderkind. You. And now we know that Collette is only still alive because the Sandman has not caught you yet."

Oliver narrowed his eyes. "The Sandman? Or whoever woke him up? Whoever sent the Falconer?"

Kitsune turned her back on the window. Slowly, she raised her hood, jade-green eyes staring out from the shadows beneath. When she spoke, he could see the points of her tiny, sharp teeth.

"Your questions might be better put to another."

Anger and confusion roiled in him. He nodded, staring at Kitsune. "I want to trust you. But I'm beginning to wonder if there's *anyone* I can trust."

"I wonder the same," she said, voice a low growl. "You are not the only one who has been kept in the dark."

"All right," Oliver said. "Let's go ask those questions, then."

He dressed quickly, grateful once again for the new clothes Coyote had supplied. Hunyadi's sword hung at his hip and he was surprised how quickly he had become used to its weight and sway.

Oliver opened the door and led Kitsune into the hall. He went to the next room and rapped on the door.

"Blue Jay won't be there," Kitsune said. "We were supposed to meet at the front desk."

"Right."

Together they went down the stairs. Oliver quickened his pace, anger rising. With all that they had been through together, the idea that Frost had been keeping secrets was infuriating. His father had been horribly murdered. His relationship with Julianna was in shambles, the wedding plans ruined. His life was in constant peril. Collette was in the hands of a monster. Maybe Frost had only come to Kitteridge to try to save them, but he'd been less than completely successful. If there were reasons behind all of this, Oliver deserved to know what they were. Hell, Kitsune deserved to know.

His boots pounded the wooden steps. Out the window in the stairwell he saw the gorge spreading out below, coming alive with the industry of morning. People and legends traveled bridges and ladders; store awnings were unfurling; small boats were bobbing at the dock on the river as goods were unloaded. All of that, he caught in a glance. What was going on in Twillig's Gorge mattered not at all. Not now.

"Frost!" he shouted as he reached the bottom of the stairs.

"Oliver, you may want to—" Kitsune began.

His hands curled into fists. He wasn't listening. Two governments wanted him dead, and now it seemed that those trying to kill the Borderkind had set their sights on him as well. And Frost was keeping fucking secrets? The time to be quiet was over.

"Frost, where the hell are you?" he shouted.

Behind the front counter, the innkeeper shot him a dark look and crossed his arms. "Sir, if you please, some of the guests may still be sleeping."

Oliver ignored him. Kitsune prowled around the foyer for a moment, sniffing the air, then went toward the tavern. Oliver followed, but she stopped at the door, peering inside.

"They're gone," she growled. When she turned, he saw the wildness had returned to her eyes. The fox-woman bit off the words. "Chorti, Cheval Bayard, Blue Jay, and Frost. Just this morning; they've been and gone."

Kitsune slipped past him, fur brushing his hand, electric to the touch. She darted toward the front of the inn again and leaped up onto the counter. The innkeeper snapped an angry curse and raised a finger to admonish her. Kitsune slapped the hand away and grabbed him by the hair, pulling his face close to hers.

"How long ago?"

"Let me go, you myth bitch!"

Oliver drew the sword, staring at the man. "When did Frost and the others leave?"

The innkeeper whimpered, but he opened his mouth to answer. Before he could, however, another voice spoke up from the front door.

"You've missed them by half an hour, I'm afraid."

Oliver and Kitsune both twisted round. Wayland Smith stood just inside the door, fox-head walking stick in his hand. If he had just entered, the door had made not a creak.

Smith nodded toward Kitsune, hat brim hiding his eyes. "You chose your path, fox."

All of the anger and tension went out of Kitsune. Oliver watched in amazement as she stood straighter, letting her cloak fall around her, and bowed her head in deference.

"As you say, uncle."

Wayland Smith raised his gaze and stared at Oliver. "You saw last night that there are spies in the gorge. There's no telling how many of those frogs escaped. Even if the Nagas did not order you to leave, you risk danger from myriad sources every moment you remain. Even if there were no conspiracy, no Hunters, have you forgotten the price on your head? Word is spreading. You ought to—"

Oliver snorted. "You've got to be fucking kidding me." He glared at Smith, then at Kitsune. "Kit, this is the guy Frost was talking to, right?"

The fox-woman did not raise her head.

"Bascombe," Smith began, as though to admonish him.

The Sword of Hunyadi felt warm and light in his grip. Oliver raised it, pointing the tip at the old Borderkind in punctuation.

"Kitsune heard your little chat with Frost this morning, old man. I'm through with secrets. The Falconer was after me and my sister, that's what you said. The legendary want us dead. You're going to tell me what it's all about, or I swear to God, I'll take your fucking head off!"

"Oliver," Kitsune whispered. "Don't."

He stared at her. "Don't? My father had his eyes ripped out by the fucking Sandman. The thing has my sister. Come on, Kit, don't you think I deserve to know why?"

Wayland Smith shook his head slowly. "You fool." He gripped the fox-head of his stick and glanced at the innkeeper. Something about the look drew Oliver's attention, and he saw that the innkeeper was looking back and forth between them as though trying to work out a puzzle.

"Now, wait a moment," the man behind the counter whispered. He pointed to Smith. "He's the one, isn't he? Oh, you bastard, trying to keep it so quiet. You clever prick."

Smith clucked his tongue and shot a meaningful glance at Oliver. "See what you've done?"

Then Wayland Smith leaped across the room, twisting in the air. He swung the stick with its heavy, carved head, and brought it down with a sickening crack on the innkeeper's skull.

The man staggered back, crashed into the wall, and slid to the floor, unmoving.

Oliver stared, sword wavering in his grasp. "Oh, Christ. What the hell did you do?"

Kitsune stepped up, fur brushing him, and grasped his free hand. "We must go, Oliver."

He gritted his teeth. "Not without the truth."

"You'll die here, then," Smith said, eyes cold and gray. "You've said too much. I killed the man for your own safety, but there's a chance others overhear us even now. And you cannot know how much Coyote may have guessed, or who else he will tell to save his own skin. Word will spread, the truth will out, and it will come to you eventually. It's safest for you if you do not know."

"Bullshit! If it concerns me, then it's *my* truth! And you're going to tell me, damn you."

He started toward Smith, sword up, watching the walking stick warily. How many fencing matches had he won? Dozens, at least. But he had never fought someone with such uncanny speed, not at close quarters.

Wayland Smith removed his hat and set it on the counter. Even as the brim touched wood, he sprang. Oliver raised the sword, parried his attack, then darted the blade forward. Kitsune cried out, but Oliver could not hear her over his own howl of rage. All of his betrayal and fear went into his attack and he twisted inside Smith's defenses, then drove the point of the sword through his shoulder, puncturing flesh and grinding against bone.

The old man grunted in pain, but grinned.

"Well, there's proof, eh?"

Gripping the stick with one hand, he shot the other out and cuffed Oliver in the side of the head like he was an errant child. Staggered, Oliver lost his balance. Smith kicked him away, the blade slipped out of the wound, and then the old man stood there, glaring at him, one hand clasped over the piercing in his shoulder. Blood seeped through his fingers.

"Uncle," Kitsune began.

"I heal," Smith replied.

Oliver was disoriented from the blow, but determined. Blood dripped from the tip of Hunyadi's sword as he raised it, ready to attack again.

Wayland Smith rushed at him with the speed of the wind. One hand gripped his wrist, keeping the sword at bay, the other grabbed his throat and he felt himself driven backward. In the span of three heartbeats he was nearly carried across the foyer of the inn. When he slammed into the door, it crashed open, and then they were at the top of the bridge that led to the inn, hanging above the Sorrowful River.

The sun splashed down upon them. Oliver twisted to escape its glare, trying to wrest himself from Smith's grasp. The old man slammed him against the thick wooden balustrade of the bridge and Oliver was bent backward, a hundred feet above the river, nothing below him but a fall that might kill him.

"You will go," Smith said, "because you have no choice. To stay is to die, but to go is to have a chance for yourself and your sister. You will see me again, Bascombe. Be assured of it."

The old man glared at him with stormy gray eyes, then abruptly released him. Wayland Smith backed away, turned, and strode along the bridge, leaving Oliver to gasp to catch his breath. He pulled himself away from the balustrade and stared for a moment at the drop below, at the community of Twillig's Gorge going about its business, none the wiser.

Kitsune stepped out of the front door of the inn. She raised her hood and looked at him from its depths, jade eyes gleaming.

"You're fortunate to be alive," she said. "Shall we be going now, and try to stay that way?"

The fox-woman turned and started along the bridge. Oliver took a deep, shuddering breath of frustration, slid the sword into his belt, and followed.

We're not alone.

Julianna stood after tying her shoe, Halliwell's words echoing in her mind. She looked at the detective, but his expression revealed nothing. Halliwell scratched at the back of his neck like a man dying of boredom and regarded her impatiently.

"You all set?" he asked.

"Yeah. Shoelaces. They come untied. It happens."

A smile flickered across his face and was gone. By silent consent they started walking again. Julianna watched Halliwell, wondering when he would comment further. Obviously there was a purpose to his behavior. He'd said those words and now he was acting as though nothing had happened at all.

But his gaze was restless. Whenever she glanced at him, Halliwell's eyes were moving, taking in the landscape around them, this copse of skeletal trees, that jutting rock obelisk.

Julianna saw the figure then, perched upon a rock fifty yards ahead. She had looked that way a dozen times and not seen the little man. Now, suddenly, he was simply there. Halliwell had noticed him, obviously. Or had felt that they were observed.

"Keep walking," Halliwell said softly.

She had slowed nearly to a stop without realizing it. Now she picked up her pace, keeping stride with Halliwell. At the same time, she did not take her eyes off of the figure who sat on the rock slab like a child, knees jutting up, elbows resting atop them. In his hands, the little man held a flute and as she watched, he set it to his lips and began to play a lilting, pleasant tune, as though to greet the morning. The melody swirled and dipped, and in spite of her trepidation, she smiled.

As they came abreast of the rock, Julianna slowed again. Halliwell stopped entirely, so she did the same. The detective stood with his hands at his sides, fingers splayed, as though he expected an attack.

They stood together and listened to the jaunty, winding music, watched the little man play his flute. He was dressed in a gray cloth tunic with a thin black rope around his waist, almost like some kind of monk. His bald pate gleamed in the sun and against the early morning blue of the sky, his nut-brown skin seemed a shadow unto itself. Her first impression, that he was old, was borne out by the many wrinkles upon his face, though his skin was taut against his skull.

But his eyes were young, and alight with mischief. As he played, he watched them, returning their curiosity. When he reached the end of the tune, he took the flute away from his lips and smiled, bowing his head.

"Very pretty," Julianna said.

"You have my thanks. A very good morning to you, travelers."

Julianna nodded. "And you."

Halliwell regarded the little man carefully. "Seems a long way from anywhere, if you don't mind my saying, sir. A long way to travel to play your flute."

The old man frowned, brown skin wrinkling even more deeply. "But of course this is not my destination, friend. It is only a place on the road, a spot to rest. But where are you headed, travelers? Forgive me for saying that you seem unlikely mountaineers. You are Lost, yes?"

"Very," Julianna admitted. It earned her a wary look from Halliwell, but she forged on. "We are attempting to catch up to some friends who are also traveling this way. They followed the river, but we weren't certain what dangers might be under the mountain—"

"And so you went over," the old man said, tapping his flute upon his knee. "It *is* dark down there."

Halliwell let out an audible breath and at last his hands seemed to relax. His whole body deflated a bit.

"We hoped to cross to the other side, to find wherever it is that the river comes out again."

The old man looked at Halliwell. He brought the flute up to his lips and blew, a little trill of music drifting off into the air. Then he lowered the instrument and grinned again, his teeth crooked and yellow.

"Ah, but those you seek will not have reached the other side of the mountain."

Julianna shivered. "What do you mean by that? Is there something in the river? In the tunnel?"

"There are many things in the dark water, lady. But you shouldn't worry. The river would carry them through Twillig's Gorge, where travelers are nearly always well met. The odds that the sentries would have killed them are very slim."

Halliwell had frozen at the implication that Oliver might be dead. Julianna understood. Her own heart had trembled because she loved him, but Halliwell was afraid because if anything happened to Oliver, they had no hope of getting home.

"This gorge," Halliwell said. "Can we reach it from here?"

"Certainly. Your present course will bring you there in time."

Julianna shivered again, this time with happiness. A town of some kind, along the river. And if she understood the wrinkled old monk properly, Oliver would have almost had to stop there.

"Thank you," she said. "So very much."

"Not at all," he replied, fingering the holes upon his flute. "The truth is freely given. But surely you must be hungry, yes?"

Something about the glint in his eyes when he said this gave Julianna pause. But Halliwell's face lit up.

"Starved," the detective said. "I don't suppose you have—"

"Certainly," the monk said.

With his flute in one hand, he leaped easily down from the rock, faster and more agile than seemed possible for one so ancient. When he stood before them, Julianna was startled by his size. He had looked small there upon his perch, but now she saw he truly was no larger than a child, perhaps four feet tall at most.

Halliwell seemed at ease, a grateful expression on his face. She wondered if the wrinkled little man's age and size had caught the detective off guard. Certainly, he did not seem to pose any threat. His music had been beautiful, his face beatific, his voice calming. He had been nothing but kind and helpful.

But what had that meant: *The truth is freely given*?

The sprightly little man slipped behind the rock and emerged with a knapsack of the same gray cloth as his tunic. He set it on the ground, unlaced the ties, and reached inside, withdrawing first a small loaf of bread and then a single banana. Crumbs fell from the bread as he held it out, offering it to Halliwell.

Julianna frowned, staring at the banana. It was perfectly yellow, ripe, with only a hint of green at the stem. There was not a trace of a bruise on it, not a brown blemish on the peel.

The old man was traveling as well. This was just a stop along the way for him. If he was carrying food supplies, unless he had taken the banana off a nearby tree, it seemed incredible to her that it would be so perfect.

Incredible.

Small, wrinkled brown hands held out the bread and the banana. Halliwell wore a neighborly smile as he reached out to take them.

The truth is freely given.

Which meant some things were not given so freely.

"Ted, wait."

Halliwell was about to pluck the food from the old monk's hands. He glanced sidelong at Julianna, one eyebrow rising in a question.

"Don't take them," she said.

The old man's eyes narrowed and he reached to put the banana in one of Halliwell's outstretched hands. Julianna lunged forward, slapping at the old man's wrist and knocking the banana from his grip. It struck the ground, where it instantly changed, transforming first into a flute, and then into a pale yellow serpent with a line of green diamond scales running down its back.

"What the hell?" Halliwell snapped, as the snake hissed and coiled, drawing its head back as though to strike. But it only swayed and watched them.

Halliwell and Julianna both backed away from the monk, staring at him. The detective's hands bunched into fists.

"It's in every fairy tale, Ted. Every legend," she said, heart hammering in her chest. Julianna licked her dry lips and stared at the old man, who only regarded them coolly, still with that benevolent expression that had lulled them. "Meet a stranger on the road, you *never* take anything from them. Nothing. Especially not food. It costs something in those stories, and the cost is always something terrible."

As they stared at him, the monk blinked once, and then he laughed softly. His grin widened.

And widened.

The sides of his face split, mouth spreading so far that the entire top of his head tilted back like it was on a hinge. His mouth stretched from ear to ear, and within were rows of yellow, crooked teeth. The front ones seemed ordinary enough, but the others were jagged fangs, long and thin, some of them broken and pitted.

When he spoke, his voice was like the hiss of the snake.

"How fortunate for you that the woman is with you," the monk said. "And unfortunate for me. I would have had your right hand in trade, friend. And her body for my pleasure, had she partaken."

Horror shook Julianna, yet the danger seemed to have passed. The man made no move to attack, nor did the hissing snake upon the ground.

"We'll be going now," Halliwell said, and he took a step backward.

The snake hissed.

The monk laughed and bent down to scoop the serpent into his hand, where it became a harmless flute once again.

"If you insist," he said, the words stretched out by the vastness of his jaws. In his left hand, he still held the small loaf of bread. "But the bread is real. Have it, if you would. Your prize for surviving. Freely given."

Julianna's breath caught in her throat. "Freely given," she said, looking at Halliwell. "I don't think he can break his word on that. There are rules."

"To hell with rules," Halliwell said, still staring at the monster. "No thanks. We'll pass."

Julianna agreed. As hungry as she was, she could not have eaten anything this creature touched. They backed away slowly, watching the little man and his sack and his grisly smile. Only when they were fifty yards away and he had made no move to follow did they turn and walk normally again. They went quickly, glancing back every few seconds.

When they had gone so far that they could no longer see the rock, or the old man and his flute, Halliwell let out a breath.

"I owe you," he said.

"Not a problem. You do the same for me, okay? We've got to keep each other alive."

"Damn straight."

Julianna put a hand on his back. The detective glanced at her, surprised by the gentle contact.

"We're going to get home, Ted. We are."

Halliwell nodded, but his eyes were haunted by the fear that Julianna was wrong.

t the eastern rim, Naga sentries awaited them. Oliver and Kitsune hurried away from the inn across that rickety bridge over the river. At the cliff wall, they climbed rope ladders that hung down from the edge. Kitsune reached the top first, but neither she nor the Naga sentries made any effort to help Oliver up out of the gorge. At the last moment, he was gripped with an urge to simply push off, to spread his arms and let himself freefall back down into the gorge, hundreds of feet, to hit the river, or worse, to crash into the roof of the inn or the balustrade of some better constructed bridge, breaking his fall and his back.

A helpless target. Better to be dead.

The Nagas held bows, just like the ones in the river tunnel, and he could hear the strings sing like harp chords as they were drawn back. The tips of arrows glinted in the sun as they followed the progress of their unwelcome visitors, ready to put an arrow in either of them. Borderkind or human, it did not matter to them. They were just doing their jobs.

The nearest Naga fluttered its wings and slithered closer to Oliver on its thick serpentine trunk. When he glanced worriedly at it, the Naga bowed its head once in farewell. A kind of deference was in its eyes, making Oliver more confused than ever.

Oliver paused to look back down into Twillig's Gorge, far below. Someday, he hoped to return to this strange place, when there were fewer secrets and fewer people trying to kill him. It had sadly not lived up to its own legend. Twillig's Gorge was supposed to be a place where fugitives fled, where anyone was safe, so long as they behaved themselves. He had read stories about Butch Cassidy's Hole-in-the-Wall, and had imagined Twillig's Gorge to be something like that.

But the world of the legendary had disappointed him. There were just as many lies, just as much betrayal and bullshit, on this side of the Veil as the other.

"Oliver. We must go," Kitsune whispered.

He looked at the Nagas. Their wings fluttered and their jaws were tight, fingers twitching as though ready to unleash their arrows. Yes, it was most certainly time to get away from here.

Kitsune touched his elbow and he turned slowly. Her face remained partially hidden by her hood, as though she had retreated back into the solitary legend she was. No trace of a smile touched her lips, and that was a good thing. Had she smiled then, Oliver might have shouted at her, angry that she had not helped him fight Wayland Smith. And he did not want that tension between them. Obviously there were relationships here that he did not understand, perhaps a hierarchy of legends, or of Borderkind. Kitsune had treated Smith as though he was some kind of king, and how was Oliver supposed to argue with that?

They left Twillig's Gorge behind.

Every time Oliver looked back, the sentries were still there, watching. He wondered if their bowstrings were still taut. Eventually he and Kitsune started down a craggy slope. When they could no longer see the Nagas, he finally felt the weight of their scrutiny lifted from him.

For nearly an hour they walked, first down that long craggy slope and then up a smaller, more gradual hill. When they reached its crest, Oliver saw that there was another—steeper, but even shorter—still ahead. Beyond that, however, he could make out the ribbon of a road unfurling across the plains ahead.

On that peak, they paused. Thanks to the mode of their departure, they had no food, no water. No supplies at all. But he was not going to complain. They had escaped with their lives—and in this case, that was enough.

He had been hungry and thirsty in the past few days. There had been worse moments. At least now they were doing something. They were in motion.

Coming to get you, Collette, he thought. *Get you away from that thing. Hang on, sis.*

As they started down, making their way carefully amongst loose rocks and scrub brush, he glanced at Kitsune. "You know where it is? The Sandcastle that Smith was talking about?"

The fox-woman nodded. "Across the hills and down to the plains, perhaps another hour's walk from here, we'll find the Orient Road. From there, I can find the Winding Way. But . . ."

"But what?"

"I thought only the legendary could travel the Winding Way. One version of the story says only tricksters can use it."

Oliver stepped down from an outcropping of rock, loose stones and dirt tumbling down the slope. He paused and looked back up at Kitsune.

"Yeah. So you said. But Smith didn't think that was as hard and fast a rule as you seem to. Why else would he tell us to go that way?"

Kitsune's focus was upon the treacherous footing below, and she did not look at him. "I don't know. But either way, our destination is east."

Oliver frowned. Too many questions, too many rules—and too many of them seemed to be different for him than they were for others. The conversation Kitsune had overheard between Frost and Smith continued to perplex him. The insinuations contained within their words burrowed into his brain like insects—voracious and maddening.

"All right. The Orient Road, then. First stop. But before we take any shortcuts that we can't turn back from, we need to talk about finding the Dustman."

The sun had begun its climb into the sky in earnest. Oliver squinted against the glare as he descended. The Orient Road was not terribly far away, but in this heat, without water, it was going to be an unpleasant trek.

"The diversion will cause a delay."

Oliver glanced at her. "Do you think we have a chance against the Sandman without help?"

Kitsune grimaced. Her jade eyes peered out from beneath the hood. The orange-red fur of her cloak gleamed in the sun, swaying around her, clinging to her as she walked. He thought about how much easier this descent would be for her in the body of the fox and wondered if she maintained a human form for his benefit.

"No."

"Then we have to find him."

"Agreed," Kitsune replied, though reluctantly. "But the Dustman is ever in motion, as though with the wind. The only way to encounter him is by chance, or by intruding upon his legend."

A small stone rolled under Oliver's weight and he slipped, nearly fell sprawling on his face down the slope. It was pure luck that he was able to arrest his tumble before that happened. His breath came ragged in his throat and he paused a moment to rest, hands on his knees.

"Intruding. Apparently I'm good at that. Of course, I don't have a clue what you mean."

At last, Kitsune smiled. It was as though some of the distance between them was dispelled. She threw her hood back and let the sun touch her face, shaking her hair out behind her.

"We must return to England. Once upon the Winding Way, it is a simple diversion. If we cannot travel that way, it will be more difficult. But one way or another, we have to pierce the Veil again.

"As Wayland said, the only way to find the Dustman is to wait for him in the nursery of an English child. His legend was born there, and the old stories keep him in their hearts."

Oliver stopped and stared at her. "Wait. Of all of the nurseries in England, all of the babies in the whole damn U.K., how are we supposed to find the right one?"

Kitsune moved with a fluid grace, stepping from stone to stone as though weightless. She passed Oliver and continued down the slope, glancing back at him over her shoulder as though taunting him to keep up.

"Not a problem at all," the fox-woman said, and the wild mischief returned to her eyes. "When the Dustman senses the presence of another Borderkind—even worse, a trickster—in his domain, he will come swiftly.

"The trick will be trying to explain it to him before he kills us both."

She laughed and spun, dancing from one rock to the next as Oliver struggled to follow.

"Wonderful," he said. "Can't anything in this world be simple?"

Kitsune paused and gave him a dark, warning look. "Legends are never simple, my friend. They appear to be, on the surface, but there are too many facets, too many fears, too many demands that human beings have placed upon every 'Once Upon a Time' for them to be simple."

And with that, she was off again.

Oliver followed as best he could, wondering how long this side trip to find the Dustman would take, and if they would survive it. He wondered where Collette was, even now, and whether she understood what was happening any better than he did. He wondered what the Sandman had done to her, there in his dreadful place.

And how long she could stand it without losing her mind.

During the night, Collette could hear a child cry. A little boy, she thought. He sobbed and whimpered and whispered "no" over and over. It had begun perhaps two hours before dawn, rousing her from sleep. In her prison chamber in the Sandman's castle, she had sat at first and tried to figure out the source of the crying. It came and went, as though at times she was nearer to the anguished boy and at others further away. She had stood and walked the circumference of her prison, had gazed up at the arched windows of the sand pit, and at the stars that showed through, even as they were bleached out of the sky by imminent morning.

She wondered if it was the Vittora, taunting her with more lunacy, but there was no sign of the thing, not a spark of light within the walls of her prison.

"Who are you?" she called into the emptiness of the castle and the vastness of the night. "Where are you?"

There came no answer. Only sobbing. But in spite of the lack of response she kept calling, speaking words of comfort, just in case he could hear her.

Her heart broke for the boy. She wanted to get to him, tried to push her fingers into the hard-packed sand of the walls, to climb, if she could, but there was no purchase. She knew that, of course. Once, and only once, just before the Sandman had appeared within the walls of her prison for the first time, she had felt the sand give way and been able to scoop away at the wall, digging into it. But since then she had begun to believe it had been a hallucination, for she had attempted it a hundred times, trying to make handholds for herself so that she could climb to the windows.

She knew the walls were solid. But the terrified whimpering sobs of the boy got under her skin and forced her to try again.

In time, all she could do was pace and try to cover her ears. The torment of hearing the child's terrified voice, and being unable to help him, was more than she could bear. She had no children of her own, but Collette wanted them, wished to find a man someday who would be a better husband than the asshole she'd married and divorced ... wished for a little boy. And here was this child, no different than the son she might have one day, sobbing in fear and despair, and she could do nothing to soothe him.

At daybreak, the child began to scream.

Collette froze, breath coming in tiny gasps. She stared at the smooth wall, the dawn's light beginning to make a warm glow of the carved sand all around her. Once, twice, three times she spun, searching for the origin of that scream.

She could not just let it happen. Could not just do nothing. Shaking, skin prickling with gooseflesh, she raced to the wall and put her palms against it. Collette closed her eyes, listening more closely than she had ever listened to anything in her life. The screaming—a chilling shriek of agony that went on and on—echoed around the chamber, but its origin was nearby.

Close, but not here. Not right here.

To the left. Her eyes still closed, she slid her palms frantically along the wall, sand scraping her skin. Again she froze, focused, listening.

Here. Just here.

The screaming stopped. She opened her eyes. The Vittora hung in the air just a few feet from her, its light flickering.

"I met her in the mall," it said, words drifting on the air, so close, as if it were whispering right in her ear. "I should have known our relationship was doomed."

During her imprisonment, Collette had retreated again and again into her favorite movies, played them on the screen inside her head. There were a handful of movies she loved with a passion, and this was her favorite line from one of them. The Vittora spoke in the voice of John Cusack from *Say Anything*, as if it could comfort her now. As if the words were anything but gibberish in the panic of this moment.

"I don't want to buy, sell, or process anything—" it began.

Collette drowned its voice out with her screams. She could not ignore its presence, the dreadful light, the knowledge that it existed there on the periphery of her imprisonment, waiting for her to die so that it could be released from the tether that held it to her. But she would not let it get in her way.

"Where are you? What is it?" she shouted, palms against the wall.

The silence shattered. The boy began screaming again, but this time he cried as well, not only terror and pain but anguish. Absolute despair and surrender.

"No," she whispered, gritting her teeth. "No."

Collette tore at the wall, grit getting up under her fingernails. The pads of her fingers scraped on the sandlike concrete. Her heart hammered. Fresh tears traced lines in the dirt on her face. She shouted back to him, pictured the little boy, wondering what he looked like, where he was, what was happening to him.

Anguish clutched her heart, and so it was a moment before she realized her fingers were digging in sand. Then her eyes widened as it came away in her hands, scoops of dry sand. It began to spill down from the wall as though she had broken through some outer shell and now it sifted to the ground, pooling at her feet.

"I'm coming!" she shouted to the boy.

Then his screaming stopped again. Collette kept digging, but fell silent. Perhaps shouting her intentions was not wise. Should the Sandman hear her, what would he do?

"Come on, come on," she muttered under her breath. Her fingers hurt. They were bleeding. But she kept digging, trying to figure out what she was digging toward.

Another prisoner. That had to be it. The boy must be a prisoner in the castle, just as she was, and now someone, the Sandman or one of those freaky hunters, was hurting him. Torturing the little boy.

Her breath came even faster as she dug. The sun was rising and now she could see clearly. She cupped her hands into claws and she dug quickly, both hands at the same time, tearing the edges of the hole to make it larger and larger, digging deeper.

There came one last, long, lingering scream of sorrow.

"No!" Collette shouted.

She thrust her hands, fingers outstretched, into the hole, into the sand, and felt them break through into somewhere else ... into open air. Holding on to the edges of the hole in the wall, she braced herself and kicked at the sand. Gray nothing light showed through from the other side. Almost darkness. But it was another room, some other chamber.

Again and again she kicked and huge chunks of hardened sand fell away, collapsing and crumbling so it spilled on both sides of the opening.

The Vittora began singing a song called "Joe Lies."

The hole she'd dug in the wall was more a tunnel, its shape an arch almost like a door or the windows of her cell. Collette's heart soared. She started through, praying it was not too late for the boy. In the darkness on the other side it was all gray light, but she saw now that it was not another chamber like hers.

It was a young boy's bedroom, a poster of the Justice League of America on the wall, a small night-light casting a dull gray glow into the room. Sand from the hole she had dug had spilled onto the carpet, but otherwise the place looked entirely ordinary, as though she had opened up a tear in this world and back into her own.

With the glare of morning sun behind her, she blinked, trying to get a better look at the figure that lay on the bed. The covers were a tangle, the spread half on the ground. The boy had his arms splayed around him, the shadows making lines upon his face.

She stood in the opening as her vision adjusted to the dim light of the bedroom. Then she saw that the lines on his face were not shadows. They were streaks of blood. And the deepest of shadows were the indents where his eyes ought to have been. Instead they were gaping, empty, bloody holes.

"Oh," Collette whispered.

All the strength went out of her and she collapsed to her knees, sand spilling all around her, down the back of her pajamas, into her hair, into the room ahead of her.

Then something moved across her peripheral vision, a shadow separating itself from the rest of the gray.

The Sandman stood just inside the room. He had remained out of sight at first, but now he swept toward her, his hideously bony form all sharp angles beneath that cloak, his fingers bent and contorted, hands held up in front of him like some bizarre insect as he moved.

From beneath his hood, he glared at her with those terrible lemon eyes.

Then he turned his right hand palm up, and she saw that he held the boy's eyes, still dripping blood and vitreous fluid, optic nerves hanging from them like tails.

The Sandman grinned and opened his mouth, showing those yellow, broken fangs, then let the boy's eyes dangle from the optic nerves above his mouth. He dropped them in and began to chew. Something damp and gleaming spilled over his lips and down his chin.

Collette could not scream. Her breath would not come. Her tears burned her cheeks and her whole body shook. Had she not already been on her knees she would have crumbled then.

"*Was that what you wanted to see?*" the Sandman asked in his rasping voice. He ran his black tongue over his teeth. "*Perhaps in the future you will learn that it is better not to look.*"

Then he held up his hand.

Power struck her. The sand she had torn away, that had spilled into the boy's room, rose up and hit her, wrapped around her, thrust her back through the passage she had dug. It threw her back into her prison so that she sprawled across the soft, shifting floor.

Collette looked up in time to see the wall repairing itself, the sand dancing up from the ground and rebuilding. In seconds, the wall was smooth again, as though she had never touched it.

Solid, again, probably.

But she did not want to know, could not imagine touching it to find out.

The Vittora hung above her, barely noticeable now that the sun had risen. It normally went away while the sun was up, but not this morning. She wondered what that meant.

Quietly, it sang its mad song.

"My daughter," Halliwell said.

"Excuse me?"

He and Julianna walked side by side. They had been traveling across the plateau for more than two hours and Halliwell felt sure they would reach the river gorge anytime now. Twillig's Gorge, the tricky little monk had called it. For the past twenty minutes they'd been on a steadily rising slope, but now he could see that it came to a crest ahead where the slope fell away like a cliff.

That would be the gorge.

He hoped so. God, he needed a rest.

Yet it was not only the gorge, or Oliver, that was on his mind. Since their meeting with the thing on the roadside, his thoughts had been of Julianna, and of home. If not for her, he might be dead now, or at least in debt to some monster, some ... demon ... on the roadside.

They were in this together. Julianna was trying to reach home just as desperately as he was, yet for her, Oliver was a part of that home. Halliwell had never quite believed Oliver was a killer, and by now he was sure of it. He only wanted answers from the man, and some help as well. But he had never looked at it through Julianna's eyes. To her, finding Oliver was everything. She needed to see him, to hold his hands in hers, to hear his voice and maybe to tell him what was in her heart.

Halliwell understood that now.

And it made him think of Sara.

"You asked me what I need to get back to so badly," he said, not turning to look at her, not wanting to see her eyes. "The answer is 'my daughter.' "

They went on another ten steps before Julianna replied.

"What's her name?"

"Sara."

"It's been a while since you've seen her, huh?"

Halliwell frowned. This time he did look at her. "It shows?"

Julianna smiled kindly. "When Oliver disappeared I was just as angry as I was scared of what had happened to him. There were so many things that I wished I'd said to him, conversations we should have had but avoided so many times. When he was gone, the idea that we'd never say those things was devastating."

Halliwell nodded. For a few seconds they walked on, but it was an easy companionship, with no weight of expectation. If he said nothing more, Julianna would not press him. Perhaps because of that, he glanced at her again.

"I don't see her much. But when I do, I never say the things I wish I could. It's like there's so much distance between these days and the old days, back when she was my little girl, that my voice just won't carry all that way. Does that make any sense?"

"It makes perfect sense," Julianna said. "But she will. You say what needs to be said, and she'll hear you."

"Yeah. Maybe," Halliwell allowed. "But first we've got to get home."

Julianna made no reply. None was needed.

Once again, Halliwell looked up the slope toward the sharp ridge there.

Two figures stood on the ridge, silhouetted in the late morning sun. Halliwell held his breath and slowed, but did not stop walking.

"I assume you see them?" Julianna said.

"Yeah."

"So what do we do?"

"If you want to go home, there's nothing we can do. We go talk to them, or try to. They've seen us by now, and neither of us is in much condition to outrace them if they want a chase."

A few more steps, and Julianna whispered again.

"They're not human."

"So I noticed," Halliwell replied. "There seems to be a lot of that going around."

Halliwell trudged onward until the figures on the ridge came into clearer focus. They were tall, thin creatures with wings, and from the waist down had the powerful bodies of snakes. In their arms, they held longbows, and each had a quiver on his back.

The creatures watched them come. As Halliwell and Julianna approached, the larger of the two slung his bow across his shoulder and slithered forward to meet them, wings rustling against his back as though at any moment he might try to take flight. The other, whose flesh was a deeper blue, nocked an arrow and drew back the bow, watching them carefully.

"Hold there," said the snake-man, slithering toward them, powerful upper body upright, wings unfurling.

Halliwell glanced at Julianna. Her chest rose and fell with short little breaths, and just from looking at her, he could see she wanted to bolt. He understood: the presence of this thing made his skin crawl. The very atmosphere of this bizarre world felt too close and claustrophobic around him; only by denying the reality of his surroundings could he fight that feeling. Otherwise it would shatter him.

Panic had been simmering in him from the moment he had stepped into this impossible world. Halliwell didn't want to think about what would happen to him if he let the panic out.

He turned his attention to the snake-man, determined not to look away.

"Good morning," Halliwell said, just as though he were walking on a backcountry road up in Maine and had come upon someone he did not know.

"State your business," the snake-man said, pale blue skin rippling with corded muscle as he swayed before them.

High upon the mountain plateau, it was hot out in the sun. But when the wind blew, it carried a chill from somewhere far off, and Halliwell shivered as the thing spoke to them. He took a protective step nearer to Julianna.

"We're ... newcomers," Halliwell replied, glancing from the snake-man to the other, whose grip was firm upon the bow. The tip of the arrow glinted in the sun.

The snake-man crossed his arms, scrutinizing them. "Lost Ones? Just arrived?" he asked, and Halliwell thought he was paying close attention to their clothes.

"Yes," Julianna said. She smiled, a quiet plea in her eyes. "We're not supposed to be here. We just ... we're trying to find someone. A friend. We were following him and we went through this door and came out ..." She looked around, spreading her arms wide. "Here. We came out here, and we couldn't get back."

The archer fluttered his wings and took better aim. They were close enough that Halliwell could hear the twang of the bowstring being drawn further.

"Not the first," the archer said. "Nor the last."

Halliwell held up his hands. "Look, we don't want trouble. We're not even asking for help. All we want to do is get down to the river."

The older, pale one narrowed his eyes. "Why?"

Julianna cleared her throat as though to get his attention. Halliwell glanced at her, realized that she was just as unsure as he was what to say next. What words would get them where they needed to be without an arrow through the heart?

"This woman is searching for her fiancé. The man she's supposed to marry," he said at last. "His name is Oliver Bascombe, and we think he's passed through the gorge sometime yesterday afternoon. He may even still be there. All we want is to find him, or to pick up his trail so we can continue our search."

Something changed in the snake-man's diamond eyes. Halliwell wasn't sure, but he thought he saw pity there.

"That is all?" the creature asked.

Julianna laughed softly, and a bit manically. "Well, I wouldn't say no to a sandwich and a cup of coffee ..."

"That's all," Halliwell said, shooting her a wary glance. "Did Oliver come through the gorge yesterday? It's a simple question. You don't even have to let us down there if you don't want. Just tell us where the river comes out of the mountain and we'll leave you alone."

The older snake-man gestured to the other to lower his bow. The archer hesitated a moment, then complied.

"Your names," the snake-man said.

"I'm Ted Halliwell. And this is Julianna Whitney."

The creature bowed his head. "I am Ananta of the Naga, and this is Shesa. Our people are the guardians of Twillig's Gorge. I am afraid that this is not a welcome time for visitors."

Ananta knitted his brows and bowed his head toward Julianna. "The arrival of your fiancé has only made things worse. Suspicion is rampant here and throughout the Two Kingdoms. Neighbors begin to distrust neighbors. With strangers, the situation is even worse."

"Wait," Julianna said, moving closer to Ananta.

Shesa raised his bow again, but the older Naga waved him away.

"You said . . . you mean, Oliver is here?"

"He was," Ananta replied. "At daybreak he departed, along with his companions. It appears that before they left, one of their number murdered the innkeeper at the Stonebridge Inn."

"Murdered?" Halliwell said. His pulse quickened. "How was he killed?"

Ananta frowned, studying him. "Violently."

He did not want to raise the Nagas' suspicions again, but Halliwell could not help himself.

"Were his eyes removed?"

Ananta and Shesa exchanged a confused look.

"What prompts the question?" Ananta asked.

Halliwell shook his head. "Never mind. Where I come from, I'm a . . . guardian, much like yourself. But it's not important now."

Not important, because the look between the two Nagas had told him the answer. The innkeeper's eyes were not taken. So whatever had killed Max Bascombe and all those children, it hadn't caught up to Oliver here. Or so it seemed.

"Do you know where Oliver went? When he left, I mean? And how long ago?" Julianna asked, the questions tumbling frantically one after the other.

Ananta gestured toward the east. "Across the Gorge. He traveled east with Kitsune at dawn. The other Borderkind who were with him yesterday left earlier, on a westerly course."

"We need to follow," Julianna said quickly. "Can you help us?"

The Nagas regarded each other once more. After a moment, Ananta slithered over to Shesa, serpentine body scraping over stone and hard-packed dirt. They conferred for a moment quietly, but Halliwell heard enough to realize they were speaking a different language. One he could never have understood.

At length, Ananta turned to face them again, his wings spreading wide.

"Shesa will remain here on guard. I will see you safely to the other side of the Gorge, and there the Nagas who stand sentry to the east will set you on the path you seek. Whether you will overtake them must be left to fate, for the Bascombe has a Borderkind with him, and there is no telling how swiftly they might travel, or if they shall remain in this world."

Halliwell allowed himself the smallest flicker of hope. If Oliver could go back, that meant he could, too. And that was one more mystery solved. When Oliver had disappeared from his family home on Rose Ridge Lane in the middle of a blizzard, Halliwell had been baffled by the question of how he had gone anywhere in the storm. Then Collette had disappeared. Oliver had shown up in Cottingsley, and then in London, with no clear explanation of how he had traveled there. But it was obvious now. He had traveled here, then back to the real world.

Home, Halliwell thought.

He glanced at Julianna and smiled, and he was sure she was thinking the same thing. The panic that seethed in him at the utter alienness of this world could only be calmed by two things: hope, and concentrating on resolving their predicament.

"All right, all right," he said quickly, practically mumbling. "That's fantastic. Thank you so much."

The Naga guard studied them, surveying their clothes again. "You truly are newcomers, then? Newly Lost?"

"We said as much," Julianna replied, though not unpleasantly.

Ananta nodded. "Come, then. Before I set you on the path, you must speak with Virginia Tsing. It is rare for the newly or recently Lost to find their way to the Gorge, but it has happened. Miss Tsing sees to them, as she will to you. There are things you will need to know about the Two Kingdoms if you wish to survive here. She will likely feed you as well. Perhaps even sandwiches and coffee, though I have never understood what humans love so much about those beans."

"They've got quite a start on us already," Halliwell said.

"Do not worry. Miss Tsing will not keep you long. Come."

Ananta slid across the mountaintop, toward the top of the ridge. Halliwell watched Shesa warily for a moment, but the younger Naga ignored him now, as though humans were beneath him. Halliwell thought that perhaps, in this world, that was precisely what such creatures thought.

Now that they were near the top of the ridge, it was clear that this was indeed the gorge. The edge was in sight. Jutting up from the broad canyon below he could see the tops of some kind of rope and metal rigging, as well as the tips of some kind of ornamental stonework.

"You have no idea how much we appreciate your help. But I wonder ... if Oliver and this person he's traveling with go back through to ... where we come from, can you show us how to get through? Is there another door that goes back?"

At the edge of the cliff, Ananta paused and looked back at her. "I am sorry. I thought you understood. You are Lost Ones now. You have crossed the Veil. And once through the Veil, the Lost Ones can never go home."

Halliwell staggered, swayed on his feet, staring at the Naga as he spread his wings, trying to make sense of the words.

"That's ... that's impossible. We have to go back."

Ananta only shrugged. "You will want to speak with Miss Tsing. She can explain better than I."

He took flight for just a moment, dropping down to a platform just beyond the edge of the cliff. Halliwell walked numbly after him. He glanced at Julianna. Her eyes were hollow.

The guardian had to be wrong. Oliver could travel back and forth.

There had to be a way. The thing wasn't even human, after all. What the hell did he know?

Together, Halliwell and Julianna went to the edge and looked down into the wondrous river gorge. There were awnings and stone bridges, ladders and walkways of wood and rope. The river went through a thriving village. The smell of food cooking down below rose to make Halliwell's stomach growl. Somewhere down there, children were laughing, and the sweet sound echoed off the walls. He saw a large, colorful florist's cart on the broad promenade beside the river, amidst all manner of shops.

Below, Ananta waited on the platform. It was connected to a strange latticework of stairs and rope bridges that led down hundreds of feet into the heart of Twillig's Gorge.

Halliwell took one last, long glance at the eastern side of the gorge, knowing that their path continued there. They had to get after Oliver and this Kitsune. That was the only way they were going to find real answers.

But Ananta began to slide his long serpent body down the stairs, holding the rails, wings tucked behind him, and after a moment's hesitation, Julianna followed.

Still numb, Halliwell descended behind them, wondering if there was any point in going on.

CHAPTER 7

ight snow fell on the tarmac at Bangor International
Airport, the gentle cascade of white illuminated by
the runway lights as the plane touched down. Sara
Halliwell stared out the window, her forehead against
the glass, and stared at nothing as the pilot taxied toward the terminal.

Everyone stood up before the seatbelt light was off. Sara stayed in
her seat. Only when the door was open and people began to file along
the aisle did she stand and retrieve her bag from the overhead compartment. It was smaller than a suitcase but larger than an overnight
bag, and heavy. With the strap over one shoulder, she listed badly to
one side.

She shuffled along the aisle, face slack, tired but all too awake. The
flight attendants stood just outside the cockpit and smiled pleasantly
as she got off the plane, then Sara was in the throng moving up the
gangway into the terminal. People hurried by her. A crewman pushed
an elderly black man in a wheelchair. She went around them, but neither of them glanced up.

Once upon a time, an eighteen-year-old Sara had driven into

Canada to go skiing with her girlfriends. It was raining lightly, just spattering the windshield, but in the dark she had not realized it was freezing rain, and the highway had become a sheet of ice. Then something about the sound of the rain on the roof of the car troubled her and she frowned and gently tapped the brake.

She had crested the hill. As she did, she saw the brake lights flash on the car in front of her. It started to skid, sliding as if in slow motion down the other side of the hill. Ahead, cars collided, one after the other, first two, then five, and then there were at least nine vehicles careening into one another with a crash of metal, gliding so gently into their collisions.

Sara had not tapped the brake again, nor had she accelerated. Instead, she had steered, carefully, skirting around a slowly spinning car and weaving through the wreckage. Even as she made it through to the other side, a car came over the hill behind her going much too fast, and the resulting crash made a thump like a cannon shot into the air.

Yet Sara had slipped through, as though she had been invisible. Untouchable. She felt that way now. Moving up the gangway and into the airport, anonymous and invisible, she was untouchable.

But fate had already touched her, after all.

Fate had been Jackson Norris on the phone just after ten o'clock last night. Just hearing his voice she had caught her breath. A phone call from Jackson Norris could only mean the worst.

When she left the gate area and walked past security, he was there waiting for her. The man was fortysomething, but the raccoon-dark circles under his eyes made him look ten years older. Haggard and tired, he looked too thin and his hair was much grayer than the last time she had seen him, back in the spring.

Still, he managed a sad smile for her as she went to him.

"Hello, Sheriff."

He held her at arm's length, like a long-lost uncle who hadn't seen her since childhood. "Sara. You look great, kid." The sheriff took her bag and slung it over his own shoulder. "And I've told you before, you're long since old enough to call me Jackson."

"Not sure I'll ever be old enough for that," she said, and she kissed his cheek even as they began to walk through the airport.

The sheriff led the way, already fishing out his keys, though it was no short walk to the parking lot.

"How's life treating you, kid?" he asked. "You still the glamour girl, taking pictures of all those pretty models in their underwear?"

Sara smiled. It was an old conversation. One they repeated over and over. "Still taking pictures," she confirmed, though for the first time since she could remember, she was traveling without her camera. She felt bereft without it, and yet also weirdly free. "Though I'll go out on a limb and say it's not quite as exciting as you make it sound."

When the sheriff chuckled, she saw the deep wrinkles around his eyes and mouth, and the gray bristle on his chin. He'd skipped shaving today. That wasn't like Jackson Norris at all.

"Because you're a girl," he said. "I don't know how a man can take photos like that and keep his concentration on the job."

"Good thing I don't have that problem," she said, not bothering to mask the sarcasm he would never understand.

They rode the elevator up to the parking garage in silence, both stewing, contemplating, worrying. Walking to the car—his Wessex County Sheriff's Department official vehicle—the sheriff moved a little too fast, as though he wasn't ready for the rest of their conversation. The real part. The unfamiliar, unrehearsed part. He put Sara's bag in the trunk and went around to unlock her door like a true gentleman. He even held it open for her.

Sara only stood and looked at him. "Where's my father, Jackson?"

He had been urging her to use his name for years. Now that she did, he flinched. The sheriff glanced away and let out a breath, then lifted his gaze to meet hers as though his head weighed a thousand pounds.

"I honestly don't know. There isn't any news, Sara. You know if there was, you'd be the first to know."

"So this law firm hires him to go look for one of their lawyers in fucking England—a guy who maybe murdered his father—he goes missing, and all you can tell me is that there isn't any news?"

Hysteria tinged her voice. She knew it, and hated it, but could do nothing about it. Once upon a time, Jackson would have chided her for her language. Tonight, he said not a word. Small town guy he might be, but he wasn't stupid.

"We know he and Julianna Whitney, who was with him, chartered a boat to take them out to an island off the coast of Scotland. It was in the middle of a snowstorm, apparently. But your father and Ms. Whitney went ashore on the island. When they didn't come back, the charter captain went looking for them, but there wasn't a trace. There was a fire on the island. The people who live there won't say how the fire started. None of them report having seen your father or Ms. Whitney. I'm not sure what else I can say."

December wind breezed through the garage. Sara shivered and ought to have zipped her jacket, but it was as though someone else was feeling it, someone else was cold.

She leaned against the car and stuffed her hands in her pockets. "Sheriff, what was my dad doing moonlighting for some law firm? I know ... I mean, I don't see him much, but we talk. He never mentioned doing anything like that. Sheriff's detective pays all right, doesn't it? So what was he doing this for? Going to England? In his whole career, he's never done anything like that. He's a cop in Maine. That's all he ever was or wanted to be. So here's what you can do. You can tell me how it happened. How did he end up going there in the first place?"

For a long moment, Jackson Norris stared at her with those raccoon eyes and a twist to his mouth like he'd just eaten something sour. Then he left the door open and walked around to unlock the driver's-side door. After he opened his door, he paused and stared at her over the roof, past the rack of blue emergency lights that were, for the moment, unlit.

"Politics, Sara."

Incredulous, she stared at him. "What?"

"I owed the firm a big favor. A lot of favors. Chances are, I wouldn't be sheriff if it hadn't been for their support. They wanted to play this investigation a certain way—do it quietly, try to protect their image, all of that—and I played along. Oliver Bascombe is one of theirs. Nobody really thinks the guy killed his father, but chances are he knows who did, or why. So when they wanted help going and fetching the lawyer in London—"

"You loaned them my father," Sara said quietly, stomach in knots.

"Not quite. They asked if I'd give him some time off, if I'd object to them giving him a freelance investigation job. I paved the way, Sara, but I couldn't have ordered Ted to take the assignment. It's not my jurisdiction. Bascombe and Cox offered him work, and he took it. Hell, kid, you know what he's like when he wants to close a case."

Sara tasted bitterness in her mouth. "Better than anyone."

Her father was a good man, but he had never been a good father. Not when it mattered. The job had always come first. And now, here she was, taken away from her life and her work because the idea that something might have happened to him made her frantic. Because, despite the distance that they could somehow never bridge between them, she loved him desperately and had never known what to do about that.

She slid into her seat and closed the door.

Only the crackling of the police radio broke the silence as the sheriff drove them away from the airport. He wasn't going to be getting many calls down in Bangor, but still he did not shut it off. Habit, Sara supposed.

How she had wished for someone to blame this on. It would be so convenient to be able to hate Jackson Norris for putting her through this, or even her father for making her think maybe they would never be able to solve the problem of the awkwardness between them.

But there was no one to blame. And nothing to do but wait, and ask questions, and hope.

The snow was falling outside, heavy flakes that drifted gently to the ground. The way the snow danced on the darkened highway ahead was mesmerizing. Sara watched it, and let herself be captivated. Taken away.

"What was that?" the sheriff asked.

Sara frowned. "Huh?"

"You said something. I didn't catch it."

For a second she did not know what he meant. Then she realized that she had spoken, almost unconsciously.

"He wanted me to come home for Christmas," she said, watching the snow, looking at the holiday lights gleaming on evergreens and strung from buildings as they drove away from Bangor. Tomorrow night was Christmas Eve.

"Guess he got his wish."

The wind was blowing from the west, or Kitsune would have caught the soldiers' scent before it was too late. Later, she would wonder if there was more to that failure than merely the direction of the wind, if the confusing feelings that swirled in her heart had distracted her. But by then, such questions would be meaningless.

It took longer than Kitsune had expected for them to reach the Orient Road. Many years had passed since the last time she had passed this way, and even then it had been from an entirely different angle. In those old times, she had not even been aware that Twillig's Gorge existed. That had been a hard journey, as she recalled, and it was a dark irony for her to learn now, so long after, that had she only traveled a few hours to the west she might have come upon that sanctuary.

But that was an old story from her life, and she did not want to dwell upon it.

More than three hours after they left the gorge, they had come to a sparse forest of ancient growth trees. Skirting its edge, they had passed a pond upon which sat the ramshackle remnants of a long-abandoned grist mill. A short way further they came upon a small house, a kind of way station from an age gone by.

Then, at last, the Orient Road.

Kitsune had journeyed the length of that road more than once. To the southwest, it led toward Perinthia. To the east, all the way into the furthest regions of Euphrasia, into the deepest and oldest parts of the world beyond the Veil. That was where her home lay, the forest where she had been born, far back in the mists of time and the ancestral memory of an entire region.

But Kitsune had not passed through that forest in two hundred years and had no desire to return. All that waited there for her was the bitter, aching memory of a more vivid, more vital time and a life full of passion and playfulness. Another age.

The present was a pale shadow of the past, but it required her attention. When the sorcerers had created the Veil, they had done so to protect the purity of the legendary worlds. Kitsune believed they had failed. It was not a pleasant thought. Indeed, these recent days it had been only the presence of Oliver at her side that lightened her heart. He was a good man, smart and strong and simple. Despite his harsh opinion of himself, there was nobility in him that was becoming more and more difficult to find amongst the legendary.

In the shadow of the tall pines, she glanced at Oliver. She knew that he was devoted to another, but Kitsune desired him. It troubled her, that desire, for she did not understand it. For a human, Oliver was brave enough, and he was charming and full of heart, but he was still ordinary. Kitsune could not make sense of what she felt for him, but that did not lessen its power.

He longed for Julianna, the woman he would have made his wife. But she was a world away, and he might never see her again. In time, his devotion to her would lessen.

Kitsune could wait.

As they passed the dusty way station, whose roof had been staved in by a fallen pine, Kitsune spared a thought for Frost and Blue Jay, and all of her kin. Part of her longed to be with them, to search for answers and vengeance in Yucatazca. But that was not to be.

She cast another glance at Oliver. He sensed her regard and looked over, one eyebrow raised. A ripple of pleasure went through her and she smiled at him. Oliver smiled back, puzzled. If he thought her enigmatic, Kitsune did not mind.

"We go east from here," she said.

Kitsune did not recall how far it was, precisely, to the stone circle where she could enter the Winding Way. For his part, Oliver did not ask, so she said nothing. It seemed more likely to her that they would be on this road all the way to the Sandman's castle in the eastern mountains, and that was ten or twelve days' walk on human feet. With nothing by way of provisions, they would have to forage or rely on the kindness of strangers. There were towns along the way, but with the

Hunters after Borderkind, and the warrant sworn out for Oliver, they would have to be very careful indeed.

These were her thoughts as they turned east on the Orient Road and set off. The old forest grew denser the further east they went, and the hard-packed earth of the road was overrun in places with grass and weeds. The Lost Ones traveled only when they first crossed through the Veil. Once they had settled, they tended to remain settled, and their offspring rarely left the places of their birth. The legendary traveled more frequently, but usually only moving amongst the larger cities of the Two Kingdoms. Farmers took their harvest to market, tax collectors gathered tithes to the monarchs, but other than those, few ventured beyond their own borders.

The road was quiet.

"It's peaceful here," Oliver said, as the breeze rustled the leaves of the trees, whose shade kept most of the day's heat from them.

"Most of this world is peaceful," Kitsune replied. "It's only those few fools who are desperate to draw blood that ruin it for the rest of us."

Oliver glanced at her, no trace of humor on his face. His brow furrowed. "Yeah. It's pretty much the same way in my world."

"I know. Legends mirror the human world far more than anyone here wishes to admit."

The hush of the wind accompanied them. Dust devils eddied up on the road. Deep in the woods, creatures skittered through the underbrush. A bird began to sing, and others replied.

Ahead there was a bend in the road, but Kitsune could hear the trickling of a brook. As they approached, she saw a stone bridge that spanned the little brook, and beyond that there was a weathered old house that looked as though it had been uninhabited for years.

It seemed the most natural thing in the world for Kitsune to catch Oliver's hand in her own, twining fingers together like any couple out for a stroll in the country. For a moment, he left his hand there, warm in hers, and it was pure contentment.

Then Kitsune's ears pricked forward. She frowned, breathed in the scents on the air, and turned back the way they'd come.

"What is it?" Oliver asked, breaking away from her.

"Hoofbeats. One rider, coming fast."

"What do we do?"

Kitsune glanced around. "The bridge."

They ran. The sound of the brook grew louder, but it was a gentle burble quickly lost in the thunder of approaching hooves.

Kitsune and Oliver reached the little bridge but did not cross. They ran beside it and down a small incline to where a swift, shallow brook rolled over gray and black stones that glistened wetly. There were far too many people, legendary and Lost, hunting them now. Better to just let the rider pass than risk being identified and having their position given away.

Her hood was back and her cloak floated behind her as she ran. Oliver thumped down into the brook, water splashing his heavy boots, and they ducked into the damp, shady hideaway underneath. Oliver's breath came fast and his exhilaration was contagious. Kitsune looked at him and felt desire overcoming her. The rugged stubble on his face and the flush of his skin made him seem wild, for a human, and his blue eyes were alight.

Hooves hammered the road, not far off now.

"You there!" a voice boomed across the brook. "Identify yourselves!"

Oliver flinched and Kitsune spun, dropping into a lower crouch, fingers hooked into claws.

On the other side of the brook, in amongst the trees, several Euphrasian soldiers moved toward them. Kitsune counted five, then a sixth appeared from the woods, hitching up his pants as though he'd just relieved himself. Four of them hung back a bit, studying them with curious bemusement, but the two at the front, both officers from the insignia on their chest plates, were gravely serious. Some kind of patrol, she presumed, though what they were doing out here in the middle of nowhere, and on foot, she could not imagine.

Kitsune glanced back to the west and saw the rider approaching. The horse galloped toward the bridge, perhaps a hundred yards away. He had no chest plate, nor a helm, but he wore a band tied around his right arm that fluttered in the wind: green and yellow, the colors of King Hunyadi.

"Come out of there! Show yourselves, now, and answer the question," snapped the nearest of the officers. He stepped into the brook and the metal sang as he drew his sword.

"What are you, Clegg, a fool? You can see it's him," snapped the other officer, older and more stout than the first. His beard was gray, but his eyes were bright with vigor.

Kitsune stood and stepped, rigid as a queen, from beneath the bridge. "Captain Clegg, is it?" she said, and her tone gave both men pause. "Are you in the habit of waylaying travelers like highwaymen and brigands?"

Clegg took a step nearer. The sun gleamed on his silver helm and on his blade. "Your name, miss. And that of your companion."

"Damn it, Clegg—" began the other officer.

"Shut your gob, Sergeant Matthias!" Clegg snapped, but he did not turn his attention away from the travelers. He was wary, this one, though not as canny as the sergeant.

"I am Kitsune," she said, and then she stepped aside, giving them their first full view of Oliver. He came out from under the bridge and stood to his full height, and they could see the scabbard that hung from his belt, and the insignia upon it that matched the one on their chest plates.

"As for my companion, as you can see, he bears the Sword of Hunyadi himself. Now you shall sheathe your blade, or his will be drawn."

The rider was twenty-five yards from the bridge.

Clegg stepped nearer still, the water washing over his boots. He raised the tip of his sword and pointed it at Oliver. "Your name, sir!"

"Captain, you've seen the sketch. It's him," Sergeant Matthias shouted. "It's the Intruder!"

With a roar of frustration, Clegg rounded on the sergeant. "That's enough of you. There are protocols to be—"

Kitsune glanced at Oliver, the thrill of mischief rising up in her, no different from the arousal that burned in her. The situation was dire, but danger was delicious.

"Fight," she whispered.

Then she lunged at Clegg, copper fur cloak floating behind her on the air as she practically flew across the space that separated them. Even as he turned, she grabbed his wrist, turned the point of his sword toward him and plunged the blade into his chest with such ferocity that his arm broke in several places.

He fell onto his knees in the brook, and blood pooled in the water.

Kitsune kept moving. With less than a thought, she transformed into a fox, splashing across the brook and barking. The soldiers beyond Matthias were shouting to one another in a panic, drawing swords, one of them rushing back into the trees.

"Come, then, myth!" Matthias called. "Traitor!"

She darted forward, his sword came down, and the fox leaped aside. The blade thudded into the dirt, and Kitsune snapped her jaws down on his wrist, fangs sinking into flesh. Matthias cried out and released his weapon, and then Kitsune was past him, running for the others.

The horse and rider reached the bridge, the clop of hooves on stone echoing off the woods and the water. But the horse neighed loudly as the rider—a messenger for Hunyadi, if his armband was genuine— drew back on the reins.

The messenger began to shout at the soldiers.

Kitsune glanced back. Sergeant Matthias was reaching for his sword, scrabbling on the bank of the brook. Oliver wielded the Sword of Hunyadi, pointing it at him as he approached.

"Stand and surrender," Oliver said loudly.

The fox growled as two of the soldiers rushed toward her. One carried a sword and the other a pike. He wielded it with the expertise of a master, and she hesitated a moment, then raced around the swordsman, putting him between herself and the man with the pike.

The swordsman swung.

Kitsune leaped at him, jaws closing on his crotch. Blood spurted from his soft parts into her mouth and he screamed shrilly. The other soldiers all shouted furiously, and that brought them running. There was no longer any hesitation. If confusion or wariness had held them back before, it was gone now.

The man with the pike kicked the screaming man out of the way, and he fell to the ground, hands clutched over his bleeding, mutilated groin. The pike waved before Kitsune, the blade feinting toward her again and again, and she realized he was only buying time for his fellow soldiers to reach her.

She transformed again, becoming human in the space between heartbeats. Her cloak blossomed around her, black hair falling across her face in a curtain as she moved.

Kitsune grabbed the pike even as he thrust it at her. With the strength of her kin, she snatched it from his hands. The soldier backed up quickly, stumbling and nearly falling.

Behind her she heard a shout, and turned to see Matthias splashing mud and water at Oliver's face. Oliver took a step back, and twisted so that it spattered only his left cheek. And as Matthias roared and jumped at him, Oliver sidestepped and drove the blade right through the sergeant's exposed throat. Metal covered the soldiers' upper torsos and heads, but their throats were bare.

Matthias could not even scream.

The horse neighed again and reared up, front hooves waving in the air. But the messenger was clearly an expert horseman and held on easily.

"Murderous bastard!" the messenger shouted. "You'll face the gallows for that."

Kitsune heard Oliver laugh.

Then a chorus of shouts was raised and she turned to see the other soldiers running toward her. But instead of the few she expected, there were more. They began to stream from the woods, where they had been encamped. She had thought it a small foot patrol, but this was an entire detachment of soldiers, several dozen at least.

She swore in ancient Japanese.

"Kitsune!" Oliver called. "This way!"

Breathless, she turned to see him charging at the messenger and his mount. The man snapped the reins and the horse snorted and turned, began to run eastward on the road. But Oliver was faster. He grabbed the horse's bridle with his left hand, sword still brandished in his right.

The animal slowed, chuffing, shaking its head, but Oliver held on.

The messenger shouted at him, tried to kick him, and drew his own sword. That was his downfall. He ought to have just tried to spur the horse on. He was a messenger, not a soldier.

Oliver parried the blow and jabbed him in the arm.

The sword fell to the ground. Oliver let go of the bridle and took hold of the messenger, hauling him from the saddle.

Kitsune fled, the soldiers charging after her. As she ran toward him, Oliver mounted the horse. The messenger began to rise, shouting in protest. Kitsune grabbed a fistful of his hair and dragged him to the ground. He tried to fight, but she struck him in the kidneys and all the fight drained from him. She untied the king's colors from his arm and took the standard with her as she raced to the horse and leaped up behind Oliver.

"You're getting quite good at this," she said.

"At what, staying alive?"

There was no humor in his face as he kicked the beast's flanks. The horse began to gallop away from the bridge and the soldiers. Some of the men tried to pursue them on foot, but fell back after only seconds, realizing they had no chance to catch the fugitives.

Two miles further along the road, with no sign of pursuit and without encountering any more troops, Oliver let the horse slow to a canter. Kitsune held on, arms wrapped around him from behind, and enjoyed the closeness.

"That was interesting," he said dryly.

"My life has been nothing but since I first encountered you."

"Funny. I could say the same."

Kitsune laughed softly, but only for a moment. As they swayed on horseback, she became aware of the heavy leather saddlebags that hung on either side of the beast. She reached over and undid the buckle on the left one, plunging her fingers in and withdrawing a small packet of letters, bound with red string, each with a seal of green wax and stamped with the insignia of the king of Euphrasia.

Her heart fluttered. Quickly she untied the string and, clutching the letters against her chest, opened the first one. The greeting alone was all that she had to read.

"Oliver," she said, her voice a rasp.

"Are you all right?" She had let go of him and now he turned slightly in the saddle.

"Quite a bit more than all right. That messenger was in service to King Hunyadi."

"Hold on, Kit. I want to put more distance between us and those soldiers. It's their service to the king that concerns me most at the moment."

"You're not thinking. Don't you want to know what a messenger for the king was doing all the way out here, three days' ride northwest of Perinthia?"

Oliver pulled on the reins. Now he turned round in the saddle as far as he could and studied her face. "What are you saying?"

"These letters are addressed to His Majesty John Hunyadi, King of Euphrasia, at his Summer Residence at Otranto."

"So he's on vacation. So what?"

Kitsune purred low in her chest and grinned. "So, foolish man, Otranto is less than a day's ride from here. We could be there by morning."

"But Collette—"

"Get a pardon from the king, and our journey to the Sandman's eastern castle will be far swifter, far easier. The Hunters still will pursue me, but you will be free to do what must be done to rescue your sister, and halfway to eliminating the death warrant that's been sworn against you besides."

Oliver took a deep breath, contemplating. "But what about the Dustman? And how will I get in to see the king?"

"Far easier here than in Perinthia, I would wager. You cannot pass up this opportunity, Oliver. The Sandman will not kill Collette as long as you're alive; we have established that. We must go to Otranto."

"And if the king just orders me captured and executed?"

"You will have to convince him otherwise."

Oliver shook his head, but then looked at her. "All right, which way?"

"Stay on the Orient Road. I'll guide you," she said, and as she did, she tied Hunyadi's standard around his bicep. Oliver was not dressed like a messenger, but they carried letters to the king.

She put them back in the saddlebag and buckled it. Perhaps they might survive another day after all.

Kitsune did not like to think further ahead than that. In particular, she did not want to think overmuch about what would happen when they faced the Sandman.

"Ride, Oliver," she said, wrapping her arms around him and pressing her face against his back. "Ride."

CHAPTER 8

I t's true, then? We're stuck here? We can never go home?"

Julianna studied Virginia Tsing's face, watched the lines crinkling around her eyes, and tried to tell herself that the woman was wrong. She had to be. But Virginia was kind and intelligent and obviously wise, which was why all of the other humans in Twillig's Gorge deferred to her as their de facto leader. There was little structure to the community, but the Lost Ones had Virginia to speak for them whenever anything came up.

"I'm sorry," the woman said, reaching out to lay her hand upon Julianna's atop the table. She glanced at Halliwell and then back to Julianna. "Truly, I am. No one ever takes the news well. But it is inescapable. The Veil is constructed imperfectly enough that sometimes people get lost, slip through to this side. But no one can ever go back—not until the Meshing, when a Legend-Born child will guide us home."

Halliwell narrowed his eyes and studied her with the scrutiny he might have given to some suspect he was interrogating. He could not conceal the desperate hope that rose in him.

"So, you're saying there *is* someone who can get us past the Veil?" he asked.

At this, the woman's expression became guarded. "Not only you. All of the Lost Ones." She shrugged, glancing away as though embarrassed. "My son would tell you it is only a story, and perhaps he is right. Even here there are legends." She tapped her left temple. "These eyes have never seen a Legend-Born child, but still I believe the tale."

With a sigh, Julianna sat back in her chair, her hand slipping away from Virginia's. Halliwell had one hand to his forehead but was otherwise nearly catatonic. From the time the Naga sentry had brought them down into the Gorge and introduced them to Miss Tsing, and through the two hours Julianna had conversed with the woman, learning about the Two Kingdoms, their rulers, and their history, Halliwell had said very little. Several times he had asked a question, mostly to clarify something Miss Tsing had told them. Otherwise he only sat in shock and stared.

Miss Tsing owned a bakery in Twillig's Gorge. The best, she claimed. Her father had been descended from a battalion of soldiers who had been swept through the Veil from Nanking, in China, many decades before, and her mother had descended from members of the Roanoke colony who had mysteriously disappeared from an island off the Virginia coast. She had never seen the world her ancestors came from. All she knew was the life and lore of this side of the Veil, and the stories of the human world that were passed down from them, or shared by Lost Ones who had come through in subsequent years.

The bakery had been started by her father in one of the storefront buildings along the Sorrowful River, right in the Gorge. There was a small stretch of the riverfront that was almost like an old European town, with florist shops and restaurants and markets, abuzz with life. A wide cobblestoned walkway passed in front of the shops, beside the river. The bakery had a patio in the front where people could sit and have tea or coffee and watch the life of the Gorge, the fishermen at work, the merchants selling their wares.

It would have been peaceful if it was not so entirely surreal. Julianna and Halliwell sipped coffee and ate pastries at a table with a rose in a vase and a white tablecloth while goblins and fairies and beast-men went about their business as though it was perfectly ordinary. And to them, it was.

Throughout the entire conversation, Julianna had learned so much that was nearly impossible to believe, and yet she had no choice but to believe it. After all, the proof was all around her. Miss Tsing told them of the legendary and the Lost, the Two Kingdoms, the Veil, and the Borderkind. She shared what she knew of a crisis that was spreading throughout the Two Kingdoms, with Hunters in pursuit of the Borderkind in a secret effort to eradicate them. A secret that was no longer quite as secret. Even as Julianna attempted to wrap her mind around that, Miss Tsing explained that Oliver was different from the Lost Ones, that he was an Intruder.

"All right," she said now, sipping at the coffee, which had a hint of exotic spice. "So Oliver was not touched by the magic of the Veil … Jesus, I can't believe I'm saying this … which means he can go back. And that's why this whole crazy world wants him dead?"

As Julianna spoke, a handsome young man came from within the bakery. He wore an apron that was covered in flour and smeared with something dark. From his complexion and his countenance, it was clear he was some relation. The man stopped at another table to speak quietly to a group of humans—Lost Ones—of varying races.

A very pale, thin man glanced over at Halliwell and Julianna and laughed softly, rolling his eyes in derision. The baker said something quiet but sharp, and the pale man fell silent.

"Just as you say," Miss Tsing told her.

"Virginia," Halliwell said, and it had been so long since he spoke that both women were startled by his voice. "If one of these Borderkind can take Oliver back, then why not us? So we went through once, and now this … roadblock … is going to stop us?"

"I'm afraid so."

Halliwell shook his head, jaw set grimly. "There has to be a way."

Even as he spoke, the baker came toward them. He put a hand on Miss Tsing's shoulder.

"There are always stories. But if there *is* a way," the baker said, "no one has ever found it in all the years since the Veil was created. Otherwise, the Lost would never have remained."

Julianna smiled at the newcomer, who seemed friendly enough. But Halliwell knitted his brows and grimaced at the man. It was obvious the detective did not want anyone dousing whatever spark of hope he could still retain. Julianna didn't blame him.

"My friends," Miss Tsing said, "this is my son, Ovid. Ovid, Mr. Halliwell and Miss Whitney."

Ovid Tsing nodded once to them politely, then glanced at the Lost who sat around the table he had just come from. There were others out on the bakery's patio as well, some of whom had been making little attempt to disguise their eavesdropping.

"I have spent my whole life on this question, Mr. Halliwell," Ovid said. He squeezed his mother's shoulder and she smiled up at him indulgently, patting his hand. "If there were a way for the Lost to return, I would know. One day you will have to accept that, but it often takes time."

"Your mother said something about a child ... what was it?"

The pale man across the patio shook his head wearily.

"The Legend-Born?" Ovid asked, favoring his mother with an indulgent smile. "Stories. Mother's generation is very superstitious."

A dreadful silence fell upon them then. Julianna could not look at these gentle, hospitable people. She looked out across the cobblestoned riverwalk and at the river rolling by. Her parents and friends would be frantic by now, believing the worst. It must be nearly Christmas, and she thought of the antique radio she had bought her father, who loved such things, and the Christmas Eve dinner she was supposed to cook with her mother. Work was not such a terrible thing to leave behind. It was all of the little things, the sweet minutiae that made up the best of life.

Halliwell stood up, chair scraping on the patio, and went to the railing to look up and down the length of the Gorge, as if searching for an exit.

"What will you do?" Miss Tsing asked, leaning in toward Julianna.

"Find Oliver. Whether I'm trapped here or not, the only thing left for me to do is to find him, to see his face and hear his voice, and from there we'll figure out what's next."

"And you, Mr. Halliwell?" Miss Tsing asked.

Julianna studied him. The detective leaned on the rail with his shoulders hunched, his muscles taut, as though he might at any moment fly into a rage. But when he turned, his expression was calm and his words measured and even. It was the eyes that gave him away. Halliwell's eyes were far away, perhaps as far away as a little corner of Maine, or an apartment in Atlanta, Georgia, where his daughter remained, never knowing what was in her father's heart.

"Julianna's right. We find Oliver," he said. "There are questions I want to ask him. Things I need to understand. And if you're wrong, and there is a way home, then I'm betting his friends will know about it."

Ovid gazed at him, only a hint of sympathy on his face. "And if I'm right, and there is no way home?"

Halliwell looked at him for a moment as though contemplating the question, then walked back to the table. He did not answer. Instead he sat down again and looked at Miss Tsing.

"All we know is that Oliver's gone east. He's got almost half a day on us. But he's going to have to stop at some point. Do you have any idea where he might go?"

The woman's forehead creased in thought. She glanced around at the other people sipping coffee and tea and eating scones and muffins and pastries at the patio tables, as though some of them might make a suggestion.

Then she shrugged. "I cannot help you. The Orient Road is to the east. If they are truly going that direction, they will travel upon that road. But your friend has a warrant sworn out for him. He will be cautious. That might slow him down. But it will also mean he is trying not to be found, unaware that some of those who seek him are his friends. There are small towns and villages along the way, but nothing of great consequence. I cannot guess at his destination."

Julianna shivered, and became aware of a chill that went all through her. It was as though she had been cold all along and only now realized it. A sip from her coffee cup did nothing to warm her. Only then did she understand that the chill was despair.

"So, what, then?" she asked, turning toward Halliwell. "How do we even begin to look for him?"

Halliwell stood up again, edgy with nervous energy. "We go, now. We'll find this Orient Road and we'll follow. If we ask enough questions, we might find someone who saw him, or even better, someone who will be able to tell us where he's headed. He's wanted, Julianna. Wanted men have only one thing on their minds, and that's how to stay alive. If we can figure out how he plans to do that, we can find him."

Julianna stood, and so did Miss Tsing. She hugged the old woman. "Thank you, so much."

Ovid shook Halliwell's hand, then Julianna's. "I wish you luck. Please, though, wait here just another minute. I will put a bag together for you, some food and water to carry on the road."

"That's very kind," Julianna said.

Halliwell looked at him and the tension between them seemed to dissolve into understanding. The detective nodded, and Ovid the baker nodded in return, then turned and went back into the bakery to fetch them food for their journey.

Virginia Tsing stepped close to Julianna. "If you do not find him, or if you should find him and return this way, come and see me."

Touched by her generosity, Julianna embraced her again, whispering her thanks.

"You'll never find him," said a small voice behind her.

Julianna turned, angry at the callousness of the words and the intrusion. She saw the fury that flashed in Halliwell's eyes and worried that he would one day lose control of himself.

But not today. The voice had come from a little girl, perhaps ten years old, who had been sitting for the past half an hour or so with two others, slightly older than she. The girl was pretty, eyes wide and precocious, skin a dark chocolate brown.

"Excuse me?" Julianna said.

"Kara, still your tongue. This business is none of your concern," Miss Tsing said.

The girl scuffed one shoe on the patio. "All right, but it's true. They don't stand a chance of finding their friend. Not without a guide. Not without a tracker."

Halliwell took a step toward her and the girl flinched.

"You know someone like that?" the detective asked, crouching down beside her.

The girl executed an elegant bow. "I am Ngworekara, sir, though I'm called Kara by most. And if you wish, I would guide you myself."

Julianna laughed softly, but not unkindly. "That's sweet, Kara. And we appreciate it. But you can't be . . . what I mean is, you're only—"

"A child?" Kara asked, those wide eyes narrowing. "You're Lost, miss, and so I can understand your doubt. But you'll learn soon enough that many of the people here are more than they seem."

Halliwell had not laughed, only studied her more closely. Now he turned to Miss Tsing. "Can she really do that? Track Oliver?"

The woman arched one eyebrow. "Who is to say? Kara has no parents. She has been here for several years and yet she seems no older. She often seems to know things others do not. If she believes she can guide you, there seems no harm in letting her try."

Julianna looked closely at the girl's face. The idea was insane. How could she and Halliwell, who knew nothing of this place, take care of a little girl while they were searching for Oliver? And yet if what Miss Tsing said was true, perhaps Kara wouldn't need much looking after.

"Are you sure?" she asked the girl. "You can do that?"

Ngworekara nodded gravely. "Oh, yes. If he can be found, I will find him."

"All right," Halliwell said. "Let's go."

Staring into the girl's eyes, Julianna felt cold again, but did not know why.

Many cities in the human world had neighborhoods that lingered from the earliest days of settlement. Often they had quaint names, but with equal frequency, the locals referred to these sections with the simplest of appellations. The Old City. The North End. The Latin Quarter.

There was a Latin Quarter in Perinthia, but it was not preserved as such neighborhoods in the human world were. At the northwest corner of the city, the Quarter consisted of buildings that had been old when Rome and Greece were young, and that had been shifted from the mundane world to the realm of the legendary when the Veil was raised. Parts of the Quarter were little more than ruins, but even the structures that were still inhabited were crumbling.

Blue Jay strode through the Latin Quarter that afternoon with Cheval Bayard and Chorti flanking him. The kelpy woman glanced around nervously as they skirted a long column that had collapsed into the street. She glanced at Chorti every few seconds, and seemed to draw courage from him, but Cheval was skittish. Blue Jay could not blame her. A gray caul of cloud cover hung over Perinthia, and a light rain fell. Even without the sunshine marking out their every movement, however, striding down the street in the middle of the day when all the Hunters were searching for Borderkind—and the authorities seemed disinterested in intervening—was about the most foolish thing Blue Jay could have imagined.

Fortunately, none of them was as famous as Frost. They were staking their lives on their lack of celebrity. Most of the city's denizens would not recognize them as Borderkind on sight. They had entered Perinthia within view of the watchtowers and no alarm had been raised. Frost reminded them all unnecessarily that there might well be spies looking out for them, but Blue Jay chose to be optimistic for once. They slipped into the city almost unnoticed.

It helped, of course, that they went immediately to the Latin Quarter. In other sections of Perinthia it was probable that they would be discovered—that locals or even the city guard might be cooperating with the Hunters and pass on the word that there were Borderkind in the area. From the stories they had heard, the news of the Hunters' mission had spread. Many Borderkind were in hiding now, or dead. Blue Jay figured the only Borderkind still in Perinthia would be collaborators or those who were insignificant enough to go unnoticed, at least for now. Or the oldest of his kin—elder cousins who were arrogant enough to believe that no one would dare to trouble them.

At the moment, they were right. The Hunters were occupied in the search for those Borderkind who dared to fight them, to strike back at their murderous conspiracy. For those—for Blue Jay and Frost, Chorti and Cheval Bayard, and any who would join them—nowhere in Perinthia was safe.

Except perhaps the Latin Quarter.

Strangers rarely entered the neighborhood, out of fear or distaste or both—and indeed, there were dangers there for those who were not welcome. Ancient creatures born with the empires of old lived in the ruins. Some thought they were simply beasts or driven mad by the passage of time, but Blue Jay had heard whispers amongst the tricksters that the monsters of the Latin Quarter were far from mad or primitive. They were only territorial, no different from the descendants of ancient Rome and Greece and the legends of those times that lived there.

Cheval Bayard flinched, glancing over her shoulder, peering up at the darkened doorway of a house. She swept her silver hair away from her face and paused, watching warily. Chorti sniffed the air, then grunted and urged her forward.

"Right, keep moving," Blue Jay said, voice low. "It's not a good idea to stand around."

"Nothing about this is a good idea," Cheval replied.

"We don't have a lot of options." Blue Jay shot her a hard look. "And you know the whispers we've heard."

She sighed. "I only hope they're more than whispers."

Blue Jay shared that hope, but did not say so out loud. They had been in Perinthia less than an hour. The moment they had arrived, Frost had slipped unnoticed into Amelia's, invisible, nothing more than a gust of frigid wind. The nightclub section of Amelia's had been closed, but the bar at the front was open, and the rumors were raging. When Frost had emerged he had shared what he'd overheard with his companions.

The rumor was that Borderkind were welcome in the Latin Quarter. The old legends who lived there did not like interference and they did not like betrayal. They were perfectly willing to stab one another in the back, but looked askance at those in power murdering innocents, and so they were happy to thwart the Hunters by harboring fugitive Borderkind.

It was possible things weren't quite as simple, but Blue Jay wasn't about to point that out to anyone in the Quarter. If the Greeks and Romans were on their side, even just to the extent of offering sanctuary, he would say nothing to jeopardize it. On the other hand, if they were just rumors, he and the others might not survive the afternoon.

The wind whistled through the ruins, making the feathers in his hair dance. Chorti kept sniffing, trying to catch a scent. Cheval had been troubled when Frost had announced that he would not join them, but Blue Jay was not concerned. Frost was just too damned conspicuous. He was around somewhere, and would aid them if necessary. But they were going into Lycaon's Kitchen without him.

Amongst the ruins, there was still a real neighborhood in the Quarter. Beside crumbling palazzos were shops and houses and an open-air marketplace where fruit sellers hawked their wares alongside jewelers, leather craftsmen, and fishmongers.

Lycaon's Kitchen stood on the corner of a nameless street, beside a brothel where a trio of ancient whores played madam to half a dozen young men and women descended from the Lost of the old world. Blue Jay glanced around uneasily at darkened windows and the stillness of rooftops, and gestured for Chorti and Cheval to precede him.

The rich scent of roasting meat wafted from the place through open, warped-glass windows. Walking inside, Blue Jay found the smell far more powerful. He normally preferred vegetables and fruits, but even his stomach growled with carnivorous yearning as he stepped into Lycaon's Kitchen. The meat and spices filled the place with their aroma.

Chorti and Cheval had paused in the foyer. The kelpy whispered something to the wild man, her elegant beauty so drastic a counterpoint to his savage ugliness. Chorti grunted, and when Blue Jay joined them, he saw the wild man lick his lips, then wipe a hairy hand across his mouth to remove the frothy drool there.

"Control yourself," Blue Jay said, voice low and dangerous.

Cheval Bayard narrowed her eyes and bared her teeth at him. "He will be fine. Look to your own self."

Blue Jay took a breath, studying her. He was a trickster, a mischief-maker by nature, but kelpies were outright killers, vicious things who ate children and distraught wanderers. Lovely as she was, hers was a treacherous beauty.

Yet her treachery did not extend to betraying her own kin to the Hunters. In that, Blue Jay trusted her entirely. And the motherly way she doted on Chorti allowed him to believe she was not purely malicious.

"Cheval," he said.

Those piercing, gemstone eyes found him.

"Be ready to fight."

The kelpy nodded. Blue Jay hesitated a moment and then stepped through the foyer into the restaurant itself. The dining room was stone and wood of an indeterminate age. The rear of the room was open to the kitchen so that the chefs could be seen at their stoves and ovens, and each time an oven door was opened, the fires that roared inside burned brightly. Chairs and tables were set up around a central court-yard open to the sky, such that, in inclement weather like this, only a portion of Lycaon's was open for business. This afternoon, for in-stance, the rain fell in a light drizzle that dampened the stone tiles in the courtyard, but there was little wind, so the patrons eating a late lunch were undisturbed.

Half of the tables were taken, mostly by humans. Amongst them were several men and women who were simply too perfect or too big to be ordinary people, and who must, then, have been legendary. Heroes, perhaps, or demi-gods. At one table, two harpies crouched without chairs, their hideous vulture bodies lurching toward their plates, pecking at the raw flesh they had been served.

Many of the dishes served in Lycaon's Kitchen were raw. It was part of his legend, after all. Once a king, he had been a cannibal who slew his guests and ate them. Upon encountering Zeus, Lycaon had tried to feed him human flesh, only to have the god take vengeance upon him by transforming him into a true animal, the first werewolf of legend.

Lycaon knew what his customers wanted. And the customer was always right. He claimed not to serve human flesh any longer, but Lycaon had been made Borderkind by the world's lingering legends of werewolves, and Blue Jay wondered if from time to time he made forays into the mundane world for fresh human game.

Beside him, Chorti grunted and tugged on his sleeve.

Blue Jay glanced at him. "You can speak. Why don't you?"

Cheval lanced him with a withering glance, as protective of Chorti as if she were his mother. "He prefers not to." Then she turned to Chorti, touching him gently upon the arm. "What is it?"

But Blue Jay had already seen what had upset the wild man. At a table in the corner were three Keen Keengs, as sorely out of place there as Chorti himself. They were Australian, and he Guatemalan, but the difference was that Chorti was Borderkind and rumored at least to be welcome here. The Keen Keengs were nothing of the sort.

When the Veil had been raised, those among the legendary who retained a connection to the mundane world—who still lived in the hearts and minds of humanity through folktales and bedtime stories—had become Borderkind. The magic woven into the Veil allowed them to travel back and forth between worlds … but only if they wished it.

Many among the legendary had wanted nothing to do with humanity, and their disdain prevented them from becoming Borderkind. But there were those, the Keen Keengs amongst them, who had wished to be Borderkind but could not, because at the time the Veil was created, the humans lacked enough belief in them.

Not all of them were bitter and unpleasant, but Keen Keengs tended not to like Borderkind very much. Blue Jay stared at the giant winged bat-men, deeply disturbed. The Keen Keengs crouched at their table, chairless like the harpies, and studiously avoided looking toward the entrance.

"Shit," the trickster muttered.

A broad-shouldered man with a cruel, bestial face broke away from conversation with a waiter and strode toward them. His hair was thick and unkempt and his face covered by a dark stubble. When he smiled at them with utter insincerity, Blue Jay saw his teeth were large and pointed. He raised enormous hands as though to punctuate his question.

"What have we here? Strangers in our midst. Which marks you as desperate, or foolish, or both."

Blue Jay stepped forward, wrapping himself in trickster magic even as he did so. A blur of azure swished in the air around him, but he did not attack with his spirit wings, nor did he transform. He might have done either, or might simply have challenged the man who approached, but Cheval prevented this by stepping in front of him and bowing to the cruel-faced man.

"Both we may be," the kelpy said, her silver hair cascading along beside her face as she bowed. She glanced up at him without rising. "But we are also kin, Lycaon. Will you not hear us speak, cousin, before deciding?"

Lycaon. Blue Jay felt foolish. Cheval had guessed, of course, but he ought to have seen it right away. The bestial features, the unruly hair, the cruel glint in the eye. This was likely the werewolf himself.

Again he bared his teeth in that false grin. His gaze shifted to take in Chorti and then Blue Jay before returning to Cheval. "I have never had much use for the kinship the Borderkind have presumed since the creation of the damnable Veil," he said, voice low, as though he did not wish to be overheard.

"Yet we have heard that you have welcomed others of our cousins to remain here until danger has passed."

Lycaon grinned now, and this time it seemed sincere. "The soft-hearts and thinkers who crafted the Veil are also those who made up rules for this kingdom, and forged a truce with Yucatazca. I don't like them. Anything that vexes them is a pleasure."

"We're welcome, then?" Blue Jay asked.

The werewolf hesitated a moment, then gestured to a table. "You're welcome to eat. Welcome to pass through. But not to stay."

That would have to do. Blue Jay nodded. "You have our thanks."

"Keep them. I've done you no great favor. You could still be eaten on your way out of the Quarter."

He turned on his heel and signaled to a waiter to attend to them. Chorti did not wait, but moved quickly to a nearby table. Blue Jay was not at all surprised, given that the wild man was practically slaver-ing at the scent of meat. After a moment's hesitation, Cheval joined Chorti at the table.

"What are you doing?" Blue Jay whispered as he went to her side. He did not take a seat, standing beside her instead.

Cheval gazed up at him. "We have been offered a moment of haven and hospitality. It might do well for us to make an effort to be less con-spicuous."

Blue Jay laughed softly and stared at her, wondering if her mind was quite intact. "It's a little late for that, don't you think?"

Already Lycaon had drawn a great deal of attention to them. He looked around and saw two of the Keen Keengs bent close, muttering to one another. The third he caught watching him, but it glanced away upon being discovered.

"This is idiotic," Blue Jay said.

He strode toward the center of the restaurant, out into the open courtyard. Warm summer rain pattered his hair and jacket, fell upon his hands as he stopped and glanced around. If the whispers were true and there were Borderkind taking refuge in the Latin Quarter, he had not seen any of them here. As he surveyed those lunching at Lycaon's Kitchen, many of them studied him in return. Human faces narrowed with concern or suspicion or simple curiosity. Blue Jay did not mind the scrutiny. In truth, he had counted on it.

The waiters studiously ignored him. If Lycaon had not slain them or thrown them out, then his staff would not trouble themselves. Only the waiter assigned to the table where Chorti and Cheval sat would pay any attention to them.

Yet there was one other.

Blue Jay raised an eyebrow when he saw Leicester Grindylow emerge from the kitchen bearing a tray of sandwiches. Grin had been a frequent customer at Amelia's and often substituted as a bartender there. But Blue Jay knew that the long-armed bogie had also been a friend of Jenny Greenteeth's, and Jenny had betrayed them to the Hunters. He wondered if Grin was also a traitor.

When the Grindylow saw Blue Jay, he lifted one hand in an amiable wave. Grin slid his tray onto the table before him and smiled at the trickster before sorting the plates out in front of the olive-skinned women at the table. They whispered to one another and looked at Blue Jay with gossip and scandal in their eyes.

Blue Jay nodded to Grin and resumed his search of the restaurant.

A pair of hooded men sat at a table near the kitchen. As an oven door opened, the heat and light of the fire inside rushing out, they glanced up. Their faces were wan and gray, eyes black, and their beards were white and braided. Blue Jay knew them on sight as Mazikeen.

Yet if there were Mazikeen here, he did not understand why they had not revealed themselves. They were not cowards, that much he knew. Which meant they had come here for another purpose, and perhaps it was in his best interest to give them their secrecy for another few moments at least.

As he searched, he noted the presence of a few other Borderkind. Several merrows sat together, feasting upon raw fish, their webbed fingers and large green eyes revealing their marine nature. Toward the front of the restaurant, bathed in the gray light that came through the pitted glass of a window, a small man sat eating something that resembled burnt poultry. His features were unmistakably Asian, yet though he was the size of a child, his face was clearly adult. As Blue Jay studied him, he turned away, resolutely refusing to meet the trickster's gaze.

Borderkind. Blue Jay was certain of it.

He started to walk toward the little man and crossed a place where the warm summer rain was frozen, icy sleet. Blue Jay flinched and glanced upward, but even as he did so he realized what had happened. The roof was open to the gray stormy sky, and Frost had passed above the courtyard, watching him, swirling in the wind and rain.

Cocky and carefree as he normally was, Blue Jay felt a distinct relief at this reassurance that Frost was with him. Cheval and Chorti might be staunch allies, but neither their loyalty nor their skill as warriors had yet been tested.

The little man glanced at last toward Blue Jay as the trickster approached. Fire ignited his eyes and streamed to the sides, flames rising toward his hair. He was no Greek or Roman legend, obviously, and so he must be Borderkind, or have presented himself as such.

Blue Jay strode to within several feet of him and bowed.

The little man with flaming eyes nodded slowly, as though in resignation.

The bang of wood on marble cracked in the air like a gunshot. Blue Jay twisted round even as Cheval called his name. The Keen Keengs had thrown their table aside. Wings spread, they lunged across the restaurant, banging chairs out of the way and driving a waiter to the ground. Chorti rose up in an explosion of fur and claws, huge jaws opening to reveal those perilously long metal teeth. The first of the Keen Keengs grabbed him and drove him to the ground with the power of its thrashing wings, long talons raking Chorti's fur.

Cheval staggered back several steps, retreating from the attack. But she was not fleeing. She transformed in the space of those steps from stunning beauty to horrid ugliness—from woman to the green-furred, muck-encrusted horse-woman form of the kelpy. She reared back and shot out a hoof, cracking the skull of the nearest Keen Keeng. The thing was shaken, but then it spread its wings wider and screamed fury, ignoring the blood that ran from the fissure in its face.

Blue Jay ran toward his companions, and once again the blur of azure wings colored the air around him. One of the waiters reached out to prevent him from joining the fray and Blue Jay spun, dancing on the air, spirit-wings hammering the waiter, throwing him back onto a table that tipped beneath his weight.

As he raced toward the Keen Keengs, he saw Chorti grip his attacker by the throat and lift him from the ground. The wild man bared his metal claws and slashed the bat-man's right wing, shredding it entirely. The Keen Keeng reached for Chorti's eyes, trying to gouge them out, and the wild man plunged metal claws into its chest and, with a splintering of bone and wet ripping of flesh, tore out a handful of pink organ flesh.

The one with the cracked skull leaped toward Cheval. Again she kicked it. This time when it stumbled back, the Grindylow caught it in his arms. Blue Jay took flight, feet sweeping above the ground though he maintained a vaguely human form. The trickster was disappointed that he would have to kill the amiable bogie.

Grin reached up, wrapped an arm around the Keen Keeng's head, and with a swift jerk broke its neck. He dropped the dead thing to the ground.

CHAPTER 9

The castle of Otranto stood on a hillside above a broad lake whose calm, silvery surface reflected back the image of the castle. It was a grim, practical structure built for the glory of war rather than pride. Round towers marked each corner and the outer walls were windowless. Near the top they were lined with iron spikes to prevent climbing. Even in peacetime, there were soldiers on the battlements and sentries on the tops of the towers and at the gate.

Hunyadi's flag waved in the breeze from a post atop the gatehouse. The king was in residence.

Oliver rode alone toward the castle on a road that curved northward through fertile farmland. Men and women worked the fields, harvesting everything from berries to barley. In the distance, the span of two entire hills displayed an orchard full of fruit trees. Pickers carried barrels to wagons drawn by horses, and children ran amongst the trees. Despite the distance, Oliver fancied that he could hear their laughter.

Small rowboats drifted on the lake, each carrying fishermen who had poles and nets. On the far side of the lake there grazed herds of sheep and cattle. Beyond that, near the forest, he saw several farmhouses spaced quite far apart, complete with barns and pens. There would be chickens and pigs and the like, he presumed. Oliver had the strangest thought—that this thriving community existed only when the king was in residence. Absurd, of course, that these people would simply disappear when Hunyadi was back in Perinthia.

In truth, it was alive with more vigor and honest effort than any place he had seen on this side of the Veil. Rather than a step into another world, it felt to Oliver like a step back in time, to a simpler era. To a man willing to put in a hard day's work, Otranto might have been paradise.

Oliver rode on, toward the gatehouse. The late afternoon sun cast long shadows across the land, and stretched the dark silhouette of horse and rider so that they were unrecognizable. The Sword of Hunyadi hung in its scabbard at his side. The letters for the king were in the saddlebag. He rode now toward a castle full of soldiers who had orders to execute him on sight. Oliver no longer bore any real resemblance to the man he once had been, but he wondered if that was because he had changed so dramatically, or because his true self had at last been given free rein.

A lawyer who buried himself in paperwork and lived in the shadow and the grasp of his father—that had been the way the world knew him. But this was a different world. The concerns that had governed his old life were no longer valid. He was desperate to save his sister, and to find his way back to Julianna. But all of the yearnings that had made a New England attorney seek out the freedom of the stage, to indulge fantasy as an actor no matter how foolish his father deemed it, had formed the basis for his survival here.

Now, once again, the actor in him had to take the stage. In order to get in to see the king, he would have to create a character, and his performance would have to be perfect. But Oliver had always felt most confident on the stage. As an actor, he could be anyone and do anything. There was freedom in that.

Kitsune had ridden behind him on the horse and had been as good as her word, guiding him along the path to Otranto. They had passed farms and residences, ridden through two small villages, and no one had attempted to question them—or even stop them—about their identity or destination. At a river crossing they had stopped at a grist mill and gratefully accepted bread that the miller's wife had made with her own grain.

When at last they had come over a hill and seen the towers of the castle in the distance, Kitsune had tugged his sleeve and told him to stop. She had dismounted and instructed him to wait half an hour, to give her that time to slip into the castle if she could. He'd rather not have had to ride up to the castle alone, but if he had any hope of going unrecognized, he could not approach the king's men accompanied by a Borderkind, and by Kitsune in particular.

Diminishing instantly to the shape of a fox, she gazed up at him with those jade eyes and then dashed down the hill and into a small copse of trees. She would work her way toward the castle and within its walls, if possible. Oliver would not know if she had succeeded until he saw her.

He rode toward the main gates. The shadows grew longer and the horse snorted with exertion.

On the shore of the lake, Oliver saw several fishermen pause in their work to watch him ride to the gate. One of them had waded up to his waist in the water and held his fishing pole with a singular nonchalance, as though catching fish was entirely beside the point and the simple act of fishing was enough.

Oliver tore his gaze away from the lake, and he slowed the horse so as not to unduly alarm the guards. As he rode toward the gatehouse— the front gates open and the portcullis within already raised—the two guards in front were joined by two more. All four wore a heavy brown leather armor adorned with the insignia of the king, and helmets of leather and iron that were unlike any he had seen before. The iron was both cap and frame, and the leather hung down on either side and buckled at the throat for protection.

The soldiers put their hands upon their swords but left them undrawn.

"Dismount!" one of them said, stepping forward.

Oliver presumed him the captain, or at least the ranking officer.

During their ride, Kitsune had familiarized him with some of the general protocol of the Two Kingdoms. When he had first crossed the Veil with Frost, he hadn't any reason to need to know such things. Now, though, he was quite glad that he did. He summoned all of the arrogance he could muster, slipping into character just as he would have on the stage.

"I dislike your tone, sir," Oliver declared, glaring at the soldiers from the superior position of his saddle. "My name is Gareth Terlaine and I ride from Perinthia with letters for the king. Letters that bear the royal seal. Matters of government are not for soldiers or couriers. We do our duty. Mine is to deliver letters. Yours is to stand aside and make way for one who bears them, as well as the colors of the king."

The soldiers all glanced at the banner tied around his arm, just as the real courier had tied his own. Kitsune had stolen the armband and Oliver thought it was the only thing that gave them even the most remote chance of success.

"Those are the king's colors," said one of the men.

The officer sneered him into silence.

"You're dressed oddly, courier. Like a peasant, more like, or a village merchant. Aside from the royal banner, you've no uniform to speak of."

Oliver smiled. They weren't entirely stupid. "Indeed, gentlemen, when your uniform is having horse shit cleaned from the breast and the seat of your pants is being stitched and you're called up suddenly as the courier on duty has fallen ill, you wear the best you have to hand, and the colors of the king. No shame in that, I hope."

Still the suspicion lingered in the officer's eyes. He held out a hand. "The letters."

"Not on your life or mine," Oliver replied gravely.

No courier in service to the king would hand over letters bearing the royal seal to anyone but the king himself, or his servant in the presence of the king. Kitsune had spent several months at court—or rather, in bed with a king—though that had been a very long time ago. Oliver hoped that customs had not changed since, but he had faith in Kitsune. She was a trickster, after all. A cunning creature.

The officer drew his sword.

Metal singing, the other soldiers followed suit.

The officer barked an order and there was a ruckus above their heads. Oliver glanced up, pulse racing, to see half a dozen archers leaning over the battlement and drawing their bowstrings back. The arrows were all aimed at his chest.

"Now," the officer commanded.

Oliver put one hand on the leather saddlebag, the courier's pouch. "I cannot place letters to the king into the hands of one of his subordinates unless in his own presence. If you'd kill me for loyalty to Hunyadi, then I suppose I shall die."

"You may at that, in a moment," the officer said. He pointed to the bag with his sword. "Take out a letter, only one, and show me the seal. You will not have to surrender it to do so."

For a moment Oliver was at a loss what to do next. If he complied, would that be a breach of protocol? Kitsune had learned some of the court customs, but hardly all. By doing so, he might well be revealing himself. But it did seem a way to follow custom and still prove the provenance of the letters he carried.

He took a breath and nodded. "Of course."

The long shadows performed a hideous pantomime of the events playing out there at the castle gates. The breeze was cool, though dusk was still a couple of hours away, and hinted at a night that would be chilly indeed. The life of the community of Otranto continued to unfold all around the castle, but here in this one spot it had come to a halt, as taut as the bowstrings of the king's archers.

Oliver unbuckled the pouch and reached in. When he withdrew a single letter, all of the soldiers tensed, prepared to fall upon him. At first only the face of the letter showed, but quickly he turned it over to show them the wax seal.

They visibly relaxed. The officer shook his head and gestured to the bowmen to withdraw. From below, Oliver could hear the strange twang of bowstrings slowly being released, arrows being returned to their quivers.

"You understand, courier, that these are strange times. Rumors are rampant of rebellion and some of the legendary conduct a crusade against their own kind. Nothing is to be taken for granted these days."

Oliver let out a long breath. He nodded, reassured by the knowledge that the king and his soldiers had far more to worry about than a single Intruder.

"I do understand. Had I any other choice than to ride here without my uniform, trust that I would not have done so, if only to avoid such suspicion."

The officer gestured to the others and they stood aside to allow Oliver to ride through the open gates and the arched passageway of the gatehouse. Two remained outside on guard, but the officer and one other, a stout, broad-chested fellow whose nose was flattened and scarred, walked alongside the horse, escorting him onto the grounds of the castle of Otranto.

A stable boy appeared, running to stand beside them, dutifully waiting for the horse to be turned over.

Oliver climbed down from his mount, then reached up and slid the saddlebags from the horse. He slung them over his shoulder and patted the horse on the side before handing the reins over to the stable boy.

"Take good care of the animal," the officer told the lad. "It's a long ride back to Perinthia."

Within the outer curtain walls of the castle, several young men worked at swordplay, parrying and dodging with a grace hard to achieve amongst those actually trying to kill one another. An old woman sat on a stone stoop outside a heavy wooden door off to one side, peeling potatoes and rattling off profanity at a cluster of pigeons who paraded nearby, pretending to be aloof while obviously expecting her to provide them with some kind of treat.

The guards led him across the grounds toward a tall, arched doorway that showed a surprising hint of Moorish influence. The wall all around the door was covered with tiny tiles that created a mural image of a one-eyed warrior standing on the body of a fallen giant, and out of the giant's flesh grew fruit trees. A naked, winged woman had plucked a yellow fruit from one of the trees and bit into it.

Oliver stared at it, trying to decipher its meaning or connect it to a specific legend, but it seemed a strange mélange of mythical elements.

The scar-nosed guard went to the door and grasped an iron ring.

He hauled the heavy door open, hinges shrieking. The officer nodded to Oliver to indicate that he should enter. Oliver glanced back across the grounds and saw that most of the archers on the battlements had vanished, though several still remained. Two stood talking to one another, but the others were watching him curiously.

"Thank you," he said.

An old man dressed in midnight blue, with the seal of the king upon his breast, appeared suddenly in the doorway to block their entry. His face was so thin he looked inhuman, and adorned with a wisp of white beard.

"What is it?" the old man said, brows knitted in consternation, lips pursed in disapproval.

"Courier, Master Hy'Bor, with letters for the king."

The old man arched an eyebrow. "Really?"

A tremor of dread passed through Oliver. The old man, some advisor to the king or court, had a stare that felt as if he could see right through him.

"Indeed," Oliver said, inclining his head respectfully.

The old man pointed a long finger at Oliver's side. "That's a fascinating sword, courier. An antique, if I am not mistaken. Indeed, I'd venture to say it is one of a kind."

Oliver held his breath, searching the man's gaze. His eyes were the same midnight blue as his robes, but there was a luminescence there that was anything but human. What was he, if not a man?

"What are you talking about, Atlantean?" the officer said, his voice not quite a sneer. Soldiers never liked interference from politicians, and that was clearly the case here.

But . . . *Atlantean*?

They were advisors to the kings—sorcerers and scholars—and they were supposed to be neutral. In another age they had brokered the peace between the Two Kingdoms, a third, objective party. But the Falconer had told Frost that Ty'Lis, an Atlantean, had sent the Myth Hunters after the Borderkind. So he had to wonder about Master Hy'Bor's true loyalties.

Later. If he lived.

"It is unique. You're right about that," Oliver replied. "A gift to me from an old man. A gift he received a long time ago from King Hunyadi himself."

The Atlantean glanced at the officer. "You've made a dangerous mistake, Sergeant."

Oliver saw the moment of confusion and hesitation in the captain and he used it. Cursing under his breath, he turned and fled, drawing his sword on the run. Shouts came from behind him.

"Intruder! Kill him, you fools!" the sergeant roared, boots pounding the earth in pursuit. "Kill the Intruder! He comes to assassinate the king!"

The words made Oliver wince. As if things hadn't been bad enough already.

The third and last Keen Keeng froze in the midst of Lycaon's Kitchen. It began to back away from them, moving out into the restaurant's central courtyard . . . into the rain.

Cheval Bayard shifted back into the lovely façade she usually wore and advanced upon him.

Chorti licked blood from his metal claws and came at the bat-man from another angle.

Across the restaurant the Mazikeen stood and threw back their hoods, moving to surround the Keen Keeng.

The waiter, Grin, stripped off the long, black uniform jacket Lycaon made his staff wear and joined Cheval.

Blue Jay nodded in approval and moved in as well.

The rain began to swirl in a dark tornado, turning to ice, and then snow. The humans in the restaurant had scattered, retreating to safety as best they could. Now the tone of their mutterings changed as they watched Frost sculpt himself a body of jagged ice from the moisture in the air. There was awe there, and a different sort of alarm.

Even in the Latin Quarter, word had come of the conspiracy against the Borderkind and the rebellion against those killers. But only now, as they saw Frost, did these people realize that they were in the midst of that rebellion. Blue Jay heard some of them talking about Frost as the leader of the Borderkind, and he wondered how news traveled so quickly. How secrets were so easily revealed.

Not that it mattered. It was true enough.

"How many others are there?" Frost demanded, moving toward the Keen Keeng. Blue Jay and the others did likewise, closing in around him. "You are no Hunter, so I want to know which Hunters are here in Perinthia. How close? And what other foot soldiers have they conscripted?"

The Keen Keeng spat at Frost.

With a gesture, the winter man froze the yellow spittle in the air and it fell to the marble floor to shatter into brittle shards.

"If they are here," a voice said, "there will be other spies. You know this without being told."

The words came from the little man with the flaming eyes. He strode now toward the circle they had made around the Keen Keeng. Pursing his lips, he whistled, and from the kitchen there came a roar. Everyone within the walls of the restaurant flinched and let out a gasp of surprise as a huge orange-and-black tiger bounded out from the back. It stalked across the restaurant, even the harpies scrambling out of its way, and brushed against the little man.

He mounted it as though climbing onto the back of a horse.

"There really is nowhere to hide, is there, Frost?" the little man said, the tiger moving beneath him, muscles taut beneath its fur. The fire flickered in the man's eyes like candle flames.

The winter man stared at the Keen Keeng, not looking at him. "Nowhere, Li."

"Then I am with you."

Frost tilted his head, icicle hair clinking together. "That is very good to know. We may have a difficult time leaving the city."

Blue Jay knew the name. Li, Guardian of Fire.

"If you'll allow me," Li said, gesturing toward the Keen Keeng.

Frost nodded. "By all means."

The tiger-rider raised his hand and fire rushed up from it, forging itself into a flaming blade. Li spurred the tiger forward. The great cat bounded toward the Keen Keeng and Li swung the fire-sword, decapitating it in a single, searing stroke.

The Keen Keeng's head fell to the ground.

Silence ensued. For a long moment those gathered in the courtyard only looked at one another, ignoring the restaurant's patrons completely. The two Mazikeen stroked their braided beards. Grin stood with Cheval and Chorti, who were checking one another over for injuries. Li stood beside Blue Jay, across from Frost.

Word had traveled faster than reality. Frost had been planning to begin a rebellion, to gather up those who would fight back, who would hunt the Hunters. But now it had begun in earnest.

A soft clapping broke the silence.

Lycaon continued the derisive, almost mocking applause as he approached the circle.

"Well done. Now leave. Begone from here, valiant idiots."

Frost glared at him, blue-white ice eyes narrowed. "You are Borderkind, wolf. They will come for you, in time."

"Not if you stop them first," Lycaon said.

"But you will not help us, even to help yourself?"

"Some of us still live here," the werewolf growled, and his cruel features became darker, more bestial, as though he might transform at any moment. "Most of you Borderkind are nomads, but I'm no wanderer. I have a home. And I want you out of it, before they destroy it to reach you."

Blue Jay chuckled softly. Rocking gently from side to side he stepped toward Lycaon. The rain spattered his face and the feathers in his hair danced in the breeze.

"Coward," the trickster said. "You'll regret this. If not at the hands of the Hunters, then at my hands, when this is over."

"As it may be," Lycaon said, and he raised his hand and gestured to the door.

One by one, they walked out of Lycaon's Kitchen and into the street, half a block from the Latin Quarter's marketplace.

Blue Jay glanced up immediately, scanning the rooftops and dark windows again. A pair of huge black birds took flight, streaking toward the city center. But they were not alone. At least half a dozen others perched on various ledges and rooftops, watching them.

"Strigae," Cheval said, coming up beside him.

Blue Jay nodded.

"Watching for the Keen Keengs to emerge," Li said.

"Or for us," Blue Jay replied. "They may have been tracking us from the moment we passed the watchtowers."

The two Mazikeen raised their hoods, hiding their gray faces and haunting eyes.

"There are Hunters in the city. Jezi-Baba and the Manticore. We have sensed Perytons as well."

Frost shook his head. "Ty'Lis grows bold, sending out Hunters that can only be commanded by Atlanteans."

"We haven't the numbers to face them," Cheval said, shifting her feet nervously, her equine nature coming to the fore.

Blue Jay had seen a wounded spirit in her eyes—her heart had never healed after her husband's murder. Much of the time she was the quiet, pensive widow, but all too often she wore the mask of a brittle, imperious bitch. He thought it might be best if she kept the façade up at all times; if Cheval drew too much attention or sympathy from the rest of them, it could endanger them all when the time came to fight. As it was, he wondered how effective Chorti would be in the midst of a real battle. If all he cared about was Cheval's safety, he would be useless to them.

We'll find out in time, Blue Jay thought. *All too soon, I expect.*

He studied the Strigae. "We'll have to face them in time, numbers or not. But I'd prefer it not be today." He looked at Frost. "We've got all the help I think we're going to find in Perinthia. Could be we'll find more on the road south. For now, let's get the hell out of here."

Frost nodded, starting northward. The other Borderkind followed, heading toward the edge of the city. It was the opposite direction from their destination, but for now the quickest route out of Perinthia was the smartest.

As they began to run, the Strigae took flight, pacing them.

"Pardon me, sirs," Grin said, long arms at his sides as he loped along. "You know we're never going to get away from the Hunters as long as those damned birds are watching us."

Blue Jay smiled grimly. "Not in this world."

The tiger trotted along the road with Li on its back. The little man had gained on the rest of them almost immediately, the tiger swift on its feet, even by the standards of myth. Now Li and his tiger turned together. Fire guttered from Li's eyes.

"Trickster, you wish us to cross the border?"

Cheval laughed softly. "That is what we do, is it not?"

Troubled, Li frowned, and the flames in his eyes burned higher. "I have not been through the Veil in a great many years."

The Grindylow shrugged. "Never done it, myself. Not once. My sort can do it, mind, but I never had the urge."

The strange parade of creatures turned onto a side street, threaded beneath a half-toppled column and through what had once been a Roman bath. Several times they spotted figures in alleys or windows of the Latin Quarter, but the people were not going to trouble them. Only the Strigae pursued them. The eyes of the Hunters.

The Mazikeen moved in silence, hands together in front of them like monks. They seemed only to walk, but covered more ground in a single step than was possible.

Blue Jay caught up to Li. "You'll love it, my friend. Their world is more corrupt than ever, but still beautiful, even so. Still stormy with love and lies and passion."

The trickster glanced around and then faltered. He came to a halt, and one by one the other Borderkind did the same. Chorti snuffled at the ground and then the air, baring metal fangs at the Strigae that circled high above them. The Mazikeen had their heads together, nearly touching, communing silently in their sorcerous way.

"Where's Frost?" Blue Jay asked.

Even as he did so there came a cry from above—a shriek that was not quite a bird's scream. The trickster turned and looked up just in time to see a Strigae fall, end over end, toward the ground. It shattered upon impact, body splintering into fragments of black feathers and ice.

Up on the edge of the roof, Frost crouched. He shot out a hand

and a spike of ice extended instantly from his fingertips and impaled a Strigae in mid-flight. It screamed, blood mixing with the rain, and then it glided lower and lower to crash to the street, dead.

Frost leaped from the roof and simply flowed down toward them, merging with the rain, becoming an avalanche of snow and ice, and then re-forming on the ground only inches away from Blue Jay.

"Beautiful," Cheval Bayard said, sliding closer to Frost. She reached out to run her fingertips along the sharp edge of his shoulder in fascination.

The winter man pulled away and glared at her, then regarded the others. "There is no choice. We cross. Only long enough to escape the spies . . ."

He gestured skyward, where several other Strigae still circled, another joining them.

Blue Jay watched the sky. "Are you sure that's wise? All of us in one place, in the mundane world, we're sure to draw attention. You saw what happened the last time."

"Perhaps we'll be lucky," Frost replied.

The two Mazikeen stared at him, eyes narrowed, pale flesh drawn over the bones of their skulls.

Some scent on the air alarmed Chorti. He ambled over to Cheval and grunted, crouching at her side. The wild man pointed a metal talon to the south, back the way they'd come.

"It's decided, then," Cheval said. "We cross. We'll make our way to the ocean, then come back through the Veil on the bank of the Atlantic River."

Blue Jay watched the way the kelpy stood, chin lifted regally, as though she led them. He glanced at Frost, but the winter man ignored her, glancing around at the others and then up at the Strigae.

"I wonder where it will bring us, crossing here," Frost said.

Li and his tiger circled the group. "You do not know?"

Blue Jay considered the question. The entirety of Perinthia had been traversed by the Borderkind, back and forth across the Veil, for centuries. The corresponding locations in the human world were well mapped. But he had never bothered to memorize the parallels. Locations in the world of legend did not correspond with the maps on the other side of the Veil. Geography and distance meant almost nothing. There was some relationship, of course, but nothing quantifiable. Crossing the Veil from Perinthia might bring a Borderkind to Britain or to the Himalayas.

Outside of the city there was a more predictable corollary. But Perinthia was a patchwork of cultures and pieces of ancient, mythical places.

"Somewhere in Italy, I'd presume. Or Greece."

One of the Mazikeen glanced at the other and nodded. "The Akrai," it said.

"Yes. The Quarter is all the Akrai," replied the other.

Chorti dug his metal talons into the street and tore it up, grunting furiously. He took a long look south, then turned to Frost.

"No more talk," he said, his voice a primal growl. "Go now."

"We go," Frost replied.

He waved a hand before him and the air began to shimmer. Blue Jay followed suit and soon all of the Borderkind were doing the same. Grin stood beside Blue Jay, shuffling anxiously. There was fear in his eyes. Li and his tiger were the first to leap through, trailing sparks and drops of liquid fire. The enormous cat bounded through a ripple in the air and passed through the Veil into the world of man.

Blue Jay waited while all of the others went. Frost, then Cheval and Chorti. The two Mazikeen. At last, Blue Jay looked at Grin, who clapped him on the back, a grateful expression upon his hideous features.

"Right, then, mate," Grin said. "On three, yeah? One, two—"

Blue Jay took his arm and the two of them stepped out of the world. The Veil was parted by the magic of the Borderkind, but still there was just the slightest resistance, like passing through a curtain of silk.

The first thing that came to Grin was the smell of the grass and the flowers around them, the trees and the earth. The sky was pale blue, and on the eastern horizon, the sun was just beginning to rise. The view was breathtaking.

" 'S beautiful, this is," Grin said.

The Borderkind stood in the midst of yet another ruin, this time of a Greek-style amphitheater, an outdoor theater on top of a mountain. It was the highest point in the area, as though whatever performances had been conducted here had wanted the gods for an audience.

Below, there stretched a city, though Blue Jay could not have said which. The theater was probably Greek, but the Greeks had influenced the world once upon a time, and the city below looked vaguely Italian, even from here.

Then he saw the volcano in the distance, gray smoke drifting heavenward from its peak.

"Where—" he began.

Frost was beside him. "Didn't you hear the Mazikeen? Akrai. We're in Sicily. The volcano there is Mt. Etna."

The trickster tossed his hair, feathers dancing on the breeze. He stretched and stamped his feet, enjoying the soil beneath his boots. Whenever he crossed the Veil, he needed a moment to become acclimated.

"We're on an island?" Blue Jay asked. He turned to look at the others. They were spread across the stones that had been laid down as a stage thousands of years before, as though they were the main attraction. "Sicily is an island. How are we going to make our way to the Atlantic coast from here?"

Frost arched an eyebrow, the ice of his face crackling. He turned his head, icicle hair tinkling musically.

Chorti threw his head back and howled.

"Somehow," Cheval Bayard said, slipping sylphlike up behind them, her silver hair blowing across her face, "I think that is the least of our concerns."

Blue Jay followed the line of her gaze, and there in the sky, he saw the terrible, angular figures with their antlers jutting from their heads and green-feathered wings spread out behind them.

"Perytons!" Li cried, fire erupting from his nostrils as he held out a hand, in which a ball of flame grew.

"At least seven," the Grindylow said. He pried a massive, ancient stone up out of the stage and prepared to hurl it.

But that was not what Chorti had scented. He scraped his metal talons on the stones and spun around like a massive dog chasing its tail. Blue Jay glanced around and then he saw, coming over the top of the hill, above the stone rows of seats that surrounded one side of the amphitheater, a pair of dreadful figures.

A hideous crone, the dawn's light illuminating her blue skin.

And a swift figure that slunk down toward them, its body as large as Li's tiger, its face a grotesque parody of humanity, its mouth impossibly wide and lined with hundreds of ivory needle teeth, tipped with venom.

The Manticore.

"They were expecting us," Frost said, icy mist drifting from his eyes. "They would not come into the Latin Quarter, but once they knew we were in Lycaon's Kitchen, they gambled that we would cross the border here."

Blue Jay sighed. "An ambush. Wonderful."

alliwell sat on a fallen tree, catching his breath. His right hand moved inquisitively over the bark and the jagged tips of several broken branches and he wondered what had taken the tree down. He would have thought a storm responsible, but there was a section of the trunk where the bark had been stripped off and deep gouges cut in the wood, as if from horns or something equally deadly. In this place, it might be anything.

He hoped that whatever had knocked down the tree was long gone.

Julianna had continued on sixty or seventy yards in the general direction of what Kara called the Orient Road. He was both embarrassed and grateful for her courtesy. They'd stopped to let him rest. His legs burned from all the walking they had done in the past two days. Halliwell often thought of himself as an old man. The truth was that he was in decent shape for his age; no old man was going to make this journey and not drop dead of a heart attack by now.

But he felt older than ever.

Kara had none of Julianna's courtesy. The little girl hung from the low branch of a tree just across from the fallen one and studied Halliwell with open curiosity and a bit of disdain. The detective—could he even think of himself as a detective in this place?—forced himself to breathe slowly and evenly and he stretched his legs, ignoring the twinging protests of his thighs and calves. His feet didn't hurt, so that was a plus. But he suspected that they would, and soon. How far he would be able to go after that, he did not know.

Halliwell returned Kara's stare, but she was unfazed by his attention. The girl swung on the branch and studied him, head tilted just to one side, like a faithful dog. He was reminded of a mental patient he had tried to interview once in an asylum in Bangor.

"How old are you?" Halliwell asked.

Kara dropped to the ground, dry grass crunching underfoot. She did a pirouette, amusing herself as children do. "I'm not really sure. How old are you?"

He hesitated a moment, on the verge of answering. Then, reluctantly, he picked himself up from the fallen tree, wishing he could sit there all day but knowing they had to move on. He brushed off the seat of his pants and shot the girl a smile.

"Young enough to make this trip but old enough to wish I was anywhere else."

Kara's dark, lustrous features expanded into a glorious smile. "You're a clever man, Mister Halliwell."

"And I'm beginning to think you're quite a clever girl."

Halliwell studied her more closely. Something in her eyes made him uneasy, and that megawatt smile did not help at all. Thus far she had proven herself a knowledgeable and skilled guide . . . or at least she seemed to be; they wouldn't know for sure how good she was until she led them to Oliver. But Halliwell felt wary around her and caught himself glancing at her almost constantly. Whoever and whatever she was, it seemed obvious to him that Kara was not quite human.

Get used to it, he told himself. *You're going to run into a lot of that here.*

But that did not mean he had to like it.

Here. He hated even thinking of *here* and *there.* It brought back the panic that churned within him. His nerves were frayed, and sometimes his hands shook. He tried to control it as best he could, knowing that Julianna had noticed.

Kara had noticed, too. A clever girl, he'd said. But there was far more to her than that. Halliwell studied her a moment longer. Kara did another pirouette and it was as though she had no idea he was there to watch her. Yet at the same time he thought she was completely aware of him, and this little dance was a performance for his benefit.

Ahead, Julianna waited. She made no gesture for them to hurry and did not call out, but her body language was signal enough. She was getting impatient. Halliwell could not blame her.

Kara led the way and Halliwell had to hurry to catch up. For her size, she moved with uncanny swiftness. He tried not to look too closely at her when she was walking, or to attempt to gauge distance visually. Something went wrong with his eyes if he did that, and a needle of pain would thrust into each temple.

"You're sure this is the way? Oliver and the ... shapeshifter ... the fox-woman, they came down here?"

The girl turned and walked backward as she replied. "I can smell them," she said, giving a small shrug. "Can't you?"

"No," Halliwell replied, knitting his brows.

"Pity."

When they reached Julianna, she gave Halliwell a visual once-over and he knew she was checking him out to see if he was okay to continue onward.

"I'm fine," he snapped, more harshly than he'd intended. He nodded, gesturing that she should get moving and not worry about him.

"All right," she said. They continued along the path and past a stand of ancient oaks. "You feeling any better?"

"I've caught my breath," he said, brushing off the question. He shot her a hard look, giving her a glimpse of the anger that he was trying to keep bottled up. After a few steps he spoke again, cautiously this time. "I'm ... sorry about that, Julianna."

As she walked, she pulled her hair back into a ponytail, using a rubber band to hold it in place. "Don't worry about it, Ted. We're in this together."

Halliwell spoke without thinking. "Thanks to your fiancé."

Julianna glanced sidelong at him. "That's not exactly fair. We don't know the whole story, but from what we can tell, Oliver didn't come here by choice and he sure as hell didn't drag us over here."

Over his shoulder, Halliwell carried the small satchel Ovid Tsing had prepared for them with food and water. He shifted it now to the other side, taking the moment to draw a deep breath and bite his tongue. Maybe Oliver Bascombe hadn't dragged them across the Veil, but he had led them here. The guy might be just as much a victim as they were, but Halliwell couldn't help blaming him, or even hating him a little.

"Ted?" Julianna prodded. "It's not Oliver's fault that we're here."

Halliwell shrugged, but would not meet her gaze. He felt the anger rising again. "You don't know that."

She stopped in her tracks and stared at him. Halliwell kept walking. When he had gained a few paces on her, Julianna started up again. She said nothing, but her jaw was tightly clenched as she fell into stride with him. Halliwell regretted that. They were stuck here together and he did not want tension between them, but he also wasn't going to lie to avoid it. Oliver might not be a killer, but Halliwell still had some pretty pointed questions for the man.

He had to have someone to blame for his fear and rage, for his panic and sorrow. Who better than Oliver Bascombe? What he wanted more than anything was to meet up with the guy and get him by the throat, up against a wall, and squeeze answers out of him.

Halliwell practically trembled with the need to lash out.

Julianna wasn't the target he wanted. As long as she didn't push his buttons, he would hold it all in. For now.

Soon they passed a ramshackle building that Kara referred to as a way station. Halliwell imagined that it must once have been exactly that—a stopover point for travelers, perhaps for coaches, horsemen, and soldiers. But though there must still have been a need for such a place, it seemed abandoned. Sometimes there were things the detective in him could not ignore, and this was one of them. He wondered why travelers in need of a place to rest would avoid this structure. Perhaps something had happened here that kept them away.

They reached the Orient Road—little more than a dirt track—and turned to the west. In time, his feet began to feel like blocks of wood. The muscles in his legs burned as though frostbitten and there were aches all through his back. But Halliwell said nothing of this to Julianna. His comments had been hurtful. True or not, he ought to have spared her those words. No way was he going to look for sympathy from her now.

Halliwell hated it, but as the day grew longer and the shadows deeper, he knew he was going to have to stop to rest again. If he could hold on a while, perhaps they could eat something from the bag that Ovid Tsing had given them.

All throughout their trek along the Orient Road, Kara had been keeping up, but only barely. Like an even younger child she stopped to investigate everything, picking up fallen leaves and letting the wind take them, climbing rocks, weaving amongst the trees on the edge of the forest. Now she joined them by virtue of a cartwheel that carried her right up beside Julianna.

"The Bascombes are special," said the girl. "It isn't as though they can help it."

Halliwell hooked his thumbs in his pockets. "What does that mean?"

"Is there something you're not telling us, Kara?" Julianna asked.

The girl looked at them, all wide-eyed innocence. "What, me?" She grinned. "Don't be silly. There are thousands of things I haven't told you. We're only just getting to know each other."

Halliwell chuckled softly. He couldn't decide if she was a complete smartass or really that innocent. Though he was wary of her, Kara also took him off guard with her oddity and nonsense, and the attitude she presented that seemed to indicate she perceived herself as the adult and the two of them as the tiresomely inquisitive children. In those moments, she helped to lighten Halliwell's mood, which was good. Anything that took the edge off of the anxious, frantic buzz in his head.

"About Oliver," Julianna prodded.

Kara shrugged, rolling her eyes. "I don't know. It's just that so many people are going to so much trouble over him. Would that happen if he and his sister were just ordinary?"

Halliwell would have pushed the question further, but Kara's face lit up with pleasure and she ran ahead.

"What the hell is she doing?" Julianna asked quietly.

He didn't know. With some difficulty, he picked up the pace and they both hurried after the girl. Evening was still a ways off, but the shadows stretched across the road now from the woods on both sides. Things dashed through the underbrush. Halliwell's nerves were so brittle that the movement startled him, every time, even as he tried to keep his focus on Kara.

Thirty yards ahead, she stopped in the road. With the waning light, it was difficult at first to see what had gotten her attention. Only when they walked up and were nearly on top of it did he and Julianna realize she was crouched over a large pile of horse shit, buzzing with flies.

The girl sniffed the air as though she wanted to inhale every bit of the aroma. Julianna grimaced and made a disgusted noise.

"What's so special about a pile of manure?" Halliwell asked.

Kara ignored him. She started off again at a trot that he was sure was meant to mimic the horse that had passed along the road recently. A giddy little noise escaped her.

"I'm not sure the girl is entirely sane," Julianna said, voice low and deadly serious.

Halliwell picked up the pace further, a strange exhilaration filling him as he pushed past his exhaustion. "You think?"

Kara continued to run ahead and passed another pile of horse shit. A few minutes later, they came to a quaint little stone bridge that crossed a narrow but swiftly moving stream.

Halfway across the bridge, Kara dropped to her knees and peered at the stone construction as though fascinated by its design. There was still something childlike about the way she conducted these examinations, but he had begun to think there was more to it than that.

"I'm not sure she's entirely insane, either," he said.

Julianna had nothing to say to that. By the time the two of them crossed the bridge, Kara had moved on to the other side of the stream.

Halliwell paused and grunted as he dropped into a crouch. He tried to see what had fascinated her so much about the stones that made up the bridge, but noticed nothing but a few muddy hoofprints. And perhaps that had been her interest after all.

"They've been here," Kara said.

Julianna ran to join her. They were just off the road on the edge of the stream. Halliwell took his time, studying the location. There were hoofprints on the far side of the bridge, dug into the dirt as though the rider had drawn back on the reins, causing the horse to slow quickly.

"What is this?" Julianna asked. "Blood?"

Halliwell snapped his head around and stared at the woman and the girl. Kara knelt in the scrub grass on the side of the road and looked more closely. She breathed it in.

"Yes. Human blood."

She can tell that just from the scent? Halliwell thought. He wished he were more surprised.

"There's more over here," he said, pointing out a spatter of dried brown on the ground by the road.

Kara stood up, then spun slowly in a circle as though she could see, with her own eyes, the scene that had played out here earlier that same day.

"There was a scuffle at the water's edge. More fighting over here. Soldiers were camped on the roadside."

"Why do you say soldiers?" Julianna asked.

"That many men all in one place. In this part of the kingdom, and without any wagons or horses, they could only be soldiers. Oliver and Kitsune came upon them here and fought them."

"Is there . . ." Julianna glanced at Halliwell and the detective saw the fear in her eyes and turned away, striding back up to the road to study the hoofprints. "Is any of the blood Oliver's?"

Kara did not respond at first, and her silence forced Halliwell to turn and look at them again.

"How could I know that?" the little girl said, wide-eyed and mystified.

"You know a lot of things that surprise me," Julianna said, the hard edge of suspicion in her voice.

Halliwell figured it was driven more by her own fear for Oliver than anything else and decided it was time to intervene. He gestured toward the flattened, broken scrub grass and the remains of a small fire in the clearing on the side of a road.

"It's obvious a group of men were camped here, at least briefly. The evidence of a struggle would be hard to miss as well. The blood tells us somebody was wounded. By the amount, and judging by Kara's assurance that it's human blood, I'm going to say at least two of them didn't survive. But there are no bodies, which also supports the military theory. They'd be unlikely to leave their dead behind. The blood's dry, but still tacky, like fresh paint. Whatever happened here did so today. And if Kara's right about Oliver and his friend using the Orient Road, then they might have been involved."

"Oh, they were," Kara said.

Julianna crossed her arms. "How can you be certain?"

The little girl held up something that was invisible in the dying afternoon light.

"What is it?" Halliwell asked.

"Fox hair. Kitsune has been this way."

Halliwell left the road again and walked toward Julianna. Her body was tensed like an animal about to bolt. The frustration and fear came off of her in waves. He felt it keenly and knew it well. It was only a fraction of the emotion he struggled to contain in himself.

"They're still alive," he said.

She stared at him. "Oh, so you're Nostradamus, too?"

The detective scratched at the back of his head. "This Kitsune, she's a Borderkind. Supernatural. Whatever. The point is, she's along with Oliver to help him, protect him. No way is she going to stand by and let him be killed. If she's still alive, then so is he. And since Kara didn't mention any puddles of Borderkind blood—"

The girl squealed and clapped her hands. "Oh, well done! I'd say you're right about that."

"So where are they, then?" Julianna asked, walking in a circle, kicking at the scrub grass, peering into the woods and back across the stream and up to the road.

Kara skipped up to the road, spun, and bowed, one hand stretched out to guide the way west, further along the Orient Road. "This way, my friends."

Halliwell and Julianna joined her and the three of them set off again.

"All right, spill," Julianna said. "How do we know where we're going?"

"You got me," Halliwell replied. "Here's what I figure. The soldiers weren't on horses. Somebody came riding up on horseback, or maybe Oliver and his friend somehow got hold of a couple of horses—"

"There was only one rider coming over the bridge," Kara corrected.

Halliwell smiled. There were a lot of things he knew, but how to figure how many people were on the back of a horse just from its tracks was not among them.

"All right. Point is, the rider came up during the fight. At some point, he pulled the reins. The horse stopped in the middle of it. It's possible they took the horse away from him."

Julianna shot him a panicked glance. "Don't even say that. If they're on horseback, we'll never catch up with them."

Halliwell wanted to tell her that at the speed he was capable of traveling, they were never going to catch up to Oliver anyway, not if Oliver kept moving. But he kept his mouth shut.

"We don't need to be faster than they are," Kara said. "Not if we know where they're going."

"And do we?"

The little girl gave him a smile that lit up the mischief in her eyes. "We do now. The horseman that came through was riding hard. One rider, alone, moving swiftly. I'd wager that's a royal courier. If so, he'd have been headed for the summer residence at Otranto. The only reason for that would be if Hunyadi is there."

Julianna uttered a soft laugh of disbelief. "Wait, you think if Oliver found out that the king was at this summer place, he'd go there? Knowing the guy's trying to kill him?"

Kara sighed and shook her head, and there was something of ancientness about her eyes then. "You don't listen. Even if your lover saves his sister, both of them will be hunted and executed unless he can secure a pardon from both kings. Having Hunyadi so nearby would likely be too tempting to ignore."

"Likely," Halliwell repeated. "What if you're wrong?"

Julianna watched the girl closely.

"If I'm wrong," Kara said, "then we have little chance of overtaking them, unless the two of you can grow wings."

Oliver ran across the courtyard of the castle of Otranto, sword in hand, the sergeant shouting at his men. The order to kill him echoed off the inner walls of the courtyard and off the castle keep. The scarnosed guard wasn't going to catch him on foot. Even the sergeant concerned Oliver only a little. The only two things he feared in that moment were sorcery and arrows. Either could kill him on the spot.

An arrow whisked in front of his face, close enough to make him falter a moment. It struck the ground with a dull thud. Several others followed rapidly, thunking into the dirt around him. If not for the fact that most of the archers had withdrawn from the wall, he would have died right then.

"Kill him!" came the cry from behind him, back by the main doors of the castle. But this time it was not the sergeant screaming for his blood. It was Hy'Bor, the Atlantean advisor to King Hunyadi.

Oliver hurtled toward the gates of the outer wall. He gripped the sword tightly, but it danced uselessly in his hand. If he stood and fought, he had no chance of survival. Serpents of ice coiled around his heart as he understood what a mistake he had made.

He would die here, and in some prison within the Sandman's castle, Collette would be mutilated and murdered by a monster. If death was imminent, he wished he could at least have seen his sister again, held her close, let her know how much she meant to him.

Anger burned in him, at himself, and at all the people who wanted him dead simply because they were afraid of the world beyond the one they knew. Where was he supposed to run? To the gates? There were guards on the other side. He was not getting out of here alive.

"Fuck it," Oliver snarled.

He spun, raising the Sword of Hunyadi. The sergeant and the scar-nosed soldier ran at him. Others were coming, climbing down ladders from the battlements and bursting from doors across the courtyard.

Out of the corner of his eye, he saw something red flash in the late afternoon sun. He heard a scream and glanced over to see one of the archers fall over the edge of the battlement and crash to the ground below. The second of them had an arrow nocked, about to be let loose, but he turned as the fox leaped at him in a blur of copper-red fur. Her jaws snapped shut on the meat of his forearm and the archer cried out in pain and tried to shake her off.

In an eyeblink, Kitsune transformed. Where the fox had been there now stood the woman. Her cloak whipped around her as she moved, the hood hiding her features. The archer tried to fight her off, but Kitsune snapped out a hand and gripped his throat, then hurled him down into the courtyard with the other. As he fell, she ripped his bow from his hands.

The last of the archers still on the battlements had turned on her now. Eyes fearfully wide, he loosed an arrow. It flew at Kitsune but she dodged easily.

With a cry of fury, she slashed the claws of her left hand across his face. The man screamed and staggered back. She tore the quiver of arrows from his back and then pushed him over the front wall of the castle. He cried out as he fell, tumbling out of sight.

All of this happened in seconds.

With no more arrows flying, Oliver had a moment to simply stand and wait for the king's guard to reach him. The sword felt heavy in his grip but he gritted his teeth and raised it higher. Beyond the sergeant and the one with the scar, he saw Hy'Bor approaching. The Atlantean sorcerer carried himself with far too much arrogant dignity to run, so instead he strode imperiously, shimmering with a strange glow that disrupted the air so that he seemed to be stepping between moments, crossing twice the distance in half the time.

"Come on, then!" Oliver shouted, and he held the grip and pommel of the sword with both hands. The wind blew and he caught the scent of flowers somewhere not far off. The incongruity chilled him.

"Take the assassin's head!" the sergeant yelled, brandishing his own sword now.

"I'm no assassin," Oliver said.

No one was listening. The sergeant came at him, sword raised. His attack was clumsy and easily parried. Oliver spun inside the man's reach and shot an elbow to the sergeant's head, knocking him backward.

With a scream of rage, the sergeant swung again, with more focus and skill this time. Oliver blocked, the blades ringing crisply in the air. The scar-nosed soldier was only steps away. Years of fencing lessons swirled in Oliver's head. He had a talent for it, but had never fought more than one opponent at a time.

Oliver feinted, and when the sergeant went to block, he slapped the flat of the blade down on the man's wrist, breaking the bone. The sergeant cursed and dropped his sword.

"Bastard!" shouted the scar-nosed soldier. He came at Oliver with little finesse but with the size and fury of a bull.

His attack was easy to sidestep. Oliver grabbed his arm and used his momentum and weight against him, turning and shoving the man so that he stumbled and crashed to the ground. With speed that belied his size, he leaped to his feet again, enraged.

When an arrow took him in the shoulder, he spun around and fell to his knees, grabbing at the shaft that jutted from his flesh.

Another whistled through the air above Oliver's head and he spun just in time to see it strike home in the chest of the Atlantean. The weird, warped shimmer of air around Hy'Bor ceased instantly. The sorcerer stared down at the arrow protruding from his chest and staggered off. He fell on his side in the courtyard, crumpling to the ground. The impact sent up a puff of dirt. But one of his hands waved in the air and then began to distort the space around it. Weakened he might be, but Hy'Bor still lived.

"Take him!" the sergeant shouted again. "Kill them both!"

"Would you just shut the hell up?" Oliver snapped.

The soldiers began to surround him and he kept his guard up, turning around in a circle, watching to see which of them would make the first move. There were three, then five, then he lost count. Had the order not been to kill him, he would have surrendered then and there. But surrender meant death, and he would rather die fighting.

An arrow struck a soldier from behind with such force that its tip poked out through his abdomen. The man started to fall and a second caught him, holding him up.

"Oliver!" Kitsune called, and fully half of the soldiers turned to face her as she raced across the courtyard with the swiftness of her breed.

"Borderkind!" shouted one of the king's guard.

Kitsune drew back the bowstring, an arrow at the ready. "Stand down. The first one to touch him, or come near me, gets an arrow through the eye."

It seemed to Oliver that the world held its breath.

Then Hy'Bor began to chant in a language unlike anything Oliver had ever heard. Fear flashed in the eyes of every one of the soldiers around him and they all drew back a step.

The Atlantean was rising. It was difficult to look at him; his body seemed out of synch with reality, as though parts of him had been stripped out and hidden away.

"Kit," Oliver began, warily.

Before Kitsune could reply, there came the shriek of stress on wood and metal and the main gates of the castle swung inward with great force. Framed in the massive gates, with the golden afternoon light streaming in behind them, were half a dozen of the fishermen Oliver had seen while riding toward the castle. They carried fishing poles and several lugged strings of hooked fish, the catch of the day. All of them were dressed in rugged clothing that had seen better days but there was an air about them that dispelled any suggestion of simple country folk.

The man in front had black hair and a neatly trimmed beard, both shot through with silver. His face was pitted with pockmarks, and though he was only a bit larger than Oliver, physically, he moved with such confidence and power that it seemed his mere presence might knock them all to the ground.

"Hy'Bor! What transpires here?" the fisherman shouted.

No one in the courtyard moved. Even the injured men, cradling broken bones or nursing wounds, ceased their self-ministrations.

The Atlantean had stopped chanting the moment the gates swung open. Now he stared at the newcomer, breathing heavily, fury dying like embers in his eyes. He plucked the arrow from his chest and a trickle of blood flowed out, staining his robe, before becoming a drizzle of clear liquid, and then ceasing altogether.

He wore a terrible sneer as he gestured toward Oliver and Kitsune. The soldiers around them flinched at this attention.

"Highness, we have an Intruder among us. You have sworn out a warrant for his death. Yet here he is, coming into your own castle disguised as a courier, undoubtedly to attempt to assassinate you."

Oliver glanced back and forth between the two men. This was King Hunyadi? This fisherman? Yet despite his clothing, Oliver believed it immediately. The man carried himself like a king and those within the walls of the castle of Otranto froze in his presence, unwilling to do anything without his leave. The soldiers were on guard, ready to finish Oliver off, but they hesitated, waiting for the king to speak.

"Undoubtedly," King Hunyadi said, but he arched an eyebrow and studied Oliver with open curiosity. When he saw Kitsune, his eyes narrowed and he nodded slowly as though he had deciphered the last line of a difficult riddle.

Hunyadi handed his fishing pole to one of his friends and left them standing by the gates. He strode toward Oliver and Kitsune. She shifted her bow so that the arrow was pointed directly at his heart, but the king neither slowed nor even seemed to notice her.

"You, Intruder, remind me of your name."

"Oliver Bascombe, Your Highness." He lowered his sword. The soldiers did not attack.

Hunyadi paused ten feet away, behaving as though he and Oliver were the only people in the courtyard. He crossed his arms, a bemused look upon his face. "Tell me, Oliver, why does a man beard the lion in its den? You're aware of the death warrant I've placed upon you?"

"Yes, sir."

"Are you a lunatic, then, coming here?"

Oliver met his gaze evenly. He started toward the king, but he held up the sword in both hands as though to present it to him.

"No, Your Highness. Just an ordinary man. A man who does not wish to die. Once upon a time another such man came to you. His name was Professor David Koenig. You granted him a year to prove himself worthy of your trust, and when he earned that trust, you gave him this sword as a gift."

A pair of soldiers stepped in to prevent him from reaching the king. Oliver knelt and laid it on the ground. He had made himself completely vulnerable now, but it was too late for fighting, in any case. His life was in the king's hands.

"I remember," Hunyadi said. He uncrossed his arms and stepped nearer, staring down at the sword. "How do you come by it?"

Oliver looked up at him. "Professor Koenig gave me this sword so that you might see it and remember, and look kindly upon me as I ask you for the same boon you granted him. One year, to prove myself worthy of your trust. He gave me this gift moments before he was murdered by the Hunters who are abroad in the Two Kingdoms, exterminating the Borderkind."

Hunyadi nodded slowly. "You may pick up the sword. Sheathe it."

The Atlantean stormed toward them. "Your Highness, you cannot trust the man! He is an Intruder, and he travels with a Borderkind witch." He gestured around the courtyard. "Some of your men are badly injured. Bascombe came disguised as a courier, who is in all probability dead, murdered by his hand, or her claws. They are your enemies."

The king considered this.

"With all due respect, sir, we are not your enemies. We are simply trying to stay alive," Oliver told him.

Hunyadi walked over to Kitsune. All throughout this exchange she had held her bow up, arrow pointed at his heart. Now he approached until the tip of the arrow touched the rough cotton of his shirt. Kitsune's jade eyes gleamed in the shadows beneath her hood. The king reached out with both hands and slipped the hood down to reveal her face.

"You are Kitsune," the king said, and it was not a question. "Your legend is a favorite of mine. The tale sings of your beauty, but you are beyond all expectation."

"Thank you, Highness," Kitsune said, revealing rows of tiny, jagged teeth.

"Your companion asks for my trust. Will you not give me yours?"

In the fading light, with evening beginning to fall upon the castle, Kitsune released the bowstring slowly and then let bow and arrow fall to the ground. She inclined her head in the tiniest of bows.

"Make her swear fealty to you!" Hy'Bor cried desperately.

Hunyadi waved this away. "There is beauty in wild things, my friend. A beauty that is crushed by placing such demands upon it. I will not try to tame the wild."

Oliver stood slowly and slid his sword into its scabbard.

King Hunyadi looked pointedly at his Atlantean advisor. "See to it that they have food and a place to wash off the grit of the road. Then bring them to my chambers."

The shrieks of the Perytons filled the air above the Akrai, the ancient Greek theater that sat on the mountaintop above Siracusa. Like harpies, they descended upon the Borderkind gathered there on the ancient stone stage. The sound of their green-feathered wings beating the air was like thunder and they moved so swiftly that even Frost barely had time to react as the Hunters fell upon them.

One of the Perytons soared down from the sky and grabbed hold of him with fingers like knives. Frost smiled, full of hatred, and sent ice spreading up the Peryton's arms, freezing its leathern flesh. White crystals of rime formed on its face.

Then the second one hit him from behind, driving its antlers into his back. The enormous prongs thrust into Frost's body, cracking ice, plunging deep into his frigid form.

The winter man screamed.

With those hideously long razor fingers they began to tear at him. Frigid water spilled from his wounds and splashed on the Sicilian soil. The air was hot and humid, and the summer day waning fast.

He looked up, the white-blue mist of his eyes obscuring his vision, and saw the Peryton above him hiss and bare its fangs. He wondered if the venom they carried could kill him.

Frost did not want to know the answer.

His fist became a single long, tapered spike of ice and he punched it right through the Peryton's chest, piercing skin and muscle and breaking bones. The icicle burst through the creature's back. The other, the one behind him, continued to attack, carving chunks out of his body.

Frost weakened as his life spilled away.

Then someone called his name. He glanced up to see a blue blur in the waning light, spinning toward him. Blue Jay danced across the ancient stone stage where tragedy had once unfolded, the magical wings of the trickster whirring around him, half visible even to the eyes of his own kind.

With the slash of his wings, he decapitated the second Peryton. Its blood was sickly yellow-green. The Hunter's head struck the ground, antlers impaled in the earth.

Frost lay on the ground, bleeding ice water, barely propped up on his arms. Blue Jay crouched by him.

"Help the others," he rasped, cold mist rising from him as he tried to heal his wounds, freezing them over with a pass of his hands.

Blue Jay shook his head. "We don't stand a chance. Look around."

The winter man did. The Perytons filled the sky. Several of them pursued Cheval Bayard, who had reverted to her true form, and was attempting to flee. As Frost watched, Li rode his huge tiger after her and leaped into the air, spheres of fire leaping from his hands and enveloping one of the Perytons. Its wings burned a moment but the fire quickly died. They could not be killed that way. Still it veered off, feathers singed. The tiger reached Cheval and spun, roaring, protecting her, keeping the Perytons at bay for a moment.

But not for long.

The two Mazikeen, silent as always, were in grim combat with Jezi-Baba, but the witch was far more ancient and powerful than they. Golden light like a summer dawn glowed around them as the Mazikeen commanded the earth to rise up around her. Deep roots of ancient trees burst through the stone stage and wrapped around Jezi-Baba, but an instant later they began to blacken and die, and fell away from her robes like cobwebs brushed aside.

She grabbed one of the Mazikeen around the throat and the same thing happened to him. His flesh withered and blackened and fell away to ash, the robe crumbling in her hands. The witch cackled and moved after the other Mazikeen. He cast a spell that lanced her eyes with that golden light and she shrieked and staggered back, hands over her hideous face.

But Frost feared it would not last.

The Manticore was wounded, half its face ripped away into a grotesque grin, flaps of flesh hanging down. Some of its teeth were broken, thanks to Chorti's metal claws. But now Chorti was down and the Manticore raked talons across his chest. The monster leaped on top of him, opened his massive jaws with their hundreds of teeth, and was about to snap his head off.

The Grindylow reached them just in time. Grin wrapped his long arms around the Manticore's head and pulled the creature off of Chorti, lifted it up, and hurled it with incredible strength at the rows of stone seats around the stage. The Manticore hit with an audible crack, but in a moment it moved, bones still cracking, resetting themselves, and it was up, beginning to stalk toward them again.

"Go back, all of you!" Frost commanded, struggling to rise. "Back through the Veil, back to Perinthia! Now!"

Blue Jay helped haul him to his feet. The trickster's eyes were dark and cold. "Are you out of your mind? We don't stand a chance in the city!"

Frost grimaced in pain. "The Hunters are *here*. All that waits for us there are the damned birds."

"How can you—"

"We don't have time to argue," Frost said, as another Peryton rode the winds, diving toward them out of the sky. "Cross the border! Go back!"

Even as Blue Jay turned, the air blurring around him, mystic wings shearing the wind and the spirit, keeping the Peryton at bay, Frost shouted to all of the others, repeating the command over and over.

One by one he saw them step through shimmering early evening light, moving out of this world and through the Veil, into the one beside it.

Only when they all were gone did he slip through the border himself. His last glimpse of the Akrai was of the Manticore and several Perytons rushing toward him, blood on claws and teeth, death in their eyes. Blue Jay spun into a blur that disappeared, winking out completely.

Then the winter man crossed over, leaving the Hunters behind.

But the hunt would only be more savage, more determined now. The Myth Hunters had spilled their blood. The had the taste and the scent.

That was all right with Frost.

He was sick of running.

liver ought to have been fascinated by the castle of Otranto. Every archway and window drew the eye. On many walls there hung elaborate tapestries that would have made him catch his breath in admiration on another day. When guards came to fetch them from the rooms where they had been brought to wash and rest, they were marched past massive double doors that opened into a vast library at least two stories high. He could not see far enough into the room to determine if it rose even higher. In an alcove in the corridor that led to King Hunyadi's presentation room, there were two glass cases in which illuminated manuscripts were on display.

But none of this provided more than a passing moment's distraction. Exhaustion had wormed its way into Oliver's bones. Until now, desperation and adrenaline had conspired to keep him going, but as he and Kitsune were brought before the king, he felt only tired and resigned.

His fate was at hand. He had done all that he could to influence it, but what happened next was no longer in his control. If it ever had been.

They were not bound, nor were they prodded with weapons as they were escorted to the Presentation Room, but there was no doubt they were prisoners. The guards seared them with hate-filled eyes and Oliver fought the temptation to challenge their bitterness. After all, any of the king's men who had been slain on the road or within the castle walls today had been victims of their own belligerence. Oliver and Kitsune had been protecting their own lives. But he was not fool enough to speak such thoughts aloud.

He had been allowed to keep the Sword of Hunyadi—an exceedingly generous gesture on the part of the king, he thought—but he had no illusions that it would save his life.

Whatever his expectations had been, the Presentation Room defied them. It was an enormous chamber in some far-flung corner of the castle that must, from the outside, have seemed a strange peninsula thrust out from the main structure. Within, it resembled nothing so much as a narrow church, with airy, vaulted ceilings, and towering, stained glass windows on three sides. Their full glory could not be appreciated after dark, with the moonlight casting a dull glow upon them from without and row upon row of candles spreading light within. There were wall sconces and oil lamps as well, but the candles were the primary light source and they cast a warm, golden brilliance throughout the chamber.

The ocean-myth motif of the mosaic around the main doors of the castle was carried through to the Presentation Room. Other mosaics had been created between each window, and the stained glass imagery also illustrated the legends of the sea. There were mermaids and selkies, monstrous kraken, and other creatures he did not immediately recognize.

At the far end of the room, a single enormous chair sat upon a platform. Fish and serpents and tentacles had been carved into the mahogany arms and legs and back of the chair, and above it three vast stained glass windows had been placed to create a triptych of the sea god, Poseidon. Upon Poseidon's head sat a golden crown whose arched points rose in the shape of waves.

King Hunyadi sat upon his chair—what passed for a throne in this room—and wore the very same crown. The Crown of Poseidon. Dozens of other people filled the room, gathered on either side of a long blue carpet that bisected the stone floor, but in the king's presence they seemed invisible. There were armored guards and robed attendants, and nearest the king there were several servants in blue and green, obviously awaiting his instructions.

To the left of the king sat Hy'Bor, the Atlantean, his primary advisor. Despite the arrow that he had plucked from his chest at dusk, the sorcerer seemed in perfect health. He was pale, but that was apparently typical of his kind. He watched Oliver and Kitsune with his lips pressed tightly together and his eyes full of malevolence.

As they strode toward the platform with its high chair, Oliver heard Kitsune growl low in her throat. Nervous, he shot her a sidelong glance, wondering if she had finally snapped. Any threat to the king now and he was sure they would be executed on the spot. Perhaps right there on the three steps that led up to the platform. For that very reason, he had kept his hands clasped behind him as he walked, making certain that no one could claim he made a grab for the sword that hung in its scabbard at his side.

But Kitsune's attention was not on the king at all. She sniffed the air and peered off to the right, toward a cluster of people Oliver presumed had gathered to plead for the king's aid or intercession on some matter or another.

"Stop," Oliver whispered.

The fox-woman glared at him, her eyes slits and one corner of her mouth lifted to reveal tiny, animal teeth. Oliver flinched at the ferocity of that glance.

"We have enemies here," she rasped, voice so low that even he could barely hear.

The sergeant whose hand Oliver had broken stood just ahead to one side of the carpet. The man's wrist was splinted and bandaged but he still seemed formidable. He frowned as he watched them whispering to one another, then raised his other hand.

"Silence," said one of the guards behind them, and Oliver tensed, believing he was about to be struck. No blow came, however, and by then it was too late for him to respond to Kitsune, for they had crossed the length of the Presentation Room.

"Your Highness, as requested, the Intruder, Oliver Bascombe, and Kitsune of the Borderkind," the sergeant announced in a loud, formal voice. He bowed his head and backed away from the carpet.

King Hunyadi studied them a moment. With his crown and silver-blue robe, he looked every inch the monarch. His blue eyes were clear and intelligent and regarded those before him as a scientist does his experiments. Yet there was still much of the fisherman in his bearing, in his broad shoulders, and in his genial, warm features.

Beside him, the Atlantean glanced out at the gathered petitioners.

Kitsune shifted from one foot to another beside Oliver, but it was not the scrutiny of the king that made her skittish. She also glanced back at the cluster of petitioners. Her hood was back, but she drew the fur cloak around her tightly as though the temptation to transform was almost more than she could bear.

"These are strange and difficult times," King Hunyadi said. He spoke loudly enough for all to hear, but all of his attention was focused on the Intruder and the Borderkind who had gained entrance into his summer residence.

"Tell me your story, Oliver," said the king. "Beginning to end."

All was silent in the room. The king had spoken.

"Of course, Your Highness," Oliver replied. A ripple of unease went through him, but he chalked it up to the weight of Hunyadi's attention. "It begins with a conspiracy, I think, but that will become obvious. And anyway, that's not how it started for me. There was a blizzard, you see, on the night before I was supposed to be married—"

In the end, it took far less time to tell the tale than Oliver would have imagined. Living it had given the events texture and substance that could not be easily expressed. Yet though the story was told in twenty or thirty minutes, its significance was not lost on the king. Hunyadi attended with great interest, nodding several times as though suspicions had been confirmed. His expression grew grimmer with each new twist of the tale.

When Oliver had finished, King Hunyadi took a deep breath and stroked his beard. He looked pointedly at Hy'Bor. Oliver had debated whether or not to reveal that Ty'Lis, another Atlantean sorcerer, had been named as the man behind the Myth Hunters, worried that he might be endangering Frost, Blue Jay, and the others by doing so. Yet, in the end, he felt he had to disclose all he knew.

Hy'Bor did not raise any challenge to his claims, but he maintained an expression of aloof disbelief that Oliver supposed was comment enough.

Even so, the way Hunyadi looked at his advisor told Oliver the king would be having a very interesting conversation with Hy'Bor later.

Oliver had also felt reluctant to reveal Collette's abduction and his belief that she was a captive of the Sandman. Their visit to Twillig's Gorge had proven that there could be spies anywhere—and with Hy'Bor standing on the platform beside the throne, he had no doubt that was the case at Otranto, too. But he had no choice. If the king allowed him to live, Collette would still be condemned as an Intruder. He had to make the appeal for both of them.

Hunyadi sniffed in apparent disapproval and turned his focus upon Kitsune. "You are Borderkind. You did not have to remain here. Hy'Bor would have used magic to restrain you, but I instructed that you be left alone. At any moment you might have slipped through the Veil and escaped whatever fate awaits you here. Why did you stay?"

The fox-woman raised her chin defiantly, her black, silken hair radiant in the glow of a thousand candles. "I vowed to help Oliver to reach the monarchs of the Two Kingdoms, to ask your indulgence and mercy. If he survives, he has pledged to aid the Borderkind in uncovering the truth of the murderous conspiracy against us. He is my friend and companion. I would not leave him."

The king nodded slowly, then turned to Oliver again.

"The sword," he said.

Oliver instinctively reached for the blade and its scabbard, intending to remove it and return it to its rightful owner.

"Guards!" Hy'Bor barked.

"No!" Hunyadi snapped, holding up a hand. He shot an angry glance at his advisor, then turned a gentler expression upon Oliver. "If David Koenig believed you worthy to bear that weapon, I will not dispute it. You may keep the sword, Mr. Bascombe. However, there are laws in the Two Kingdoms, and by now you are well familiar with those concerning Intruders. They are dangerous to our way of life. You and your sister, sir, are dangerous to us.

"You are also correct that Intruders may, in certain circumstances, be given clemency. This may only happen with a joint order by the monarchs of both kingdoms. To that end, I grant you the same boon that I granted to the wise Professor Koenig. One year, Mr. Bascombe, in which you and your sister must prove yourselves worthy of the trust of the Two Kingdoms. If my friend the king of Yucatazca allows you the same boon, at the end of that year we will determine together if the two of you will be allowed to live. Otherwise, a new death warrant will be sworn out for both of you.

"I must also caution you that should the king of Yucatazca not grant you this boon, the warrant for your death in Euphrasia will be reinstated. Of course, at that point it will hardly matter, as you will likely already have been executed."

Hunyadi grinned broadly, morbidly amused.

Oliver stared at him, a smile blossoming slowly on his own face. It took a moment for the words to truly sink in. There were still enormous obstacles to overcome, of course. Another king to persuade. Not to mention the search for some deed that would prove his trustworthiness and make this mercy permanent. But it was a beginning. For the moment, he was still alive.

Beside the king, Hy'Bor scowled.

The Atlantean raised a hand, pointed a finger at the gathered petitioners. "This will not do. Kill them."

Kitsune spun, snarling. She whipped up her hood, the copper-red fur obscuring her face. Then she dropped into a crouch and diminished instantly into the fox.

Hunyadi shouted to his guards as he stood, and he reached out for his advisor. The king produced a short sword from within the folds of his robe. Hy'Bor was a sorcerer; sickly yellow light began to glimmer all over him, to gleam in his eyes and crackle around his hands.

The Atlantean lunged at his king.

Oliver saw no more. He twisted around at the sound of a mighty roar that erupted from amongst the petitioners. Two massive figures stood and threw off brown, hooded, monastic robes to reveal themselves. They were lumbering, slavering things, wild boars that walked on two legs, tusks jutting up from their lower jaws, jaundice-yellow eyes glaring with homicidal frenzy.

"What the hell are they?" Oliver shouted as the other petitioners screamed and began to scatter.

Kitsune had become the fox by instinct. But now she changed again, regaining her human aspect, standing beside him.

"Battle Swine," she said flatly. "Stupid, but fierce."

"Wonderful."

Guards with swords drawn shoved people out of the way, working their way toward the Battle Swine, but the Hunters were already moving. One of them gored the first guard to reach him, tusks puncturing leather armor easily. He tossed the soldier aside, blood staining ivory.

Oliver drew his sword.

Kitsune grabbed his wrist. "No. You achieved what you came for. There's no point in staying."

Her grip on him firm, she waved her free hand in the air and it began to shimmer, just beside her, a slit in the Veil appearing. Kitsune stepped through, pulling Oliver after her. The Battle Swine were shrieking, snorting, and hacking at innocents and guards alike as they rushed to fulfill their orders. They were close enough that Oliver wrinkled his nose at the stench, perhaps ten feet away. One of the Swine plunged his own sword into a guard that put himself between it and Oliver, and blood sprayed from the wound, spattering Oliver's boots.

Kitsune hauled him through.

In the last moment, Oliver glanced up at the throne. King Hunyadi had driven his short blade into Hy'Bor. The magic that animated the Atlantean had been snuffed like a candle flame. Behind Hy'Bor was an eight-foot, hideously ugly troll. Where he'd come from, Oliver had no idea, but it made him realize that Hunyadi had suspected Hy'Bor's treachery and had been prepared.

The troll had crushed Hy'Bor's skull between his hands. Oliver suspected it was not the king's blade that had ended the traitor's life.

Hunyadi glanced at Oliver and gave a small nod as if to spur him on. Then Kitsune and Oliver were gone from the Presentation Room, from Otranto, and from the world of the legendary.

For just a moment, he felt the membrane of the Veil, or at least the pressure of it around him. The substance of reality warped and his eyes could not process what they were seeing. He squeezed them closed, staggered, and as he fell forward he felt a gust of frigid wind.

Oliver dropped to his knees on frozen ground covered by a thin crust of snow. He shivered with the cold and opened his eyes. The shift of location, of reality, had become almost familiar, but this was something different. They were in the mountains somewhere in Europe, above a lake that seemed quite similar to the one at Otranto, down in the valley below. But the lake was frozen and snow covered the mountaintops. The sky was a lustrous blue, perfect and clean. It was afternoon and the sunlight gleamed on the pure white snow.

"I'm not certain where we are," Kitsune said, walking several paces in the general direction of the lake.

Oliver laughed. "I don't care. I really don't. We're home. In my world. For the next few minutes, I'm just going to . . ."

He could not even finish the thought. This was a brief respite, he knew. Collette needed him. The Sandman held her life in his hands. Wherever this was, Switzerland or Germany, he figured, but wherever, they couldn't stay. But for just a moment, he had to relish it. Hunyadi had granted his boon, spared him and Collette for now. The conspiracy beyond the Veil had begun to unravel with the revelation of Hy'Bor's treachery. They'd escaped the Battle Swine.

"Pigs," he whispered to himself, and he chuckled, shaking his head. "Fucking pigs."

Then he sobered. Grimly he rose and strode after Kitsune. She turned to glance at him, then returned her attention to the frozen lake below.

"We have to go to England. All the way back to England, from wherever here is," he said. The Dustman could only be encountered in an English nursery, and the knowledge was heavy upon his heart. "It's the wrong direction, Kit. I know there's nothing we can do without his help. But for Christ's sake, it's the wrong direction."

Kitsune turned to him. With a mischievous grin, she reached up and touched the tip of his nose.

"I have an idea."

The night sky caressed Blue Jay as he rode the wind higher. Dark as it was, the moon was bright enough that he could see his companions emerging from a dense forest onto a hillside. A valley lay below and they descended the hill without hesitation, headed southwest. The icy edges of Frost's profile gleamed and sparkled in the moonlight, and the others followed. His injuries had been nearly healed within minutes of their return to Perinthia, and now, hours later, there was no sign that he had ever been wounded.

Frost had been right. Crossing back through the Veil from the Akrai had put them in the midst of the Latin Quarter of Perinthia again. They had been spread out, so that it took precious seconds for them all to gather again in the ruins of the Greek and Roman city. Strigae perched on the peaks of buildings and shattered rubble, and the black birds began to caw loudly, a shrill cry like children being stabbed. It filled the air. Legends in the Latin Quarter had pulled their shutters quickly or raced to hide in shadows.

But they were only birds.

There would be no retreat for the Hunters. Ordinary legends, they could not slip away through the Veil the way Borderkind did. They could not cross between worlds without a door.

The Strigae hadn't stood a chance. Dusk had settled over Perinthia. Though Frost and Chorti had been injured, they were not so badly wounded that they could not trouble annoying birds. Frost impaled the nearest Strigae with a spear of ice that jutted from the palm of his hand. The others cried out and their wings beat the air as they tried to flee.

Blue Jay had slain two of them himself. Grin had climbed an old palazzo with three quick bounds and grabbed hold of a Strigae, then snapped its neck with a quick twist. Li burned three of them right out of the air with gouts of flame that spewed from his throat, breathing fire like a dragon. The tiger had broken one in its jaws. Two or three of the Strigae had escaped, but Blue Jay had pursued them for a mile to be sure they would not follow, and as he suspected, they had not even slowed in their flight of terror.

As the evening deepened, the darkness gathering its cloak around Perinthia, Cheval Bayard had slain the sentries at two of the watchtowers on the edge of the city. They had left Perinthia without raising an alarm on the northern end, but by the time the dead sentries were discovered, they would already have circled around and started southwest, away from the city.

As a bird, Blue Jay had flown far above them throughout the journey, circling, watchful for any threat or pursuit. They had given a wide berth to the village of Bromfield. There would be no help from the Lost Ones who lived there, and certainly not from any of the legendary. They could expect little help wherever they went, but Frost and Oliver and Kitsune had stopped in Bromfield on their way to Perinthia and doubtless there would be spies in the village on the watch for Borderkind.

No one could be trusted.

As a trickster, he understood that, but Blue Jay wondered if the others truly did.

Once past Bromfield, the motley collection of Borderkind had traveled briefly on the Truce Road, where the going was far smoother. But as the night deepened and the creatures of darkness roamed across the land, there would be too much risk of an unpleasant encounter. Also, by then, Frost and Blue Jay had been certain the Myth Hunters would have made it back through some Door in the Veil. It would likely be many hours before any of those searching for them could catch up, but it was better not to take chances.

So they had struck out from the road, journeying first through farmland and then up into the hills and then deep in the Cardiff Forest. Blue Jay lost sight of them for much of their trek through the woods but he continued to circle and to travel southwest. He had seen night birds flying—several owls, but no Perytons and no Strigae. On the road there had been private carriages, but this far from any frequented path, only the wild legends were about. Goblins and sprites and the occasional giant might live in the forest, but they would not have anything to do with the conspiracy against the Borderkind.

Even so, the moment he saw them emerge from the forest and start down the grassy hill into the valley, Blue Jay felt a wave of relief sweep over him. He could easily make out the shambling form of Chorti. Cheval Bayard drifted along beside him, ghostly in her translucent gown, silver hair picking up the shine of the moon. Chorti's wounds would heal, but she doted on the monster in the meantime.

The tiger stalked along behind them with Li upon his back. A gray specter followed: the single surviving Mazikeen. He moved as though floating just above the ground, never hurrying, never lagging behind. Blue Jay was unnerved in the presence of the sorcerers. He understood magic—hell, he *was* magic—but warping sorcery was something different entirely.

Last came Leicester Grindylow, who moved not at all like the ape Blue Jay considered him. He forgot that Grin was a water bogie and quite agile. The boggart never stayed precisely at the end of the line. He moved from side to side, swiftly and quietly, watching their backs.

Any doubts Blue Jay might have had about Grin's loyalty had dissipated. The boggart was faithful, and smarter than he looked. In short order, he had come to trust the boggart more than any of the others, even Frost.

Once again, Blue Jay flew a circle. As he did, he thought he saw, far behind him, a single dark mark against the night sky.

The bird descended, swooping down from the dark. He passed over the trees, wings straight out, and then he was out over the grassy hillside, propelling himself after the Borderkind. When he reached Frost, he circled once around the winter man's head and spread his wings. They became arms, and he set his feet down upon the grass. Blue Jay smoothed out his thick cotton shirt and shook his head. His long, braided, black hair fell down his back, and the feathers tied there danced in the breeze.

"Are they following, then?" Frost asked. In the moonlight, his jagged ice features looked blue.

"I'm not sure," the trickster said. "I thought I might have seen something. But we're far enough away now and moving closer to the Atlantic Bridge. No reason not to cross the border so that there is at least part of our trail they cannot track."

Frost concurred.

The small group of Borderkind gathered around, there on the hillside. The Mazikeen inspected Chorti's wounds silently and muttered a few words in his ancient tongue. The wild man grunted and actually smiled in relief, soothed by the spell.

This done, they all crossed together, that strange new family of Borderkind.

They left the long night of legend behind.

In the mundane world, dawn was on the eastern horizon. The seven Borderkind and the massive tiger stood on the shore of a broad half-frozen lake whose exposed surface rippled in the chill morning breeze. In the dawn's light they found themselves surrounded by rolling fields and hills, with mountains in the distance.

A small town sprawled nearby, rows of white houses and shops with gray-black shingle roofs. It was a simple place, unchanged from a long ago time, and on that winter morning it was pale and faded, as though every home had its share of ghosts. The only brightness in the entire panorama was the twinkling of Christmas lights on several of the larger trees, but even that seemed halfhearted.

Cheval Bayard stepped away from them, leaving Chorti on his own. The town earned merely a glance. The lake drew her attention instead and she stepped into the water, crushing a thin shell of ice that had formed. A sensual shiver went through her and Blue Jay relished the sight. Contact with the water gave the kelpy great pleasure.

"Where are we?" Cheval asked, turning to look at Frost.

They all regarded Frost. No formal command had ever been given or taken, but he led them. Even the Mazikeen, alone now in his silence, looked to the winter man for instruction.

Frost glanced around, hesitating. He didn't want to say it, but Blue Jay saw in his eyes that he had no idea where they were. Li ran his fingers through his tiger's fur, the two growling softly to one another—

serious and proper, they seemed two halves of a whole, complete unto themselves.

They all seemed slightly baffled, but then Grin spun around once, nodding as though to himself.

"Can't say for sure, but if I was the sort, I'd wager we're in Wales. Kind of gray, but pretty. Mountains. We headed off west, so, Wales. We keep going west, or south ... or any direction but east, really, and we'll hit ocean, yeah?"

The winter man held up a hand, feeling the wind. "Due west."

And so they went, that strange parade, across thirty miles of the hills and fields of Wales, moving faster than ever they could have with Oliver or any human along for the journey. The sun had been up less than two hours when they came to a rocky coastline where the wind whipped at them and the waves crashed furiously upon the shore. Several houses were in sight, but as they approached the Irish Sea the sky had become overcast and now hung low and grim above them. All throughout their journey they had easily avoided being sighted by humans. It was not difficult in a country as quiet and desolate as this. And now, on the shore, it mattered little if they were seen by an old Welshman or some young housewife.

Who would believe them?

The waves crashed on the rocks and spattered them all with frigid sea spray. Li's tiger kept well back from the water, growling at the raging surf. The Guardian of Fire sat astride him, watching Frost impatiently.

Cheval stood with her feet in the water, stroking the fur on the back of Chorti's neck as he leaned into her, the largest, most ferocious pet anyone had ever had. Or so it seemed. But they all knew differently. The two shared a rare friendship that any would envy, if it had not been based on grief and loss.

The Mazikeen kept his distance, lost in his flowing robes. Blue Jay tried to catch his eye, but the sorcerer resolutely refused to meet such direct scrutiny. He stroked his beard and kept his gaze out to sea. Blue Jay wondered what created that distance the Mazikeen kept between themselves and others. What was this guy thinking?

Frost strode up beside Blue Jay. He seemed quite recovered now. "Are you ready to cross?"

"Is anyone else getting tired of this back and forth?" Blue Jay asked, looking around at the others.

Grin leaped from one large rock to the next like some reckless child, spinning toward his kin.

"Unless we're very unlucky, this ought to be our last jaunt through the Veil for a bit, yeah? You worry too much."

Blue Jay blinked in surprise. He was a mischief maker, a trickster. In all his ages, no one had ever accused him of worrying too much about anything. But that was the world they were living in now, wasn't it?

Frost laughed softly and shook his head, icicle hair chiming. "Oh, yes, because we've been very lucky so far."

The trickster turned to the winter man. "We're still alive, aren't we?"

Frost sobered, all trace of amusement gone. There was a brief pause and then he turned to the others.

"Shall we go?" he said, as though it were the simplest thing in the world.

And in a way, Blue Jay supposed it was. After all, what choice did they have? One by one they slipped through the Veil again and now found themselves on the eastern bank of the Atlantic River, far, far north of the main bridge. There were other bridges, of course, but they were all in agreement that crossing the river that way was a terrible idea.

Cheval and Grin swam, both of them ecstatic to be in the water, even briefly. Frost whipped up a cold wind and let it carry him away as a gust laden with sleet. Blue Jay could fly, but that left Chorti, Li, and the tiger. The Mazikeen muttered something in a low voice and gestured for the trickster to move along. Blue Jay presumed he planned some magic or another and the sorcerer's presence unnerved him, so he spread his arms into wings and took flight.

When he landed on the opposite bank of the broad, churning river, he was the last to arrive. Somehow the Mazikeen had gotten the others there before him. The tiger seemed disoriented, snapping its jaws at the air, and Chorti's eyes were glazed as though he was drugged. Li kept far away from the Mazikeen after that.

They set off toward the southwest, Frost once more leading the way. There was a great deal of open land between here and Yucatazca and a few small villages they would avoid, just as they would only travel on the Truce Road for the few seconds it took to cross it.

Blue Jay walked beside the silent sorcerer and studied his gray features. "You're really freaking me out, you know that?"

The Mazikeen glanced sharply at him, eyes narrowed. "I mourn. My brothers are dead. Your kin are being slaughtered, yet you laugh and smile. Why do you not mourn?"

"Whistling in the dark, my friend. Whistling in the dark."

The Mazikeen wore a quizzical expression but Blue Jay did not bother to explain. He picked up his pace, nodding to Li as he passed. The tiger ran its tongue over long fangs and eyed him hungrily. Li cuffed the back of its head and the tiger snapped at him but did not falter in its stride.

"I had a thought," Blue Jay said as he caught up to Frost.

The winter man glanced back at the others. They were far enough ahead that their words would not be overheard. "Yes?"

"If we adjust our course slightly southward, it would affect our travel time only a little and put us on a path to pass right by the Sandman's castle. The one where you and Kitsune and Oliver found all of the dead Red Caps."

The wave of cold that emanated from Frost in that moment made Blue Jay shiver and his teeth clack together. His eyelashes felt as though ice had formed on them. Blue-white mist rose from the winter man's eyes.

"Why would we want to do that?" Frost asked.

Anger flashed through the trickster. "Oliver's sister is his captive, as you well know. We don't have a way of knowing if Oliver and Kitsune have reached the eastern castle. If we have an opportunity to help and we're so close, it seems—"

"The Sandman could have Collette Bascombe anywhere. You are correct that we have no way of knowing what has transpired since we parted company with Oliver. But we cannot delay our own efforts another moment, or risk ourselves in any other cause. Oliver and Kitsune have one objective, and the rest of us have another. Or has it not occurred to you that at this very moment, and every other minute that has passed since we set out, other Borderkind may be dying?"

"Of course it has," Blue Jay snapped.

Frost glared at him, eyes colder than ever. "Keep your focus, Jay. We'll travel south through the Oldwood, amongst the wild legends, all the way to Yucatazca. They may think to search for us there, but they'll have a terrible time finding us, and no cooperation in the hunt. All that matters now is reaching Yucatazca."

His gaze became distant, as though he watched some faraway event, or a future unfolding within his own mind.

"All that matters is my hands around Ty'Lis's throat."

On Christmas Eve, Sara Halliwell stood in the living room of her father's house—the house she had grown up in—and stared out the frosted window at the snow-covered yard. Once she had made snow angels there, had learned to ride a bicycle in the street, had pushed Terry McHugh down in the driveway when he tried to kiss her.

Home.

God, how long had it been since this place felt like home? It was more the ghost of home, the specter of a bittersweet past. The oldest memories were precious to her. Christmas lights in the windows while she snuggled deep under her goose down comforter, raking leaves with her father, spraying her mother with the hose on a long summer day with Daddy watching the Red Sox game on the little TV in the kitchen.

But the more recent memories were different, just a series of awkward pauses and distant looks, of a mother and father who had forgotten how to talk to one another, and consequently, to their daughter. By the time Sara came out to her parents, the fact that she was in love with another girl was barely a blip on the radar of their estrangement. It couldn't have improved things, but she didn't think it had made them any worse.

Living in Atlanta, away from them both, had been wonderful at first. Sara had found her mother much easier to get along with from a distance. But her father was another story entirely. How could she have imagined that it was possible for this man—this cop, so completely defined by his occupation and stolen away from his family by the job—to become more distant? Yet he had.

That's right, she told herself. *Keep blaming Daddy. Distance is the space between two people, but it only takes one to reach out and close it.*

Sara sighed, breathed in, and her heart was seized by grief and loneliness unlike anything she had ever felt. The place smelled of him, of all the times he hugged her when he'd come home from work, or bent over to kiss her forehead as she lay in bed, when the job brought him home too late. The faded scent of cologne and cigars was in every curtain, in the furniture and the carpets. He did not smoke cigars anymore, except maybe for the occasional holiday, but the aroma remained. It was such a man smell, such a Daddy smell, and it was both foreign and precious to her.

How could you have let this happen? she thought, and couldn't be sure if the admonition was directed at her father, or herself. All the time that had gone by, all of the phone calls asking her to come home, and at last she had been drawn home for Christmas when it was too late.

Out the window, she could see the gleam of Christmas lights that had been strung across the frames of neighboring houses. The old Standish house still used the multicolored ones in their trees and above the door, but where the Quinns had once lived, the new family used those bright white lights that she thought were so cheerless and sad. Still, the effect of the various decorative lights all along the street gave a holiday warmth to the scene, gleaming off the snow.

But inside Ted Halliwell's house, there wasn't even a tree. He hadn't bothered with lights or decorations of any kind. Sara understood. He had asked her to come home and she had said no, so what was the point of decorating? He wouldn't do it for himself. Someone would invite him over for Christmas dinner—Sheriff Norris, maybe—and he'd probably go, but there would be no celebration for him.

No. Stop it. Don't you feel sorry for him. He could have been different, could have changed it anytime he set his mind to it.

But that was the tragedy. Her father had tried to change. Sara could not escape the truth now. How many times in the past few years had he reached out to her, tried to heal the past and bring them closer together, and how many times had she put him off, telling herself she wasn't ready to forgive him yet for not being there for her?

So many.

She reached out to trace her fingers through the frosty condensation on the window. Christmas Eve existed out there in the world of Bosworth Road, but here, inside, it was so far away.

"Where are you, Dad?" she whispered to the winter night.

Somehow, she had to find out what happened to him. She could haunt Jackson Norris, but knew the sheriff wasn't going to have any answers for her. If she wanted to know what happened, she had to go and talk to the people at Bascombe & Cox, who'd sent her father and Julianna Whitney to London, searching for the missing lawyer.

But it was Christmas Eve, and nobody was going to be looking for her father or even thinking about him much for the next two days. Nobody except her. The time between now and December 26 stretched out before her as an endless void. She could do nothing but wait for the rest of the world to celebrate and revel in love and holiday spirit, and that helplessness was a terrible weight upon her heart.

Sara needed to understand what had happened. Her father had always felt so far away from her, even when they lived in the same house. Yet in some strange way, she felt closer now, as though if she turned at the right moment and glanced into the corner, she would see him in the shadows. It was as though, if she reached out at the right moment, she would be able to grab him and pull him close. That was something she had not done since grade school, but now she felt like she could hug him without resentment getting in the way, if only she could find him.

Her father was still alive. She refused to believe otherwise. But it felt like his ghost haunted the house.

Sara turned away from the window and strode to the enormous bookshelf that stood against one wall. There was a CD player there and she turned it on. Christmas Eve it might be, but there'd be no holiday music for her. She pressed Play and blinked in surprise when the music started, because she recognized it immediately. Diana Krall sang "I'm an Errand Girl for Rhythm." Sara had this CD herself. She favored cute little folk-rock boys like Jason Mraz and Jack Johnson and jazz-pop from Jamie Cullum, but there was something so beautiful and sultry about Diana Krall's voice that Sara fell a little in love with her every time she heard her sing.

To discover that her father listened to Diana as well gave her a chill.

She opened the liquor cabinet beneath the bookcase, took out a tumbler, and poured herself a Seagram's 7 and 7-Up. Her father had called it the "medicine cabinet." This was his drink. Sara would have preferred it on the rocks, but did not feel like going into the kitchen for ice.

Taking a deep breath, she sipped the whiskey. It burned the back of her throat, but it warmed her nicely.

Sara closed her eyes and raised the glass, silently toasting her father and cursing the irony that it had taken his disappearance to make her feel close to him for the first time in well over ten years.

"Merry Christmas," she whispered, and took another sip of whiskey.

CHAPTER 12

liver and Kitsune sat together in a compartment on board a train bound for Vienna. Near the mountain lake where they had come through the Veil they had found a small village, brightly decorated with Christmas lights. It had seemed in its way just as mythical a place as the lands beyond the Veil, with its covering of snow and the smoke swirling from fireplaces and the smells of cooking food that came from the inn where they had found the information they needed.

They were in the mountains above Salzburg, Austria. With his American Express card, it was simple to get bus tickets into the city. The countryside had been beautiful, and the city, with its hilltop fortress looming above cobblestoned streets and grand architecture, equally lovely. Oliver had stood with Kitsune in a broad plaza and felt a longing for a simpler day, a time without danger to himself or those he loved, when he could just wander this peaceful, charming city. But if he did not hurry, he might never have a day like that again.

There was magic in the city, this time of year. In some indefinable way, the world of legends had begun to feel more ordinary to him over time, and this place, the mundane world, seemed somehow more fantastic and surreal.

He wished Julianna could have been there with him. She would have seen the simple magic of the place in a way that he knew Kitsune never could. During law school, and in the years since, they had fallen into the habit of purposefully getting themselves lost while driving. Whenever they were on their way somewhere—down to Boston or Portland or in the mountains—they would knowingly take wrong turns, just to see where these strange, unfamiliar roads would lead. Regardless of which one of them was driving, these adventures would begin spontaneously, and they would explore together.

The irony was not lost on Oliver; he only wished that Julianna had been along for this—the ultimate wrong turn.

Though he was an ocean away from home, just knowing that he was in the same world as Julianna was painfully bittersweet. He wished he could just book the next flight to the States—hurry back to her—but he did not dare, as long as monsters and Hunters still pursued him. His father was dead, and Collette the Sandman's prisoner. If he brought such horrors to Julianna's doorstep, he could never have lived with himself.

In Salzburg, Oliver and Kitsune had gone shopping, hurrying through various shops for clothing and a heavy canvas duffel bag. On the bus it had been simple enough to hide the scabbarded sword, at first in Kitsune's cloak and then wrapped in Oliver's pea coat. They had stored it in a locker in the train station. But there was no way that they were going to be able to get on the train with the weapon wrapped in a coat.

After their shopping spree, however, Oliver had buried the sword amongst the new clothes and toiletries in the duffel bag. As long as no one searched the bag, he thought they would be all right. If they'd had to fly instead of taking the train, there would have been complications because of the sword. Declared as a gift, and kept in checked luggage, he might have gotten it through—people brought swords home from Toledo, in Spain, all the time.

Still, it was simpler to stick to the train, particularly since neither of them had a passport.

He would have liked to check into a hotel for a few hours—to take the time to rest and bathe. Stubble covered his chin and the stale smell of his own body and dirty clothes filled his nose. But Oliver knew they could not wait. His one phone call was to a hotel in Vienna, to make reservations for the evening. The American Express had gotten quite a workout in a few short hours, but he had made one final purchase: their tickets for the next train for Vienna.

Only then—he and Kitsune resting comfortably against each other and drinking hot chocolate in the Vienna train station—did Oliver glance at a newspaper and realize what day it was. Or, by then, what night.

Christmas Eve.

He had sat up awkwardly and moved away from Kitsune, giving her an apologetic smile, making it appear that he only wanted to pick up the paper for a closer look. But he avoided her gaze for several minutes after that.

What was Julianna doing tonight? With all that had happened at home in Kitteridge, could she be celebrating Christmas with her family? Was that just arrogance on his part, to think that she would not?

God, how he missed her.

His breathless race through Salzburg's streets and shops with Kitsune had been, despite the circumstances, a strange pleasure. She was extraordinary. And yet as much as Oliver embraced the existence of magic, he also longed for the ordinary. The world beyond the Veil thrilled him with each new discovery, and knowing that it all existed satisfied a yearning that had been in him since childhood.

But more and more, his thoughts were of home.

Kitsune was exotic and astonishingly sensual, and the obvious attraction she felt toward Oliver amazed him. To spark the interest of a creature of magic and myth changed, just a little, the way in which Oliver viewed himself. It was a confirmation of all that he had ever believed, that within him there existed a man capable of more than life as a dutiful son and staid attorney would demand.

But he longed for the familiar comfort of Julianna's arms, and for that look in her eyes that said that she saw right into his heart and knew him better than he knew himself.

Magical or not, Kitsune would never be able to do that.

It was Christmas Eve, and he yearned with all of his heart to be at home in Kitteridge, sitting in front of a fire with Julianna in his arms. All of the confusing things he felt toward Kitsune could not change that.

Guilt about the feelings she stirred in him made Oliver separate himself from her for a few minutes, but it was a useless gesture. Their journey lay ahead of them, and they would travel it together.

Now they sat together on the train, the fox-woman stealing glances at him that alternated between curious and suggestive. The mischief in her eyes was a constant, silent invitation. Yet even then, he kept his mind on Julianna.

Ever since they had crossed the Veil into his world again, he had intended to call Julianna. The day had been frantic, but when they arrived in Vienna, he would have the perfect opportunity. The more he considered it, however, the more he realized how selfish the impulse was. He needed desperately to hear her voice. But what would it accomplish, except to give her false hope that he might be home soon to sort out all that had happened?

When it's over, he thought. *When it's all done, I'll tell her everything.*

The train steamed through the Austrian countryside and Oliver gazed out the window, breathless at the beauty of the place. Only dim lights glowed in the compartment and he did not bother to turn on anything brighter. Perhaps there was romance in that glow, but he focused on the ambience of Christmas that he saw in each town and village the train passed.

They stopped at a station and there were lights and ribbons everywhere. People on the train platform smiled at one another. He saw two conductors sipping coffee or something even more merry.

Kitsune's scent filled him. Oliver glanced down and saw that their hands were entwined, and was not at all sure how long they had been this way. She smiled playfully at him, and arched an inquisitive eyebrow, as if to ask *"What's next?"* His pulse raced even as he gave a shake of his head and chuckled softly. He chose to take her flirtation as more mischief. If it was more than that, he could not acknowledge it. That would lead to awkwardness, and perhaps a conversation he did not wish to have.

Beside him, Kitsune purred.

Once again, Oliver laughed. Her eyes sparking with that same playful glint, she joined in. They shared that moment of amusement as though the whole thing was a game between them, but they both knew that it was not. Oliver was grateful that Kitsune did not push the game to the next level. He could not help but be aroused by her, but it could never go further than that.

With a lurch, the train lumbered out of the station, picking up speed.

The door to the compartment rattled with a chill December wind that whipped through the train. The lights flickered. Eyes closed, Kitsune burrowed closer to Oliver and he did not pull away. He let her mold herself to him, but fought the temptation to put his arms around her.

Kitsune settled comfortably there, the trace of a smile at the corners of her mouth. Her eyes remained closed.

Merry Christmas, he thought to himself.

The train rattled through the darkness toward Vienna. Again, the lights flickered. There came a thump against the compartment door.

Kitsune stiffened in his arms, not sleeping at all. Her eyes snapped open. Oliver stared at the door. Had someone knocked, or just bumped against the door while walking through the car? The train rocked back and forth. Someone might easily have lost their balance and been thrown against the door.

A second thump shook the door, followed by a scratching sound, as though steel wool were being scraped along its outside.

"What the hell?" Oliver whispered.

Kitsune sat up and Oliver let her go. The two of them were very still, straining to understand the nature of the sounds outside the door. So that when the knock came—an ordinary sort of knock, three raps in quick succession—they both started in surprise.

Cautious, Kitsune rose and started toward the door.

"Yes?" Oliver called.

A voice replied in German, and then in English. "Passports, please."

He let out a breath, only then realizing how quickly his pulse was racing. A dozen possibilities suggested themselves to explain the sounds they had heard, including something as typical as two people trying to get by one another in the narrow passageway outside the compartment. Living in constant danger had made him paranoid.

Kitsune glanced at him, jade-green eyes gleaming, her features tense. Oliver shook his head and gestured for her to step back. She went to the seat opposite the one they had been sharing and unzipped the duffel bag, reaching inside.

If it truly was the conductor outside the door, Oliver and Kitsune had already discussed the pantomime that would ensue as they searched for their suddenly misplaced passports. At worst, they would be left off the train at the next stop.

But the sounds they'd heard against the door concerned him. He glanced again at Kitsune and saw her sliding the Sword of Hunyadi from the duffel. Clearly, the sounds worried her as well. There was no telling what might be beyond that door.

"Passports, please," the voice demanded, with another rap on the door. "Open, now."

A ripple of unease went through him. The voice did not sound right. It was not simply the matter of a foreign accent. The words seemed muffled.

"Open it," Kitsune whispered from behind him.

Oliver turned toward her. She sat beside the duffel, holding the sword down behind it, hidden from view.

He hated to do it, but she was right. On the chance it really was the conductor, they would be ejected from the train for certain if the crew had to force the door open.

"Coming," Oliver called as he walked to the door.

He unlocked it, then slid it open, tensed to jump back if attacked. The first thing he saw was the conductor's hat on the woman's head. In the passageway, lights dimmed for nighttime travel, he could make out none of the details of the conductor's face. But it eased his tension a little to see that hat.

"Sorry. We were napping a bit."

"Of course," said the conductor.

In the dim light, her grin was Cheshire Cat broad. Oliver heard a strange sound coming from her, a kind of rustling that came from beneath the long blue coat with the railway's insignia on the shoulder and breast.

Opening the door had been a terrible mistake.

She pushed off the conductor's coat. A terrible rasp came from her body, which was covered with hair so thick it seemed like the yarn on a rag doll's head. But it twisted and coiled and lashed out and something jabbed Oliver's left forearm. He cried out and staggered back, and the cablelike tendrils that covered her body thrust out toward him, each of them tipped with a curved stinger.

His arm ached where she'd stung him and began to feel hot. Some kind of venom was moving through him. Oliver wondered if it was fatal and how many stings it would take to kill him.

On instinct, he grabbed the door and slid it shut. With all of his weight behind it, he drove it home, crushing several of those tentacles in a small gap between door and frame, but the stingers did not withdraw. They thrust out at his hands as though they could see him. Oliver swore but did not pull away. One of the stingers grazed his left wrist. He opened the door a few inches and slammed it again. A tendril was cut off and fell to the floor, leaking greenish ichor.

"Help me!" Oliver said through gritted teeth.

"Step back," Kitsune commanded, her voice deathly calm.

"Are you crazy? I'm going to lock the door!"

A bouquet of stingers erupted through the narrow opening in the door, pressed themselves against the door edge and the frame, and then the handle was torn from his grasp as the stingers forced the door open with such violence that it rattled and slammed and he heard metal tear.

"Oliver, step back!" Kitsune shouted.

In fear he threw himself away from the door, falling backward onto the duffel bag as the Hunter swept into the room, stingers stabbing at the air all around her. The tendrils curled like a basket of snakes upon her head. Somewhere in that mass of darting stingers was a face, but all he could see were clear, perfect, blue eyes and that Cheshire grin.

"So pleased to make your acquaintance," the Hunter said, and then it laughed, the coldest sound Oliver had ever heard.

Kitsune tossed him the Sword of Hunyadi, still in its scabbard. He lay on his back on the bench seat and snatched it out of the air. He began to draw it even as Kitsune attacked the woman.

The fox-woman did not alter her form. Fur cloak rustling around her, she lunged at the Hunter. Stingers darted out, jabbing into the shadows within her cloak. Kitsune whimpered through gritted teeth, and Oliver wondered how many times she would be stung, how many it would take to kill a Borderkind. But the fox-woman was fast. She grabbed the Hunter by the throat and used her free hand to rake the creature's abdomen with vicious claws.

Then, Oliver was in motion. He slid the scabbard fully off the sword as he stood. Without a word he moved behind Kitsune and thrust the blade past her and into the mass of angry stingers.

The Hunter hissed, but the smile remained, as though the pain was a pleasure to her. Some of the stingers wrapped themselves around the blade and Oliver felt them pulling it, trying to tear it from his grasp.

"Move her!" he snapped.

Kitsune understood. Fewer stingers were jabbing her now but already there were angry welts rising on her flesh. She gripped the Hunter by the throat and twisted her toward Oliver, who used new leverage to shove the sword deeper, to twist it. The Hunter cried out and the stingers faltered for a moment.

He caught Kitsune's eye, saw the fox-woman glance toward the window. Oliver nodded, and together they half lifted, half pushed the Hunter across the compartment. With all of his strength, Oliver used the sword to drive the thing against the glass.

It cracked.

The stingers began to twist again, darting at his hands, at the sword, and at Kitsune's fur and hands, at her face.

They hauled back and slammed the Hunter against the glass again, using her skull as a battering ram. The window splintered and the Hunter's head crashed through, scattering a million tiny diamonds of safety glass out into the night and the wind as the train hurtled through the darkness. But it was made to push out in case of an emergency, and the collision pushed the whole window from the frame.

With the Hunter partway through the broken window, they gave one final push as Oliver slid the sword from her body.

With a scream of hatred and pain, the creature tumbled out the window and struck the ground, rolling into a ditch alongside the tracks at a speed that must have snapped bones and torn muscles. The wind screamed into the compartment and Oliver and Kitsune stood and stared out into the night, buffeted by the speed and the wind. Her hair and cloak flew around her. He glanced down at the viscous green blood on his blade.

"What was she?"

"I have no idea."

Oliver glanced at Kitsune.

She gave him a sharp look. "No one can know every legend."

But he had already forgotten his question. The welts raised on her cinnamon skin were bright red. There were at least two dozen that he could see, and undoubtedly more on her chest where the stingers had jabbed through her shirt.

Kitsune swayed on her feet. "You don't look well," she said.

Oliver smiled. The heat of his own stings burned through him and made his face flush. He felt feverish and there was pain in his hands and arms where the Hunter had stung him, but now a kind of numbness was descending upon him.

"Do you think we're going to die?"

Kitsune frowned. "I told you, I do not know her legend."

Shouts came from elsewhere in the train car. Oliver blinked. They had to get out of there. Had to, in fact, get off the train at the next stop. If this Hunter had found them, others must know they were on the train. And though it was a lesser concern, the condition of their compartment would likely summon the police.

"Let's go," he said.

He turned and bent to pick up the scabbard. Only as he rose did he realize how slowly he was moving, how sluggish his muscles. His whole body had begun to feel frozen, as though it was fighting against him.

Oliver forced his limbs to move, put the sword back into its scabbard, and dropped it into the duffel. He did not bother to zip it, slipping its strap across his shoulder. The numbness and stiffness of his body was increasing.

Kitsune stood at the ruined door of the compartment, looking out into the hall.

"Anything?" Oliver asked, his words slurring, his mouth leaden.

"Passengers, but they're scared. Keeping well back," Kitsune said. Her head bobbed sleepily as she spoke, like she was drunk.

"Go."

Slowly, Kitsune staggered into the corridor. Oliver followed. How they managed to make it into the next car, and the next beyond, without a conductor stopping them, he didn't know. Only when he remembered the conductor's cap and jacket that the Hunter had worn and realized that at least one of them was dead did he understand.

When they found the ruined door and the broken window, they would come looking. He only prayed that he and Kitsune would be off of the train by then. For now, though, they kept moving until the sluggishness in his muscles became too much. Then he started to knock at every compartment door they passed. When he got no answer, he tried the door. Two of them were locked, which meant someone was inside, asleep. But the third one opened.

It was empty.

They staggered into the compartment. Each fraction of a movement was like swimming in wet cement. Oliver collapsed on the floor. Had Kitsune been human, he was certain she would have fallen before him. As it was she had only enough energy to close and lock the door before spilling onto the cushioned bench.

"Paralysis," Oliver said. Or thought he said. He was not sure his mouth had properly formed the word. It was becoming difficult to breathe.

The Hunter's sting paralyzed her victims, presumably long enough for her to kill them. Unless the paralysis was only the first stage of the venom's effect, and death would result momentarily.

Completely immobile, they could only wait.

Kitsune recovered more quickly than Oliver. He was only human after all. Though they needed to reach Vienna for her plan to work, Oliver insisted that they get off as quickly as possible, before any of the train personnel figured out that the compartment they were hiding in was supposed to be empty, and that they had been the ones in the ruined compartment. Neither of them was in any condition to answer questions, or any mood, and Oliver still had no passport.

As she helped him from the train, carrying the duffel bag over her shoulder, they had both been too focused on the task at hand to register the name of the station. Wherever they were, it was no Salzburg. The town had none of the quaint, picturesque charm of that city. It was a dreary place full of garages, warehouses, and old factories.

They needed a car, and a map. Oliver had said they couldn't be more than an hour or so from Vienna. Kitsune watched the skies and the windows of darkened buildings as they left the train station, wary of further attack. None came. In the train station, Oliver had found a ticket agent who spoke enough English to tell him of the car rental operation two blocks away, but it was a small town, the man had said, and Christmas Eve, and he did not know how late they would be open. There was no airport here, after all.

Now they strode through the dirty street and a freezing rain began to fall, tiny pinpricks of ice. Oliver had something in his hand, held between his fingers like an old conjure-man's worry stone.

"What've you got there?" she asked.

He opened his hand and she saw the fat seed that the Harvest gods had given him.

"Sort of a lucky charm," he told her.

Kitsune arched an eyebrow. "Not very effective, is it?"

Oliver slid the seed back into his pocket. "We're alive."

"There is that."

Oliver smiled and took the duffel from her, obviously feeling much recovered. The cold made her feel alert and helped to shake off the numbness from her. Kitsune put up her hood, her fur protecting her from the sleet, and reached out for Oliver's hand. He flinched a bit, then cast an apologetic glance at her and slid his fingers into hers.

"The lights are on," he said, the hope in his voice the first real energy he'd shown since the creature's venom had begun to wear off.

They picked up the pace, hurrying up to the little parking lot. The rental agency had a brightly lit orange-and-blue sign, but it was set up in what appeared to be an abandoned gas station. Kitsune did not spend a great deal of time on this side of the Veil, but she knew the world well enough not to like it very much. There were places of great beauty, and there was real magic in the human race—some of them, at least—but there was also despair and filth, and this town reeked of both.

Inside the squat little rental car building, a thick-necked, red-faced man sat behind a counter smoking unfiltered Turkish cigarettes whose herb-redolent stench choked the air. Kitsune hung back away from the counter, feeling the shroud of smoke covering her fur, and wrinkled her nose in distaste. The middle-aged bull of a man took a long draw from his cigarette and watched her with a gleam of cruel lust in his eyes. Only when Oliver had made several attempts to speak with him did he at last pay attention and then a horrible distaste curled his lip, as though they had come into his place of business covered in offal.

The man held up his hands in surrender. "No English."

Oliver shifted the duffel bag to his other shoulder and glanced at Kitsune. "And I don't speak German." Again he focused on the man behind the counter as he reached into his back pocket and withdrew his wallet. He slid his American Express card out and snapped it down onto the counter.

"You don't need to speak English to understand me. *Car. Vienna.* One night. *One,*" and now he held up a finger, "*nacht.*"

He tapped the American Express card.

The man behind the counter continued to regard Oliver as though he were some sort of leper, for at least a count of ten before finally reaching out and picking up the credit card and studying it. Then he looked up.

"I.D."

"See," Oliver said. "What language barrier?"

He handed the man a pair of cards, one of which was the international driver's license he'd gotten in London. Kitsune felt sure the man would demand a passport, but after glancing at the license he picked up the credit card again, placed it beside his computer, and began typing, eyes on the monitor. The *tak-tak-tak* of the keyboard made her head hurt. The welts where the Hunter had stung her were little more than blemishes now, but they ached fiercely.

The man finished inputting information into his computer, then sat back and watched the screen, waiting for something. Approval, perhaps.

Then the man blinked and all trace of the hostility he had shown vanished. When he glanced at Oliver, it had been replaced by a kind of wary deference. He held up a finger to indicate that they should wait, and picked up the phone.

"What is it?" Kitsune asked.

Oliver shrugged. "Probably has to get phone verification on the charge or something. Nothing to worry about."

The fox-woman pulled her cloak closely around herself, not at all convinced. The man's demeanor had changed, his body language too, and though in the miasma of Turkish cigarette stench it was difficult to be sure, she thought his scent was also different.

In the short, hard-edged language of his countrymen, the rental agent spoke to someone on the phone. When he hung up, he showed them a placating smile whose falseness was inarguable.

"Oliver," Kitsune cautioned.

He nodded, as if to reassure her. The man held up a finger again, indicating that they should wait, and then he went back to typing information into the computer. Every few moments he would frown as though what he read on-screen was not to his liking.

"What's the problem?" Oliver asked.

"No," the man said, smiling again. "No problem."

He understood that much. Pulling himself away from the computer he looked out through the dirty glass of his little building and studied the cars in his parking lot, then ran his fingers across rows of keys hanging on hooks on the wall. The man continued to puff on that horrid cigarette and the smoke choked Kitsune's lungs.

"I cannot breathe in here," she said. "I'm going to wait outside."

A bell dinged above the door as she left. Odd that she hadn't noticed it when they entered. On the concrete curb in front of the rental office she stood and glanced out across the small fleet of rental cars at the town beyond. There was nothing left here of nature or magic, only the worst that humanity brought to the world. Pavement and metal and brick, smoke and garbage and cars spewing dark exhaust. Whatever magic there was in the season of this holiday of Oliver's, it did not show itself here.

Several times she glanced back inside. Oliver stood tensely by the counter, glaring impatiently at the rental agent. The thick-necked man seemed nervous, and more than once she saw him peering out through the dirty glass at her, at the cars.

No. That was wrong. He was looking to the street.

Kitsune's heart clenched. She spun, peered into the darkness of the town, and saw blue lights flashing in the distance. Her travels through man's world had crossed centuries. Though they had been infrequent of late, she had been here often enough to know what those lights meant.

She pushed through the door with such force that the glass shattered. The man shouted as though he'd been shot. Oliver turned, staring at her as though she'd gone mad.

"He's called the police."

Oliver blinked. "What? Why?"

Kitsune shook her head. "I don't know, but there will be time to discover that later. We must hurry if you want to get to Vienna tonight."

She left unspoken the fact that if they did not reach Vienna soon, the plan would have to wait until the following night, and that would be another entire day's delay before they could reach Collette.

Anger flared upon Oliver's face. The rental agent was a big man, broad across the shoulders, with enormous hands, but when Oliver slammed his hand on the counter the man backed away instantly.

"Why?" Oliver shouted.

The man began to curse at him in German, throwing up his hands. Spittle flew from his mouth and his red face turned purple. Oliver swore, swept up his I.D. and credit card, then reached over to snatch a ring of keys from the wall, the heavy duffel bag banging the front of the counter as it swung forward.

The man tried to grab him but Oliver was too quick.

"Hurry!" Kitsune called.

They ran out of the little building. In the low thrum of city noises there were no sirens, but the lights had grown brighter. Down the darkened street, slicked with freezing rain, the police car was coming.

"How do we—" she began.

Oliver held up the keys, touched a button, and one of the cars chirped, its taillights flashing. They ran to it. The blue lights swept closer.

"Just get in and get down," Oliver said.

The car was in the second row, third in from the end. Oliver pushed the duffel in and they tumbled inside, shutting the doors in the very same moment that the police car pulled into the car rental lot. They sat in the darkness, both of them breathing hard, as the police car stopped right in front of the little building.

A single policeman climbed out, glanced around once, and walked to the door. He stared at the broken glass and then entered.

Oliver put the keys in the ignition.

"Wait," Kitsune said.

She opened the door, cursing the momentary flash of the dome light, and shut it quickly behind her. Then she was moving across the lot with an inhuman swiftness, racing along on fox feet. Inside, the car rental agent was shouting at the police officer in guttural German, gesturing wildly to the cars in the parking lot. The policeman snapped, pointing at the man, not pleased at all with being spoken to in such fashion. He held up a hand, wanting to make sure the rental agent stayed inside.

Cautiously, the police officer opened the door again, shoes crunching shattered glass.

By the time he stepped out of the little building, Kitsune had slashed both of his rear tires with unnaturally sharp claws. Unaware, he began to walk toward the darkened rental cars, brandishing a flashlight.

The fox dashed across the lot.

From fox to woman, she stood in a crouch and opened the car door. The dome light went on again.

The cop saw the light and started to shout.

"Drive!" Kitsune cried.

The engine roared as Oliver turned the key, and she practically fell into the car as he put it in gear and tore out of the parking space. The policeman shouted after them even as he ran back toward his car.

Seconds later they were out onto the street, racing into the darkness and grime of an unknown Austrian town, headed for Vienna in a stolen car.

The policeman would not be able to give chase. There would be others, Kitsune knew, but if they could get out of this little industrial town without being caught, she felt sure they would reach Vienna.

"What just happened?" Oliver said, and she was sure the question was directed more to himself than to her, so she did not respond. "Why are they after me?"

Kitsune said nothing, only watched the troubled expression on his pale features as oncoming headlights washed over them. She reached out and put a comforting hand upon his thigh. They drove in silence, the echo of unanswered questions drowning out anything else they might have wished to say to one another.

he Vittora no longer spoke, not even nonsense words. Even the insinuating tone of its quotes from her favorite films had ceased. Collette sat propped against the grating sand wall of her strange cell, turned to one side, legs drawn up beneath her. She had made herself very small, there in that rounded prison. The moon and starlight that came through the high, arched windows provided no comfort. As though she lay in her bed at home and could burrow underneath the bedclothes for protection and privacy, she huddled there, lost in thought.

Her mind wandered, lulled and lured by the voice of the Vittora. It no longer spoke to her, but that did not mean it was silent. Rather, its voice had become a ceaseless song, a high, childlike, singsong melody that segued from "Over the Rainbow" to "As Time Goes By" to "In Your Eyes" and on through others before starting all over again. This perversion of the music from her favorite films had begun to tear down her passion for those cherished memories. The incessant humming was quickly becoming the soundtrack for her madness.

The Vittora, she'd been told, comprised all her hope. Its separation from her flesh was harbinger to her doom. Yet as she drew her limbs even more tightly to herself, it occurred to her that the Vittora might be the place she was storing the fear and hysteria that she ought to have been feeling.

In that moonlit pit, she sat in her filthy pajamas with sand in every conceivable crevice, the stale smell of her own body in her nose, and the stubble of her unshaven legs prickly under the cotton. The Vittora was a tiny sphere of light, no larger now than a baseball—a golden glow that flickered and swayed on the other side of the chamber as though taunting her.

But as much as she hated the thing and wanted to snuff it out completely, Collette felt certain that as long as the Vittora remained, she would not succumb entirely to terror. As long as the Vittora remained, she could think.

A vast abyss seemed to open up beneath her. Collette felt the pull of it, as though she teetered on the edge and would tumble into it any moment.

"Up," she whispered.

With that single syllable, she placed one hand on the wall and practically leaped to her feet. The Vittora hummed the tune for the Lollipop Guild and Collette laughed under her breath. Images of the Munchkins of Oz blossomed in her mind but were quickly replaced by small children, mutilated by the Sandman.

"Fucker." Her voice was a dry rasp. It seemed she had not had anything to eat or drink for a while, and presumed that her captor was punishing her for spying on him or trying to escape, or both.

The question is how, she thought. *How the hell did you do that?*

The Vittora sang softly, as though to itself. Collette turned her back on it, half wishing the thing would simply disappear despite what that might mean. She stared at the gently curved wall, at the glitter of small bits of quartz or other reflective mineral in the sand.

Brow furrowed, she reached out and pressed the tips of her fingers against the wall. Nothing. It was entirely unyielding. Adding pressure, she tried to dig her fingers in, staring at the sand, at her ragged fingernails. Gritting her teeth, she put her weight into it, trying to drive her nails in. A little dart of pain shot up her ring finger and she hissed and pulled away, sucking on that finger, wondering if she had torn the nail.

Where was the door?

With only her palm, she brushed against the hard, abrasive surface of the sand wall, but it was truly like cement. She had been around and around her cell, probing for another soft place like the one she had discovered before, and found nothing.

Home. Collette had felt it, sensed it, tasted and smelled it. That bedroom, where the child had been horribly murdered, existed back in her own world. The place she was supposed to be. The Sandman could pass back and forth between the two worlds.

"So did he let me through, or did I dig my own way?" she whispered to the wall, to the night.

The Vittora paused and for a moment she thought it would give one of its nonsense replies, but then it began humming again, a shrill melody that she recognized from childhood, from some Disney film or other, though she could not place it precisely.

She ignored it.

Focused on the wall, she tried again to press her fingers into the sand, working the tips against the wall. Grimly determined, she slid her fingers across the hard surface, testing again and again. Useless. The wall was only a wall and her fingers could not penetrate.

It had to have been the Sandman, making the sand malleable, giving her the chance to follow. The creature had allowed her to dig away at soft sand and find that door and see what she had seen.

But then, why was he so furious?

The question lingered. She remembered quite well the way it felt to plunge her fingers into the yielding sand and to excavate that door that led out of her prison. It had certainly *felt* as though she was doing it herself.

Collette took a long, shuddering, exhausted breath and pressed her forehead against the wall. The sand scraped her skin, but in frustration she pressed harder and began to slide her forehead to the left, welcoming the sting, the million little shards of pain. She hissed in through her teeth, but then she just stood like that, head leaning on the wall, hands pressed against it on either side of her. The Vittora hummed high and shrill, and now she knew the song.

"I've got no strings ... to hold me down," she sang along, voice quaking.

With a shout, she struck the wall. Pain jammed her knuckles.

Something shifted elsewhere in the cell. Rustled. Collette spun and glanced around. The Vittora had stopped its childlike humming and had shrunk to a mere pinprick of illumination. In the light of the moon, she stared around at the haunting gloom of the rounded cell and saw that she was indeed still alone.

The sound came again. A shifting rustle, something familiar about it.

And then she knew: *feathers.*

Collette craned her neck back and looked up. One of the skeletal creatures she had seen before was crouched in an arched window, green-feathered wings black in the moonlight. Its enormous tangle of antlers hung heavy upon its head. She blinked a moment, allowing her eyes to adjust, and she could barely make out the gleam of its eyes.

"What do you want?" she demanded, hating the tinny, frantic sound of her voice.

The Hunter only perched there, limbs jutting at harsh angles. After a moment it gave a birdlike cock of its head and seemed to study her even more closely. A shiver went through Collette. Its antlers threw moonlight shadows down upon the floor of the cell like the twisted branches of some looming tree outside her bedroom one stormy night.

But there was no storm here. No sound, save a barely audible wind and the rustle of its wings as the Hunter shifted its weight again.

"Stop ... why are you just staring at me like that? What do you *want*?"

It spread its wings and rose, legs tensed, about to take flight.

"No, wait!" she cried. "Please!"

The Hunter paused, regarding her once more. Curiously, it cocked its head again and wrapped its wings around itself like a cloak.

"I know ... I know you won't help me," she said. No, she wasn't that much of a fool. This thing wanted to kill her, maybe even eat her, if it was into that. Only the fact that the Sandman wanted her for bait kept the thing from dropping down on her right now.

"But, look, can you just tell me why?"

Silhouetted in the arched window, antlers black streaks across the moon, it lowered into a crouch again. She thought it might actually come down to join her in the pit then, but it remained where it was.

"Why?" the thing repeated, its voice harsh and stilted, as though its mouth was unused to forming words.

In despair, she nodded. "Just ... why? Why do you want Oliver dead? Why me? Why ... damn it, why us? It's all riddles and innuendo, and if I'm going to die and my brother is going to die, I'd really like to know why."

The thing sat for so long staring at her that she was sure she would get no answer. It bent its head and scraped its antlers against the arched window frame, slowly, as if in thought.

Just as she was about to act, to plead, or to scream in frustration, the Hunter spoke.

"You will die because you were never meant to live," it said in that stilted voice. "You will die because if you are allowed to continue, neither of our worlds will ever be the same. The Bascombes. Creatures of disaster."

Collette could manage only shallow breaths. She stared at the thing. "Creatures of ... what are you talking about? We've never done anything to hurt anyone! We're just ... we're just people. *Boring* people, for Christ's sake!"

And then she couldn't hold it in anymore.

"Please! Oh, God, please just get me out of here! We'll go away. Oliver and I, we'll just disappear, change our names, whatever. Nobody in this place will even know we're still alive. Just let me out, please! Please!"

Even as the words left her lips she hated herself for them, hated the weakness in her. But desperation was all that she had left.

The Hunter spread his wings again. She thought he would fly away for sure now, but a tiny spark of hope remained and she wondered if instead he would fly down into the chamber and pluck her from her prison. It was a foolish hope, she knew, but could not help nurturing it just for a moment.

When he pulled his wings in again, pinioning them against his back, she saw the gray-cloaked reaper behind him.

The Sandman had come, and even the Hunter seemed unaware.

Swift hands reached up, grabbed hold of the Hunter's antlers, and twisted. Bones snapped and flesh tore wetly as the Sandman ripped the Hunter's head from his shoulders.

The thing tumbled into the pit with her, wings fluttering as it struck the sand and twitched, wings attempting to move though the body had no head. It shifted toward her several inches and a spurt of blood jetted from the ragged stump where its head had been.

Collette was frozen to the spot, but even had she been able to flee, there was nowhere for her to go.

The Sandman stepped away from the window's edge and *spilled* down into the chamber, flowing in a careful avalanche along the wall and then rising up across the cell from her. He held the Hunter's head in his right hand, antlers clutched in his fist.

"I told them; I tell them all," he said, "we do not speak to the prey."

The head fell from his grasp and the sand swallowed it up hungrily, as if it had never been. Then the sand began to slip around the corpse as well. Soon the Hunter would be a memory, a fossil buried deep, and Collette wondered what else had been swallowed up by the sands of this place, this prison.

Then a strange sound reached her—a rasping, grinding noise— and abruptly she realized it was the terrified sound of her own breath. Collette shook all over, heart racing as it had when she had woken from night terrors as a child. But there was no waking from this.

"Please," she said at last, hating the word more than ever, despising this creature, whom she knew had no understanding of mercy.

The Sandman seemed to fly or flow the short distance between them. His long spindly fingers wrapped around her head, a terrible vise that made her skull feel as though it would pop. She opened her mouth, and the scream that tore from her throat felt like the last vestige of her hope departing. But she lived. She reached up to batter at his arms and his face.

Beneath his hood, he stared at her with those dreadful lemon eyes.

The Sandman drew her close. Collette shrieked her throat raw, fighting him, clawing at him, but he pulled her inexorably toward him. Lemon eyes wide, locking her gaze with his own, he drew her near until their faces were only inches apart.

His lips parted. A pink-brown tongue snaked out. He held her head so tightly, fingers pulling her skin taut, that she could not close her eyes. He ran a tongue like sand across her right eyeball.

Piercing screams filled the chamber. She felt him let her go, felt herself fall to the ground, contorted in a frenzy of revulsion and pain, one hand over her eye.

Darkness claimed her. Blessed unconsciousness, her only escape from the Sandman, from her terror and pain.

And then, unconscious, the nightmares began.

Julianna felt certain she could not walk another step. Yet each time this certainty rose in her mind, Kara would insist they had only a short way to go and she would find enough strength to make it around the next turn or over the next rise. The little girl kept both Julianna and Halliwell going with this persistence and false hope, and yet it seemed like there might be more to it than that. The girl had inhuman endurance, which was not too much of a surprise; Julianna was sure she was no ordinary little girl. But Kara seemed to be able to lend it, at least a little bit, to them, and for that, Julianna was grateful.

"Really. Truly. I can't keep going. We have to camp for the night. I need to rest, to eat something," Julianna said.

Halliwell staggered along beside her as though he had just dragged himself from his grave, or was stumbling toward it.

Kara flashed her bright smile and pirouetted in front of them, a sweet, beautiful Pied Piper, luring them along. "You must trust me. It is just over the next rise. If your Oliver is still alive, he will have stopped here. They may have cut his head off already, but he'll have come to see the king."

"Just over the next rise?" Julianna asked dubiously.

Halliwell grunted derisively.

"Yes," Kara insisted, making a face. "Don't you believe me?"

Julianna laughed softly. "Not a bit. I know you are doing your best to help us, sweetie, but I'm telling you now that if I can't see the castle from the top of this hill, we're done. We're stopping to rest, and sleeping till dawn."

Kara sighed. "As you wish."

The night was warm but the breeze was cool, and as exhausted as she was, Julianna shivered with each gentle gust. She wanted a sweatshirt. She wanted a soft bed and a pot of coffee and her TV remote control. Her stomach grumbled and she realized she also wanted cinnamon danish. Nothing else, at that moment. Not a steak or a piece of swordfish; not ravioli or sugary breakfast cereal.

"My kingdom for a cinnamon danish," she whispered.

Beside her, Halliwell uttered a bitter bark of a laugh. "I could go for pizza right now. With enough pepperoni to give me a heart attack."

The disturbing thing was that Julianna felt sure he meant it. Halliwell's eyes had lost the frantic quality they'd had for quite some time, but now they were simply dull, as though something had gone hollow inside of him. When he implied that he would welcome a heart attack, she knew it was not a joke, though he tried to play it off as one.

"I'm sure we're almost there, Ted," she lied.

He gave her a false smile. "Great. And then what?"

Julianna had tried already to lift his spirits, to no avail. She hadn't the heart or the energy to play the optimist again, so she said nothing.

Kara reached the top of the hill and paused to wait for them. She executed a neat, courtly bow.

Julianna crested the hill and stopped, steadying her breath. Below them were scattered farms and small cottages and a vast lake. And on the hill above the lake, directly across from the one on which they stood, was a walled castle with torchlight burning inside.

Halliwell joined them atop the hill.

"The castle of Otranto, my friends," Kara said.

"Oh, thank Christ," Halliwell muttered, and the frantic look was back in his eyes.

Julianna thought that was probably a good thing. She wasn't sure how much longer Halliwell could go on without snapping—or just shutting down completely. The search for Oliver was the only thing distracting him from the truth of their predicament. Halliwell resolutely refused to believe that they were trapped here. She hesitated to think about what would happen if, when they caught up to Oliver, he confirmed that they could never go home again—that Halliwell would never speak to his daughter again.

For now, she just had to keep him going. As brusque as he had become, Halliwell was a good man. If there was a way to get him home, Julianna hoped they would find it, for both of their sakes. In the meantime, she had to manage him as best she could.

"Time for some answers," Julianna said.

Halliwell said nothing.

Julianna stared at the archaic outline of that structure upon the hill, and the possibility that Oliver might be inside struck her deeply. If he had come here, if he was still alive, he might well be inside still. What she would say when she saw him, or what any of them would do afterward, she did not know. But she would worry about that later. Right now, just to see him would be enough.

"Let's go," she said, starting down the hill.

Halliwell grunted unhappily, but followed. Kara did a cartwheel and then sprang up, leaping and dancing her way down.

It was nearly half an hour before the three of them trudged up to the main gates of the castle. They had not gotten within a hundred feet when the two guards in front of the gatehouse called out to them to halt, and several archers appeared in the embrasures on the battlements above, arrows pointed at the travelers.

"Good evening, friends," Kara said, bowing with a flourish. Her smile was that of a little girl, but her courtly manner belied her apparent age.

"What do you want, little one?" asked a guard. His fingers flexed upon the grip of his sword but he did not draw the weapon. There was an Asian cast to his features, but the guard beside him had long reddish-blond hair and a thick beard, like some kind of Viking.

Halliwell started to speak, but Kara gestured him to silence and, to his credit, the detective hushed. It surprised Julianna that Halliwell—

always curmudgeonly, and, of late, quite brittle—would take instruction from this slip of a girl. But it was clear he had realized she was no ordinary child.

The playful tone and expression disappeared from Kara's face. This time when she bowed it was only with a nod of the head.

"I am Ngworekara, proud soldiers. My companions and I are weary travelers seeking safe haven for the night. Also, with profound respect, we request an audience with His Highness, King Hunyadi."

The Viking grunted and his upper lip curled. "It's a bad night for strangers to visit."

The other guard, handsome and grim, shot a dark look at the Viking and kept his hand upon the grip of his sword. "Move along, girl. All of you."

Kara lifted her chin as though she'd been insulted. "Have pity, friends. They have only recently slipped through the Veil and the idea that they can never return home weighs heavily upon them. We are in pursuit of a third, the only friend they have in the Two Kingdoms, himself a recent arrival, and we have reason to believe he has passed this way."

The handsome guard cocked his head and studied her, then took a hard look at Halliwell and Julianna as well. "What's his name, this man you pursue?"

Julianna took a small step forward, drawing the guards' attention. "His name is Oliver Bascombe. I'm going to guess it sounds familiar to you, since the king's put a price on his head. But if we're right, he came here today looking for some mercy. All we want to know is if he found any, and if he's still here."

From the guards' reaction, it was obvious they knew precisely what she was talking about. Julianna allowed herself a tiny bit of hope, but the guards were clearly troubled by her words, and so that tiny bit was all she could muster.

But Kara glanced back at her and smiled, and that comforted her.

The Viking studied the trio at the castle gates and then glanced up to the archers above them on the wall. "Tage, go and get Captain Beck and return immediately."

The nearest of the archers—apparently this Tage—lowered his bow and nodded, disappearing below the battlements. Kara raised her hands.

"Gentlemen, what is the trouble? Our request has been put forth as politely as possible. As subjects of His Highness, we desire some response."

The handsome guard narrowed his eyes. "Oh, you'll have it." Then he drew his sword.

Halliwell went for his gun, eyes flashing with violence, as though he had been waiting for just such a moment.

"No!" Julianna snapped, grabbing his hand, preventing him from drawing the weapon.

Both guards drew their blades with a chime of metal. Kara froze, hands still in the air. She lowered them slowly, palms forward.

"Calm down, my friends. There is no need for drama."

Julianna held on to Halliwell's wrist. His chest rose and fell and he glared at her. His jaw clenched and unclenched, and she could see that he did not want the moment to pass. He invited conflict, bloodshed—even death—as just another distraction, and a way to vent the despair and fury that was eating him up inside.

"Ted—" she began, warily.

"This was not the world's most cunning plan," he rasped. "Just walking up and telling them what we want, knowing how much trouble your fiancé is in . . ."

"We don't have time for secrets, Ted. We're not spies. I'd rather die for the truth than a lie."

Halliwell relaxed his hands, let them fall to his sides, and Julianna released his wrist. Together they turned to watch the two guards who stood with their swords drawn. The tableau of these hulking men with their blades gleaming in the moonlight, standing there in the dark as though defending themselves from a pretty little girl, was unsettling as hell. The line of archers on the wall, ready to pin them all to the ground, only made it that much worse.

"If it's all the same to you," Halliwell muttered, "I'd rather not die at all."

Julianna nodded. "Yeah. Well, at the end of your days, when the

Reaper comes to collect, that's what you should tell him. Let me know how that goes, will you?"

With a groaning creak of hinges, the gates of the castle's outer wall swung inward. Chains rattled, and they watched the portcullis grate rise upward. A small cadre of leather-armored soldiers of varying race and gender—Julianna counted nine—emerged along with a tall, formidable woman whose ebony skin was the deepest black Julianna had ever seen. Her cloak, tunic, and heavy trousers were all black as well, which only served to make her skin seem all the darker. She carried herself with the grace and dignity of a goddess, and with such power that the sword that hung at her side seemed an afterthought.

Kara went down on one knee before her.

Julianna and Halliwell glanced at one another, wondering if they ought to do the same.

"I am Captain Damia Beck," she declared. "Primary advisor to His Highness, John Hunyadi. I'd have your names, travelers."

"I am Ngworekara," Kara began.

Captain Beck arched an eyebrow and gazed down at her. "So I'm told. Curious and a bit troublesome, that is. How many parents would give their child such a mischievous name?"

Julianna frowned. What was the woman talking about? She might have asked, but then Captain Beck turned her formidable gaze upon her.

"And you?"

"Julianna Whitney."

Halliwell crossed his arms. "Detective Theodore Halliwell."

Beck's placid features rippled with curiosity. "Detective? Interesting. Yes, we get one of you from time to time. Always looking in the places no one else bothers to see, so they stumble through. But you're not a detective here, you do know that, Mister Halliwell? You're in the Kingdom of Euphrasia now, the realm of Hunyadi."

"So I'm told," Halliwell replied.

Captain Beck smiled. "Excellent. Then you won't mind handing over your gun."

Halliwell flinched. He looked at her more closely. "I'd rather hang on to it, if it's all the same to you."

One of the archers above barked an order and they all leaned over the wall, bowstrings humming as they were drawn taut. Julianna held her breath.

But Beck waved a hand and they all relaxed. Her face lit up with a knowing smile. Her hands disappeared inside her robe in the single blink of an eye and she produced a pair of gleaming silver revolvers. They glittered in the moonlight.

"Guns are crude," Captain Beck said. "We do not like them here. In fact, very few are allowed to carry them. They're a product of the human world and never manufactured here."

She gestured with one of her pistols. "Well, almost never. Now, please, let's not make any trouble. You want to speak with the king about Oliver Bascombe. I may be able to arrange that. But not while you have a gun. I'm sure you understand."

Halliwell glared at her. Julianna could see the doubt in his eyes, see him weighing the odds of them getting out alive if he refused. Pure stubbornness. The odds were a billion to one and it shouldn't have taken a millisecond to consider them.

"I suspect Miss Whitney and your guide could meet the king without you, Detective," Captain Beck added, cocking both pistols and aiming them at Halliwell's head.

A humorless smile touched his lips. Halliwell pulled his gun slowly and held it out, butt first. Captain Beck nodded, and the guard who looked like a Viking came over and took it from him. He handled the thing as though it were a dead rat he'd just found in his basement.

"This way, please," Damia Beck said.

She holstered her pistols in the darkness within her cloak and turned on her heel, striding through the gates. Julianna blinked, surprised it could be so simple. But the soldiers split into two groups, making room to let them pass. The archers withdrew from the walls above.

The Viking tossed Halliwell's gun to the ground just beside the gate. "It'll be here when you come out. If you come out."

Halliwell ignored him and started after Captain Beck. Kara and Julianna followed as well. With no other escort—as though they represented no threat at all—they were allowed to pass through the gates and across the courtyard to the castle itself.

Inside the stone corridors, lit by torches and lamps, Damia Beck looked both more beautiful and more formidable. Her cloak swirled around her as she walked.

"Excuse me, Captain," Kara ventured.

Beck glanced back at her. "Yes?"

"It's just ... I'd heard that the monarchs of the Two Kingdoms always had Atlantean advisors. You hardly look Atlantean."

Captain Beck sniffed dryly. "People are often not what they seem. But you're correct that I am not Atlantean. That ... policy ... is currently being reconsidered. My elevation to primary advisor is fairly recent. It has been a difficult day, here at Otranto. Your arrival is ill-timed. But we shall see what His Highness wishes. What the future will hold, no one may know."

Julianna trudged along behind Kara and the captain. She glanced back several times at Halliwell. His gaze had turned cold again, and his expression was grim. He moved as though they walked to the gallows, the spark of hope gone. She wanted to tell him not to lose faith, that he would see his daughter again. But Julianna knew how hollow that would sound.

Captain Beck was right. No one could know the future. And, at the moment, theirs was very much in doubt.

Oliver Bascombe had done many foolish things in his life, but he did not consider himself a fool. Others might, perhaps, but even those who would happily recall his least admirable moments would never have called him stupid.

He had driven the stolen rental car—though since he had given the clerk his credit card number, he didn't think it could technically be considered stolen—through the winding streets of Vienna until he had found a bank with an ATM machine. With his card, he withdrew the daily limit on his account, and then took a cash advance on his credit card as well. If someone had flagged his card and the police were looking for him, they might well trace him to Vienna and even to this bank, but that was as far as they would get.

Kitsune had stayed in the rental car until he signaled her, and then she had abandoned it on the curb and joined him on the sidewalk. They had walked a dozen blocks or so. The night was astonishingly beautiful. A light snow fell, bringing with it a kind of winter hush that muffled the sounds of the cars and the grind of the city. Somewhere a chorus was singing Christmas songs. A rainbow of lights gleamed all through the streets from decorations on buildings and in shop windows and strung from lampposts. People laughed together and couples held hands as they passed. In the cobblestoned square in front of a great cathedral, a solitary couple waltzed alone.

How Oliver had envied them.

They had walked a distance from the abandoned rental car before hailing a cab, wanting to make it as difficult as possible for anyone who might track them—no matter what side of the Veil their pursuers might come from.

Now Oliver sat in an uncomfortable chair in a hotel room in a neighborhood that did not have any gleaming Christmas decorations, a place where no voices were raised in song. In college he had backpacked with Bob Dorsey from Amsterdam to Prague, traveling by train and staying in grimy youth hostels filled with cockroaches. It had been his own money—cash Oliver had earned tutoring—and it felt good to do something that wasn't reliant on his father's money. The filth had been amusing to him back then.

Now it was just filth.

This place was not nearly as bad as the worst of those hostels, but it was decidedly unpleasant. The stuffing in the chair had worn thin, the fabric faded and ragged. The carpet was no better, neither the curtains. But here, at least, no one tried to arrest him or have him killed. For the moment, he could not ask for more. A rest and a shower, that would do.

Until the hour arrived to put Kitsune's plan into action. At that point, it would begin all over again. Yet there was no other way. Or, at least, no way that would not have taken days longer. It was hard to stomach even this short delay, knowing that Collette lingered in the custody of the monster who'd murdered their father and torn out his eyes.

The drive into Vienna had given him time to plan: find the ATM, get some distance from the abandoned car, take a cab, locate a hotel shitty enough to have a room they could use on Christmas Eve and for which they could pay cash. That explained all of the hookers going in and out of the lobby.

If the police were searching for him, there were only two possibilities he could think of. Either they wanted him in connection with the events on Canna Island—the murder of Professor Koenig and the fire that burned his home—or Oliver was a suspect in his father's murder.

It never occurred to him that they might want to question him on both matters, and that there might be more—that there might be worse. In fact, it never occurred to him that there could be anything worse than being a suspect in the murder of your own father and the disappearance of your sister.

So they had checked into the hotel and taken turns showering, and now Kitsune lay on the bed, curled up beneath the comforter, having left plenty of room for Oliver. But he forced himself to stay in that uncomfortable, worn and faded chair and watched CNN, trying to avoid the bright jade eyes that would drift from the television screen every so often to cast him a glance full of equal parts curiosity, desire, and disappointment. He did his best to focus on the telling nature of CNN's international newscast, which truly did provide news from around the world; at home, the news was weighted a hundred to one in favor of American coverage.

When the story began, he did not realize it was what he had been waiting for, and yet he was riveted with horror by the story of the murder of twenty-seven children at a German orphanage. Even the word "mutilated" did not register except to make him shudder with revulsion and wonder what sort of monster would do such a thing.

Then the report began to link other cases to that German atrocity. Prague. Toronto. Paris. New Orleans. San Francisco. In those cases, only one or two children had been killed, but all of the murders had been in the last few weeks, and according to local authorities as well as U.S. and European officials, the mutilations in each case were similar enough to make them believe some kind of cult was involved.

There did also seem to be a connection to another series of murders and mysterious disappearances, however.

Oliver's mouth opened slowly, his eyes widening. His father's face appeared on the screen. The murder of Maximilian Bascombe shared disturbing similarities to those of the dead children, as did that of Alice St. John, a little girl from Cottingsley, Maine. Both of Bascombe's children had vanished ...

"But authorities on two continents are searching for *this* man, Oliver Bascombe, son of the late Maximilian Bascombe, for questioning in regard to this international string of heinous crimes and also concerning the murder of a retired college professor, David Koenig, in Scotland. Yet the mystery only deepens. Confirmed sightings of Oliver Bascombe in London and Scotland prompted independent investigators Ted Halliwell and Julianna Whitney to travel from Maine to the United Kingdom to seek him out, only to vanish themselves on the night of David Koenig's murder. If you have seen this man—"

The words continued but he could not hear anymore. It was as though he had gone deaf.

Oliver brought both hands to his forehead. His mouth hung open and his body shook as he drew in tiny gasps of air. Slowly he slid from the chair and his legs folded beneath him. He contracted in upon himself, leaning against the wall, trembling with denial and hopelessness.

It was her scent that made him aware of Kitsune's presence beside him. She had curled up on the threadbare carpet and tried now to comfort him, but when she touched him he flinched and contracted further, trying to burrow deeper within himself, perhaps hoping in some way that he might disappear completely.

If she spoke to him, he did not hear. Though she did not try to touch him again, she remained there, curled on the floor nearby as though she could absorb some of the pain from him.

A vast gulf had opened within Oliver. Hollow, he huddled there and waited for the emptiness inside to fill again, at least enough so that he could stop shaking; so that he could get up and get on with what had to be done.

He feared that it never would.

alliwell retreated deep within himself. It felt to him as though he operated his limbs from a great distance. Even looking out through his own eyes, everything seemed far away. And down in that place deep inside, he nursed a growing hatred of Oliver Bascombe. More and more he had become convinced Oliver was a victim, just as he and Julianna were, but that no longer mattered. He had simply grown tired of following the man, of chasing this phantom who bumbled on ahead of them through a world of impossibilities, and upon whom they had hung all of their hope.

There it is, Halliwell thought. *That's why you hate him ... because you need him, and you know damn well he doesn't have a magic wand. No ruby slippers here, Teddy. No way to click your heels and go home.*

He thought the world of Julianna, but with every passing moment he drew further away from her. The distance helped. If he let himself be charmed by her wit and intelligence and sincerity, it became difficult to hate Oliver. Yet much of his bitterness was on her behalf.

Julianna believed that once they found her fiancé, everything would be all right. Somehow, they would get home.

The truth left a black streak across his heart. There were no ruby slippers. Halliwell wanted so desperately to believe they would get home, and this world bristled with magic, so perhaps it was possible. But following Oliver around the Two Kingdoms seemed bound to get them killed.

Not that they had any other option. And even if they had, the time to divert from this path had long since passed. They were committed now.

All three of them—Halliwell, Julianna, and the girl, Kara—had been locked into a single large room. It had been well appointed, with soft, comfortable chairs, a balcony too high to leap from, and a pair of sofas. Halliwell had rested a bit, but had been unable to fall asleep. How could he shut down his thoughts, quiet his fears? Eyes open, he could only lie there and think of never seeing Sara again. The more he tried to push thoughts of his daughter from his mind, the more impossible that became.

Julianna and Ngworekara had gone out on the balcony for a time, then the girl had stayed out there while Julianna came in, curled up in a chair, and instantly fell asleep.

She woke with the metal clank of the lock turning. The door had swung open and Captain Beck had entered, leaving a quartet of guards in the hall. All of which had led them to the here and now.

Kara led the way, flanked by two grimly silent soldiers who seemed immune to the girl's mercurial charm. Julianna and Halliwell followed side by side, with Beck and the other two guards behind them. The captain kept right on Halliwell's heels and he felt her presence keenly. In all his life, he had never encountered a woman so beautiful and so deadly. Captain Damia Beck looked as though she'd been carved out of ebony and she moved with utter confidence, but he had no doubt she would kill him without blinking if the order came.

"He's been here," Julianna whispered.

Beck cleared her throat, perhaps coincidentally, but Halliwell felt sure it was an admonition. He ignored her, glancing at Julianna.

"How can you be sure?"

She smiled softly and arched an eyebrow. "Aside from the way we're being treated? I just feel it. I know him, Ted. Have known him, in fact, most of my life. He's been here."

Julianna said nothing more. They followed Kara and the two guards around a corner, down a long set of stone stairs that gently curved to the right, and arrived at a pair of wood and iron doors that looked like they could withstand just about anything.

A diminutive soldier, a woman with olive skin and dark eyes, stood at attention at the sight of Captain Beck.

"His Highness, King Hunyadi, awaits," the small soldier said. Then she grabbed hold of the door handle and swung it open with strength that belied her size.

They were ushered into a long, narrow room extensively decorated in an oceanic theme, with art depicting nautical scenes and marine life. A great many candles were arrayed around the room, but they remained unlit. The light from the lamps and torches on the walls cast the room in an eerie, pulsing glow. Fully two dozen soldiers were already inside the room when they arrived, lined up at attention on either side of a raised dais at the far end of the room, beneath a massive stained glass depiction of Neptune or Poseidon.

On the dais was a chair. But the king wasn't sitting.

At least, Halliwell assumed the guy was the king. He stood with his arms crossed as though he had been awaiting their arrival with impatience. With his thick beard and graying hair, he could have been the father to the Viking soldier they'd met at the castle gate.

Kara, Julianna, and Halliwell were halted by their escort. Captain Beck strode forward and bowed with a flourish.

"Your Highness, may I present—"

King Hunyadi leaned on the back of his high chair and studied them. "I know who they are, Captain." The king stared at Kara a moment, then looked at Julianna and Halliwell in turn. "The question is, do they?"

"Forgive me, Your Highness, but what the hell does that mean?"

Halliwell blinked and turned to stare at Julianna. Whatever distance he had cultivated evaporated in that moment. The way she looked at the king, it amazed Halliwell that she was not executed on the spot.

Instead, Hunyadi smiled and shook his head. "Ah, Miss Whitney. I can see why Bascombe wants to marry you."

Julianna gave a tiny gasp and Halliwell was sure he saw her shudder at this confirmation that Oliver was alive. Whatever she might have believed, this was the first real indication she had that her faith was well founded.

"Then he's been here?"

The king nodded thoughtfully. He came around his chair and sat down, then leaned forward, elbows on his knees. With that gesture, he seemed like such an ordinary man that Halliwell found himself instinctively trusting him. The whole atmosphere in the castle was a comfort to him, given the circumstances. Some of the animalistic panic that churned in him retreated, and he took a steady, even breath.

Twillig's Gorge had been chaos. But this . . . there was order here. He was a former military man and a police detective. He could understand hierarchy. It calmed him.

"Your Highness, if I may—" Kara began.

Hunyadi's gaze turned dark. "No. You may not."

The king ignored her then, studying Julianna and Halliwell. Several times, he seemed about to speak—so that when at last he did, it was obvious he had come to some decision.

"Detective Halliwell, what are your intentions toward Bascombe?"

"I'm sorry?"

"What will you do when you catch him?"

Halliwell shrugged, hoping that neither his dark thoughts nor his desperation would show in his expression. "I don't know. We're going to help him get his sister, Collette, back. After that . . ."

Julianna stared at him. Ted looked away.

King Hunyadi's gaze commanded his attention. "You are aware, I'm sure, that there is no way for you to return to your own world?"

"We're aware," Julianna said.

"That's what we're told, at any rate," Halliwell countered. Whatever calm he'd felt moments before had been burned away by the king's words. Hunyadi was the ruler of this nation. If there was any way back, surely he ought to know. But Halliwell set his jaw and glared, still refusing to surrender to the consistency of this assertion.

He could not.

The king nodded slowly, studying him. "One day, my friend, you will have no choice but to accept the truth of it. When the day comes, perhaps we can speak again. A man with your training could be of great use to me. But that is the future. Let us discuss the present."

He smiled at Julianna. "By now you've realized that your Oliver was, indeed, here at Otranto. He travels with a Borderkind called Kitsune. When they left my presence, both were still alive. I presume they remain that way and make their way even now toward the Sandman's castle in hopes of destroying the fiend and retrieving Oliver's sister from her captivity there.

"However, their visit here was not without incident. Beneath my very nose they were attacked by the Hunters. They survived only because Kitsune was swift enough to take Oliver across the border between worlds. They went through the Veil."

Halliwell felt ice form in his gut. "They're back in the world?"

King Hunyadi nodded. "Oliver is not restricted the way you are. He is an Intruder. But he has asked for a boon—a year to prove himself worthy of my trust—and I have granted it. Already, I believe he may earn that trust. The tale he told of a conspiracy against the Borderkind, and the threat presented by Ty'Lis of Atlantis, was proven by the assault upon him and his companion in this very chamber. Captain Beck has graciously accepted the position of advisor after I was forced to ... eliminate the Atlantean presence in my own court."

Halliwell frowned. Kara had begun to fidget like an even younger child where she stood at the foot of the dais, between the two guards who had escorted her in. She huffed and crossed her arms in petulant boredom.

The king either did not notice, or chose to ignore her.

"My agents had brought me tales of the travails of the Borderkind, but I confess I had only begun to realize the extent of the conspiracy and certainly had no idea what powers might lie behind it. I am indebted to Mister Bascombe for enlightening me. And now that you are here, I shall repay that debt."

Kara twirled her hair in her fingers. "Really, Your Majesty, that isn't necessary," she said.

Hunyadi pinned her with a glare. "Oh, but it is. Entirely necessary. I repay my debts."

Again he looked at Halliwell, then sat back in his seat, elbows on armrests, fingers steepled before him. His gaze shifted to Julianna.

"You will sleep here tonight. I will provide you with horses. At dawn, you'll leave in the company of a dozen of my soldiers. They will ride with you to the Sandman's castle either to aid Oliver or to learn his fate. Captain Beck herself will lead them."

The relief and gratitude on Julianna's face was contagious. "Thank you. Thank you so much."

Halliwell took a deep breath, nodding slowly. "We're grateful, but with the lead Oliver already has, would it be ..." He'd been about to say *wise*, but thought better of it. "Wouldn't it be better to leave right away?"

King Hunyadi glanced at him. "Of course. But Kitsune has taken him through the Veil. There is no way to overtake them. Your only hope is to reach Oliver's destination before he gets there himself. As he explained it to me, they plan to recruit a powerful ally before continuing on. That effort should divert them at least for the night, if not longer. And let us be honest with one another, Mister Halliwell. Neither you nor Miss Whitney is in any condition to continue on your journey without rest."

It was Halliwell's nature to argue with such a statement, even if it had come from Sheriff Norris. The panic rose up in protest, anguished and desperate, making his whole body tense with the need to shout and move, to continue the search for an answer. But this man was the king of the country they found themselves in. And he was right.

"We appreciate your generosity," Halliwell said.

The king remained grim as he studied them. In front of Halliwell, Kara shifted impatiently.

"Excellent. Then only one thing remains," Hunyadi said, and he nodded once toward Captain Beck, whose own expression was equally grim, the lamplight playing across her ebon features.

Beck reached into the shadows of her cloak and drew out her twin silver pistols. Halliwell shouted and reached for Julianna, putting himself between her and those guns.

He need not have worried.

Captain Beck leveled both pistols and began firing. The first bullet struck Kara in the back, even as the girl tried to turn. The pretty little girl contorted, still on her feet, as the bullets tore into her, spraying blood across the floor. She would have fallen sooner, but the impact of each bullet drove her back another step and kept her from collapsing.

Julianna shouted and tried to pull away from Halliwell, to run to Kara, but he grabbed hold of her and would not let her move, afraid that the next shots might be for them.

Instead, Julianna collapsed into him and he held her. Together, in the fading echo of the bullets, they watched the little girl fall to the ground with a wet thump. Blood pooled, and tongues of smoke licked from the barrels of Captain Beck's guns.

"Jesus Fucking Christ, what the hell is wrong with you people?" Halliwell roared, his mind trying to deny what he had just seen.

Captain Beck turned her guns on him, her eyes emotionless. For the first time he noticed a thin scar above her right eye, the only blemish on her perfect face.

"The Hunters who are murdering Borderkind are also searching for Oliver Bascombe," the king said, stroking his beard calmly, eyes locked on Halliwell. "They are not above subterfuge. Ngworekara had her own purpose in guiding you. In her land, she was queen of demons."

Halliwell blinked. Demons?

"She was a little girl!" Julianna screamed, pulling away from Halliwell and stalking toward the dais. Captain Beck got in the way and Julianna stopped, but still she stared at Hunyadi in disgust.

"No," said the king. "She was not."

In confusion, Halliwell stepped forward. Even as he reached for Julianna to pull her back, they both looked down at the bleeding corpse of the little girl who had guided them this far.

Her skin no longer looked human. And her face ... Tusks thrust from her mouth and an elephantine trunk hung down where her nose and mouth had been. Short, bristly hair stubbled her skull.

"Oh, hell," Halliwell whispered.

Julianna clapped a hand over her mouth and turned away.

The Borderkind forged their way through the rain forest, the air thick and close, so dense it seemed more akin to striding along the ocean bottom than crossing terrain above sea level. Coils of moss hung down from branches, and in the heat and humidity and the lightly falling rain, the whole forest churned with the rich smell of vegetation, of life. Through the canopy of treetops above, the late morning sky was a blue-white haze.

The winter man led them, moving through the brush swiftly, but heavily. He did not belong in Yucatazca. The heat and humidity wore not only at his spirit but at his physical self as well. It *eroded* him. The weather could not destroy him, of course; winter itself comprised his core. But here in the rain forest, his form became leaner and sharper, until he stalked mantislike through the trees, freezing the moisture on the leaves he brushed against.

The climate put him in the foulest of moods.

Blue Jay hung back, lingering at the end of their little parade, watching the rain forest for sign of some threat. The others were strung in a line between them: Cheval Bayard and Chorti, Li and the Mazikeen.

Despite his heavy robe, the Mazikeen seemed to drift ghostlike through the heat and dampness. A sense of doomed resignation enveloped him. Frost wondered if this was grief for his lost kin, or some deeper sense of impending catastrophe.

They would never reach Palenque, the capital, without coming under attack. Difficult to accept, but there it was. There were simply too many of them to avoid detection. When he had begun to formulate his plan, he'd envisioned a small army of Borderkind, never imagining that so many would have been murdered or fled before he could repay his debt to Oliver and discover the identity of their enemy. A small army would have been useful. But with every mile they traveled into Yucatazca, Frost became more and more convinced that it had been a mistake to set out with half a dozen allies. Without the strength of a larger force, he'd have been better off alone, slipping into Palenque as a silent assassin, a cold breeze that slit the throat of Ty'Lis.

But there was nothing to be done about it now. They were allies, and committed. The winter man was determined they would make an attempt at stealth, but he felt certain it would fail. The seven of them tromping through the rain forest—they could hardly fail to attract attention.

With a low growl that seemed to vibrate the ground, Li's tiger padded past Frost. On his back, Li turned toward the winter man.

"Do you see it?" asked the Guardian of Fire.

Ahead, above the canopy, hazed in damp air and roiling heat, thrust the pinnacle of a pyramid. Unlike the Egyptian sort, the structure had a broad, flat top, upon which was built a small square temple. Wide stairwells—fifty feet across—led up the outer walls, steps to allow the high priests to climb to the sky, to be nearer the gods.

Frost had been so lost in thought that he had not, in fact, noticed. Perhaps a dozen large, red-winged birds soared above the pyramid, circling lazily. It was difficult to see from this distance how large the clearing around the pyramid might be, but if there was a temple, he knew there was likely a village, and if a village, likely there was water. Despite the level terrain, Frost suspected a river or at least a stream.

He turned to regard the others as they gathered around.

"It's half a day to Palenque from here, if the Mazikeen is correct. I do not know how long we can remain undiscovered, but it seems wise to go around any settlements. We'll move east, keep forest between us and whatever people worship at that temple. From here, it's going to—"

The growl of the tiger alerted him first. The winter man glanced at the animal. Upon its back, Li narrowed his eyes and the fire that flickered there burned higher as he glanced around, studying the forest. Rain hissed into steam where it struck Li.

Chorti grunted and began to turn in a circle, slowly, also searching for the source of whatever it was that had unsettled him. He edged protectively closer to Cheval.

"What's this, then?" Grin mumbled low, almost to himself.

Frost looked past them all, at Blue Jay. The trickster closed his eyes and tilted his head back, listening to the patter of the rain and whatever other sounds were in the forest.

"Jay?" Frost said.

The trickster shrugged. "Not sure. Something, though. Something dark."

"What do you say, sorcerer?" Frost asked the Mazikeen.

The hooded man reached up and tugged the iron rings in his beard, brow furrowed in thought. "No sorcery. Whatever comes this way is not familiar to me."

Frost peered into the trees around them. Li rode the tiger into the forest, weaving in and out of trees with stunning quiet, prowling in search of their watcher. The winter man did not wish to wait any longer.

"Let's move on. We will circle the settlement, as planned. All of you, be wary."

The Borderkind began to move, continuing southward through the rain forest. The hazy sky seemed far lower suddenly, as though it were slowly collapsing in upon them. The rain fell upon each of them, hissing as it touched Li and the tiger, but merely dappling the others.

Something watched. They had a Mazikeen among them, and creatures with remarkably acute senses. Whatever it was, they ought to have been able to sense it.

Wings fluttered above him, and Frost glanced up to see the small bird dart above his head. Blue Jay felt safer in that form, Frost knew. Cheval moved through the trees as though dancing. Her rain-dampened hair clung to her face and coiled in wet strings upon her shoulders. Chorti stayed close to her, metal teeth bared as though every raindrop posed a threat.

Now it was the Grindylow who hung back. Even as Frost glanced at him, Grin paused and turned slowly, backtracking with his eyes.

A noise had been growing, distant at first but moving closer, a high-pitched flutelike whistle. Frost saw no sign of its source but knew it was only one more reason to continue forward. The alternative was unacceptable.

First, though, they had to get past whatever Grin had seen in the trees. He wanted to see it for himself. The ground around the winter man froze, ice spreading from his feet onto the grass and leaves and the stalks of plants. His eyes narrowed. Again he spun, mist rising from his eyes, and then he saw it ahead of them, standing amidst the trees as though to block their way through the rain forest. At first glance it seemed like a man riding horseback, but it was nothing so mundane.

"Black Devil," Chorti grunted.

The winter man stared at the centaur—some sort of local legend. It had the body of a stallion, but where its head ought to have been was the upper body of a man. Yet that was only illusion, it was neither one thing nor the other but a third creature that shared elements of both. Its skin was black and smooth and ridged with cords of muscle. Slick with rain, it gleamed in the haze of the Yucatazcan day.

Frost caught scent of its musk.

The whistling noise became louder . . . moving closer.

"Either it moves," Cheval said, gliding past him, "or we kill it."

Li urged his tiger forward, blocking her with its sinewy body. The little man glared at her. "Do you really think it is alone?"

"Ah, bloody Hell!" Grin swore, as if in answer.

As one they all glanced back at him. He ignored them, staring still into the forest they had just traveled through. Two more of the Black Devils were moving out of the trees, hooves noiseless on the wet ground.

The winter man studied the centaur ahead of them, took a step toward it. "We don't know they're enemies. Even if they are, they might not be Hunters."

Blue Jay circled around his head, wings fluttering, and with a blur of color that seemed darker against the rain, transformed once again into the jean-clad trickster. The feathers in his hair lay flat and damp against his head. His eyes were clear and bright with danger.

"Something else is coming."

The tiger growled. Li shifted anxiously upon its back. The Mazikeen appeared suddenly at the winter man's side as though he moved between moments.

"They are Minata-Karaia. We must leave the forest."

Frost heard the whistling. It grew louder still.

The Black Devils moved through the trees in a slowly closing circle, but they were only three. Around the winter man, the rain turned to snow. He was weaker here in the tropical climate, but not entirely without power.

"Get to the pyramid!" he snapped. "Kill anything that gets in your way!"

As one, they turned south. Blue Jay took flight again, diminishing into a bird and darting up through the branches. Li and his tiger bounded into the trees with Grin and Chorti crashing through the forest behind them. Cheval Bayard was all green and silver streaks, shifting in an eyeblink from woman to horse. Frost could have summoned a chill wind to carry him, but he dared not exert himself so much in this weather. Instead he ran, slicing through the forest again.

Out of the corner of his eye, he saw one of the Black Devils careening through the trees to cut him off. He tensed, dagger fingers hooked, prepared to slaughter the thing if it attacked. But before he could even pause, Cheval was there. The kelpy thundered through the trees, snapping branches before her, and collided with the Black Devil, knocking the centaur off of its feet. Before it could fight back, she began to beat it with the hooves of her forelegs, breaking bones and pulping its skull. The Black Devil screamed, then fell silent.

The winter man kept going, grateful and impressed. He had underestimated Cheval, and vowed not to do it again.

Another bestial cry came, off to his left, and he glanced over to see a Black Devil writhing on the ground, bucking against the earth in obvious agony. Over it stood the Mazikeen, one skeletal hand extended from beneath its robe, the air shimmering between its fingers and the centaur's flesh.

The last of the Black Devils galloped behind him, its hooves pounding the forest floor, but Frost was not concerned. On its own, a single Black Devil posed no challenge to the Borderkind.

Ahead, in the trees and through the sheen of light rain, he saw Chorti and Grin rumbling through the rain forest like enormous children playing some sort of game. But the whistling sound had grown louder still, and the name the Mazikeen had used, Minata-Karaia, was echoing through the winter man's head. What were they? The sound was unfamiliar, but if the sorcerer said they had to flee, he knew they must be terrible indeed.

Branches whipped against him, snapping on his frozen form. All around him, snowflakes whipped in a light breeze, the rain no longer reaching him. Frost darted around trees and leaped—flowed—over fallen logs.

Up ahead, he heard Li's tiger roar.

Something shifted in the forest beside him.

A tree.

But not a tree. He looked up and his eyes widened at the sight of the creature as tall as the tallest tree, fruit hanging from its strange branch-arms, its head a thick wooden knot that jutted up from the trunk of its body. There was a hole in its head, and even as it bent to grab at him, the air rushing through that hole screamed into that terrible whistling noise.

With merely a thought, Frost became the winter storm. There in the rain forest it was little more than a cloud of frigid mist, but as the Minata-Karaia reached its tree-fingers into that cloud, the entire branch froze solid. When the creature moved, that whistle announcing its motion, the branch snapped off.

Frost drifted only a dozen feet before taking form again, a sliver man, narrow ice carved like a stick figure. He could not keep up the storm for long. Now he ran again, but this time his gaze searched the trees above and he saw them moving. The whistling grew louder. The Minata-Karaia came after him through the harmless, unmoving trees.

Li's tiger roared again, the sound echoing through the rain forest. There came a howl that could only have been Chorti. Then Cheval thundered past, her hooves pounding the ground. Frost would have tried to swing up onto her back, but by then the Mazikeen was beside him as well, not running but rather floating along a few inches above the forest floor.

Together, they burst from the trees out into the vast open plain around the settlement. Small huts and white-washed buildings were clustered on the far side of a narrow river, little more than a stream. On the near side was the pyramid.

The Borderkind charged out across the open ground, leaving the trees behind. Chorti had blood matted on his furry back. The Grindylow rested on his fists like a mountain gorilla and spun to face the others. Li leaped down off of the tiger, spheres of fire bursting from his hands, ready for battle. Blue Jay danced down from the sky, spinning until he was a man again, his boots alighting upon the ground. Cheval reared back, the battle cry erupting from her throat not quite a neigh.

Together, Frost and the Mazikeen turned to look back the way they'd come. The Minata-Karaia shuffled to the edge of the rain forest. Only when they were moving was it obvious they were not trees, but then it was very, very obvious. They were not even tree-men, but giant, narrow creatures with dark, brittle flesh like bark and long, long legs. They were a race of giants perfectly created to camouflage themselves in a jungle or forest, save for that horrid whistling their heads made as they moved.

But they stopped, unwilling to come into the clearing, at least for the moment, and so the whistling stopped as well. They made odd Hunters, these things who would not pursue their prey. Frost saw perhaps fifteen or twenty of them, just standing there watching as though they were the audience at some kind of bizarre Roman forum.

A single Black Devil trotted from the woods, but it was not looking at them. Its gaze was on the sky.

Then Frost knew.

The Minata-Karaia *were* the audience, but they had also been shepherds, herding them into a real forum, a gladiatorial ring. He turned and looked up at the top of the pyramid where those red-winged birds—blood-winged carrion birds who bathed in the lifeblood of sacrificed prisoners—had begun to land atop the temple roof, also watching, also waiting.

The Borderkind moved nearer together, forming a tight, defensive circle.

"I sense magic," the Mazikeen said, glancing at Frost with black eyes.

The winter man nodded. "Yes."

"It seems we did not run fast enough," Cheval Bayard said, pushing silver hair away from her face.

Blue Jay spread his arms, the blue shimmer of deadly, invisible wings beneath them. "I don't know about the rest of you," he said, "but I'm tired of running."

Leicester Grindylow pounded his fists on the ground. "Too right."

The tiger roared.

In the air, familiar figures soared and circled, green-feathered wings spread wide, twisted antlers dark scrawls against the hazy sky. The Perytons had arrived.

The Manticore emerged from the temple atop the pyramid and began to prowl down the steps. Jezi-Baba followed. From this distance, they should not have been able to hear her laugh, and yet it rolled across the field of battle like distant, insidious thunder.

he British ambassador's residence in Vienna was a late nineteenth-century structure in the classical style, though rather subdued, considering that its architect had also designed the Gothic church that stood only a stone's throw away. The windows of the first story had an oddly bunkerlike quality that made them spectacularly unattractive, though the enclosed balcony and stone-gabled windows of the second story quite made up for this. Overall, the effect was one of proud austerity. The arched entrance doors were set off center, but so large that they must have opened into some interior garden or courtyard.

In the dark of that Christmas Eve, after midnight, Oliver stood shivering in a shadowed doorway across the street from the embassy, stomping his feet to warm his legs and hugging himself against the cold. This was insane. Kitsune's plan simply could not work.

Yet if she had failed, where were the shouts? Where were the gun-shots? He had to remind himself that the world had changed, that magic did indeed exist. In the political climate of the modern world, it should not have been possible for Kitsune to slip into the building undetected. But with myth, anything was possible. If Oliver had not been convinced of that before, he certainly was now.

"Where are you?" Oliver whispered to the night.

As a fox, Kitsune had slipped across the street and alongside the embassy. On Christmas Eve, this late at night, Vienna slept and waited for morning—for celebration, for bells and elation. No security had been visible outside, and little traffic prowled the streets. Only the lithe creature who was not at all what she seemed.

Silently, the fox quickly scaled the outer wall of the embassy. She had leaped from one stone-gabled window frame to the next, and then the next, and then moved up again. Claws noiseless on the wall, she had climbed like a squirrel to the third floor, where a window stood open just a few inches.

Then Kitsune had disappeared into the ambassador's residence.

Oliver stood watching the building now, an afterimage lingering ghostlike on his eyes. It was as though he could still see Kitsune slinking up the wall, still see her slipping through the window. The idea that this might have been his last glimpse of her settled more heavily on him with each passing moment. Most of the windows were dark, and those without light remained that way. Nothing seemed to stir within.

His heart should not hurt so much at the thought of losing Kitsune, but it did. It did. Not only because he had grown more than fond of her, but also because without her, he would be alone.

His breath quickened at the thought. *Alone. And what then?*

Even as the question echoed in his mind, something shifted in the shadows alongside the building. Oliver narrowed his gaze, unsure, and then he saw a deeper darkness there, a figure protruding from a newly opened window. An arm stretched out and a hand beckoned.

A soft laugh escaped Oliver's lips. He shook his head, amazed, and darted across the street. Alongside the residence he glanced about in search of any sign of security. Only then did he spot, far along at the rear of the building in a pool of light from a streetlamp, a small object on the ground. Narrowing his gaze he saw it was a flashlight, but its owner was nowhere to be seen.

At the window, Kitsune shot him a frustrated look and waved him closer. Oliver took a breath, scanned the windows on that side of the building—all but two of which were dark—and slipped up to the window with all the stealth an ordinary man could manage. From the darkened room Kitsune stared out at him, jade eyes preternaturally bright beneath the copper-red fur of her hood.

Again she beckoned, stepping back into the room. Oliver undid his belt and removed his sword and scabbard, handing them up to her. Then he took one final look around and grabbed hold of the window frame with both hands. With a single swift motion, he boosted himself up and slid the upper half of his body through the open portion of the window. He paused a moment, then reached down for the floor. When his fingers touched carpet it was simple for him to slide the rest of his body into the room.

On the Oriental rug he lay a moment, breath coming too fast, and thought about what he had just done. He'd just broken into the British ambassador's residence. With a sword. On so many levels, this was a terrible idea. Yet he was past regret and past caution. All that remained was what was necessary.

Oliver sat up and looked at Kitsune. She had her back to him as she slid the window shut and the light from outside lit up a fringe of fur that traced the edges of her body. He caught his breath.

Crazy. No other word for it.

"How the hell did you do this?" he asked.

Part of the answer presented itself in the desk that had been moved aside and which she silently slid back into place. She had cleared the way for Oliver to enter. But he thought of the flashlight at the back of the building and had to wonder.

Kitsune put a finger to her lips, eyes alight with mischief.

"You didn't ... hurt anyone?"

She raised an eyebrow and then moved up beside him. "Of course I hurt people," the fox-woman whispered in his ear, the scent of her musk strong. "Two guards, one at the rear of the house, so we won't have any trouble getting out of here, and one guarding the stairs that lead up from these offices to the residential quarters. And I persuaded one of them to provide the code for the alarm, while he was still conscious. I'm a trickster. Such things are not a problem for me. You, on the other hand—we needed the alarm code.

"But I haven't killed anyone, Oliver, and it would be nice to keep it that way. So, hush."

He took his sword and scabbard back and slid it onto his belt, knowing it was sheer idiocy but refusing to even consider leaving the weapon behind. It represented more than mere protection. It was a calling card from David Koenig, and from Hunyadi as well. He could not afford to lose it.

Oliver took a long breath, steadying his nerves. "Do you really think this will work?"

Kitsune went to the door of the book-lined office, but paused with one hand on the knob and the other on the polished cherrywood of a bookshelf. She glanced back, brow creased in a deep frown.

"It feels a bit too late for that question. But it should, Oliver. Rules have power. Laws, too. Not just the power they have when they are enforced, but the power of belief. When people accept and respect the rules, that makes them real. According to the laws of your world, though entire nations separate us from the United Kingdom, we're standing on British soil. The legend says the Dustman visits the bedchambers of British children. And here we are. The Borderkind are territorial. The Dustman will probably sense me here, and when he does, he will come."

Oliver paused, listening to the hissing of the heat and the shifting tick and pop of the embassy. "And what do we do then? How do we know what kind of creature he is?"

Kitsune smiled. "That part is up to you."

Without giving Oliver a moment to protest further, she opened the door and poked her head out. The hood hid her face and so he could only assume she made certain the hall was clear before slipping from the room, cloak swirling around her.

After a moment, he followed her, passing through high-ceilinged, ornate drawing rooms filled with portraits of emperors and kings.

Kitsune had been in the ambassador's residence long minutes

before she had found the best point of entry for Oliver. During that time it was obvious she had been upstairs already. The guard was nowhere to be seen, undoubtedly put aside in some corner room where no one would discover him until morning, or until he raised an alarm upon regaining consciousness.

The door at the top of the stairs was unlocked. Kitsune had been very busy indeed. It creaked softly upon opening and she glanced back and gestured him to silence a final time—needlessly—before entering. A light burned in the hall bathroom, perhaps to guide the way for nighttime wanderers, and another in a sitting room at the far end of the corridor. Kitsune ignored this, and so Oliver assumed it was empty.

The fox-woman led the way to a curving staircase that wound up to the third floor. Oliver followed, several of the stairs creaking lightly beneath his step. A carpet runner kept his tread otherwise silent and he was grateful. Nervously, he slid his hand into his pocket and rubbed the seed of the Harvest gods between his thumb and forefinger. It had grown into a habit for him.

From his entry into the embassy until the moment they stood in the open door of the nursery it had been perhaps four minutes, yet each passing second grew longer, and none so long as that in which Oliver first laid eyes upon the little girl who slept in the floral canopy bed. The ambassador's daughter—he knew only the family's last name, Hetherton—lay curled in the bed, a plush doll crushed against her, hair spread upon her pillow, burrowed deeply beneath her covers.

Christmas Eve. In a matter of hours, she would wake in search of her presents. His mind busily wove fictions about Santa Claus and his helpers in the event that their entrance roused her. Yet he prayed that did not become necessary.

All of this was so wrong, and nothing more so than sneaking into the room of a little girl—she couldn't have been more than three—while she slept. The magic that he still felt in his heart at the thought of Christmas Eve only made it that much worse.

Oliver hesitated. The little girl's breathing seemed so loud. Her expression was soft and innocent, her lips parted in total surrender to sleep.

To the Dustman.

Kitsune snatched up his fingers and drew him into the room. Oliver swallowed hard and stood staring down at the girl as Kit closed the door all but a few inches. Drawing her cloak around herself, Kitsune diminished, becoming a fox in the space between heartbeats. Each time she did this Oliver felt a second of vertigo, as though he might fall into the space left by the sudden absence where she had been.

The fox trotted to a place at the foot of the girl's bed. Oliver frowned at the lack of any sound from her passing, not even the scratch of claws upon the wooden floor, but he ought not have been surprised. Kitsune rarely made a sound, her feet seeming barely to touch the ground. The fox stood at the foot of the bed and twitched her tail as though it was a beckoning finger. She nodded as if to urge him to join her, and so he did. If the girl did stir, it would be best not to be within her view. Careful not to let his sheathed sword bang against the wood, Oliver lay quietly on the floor, hidden.

Kitsune circled him twice like a dog searching for the perfect spot to lie before the fireplace. At last she settled in front of him, backing up, nuzzling into him as though she were indeed a pet. Oliver's throat went dry. The strangeness of the moment enveloped him. In the silence of the embassy he lay there. Low and primal, the fox purred in a way that was not at all feline. This was the purr of a lover.

She shifted her head, copper fur brushing against his arm. The fox glanced at him with jade eyes.

There, against him, the magic transformed her again. Fox became woman so suddenly that he started, then held his breath waiting to see if the child had been disturbed. Kitsune gave him half a smile, one corner of her mouth lifting. Her hair hung down from within the hood, a cascade of black velvet. It touched his arm, just as her fur had. The heat from her body had reached him before, but now she felt like a furnace so close to him.

"What about the Dustman?" he whispered, barely vocalizing, afraid to wake the girl, afraid he wouldn't be able to speak.

"If he could sense me, he will have. He'll come."

She edged nearer, her body up against him, every contour felt in sharp relief.

Kitsune reached up to trace his face.

"Oliver," Kitsune said. "There is magic in you."

She brought her mouth up to be kissed.

Oliver shivered with lust and fascination. "Kit."

"Ssshhh," she whispered.

He drew back to catch her gaze, and then shook his head. No. He could not do this. No man could have been there with Kitsune, in that moment, and not desired her. It would have been so easy to surrender to that. But he owed Julianna more than this.

Julianna had gone searching for him, and according to the news, she had vanished as well. He had done his best not to think about what might have become of her. With every part of him—from muscle to spirit to breath—he felt the longing for Julianna. All he wished for was to hold her in his arms and know that she was safe, not only for her benefit, but for his own selfish needs as well. No one could look inside him the way she could. When he felt despair or fear or doubt, no one could raise him up from that the way Julianna had always been able to.

Thus far, he had not allowed himself to consider the obvious possibility—that the Sandman had taken Julianna as well as Collette. He knew his sister was in the monster's hands, and so before he could consider the next step, he had to save Collette. Until then, he could only hold Julianna in his heart like a talisman, to keep away despair. In his mind he could still see her there on the end of the jetty, all the way back in the summer before high school began. He kept that image clear in his thoughts, polished and shining.

"Kit, I'm sorry," he whispered.

Or thought he did. He might not even have spoken the words aloud. Regardless, Kitsune understood well enough. Anger and betrayal flashed in her jade eyes. Her brow furrowed and she glanced away, though she did not move. Her body was still pressed tightly to his.

"I understand," she whispered. "You must have time."

But he shook his head. She should not speak. For something was stirring in the room. A sound like a breeze rustling leaves far away reached him and a soft wind blew across the floor, eddying and swirling. It was not the girl that stirred.

Grains of sand danced across the wood floor. It began as a light spray, but soon a fine covering lay upon the floorboards, a dust devil of sand. When it began to rise, to sculpt a form, Oliver went rigid. He knew this was not their enemy, not the creature who had taken Collette, but it was an aspect of the same being. How could they predict what was to come?

The breeze died and a bit of sand scattered upon the floor.

The Dustman had arrived.

On Christmas morning, Sara Halliwell woke with the dawn. Warm sunlight streamed in the windows of her father's house. She had slept on the sofa in the living room, falling asleep there in front of the fire. Sometime during the long night she had awoken in the dark with only embers glowing in the fireplace and the gleam of Christmas lights outside from other houses in the neighborhood, and she'd been tempted to move to her father's bed.

But Sara stayed on the sofa instead, too tired and unnerved to move, troubled by the suspicion that sleeping in her father's bed would constitute some strange admission that she thought him gone forever.

When the light of Christmas morning woke her, she turned over, burrowed into the sofa, and tried to go back to sleep. Her eyes burned and her head felt stuffed with the cotton of exhaustion, but no matter how early it was—surely no later than seven—she could not force herself to go back to sleep. Her neck ached and her mouth felt dry.

How easy it was to remember other Christmas mornings, when she had awakened before dawn and run to her parents' bedroom, jumping up and down upon their mattress and demanding that they rise and escort her to the living room—to the tree and the many beautiful packages that lay beneath.

In those days there would be plastic candles burning with warm orange electric light. Those orange bulbs comforted her. But this morning the house was dark. No Christmas tree, no orange glow in the windows. When she forced herself to rise and look outside, the whole town lay blanketed in crisp new-fallen snow. The blue sky was perfectly clear and the sun shone brightly on the snow, giving the whole world a feeling of unreality, as though the town itself existed inside a snow globe.

Christmas had arrived.

But not in here, Sara thought. *Not in this house.*

Even with the glare off of the snow, the sunshine could only reach so far and could not dispel the gloom in this house, in her heart.

With no hope of retreating back into sleep, she went to the kitchen and moved slowly through the motions of preparing breakfast. She expected to find very little that was edible in the home of a fifty-something, divorced police detective and received a pleasant surprise when she discovered four eggs that had not fossilized, as well as a package of bacon and a half-eaten slab of cheddar cheese that had yet to turn green.

Sara fixed a palatable omelette with those remnants. She wished for toast but refused to attempt the crusty bread, even with its edges cut off. Spots of bluish mold had begun to grow on it. One final bit of luck presented itself in an unopened container of cran-apple juice. Not her first choice, but it would do.

"Merry Christmas," she said, her voice a bitter whisper, and she toasted the empty house with warm cran-apple juice in a Bugs Bunny glass that had been—in the once upon a time of her own childhood—a jelly jar. Why her father had kept it mystified her.

He never throws anything away, she thought, and did not allow herself to wish for another reason, a deeper meaning and connection.

In the kitchen, drowning in silence broken only by the drone of the refrigerator, she stared around the room at the peeling floral wallpaper and the faux-tile linoleum floor and the lazy Susan on the table that carried salt and pepper and napkins—who did he ever have to spin it for? The answer was obvious. No one. The lazy Susan never spun, because there was only ever one person at the table.

The morning slipped by in a fugue of waiting. Sara felt both a terrible restlessness, her every muscle a frightened animal about to bolt, and a crippling malaise of the spirit that turned her into a ghost in her father's house. She washed her own dishes and the frying pan by hand, then went out into the living room and began to sort through the mail that one of the investigating officers had left in a neat pile on the coffee table. A single postcard—a wish-you-were-here sort of thing from one of his fellow officers with large-breasted girls in bikinis on the back and a Florida postmark on the front—lay atop days' worth of junk mail, credit card offers, promotions, and bills. Amongst them were precisely five Christmas cards, two of which were from old friends her father hadn't seen in so long that Sara would not have recognized them on the street. One was from Sheriff Norris or, rather, from his wife, Sophie. The fourth had come from Sara's mother, and it stunned her—mainly because she had been unaware that her parents still exchanged Christmas cards.

Don't be an idiot, she chided herself. *Mom sent one. Doesn't mean Dad did.* No, Ted Halliwell had never been that kind of father. He loved her, she knew that, but there were never any grand gestures from old Ted. Not even small gestures.

The fifth card had come from Sara herself. She wondered if her father would ever return to open it. It lay on the coffee table like a smoking gun, evidence that this was no nightmare, that he was gone.

The restlessness in her grew worse and somehow so did the fatigue. Sara checked her cell phone several times to see if she had any messages, but there were none. Christmas day, and everyone was off celebrating with their families. She existed in their worlds only peripherally on this day, outside of everything they cared about. Those friends who had been calling since learning of her father's disappearance would forget about her today, and Sara was surprised to find that she did not begrudge them this freedom. If they needed peace on this one day, out of all of them, who was she to intrude?

For nearly two hours she set about tidying her father's house. She was far from the neatest or most meticulous girl. When she had girlfriends, she spent nearly all of her time in their beds instead of her own. The sort of girls she was attracted to were almost invariably scared off by her slobbishness before they even had time to fall in love with her, so Sara tried to hide it well.

Yet here she was, cleaning.

But what else could she do?

Shortly before noon she plunked herself down on the couch and blew a stray lock of unwashed hair out of her face. *A shower,* she thought. *God, how nice would that be?*

Sunken into the cushions, she found her gaze straying to the stereo system that had been inserted amongst books and plants on a tall shelf against one wall. Any distraction would do, and so she rose and went over and turned the radio on. A static hiss filled the room and Sara glanced stupidly at the speakers for a moment as though they were at fault, then began to turn the dial.

The first channel she could tune clearly played an old Sinatra Christmas song. A shudder went through her and she twisted the knob. The next station had Bruce Springsteen singing "Santa Claus Is Comin' to Town." The one after that, a holiday song from Mariah Carey. Sara gave it one final chance and found the jazzy piano that Vince Guaraldi had written and recorded for "A Charlie Brown Christmas."

That last one brought a tear to her eye and made her bite her lip. She swore and punched the power button off, furious at her father for allowing her the bittersweet memories of her childhood and then tainting them with years of awkwardness and misunderstanding.

She stood leaning against the bookshelf, forehead resting against the smooth wood, and was in that very position when, a moment later, she heard the slow, purposeful crunch of tires rolling over snow. Sara glanced out the window to see a police car pull into the driveway and stop.

Jackson Norris climbed out of the driver's seat.

Relief swept through her, but then she saw the expression on the sheriff's face and she knew he had not come with good news. His features were as rigid as a mannequin's, yet sympathetic.

Her blood ran cold as she went to the door and opened it, watching Jackson come up the front walk.

"Sara," the sheriff said when he saw her there. " 'Morning."

Jackson Norris was a competent sheriff for the most part, but Sara had always wondered just how smart the man was. When he declined to wish her "Merry Christmas" or even "good morning," though, Sara had all the proof she would ever need that the sheriff was no fool. Only a sadist or a fool would have wished her "Merry Christmas" this morning.

She nodded toward him, standing silhouetted in the doorway, blinking from the glare of the sun streaming across the perfectly blue sky. Somewhere else, probably nearby, people were enjoying the perfect Christmas weather. Children would be sledding in the new-fallen snow, fathers would be out shoveling.

As it should be on this day of joy.

"Jackson," Sara said, nodding to the sheriff. "You have news?"

Down the street a couple walking their dog had stopped to chat with a neighbor who was behind the wheel of a minivan. They were far enough that she couldn't have heard what was said, but she saw the way they pointed in her direction, expressions full of pity.

She resisted the urge to scream.

The sheriff shifted his weight from one foot to the other, glanced over his shoulder at the whisperers, and nodded toward the home's interior.

"Maybe we ought to talk inside?"

"Oh," she said, voice small. Sara shook her head. "I'm sorry. Yes, please come in. I'm just … not myself."

She stood back to let him pass and closed the door behind him.

" 'Course you're not. Don't worry about it," the sheriff said. He scratched at the back of his head and glanced around as though expecting someone to be there.

Maybe he's just not used to being here when Dad's not home, Sara thought. Or perhaps it might have been that Jackson Norris wasn't accustomed to making social calls at the Halliwell residence in recent years.

"Can I get you something?" she asked, slipping her hands into the soft cotton pockets in her pajama pants to keep them from fluttering about. "Water? Cran-apple juice? I'd offer you some coffee, but there's nothing here I'd serve my worst enemy."

The sheriff managed a wan smile. "No, thanks. I only stopped by for a minute. Wanted to check on you. I can imagine how hard this day is going to be, and I just wanted to remind you that you're not alone. I'm here if you need me."

Numb, Sara nodded. "I appreciate it."

But Jackson Norris wasn't in any hurry to leave. He frowned.

"What is it, Sheriff? You've got a lead on my father? What's on your mind?"

Jackson shook his head. "No. Nothing on your dad. It could be nothing, honestly, but ... well, I thought you should know we've had another Oliver Bascombe sighting. If Ted's disappearance really is connected to the Bascombe case, finding this guy could give us some answers."

She forced herself not to hope.

"Where is he? Where did they find him?"

The sheriff couldn't meet her eyes then. "Austria. I know it sounds crazy. First London, then Scotland, now Austria. He's not technically a suspect in anything, just a 'person of interest.' They put a watch on all of his credit cards and got a bunch of hits on his American Express. Figured they had him on the hook then, had all the credit companies freeze his cards. Now that they knew where he was, they didn't want him going anywhere else. Next time he tried to use his credit card, it didn't go so well. Bascombe took off, apparently. But the clerk picked out a photo of him, so it wasn't just some thief trying to use his card. It was the real deal.

"They're going to track him down, Sara. Get some answers."

For several moments she breathed in and out through her teeth, a sick twisting in her stomach making her fear she might throw up. With difficulty she nodded and thanked the sheriff for coming, for caring.

"You'll let me know when they've got him?"

"Of course. The very moment," he assured her.

Then he was gone. Sara stood in the open door and watched him pull out of the driveway and roll off down the street, tires slushing on the road. She stayed there for half a minute, until at last she retreated into her father's house once more.

Seeking solace, Sara went to the radio again and turned it on. A pleasant version of "God Rest Ye Merry Gentlemen" was in progress, harmonies lush and lilting.

At the sofa, she sat and held between two fingers the unopened card she'd written to her father. For a time she carried it around, setting it on the mantel or the lamp stand or on top of the television, somewhere he was likely to discover it in his wanderings around the house.

As if it were that large . . . as if he had just become lost in his own home.

So much remained unsaid between them and she desperately wished for a chance to fix that.

The phone rang, startling her, and she stared at it as though it were some exotic beast. Who would be calling her father's house on Christmas day that did not already know he had disappeared?

The answering machine picked up the call and she stared across the room, mesmerized by the sound of her own father's voice in the greeting message.

"You've reached the home of Ted Halliwell. Please leave a message."

Simple as that. Uncomplicated. That was her father. Hearing his voice like that lent her a comfort she would never have imagined. When the beep came, her mother's voice took over, leaving a message meant for her, exhorting her to pick up, to call her if there was any news.

As though she would have done anything else.

For now, though, she let her mother talk, let the answering machine deal with her. Ignoring her mother, Sara went to the couch and lay back on it, listening to Christmas carols and wondering.

Waiting.

The Perytons swept down from the sky, eleven strong. Jezi-Baba floated down the steps of the pyramid as though gliding on the wind, but the Manticore was faster. It raced down those high stone stairs practically sliding on its belly, hissing death through rows of needle teeth.

The open plain around the pyramid had become a killing field.

Cheval Bayard stood, paralyzed with uncertainty. The giant tree-like men that had herded them into this clearing stood at the edge of the woods but did not come any further. The bloodred birds that had soared in circles around the top of the pyramid had settled down on its peak.

"Cheval!"

Flinching, she glanced over to see Chorti lumbering up beside her. The wild man gnashed his metal teeth and bared iron claws. It steeled her resolve, having him there. They had fought side by side against marauders and mercenaries—killers all—first to protect their lives and avenge her husband, and then to safeguard Chorti's family home. Always they had prevailed. Scarred and bloody, they had stood at each other's side.

"Fight!" he growled.

She shifted, her bones cracking and stretching as she cast off her human mask and transformed into the kelpy, long horse's legs unfolding beneath her.

At the pyramid, the Manticore leaped the last half-dozen steps and tore across the clearing toward them. Jezi-Baba cackled and began to sway even as the blue-skinned hag floated in the air ... then she shimmered like a ghost and vanished.

The Borderkind tightened into a battle circle, all of them with their backs to the center. She heard Frost and Blue Jay shout, and a blast of fire shot into the air. Li, the Guardian of Fire, had begun the war.

A green blur dashed from the sky. The Grindylow tried to bat it away, but the Peryton sank its claws into him. Grin shouted in pain as the thing carried him up into the sky, blood spattering the ground below. The Grindylow swore loudly, roared in pain, and beat at the Hunter, but then Cheval lost sight of them amidst the angry swarming of the Perytons.

Leicester Grindylow was gone.

Another Peryton dipped from the sky. Cheval launched a kick at it. Her hoof glanced off of its body with a crack of bone, but the Peryton kept flying, baring its long black talons. Its antlers hung heavily upon its head and the sharp prongs lowered.

Chorti thundered across the ground and leaped, barreling into the Hunter as it flew toward her. The Peryton and the wild man rolled in the grass and dirt. The Atlantean beat him with its wings, trying to gouge him with its antlers. Chorti's metal claws flashed in the sunlight as he struck out, razors scoring antlers and flesh. One of the Hunter's antlers snapped off and the taut skin of its head tore, gashed to the bone.

Then it shook Chorti off and leaped upward, wings carrying it skyward again.

The defensive circle had shattered. All around Cheval the Borderkind were at war, the Perytons screaming unintelligibly, green-feathered wings blotting out the sun.

As one, Cheval and Chorti moved together, eyes turned to the sky. "Well done, my friend," Cheval said.

She spared a glance at him and saw the smile that split his savage features, revealing those shining metal fangs. Proud of himself, pleased by her praise.

The Manticore struck from behind, careening into Chorti and driving him down. The impact drew a cry of pain from the wild man. One of his arms lay trapped beneath him and with the other he flailed behind him, trying to dislodge the weight of the Manticore. But the thing's ferocious speed was too much.

Half on top of Chorti, weight pressing him down, the Manticore opened its maw so that its nearly human face unhinged. Its jaws snapped open, impossibly wide, and it thrust downward. Rows of razor teeth closed upon the back of Chorti's head like a sprung trap, and the Manticore bit off the rear of his skull, wrenching away skin, bone, and brain. The beast threw its head back and gulped it all down.

Cheval could only stare as it took a second taste, nesting its muzzle in the open back of her friend's skull, sucking and gnawing at the viscera there.

All the will and strength went out of her. This simply could not be. Then it turned on her.

Her flesh seemed to shift of its own accord. Cheval transformed again, taking on the human form that so captivated men and women alike. The river was so close. She could smell it, could practically feel the water enveloping her. If only she might reach it she knew that she would be safe, and some instinct told her that she might distract the Manticore with this change.

It *did* hesitate and sniff the air.

Cheval quivered in terror, about to bolt.

The Manticore smiled. Its teeth were stained with Chorti's gore. At the sight, grief closed in around her, oppressive and terrible. In some way, having Chorti at her side had kept her from feeling the loss of her husband as keenly as she would have otherwise. Trusting him, having faith in him, she had never been alone.

Now he was gone.

Cowards run, she thought. *Chorti would not have run.*

With a harpy's shriek she ran at the Manticore, about to change once again. In her mind's eye she could see herself shifting forms, kicking out with her hooves, knocking the beast back and trampling it until its bones were powder.

A shadow blotted out the sun above them. Both Cheval and the Manticore glanced up to see green feathers plummeting toward them.

But the Peryton did not spread its wings, did not swoop in for the kill. It struck the ground with a sickening, wet thump, and only then did Cheval see the figure with which it had been struggling, the hugely muscled creature that had pinned the Peryton's wings and ridden it down from the sky.

Leicester Grindylow rose from the Peryton's corpse.

The Manticore turned toward Grin, baring its fangs, about to lunge. In the same breath, Cheval *shifted,* transforming, and lashed out with her hooves. She struck the Manticore in its side, knocking it sprawling on the ground. Quick to recover, it rose painfully, injured just enough to take away some of its ferocious speed.

The monster was not fast enough. It crouched to lunge at Cheval.

Grin jumped upon it from behind, wrapped his obscenely long, sleek arms around its neck, and twisted, tearing the Manticore's head from its body.

CHAPTER 16

i knelt in the grass beside his tiger. The creature shuddered, her damp eyes locked upon his own, as her heat and blood ran out and soaked into the earth. The tiger's eyes held no fear, only sadness.

The charred remains of two Perytons lay upon scorched earth not far from where Li knelt with his loyal beast. Perhaps a dozen feet further, the Black Devil lay upon the ground, eyes glassy and still. The tiger had killed it, but received terrible wounds in return. The Black Devil's throat had been torn open and already flies buzzed around the wound. A single insect began to circle above Li's tiger and the Guardian of Fire glared at it, flames spilling from his eyes and incinerating the fly instantly.

A horrid chuffing noise began to come from the tiger's throat.

"No," Li whispered, in the ancient language of his kin. "Do not go, my friend."

The little man ran his hands over the tiger's fur, felt the soft velvet and the heat of the animal's body, felt her tremble in pain and confusion. Tears began to slide down Li's cheeks, liquid fire that dripped upon the ground. The grass began to burn. The fire from his blazing tears spread, but he willed it away from his friend.

The tiger grimaced, black lips pulled back from her bloodstained teeth, and then went still, chest compressing as she exhaled her final breath. In a single moment, the light in her eyes vanished and they became glazed and dull.

Li felt her heart cease its beating. He bent over the tiger and embraced her, but made no more effort to keep the fire away from her remains. Fiery tears spilled upon her and her fur began to burn. Liquid fire spread quickly, engulfing both of them.

With a scream to ancient gods, Li stood and turned to seek out more of the Hunters, to destroy those responsible. His ears were full of the roar and crackle of the flames that raged around his fists and engulfed his upper arms. Fire spilled from his eyes and jetted from his nose, and when he screamed it erupted from his open mouth.

But he was diminished now, both in power and in spirit. The passing of the tiger had leeched so much from him that he felt old and weak. The fire that blazed within him still burned, but had lost some of its heat.

Still, he was a warrior. And the fire in his heart cried out for vengeance.

Off to his left he saw Cheval and Grin attacking a fallen Peryton. Above him, a blur of deeper blue spun across the sky, and green feathers floated down with a rain of Peryton blood. Li ignored them both. Ahead of him, Frost struggled with one of the Atlantean Hunters. He had managed to tear one of its wings off, but the winter man was out of his element here. The heat of Yucatazca weakened him. He ought to have been able to kill one Peryton with ease, but Frost had managed barely to root himself to the ground and now he grappled with the Hunter.

The Peryton slashed at Frost with its talons, gouging ice. Frost hissed in anger and pain and reached up, fingers wrapping around the Hunter's antlers. The ice of his hands spread, quickly weighing down the Peryton. It bent under the weight of the ice and its own antlers. The creature shouted and thrashed its body, cracking the ice that had formed upon it, shattering Frost's fingers.

The winter man did not so much as moan. Instead, he formed what remained of his left hand into a single dagger of ice and, with all his strength, impaled the Peryton upon it. The Hunter shrieked and bled, then died.

The last of the creatures shouted in fury as it dove from the sky toward Frost, intent upon his death.

Li screamed in return, a battle cry filled with all of his love for the tiger and all of his grief at her loss. The Guardian of Fire felt flame burst from him as though some volcanic explosion had come from his hands and his heart. Never again would he burn so brightly or with such heat as he had—he had lost a part of himself—and perhaps his command of the flames had lessened, but still he was the Guardian of Fire.

The last of the Perytons crashed to the ground in flames, twitching and dying.

The winter man felt weighted down with sorrow and frustration. He'd had enough of fighting, enough of death. Jack Frost had never been a warrior, but he had not been given a choice. That he had discovered himself quite capable of such horror provided little comfort.

The pyramid stood still and silent and Frost glanced toward it to see if any more enemies would emerge. But nothing stirred there save the bloodred birds that now took flight. He paused to see if they would attack, but they only circled, carrion birds above a field of battle, awaiting their meal.

Though the Minata-Karaia, those bizarre treelike creatures, still watched from the edge of the forest, they made no attempt to attack. The Perytons had been slain.

Grin and Cheval dragged Chorti's broken corpse between them toward the blazing pyre Li had made of his tiger. Cheval, bent with grief, cast a pleading, hollow-eyed glance at Li, who nodded once, simply. As Grin helped her heft the wild man's shaggy, blood-matted remains into the fire, Frost saw that half of his skull had been sheared away.

Had he been able to spare even a bit of water, the winter man might have wept.

He staggered toward Li, but did not dare go too near to the Guardian of Fire while the other Borderkind's hands and eyes still burned. Li looked pale as ash, and his flesh was spotted with places where the skin glowed like fireplace embers. Something had happened when his tiger had died, changing Li and the fire inside him, weakening both flame and flesh.

Even so, the heat from within him rippled from his flesh in waves, shimmering in the air, and the winter man kept his distance. He'd had enough of heat.

When night fell, Frost would be better. The sun plagued him. The river water would be cool and could replenish him for a time, but not yet.

A small blue bird flew down from the sky and alighted by his feet. For a moment it hesitated as though wishing it might rest, but then the bird spun into a blue-streaked cyclone and, a moment later, Blue Jay stood beside Frost. The trickster gave him a mournful look and then slipped his hands into the pockets of his jeans.

"You'll be all right?" Blue Jay asked, glancing down at Frost's shattered hands.

The winter man nodded.

One by one, the surviving Borderkind began to walk toward the pyramid, while the silent Minata-Karaia watched, the air filled with the quiet whistle of the wind through their hollow heads. The pyramid was not their destination, however.

At the base of the pyramid's steps—steps high enough that they must have been built to be scaled by a god—a ball of black flame burned. The ebon fire flickered in the air, tendrils rising a dozen feet from the ground. Within the black flames, two figures stood rigid as flies trapped in amber.

Frost and Blue Jay reached the sphere of darkness only a moment before Grin and Cheval stepped up to it on the other side. Li joined them an instant later, the flames around his hands having subsided, though fire still danced in his furious eyes, and those ember patches still flared upon his pale skin.

Black as it was, enough light passed through the circle of flames that they could identify the figures within. The Mazikeen had his long, slender fingers wrapped around the throat of the witch, Jezi-Baba. Her neck was broken and her head lolled to one side, yet even in death she killed him, her blue-skinned hands buried to the wrist in his chest. A rictus grin split her features, showing pitted stone teeth and a lunatic's amusement.

"He lives," Blue Jay said, voice low.

They all moved nearer the flames. Though the black fire hissed and crackled like the blaze in a hearth, no heat came from it. Rather, it felt cold as the first snow of winter.

The Mazikeen's eyes moved. The sorcerer glanced at each of them in turn, even as the black flame began to consume his flesh. His robes burned with it.

"Go," the Mazikeen said. "My brothers will find you."

Yet, even with his urging, they stood and watched him burn. Frost had begun to think that the black fire had been Jezi-Baba's magic, but the moment the fire engulfed the Mazikeen's face, the witch's entire body disintegrated, crumbling to blue-black ash.

For a long moment he said nothing. At length he turned and surveyed the grim, mournful faces of his comrades, his kin.

"We must head for Palenque with all speed. Other Hunters will come soon."

Cheval stared at him, shaking her head. "No. Can't you see that you're only leading us all to our deaths? This is madness. We cannot hope to succeed when so many stand against us."

Her hands trembled and she cast her gaze downward, swiping at the tears that began to slip down her face. "You're only killing us faster than the Hunters would have. There's nothing left now. We should find somewhere to hide. Let someone else fight them—"

Frost did not take a step nearer or make a gesture. He only spoke one word.

"Who?"

Cheval flinched, raised her chin, and stared at him defiantly. Her features were taut with sorrow. "We cannot—"

"If not us, then who?" the winter man demanded. "I know you

mourn, Cheval. Perhaps you do not have it within your heart to continue. You wish, now, to do nothing but crawl into a cave and hide, but I tell you this: the Hunters will not stop. You might live longer in hiding, but when the rest of us have fallen, they will come for you, too. And then Chorti will have died for nothing."

Cheval glared at him.

Frost turned and strode toward the river, needing the cool water to sustain himself. It would not return him to his full strength, but it was the best he could hope for here.

One by one, the surviving Borderkind followed, their fallen comrades still burning on the battlefield behind them. Cheval Bayard came last, but then hurried to catch up to the others.

The bloodred birds descended.

The Borderkind did not look back.

Oliver could not breathe. The ambassador's daughter slept on in her floral canopy bed. The two-year-old's gentle breathing was the only sound in the room save for the eerie scratch of sand eddying across the floor in an unnatural breeze. Kitsune's body stretched languorously against his, warm and pulsing with the beat of her heart, but he sensed that even she now held her breath.

In the center of the room stood a tall figure in a black bowler hat and a dark woven greatcoat with a high collar. Its hem nearly reached the floor. The figure had tombstone-gray flesh and a thick, drooping mustache. There was about him the sense that this was a man from another age, a time past. His hands were overlarge, the fingers long and slender and somehow *wrong*. When he moved them, as he did now, raising one to point a stern finger at them, grains of dust sifted off his hands, falling to the ground.

"You are trespassing," the Dustman said, his voice deep and sonorous, with an edge of gravel.

Oliver swallowed, his throat dry and tight. "Yes, we know. But with good reason."

He would have gone on, but Kitsune held up a hand to silence him. She turned, slowly pulling her legs beneath her, and bowed low in a manner more customary in the land of her own legend than in that of the Dustman. His English accent was clear.

"We beg your pardon, sir," Kitsune said. "We do not wish to incur your wrath, only to have a few moments' discourse."

Beneath the rim of his bowler, the Dustman's eyes glittered like stars; pinpoint white amidst deepest black. He raised both hands and dust sprinkled to the floor, where it began to swirl upward, raising a cloud that reached toward them as though he were a puppeteer holding its strings.

"Wait. Stop!" Oliver said, voice rasping in panic even as he tried not to wake the little girl. "Just talk to us. What harm will it do? The Borderkind are being slaughtered. She's here as your kin, not your enemy. Do you really want to help the Hunters finish the job?"

The Dustman cocked his head to one side and regarded them both. Cold radiated from him, and Oliver shivered.

On her bed, the ambassador's daughter began to stir. She reached a tiny hand up to rub the sleep grit from her yet unopened eyes. Oliver and Kitsune fell completely still, but the Dustman gestured toward her and a tendril of the dust that swirled around his feet reached out toward her, breezed past her face, and the girl's arm slid down. She did not stir again, and her breathing grew deeper.

"Continue," the Dustman said. He slid his hands into the pockets of his jacket, an oddly human gesture. But the more Oliver looked at him, the less human he seemed. The Dustman did not breathe. The air that he expelled with his words was a breeze through a hollow cavern, and when he turned his head, the substance of him, flesh and mustache and hat and coat, shifted like sand.

"May we rise?" Kitsune asked.

Oliver studied her. The subservient tone was quite unlike her, but he saw the spark of something in her gleaming jade eyes, a dark, calculating intelligence. It ought not have surprised him. She was a trickster and had a great deal at stake here—not only on Oliver's behalf, but her own as well. When Collette had been rescued, the Dustman might make a powerful ally in the war against the Hunters.

The Dustman nodded, glittering eyes eclipsed for a moment by his hat brim. Oliver let out a tiny breath of relief to be spared his attention even for that moment.

"Tell me your tale," he said in that gravel voice. "Whispers have reached me about the Hunters, but I would know more."

So Kitsune and Oliver began, taking the story in turns. They told the Dustman of the conspiracy to murder the Borderkind, of Oliver's first meeting with Frost and their flight from the Myth Hunters, of the losses and betrayals they had suffered on the road to Perinthia and later to Canna Island, of the death of Professor Koenig and the massacre there. Oliver touched the hilt of the Sword of Hunyadi to illustrate the tale, but he made no attempt to draw the blade for fear the Dustman would misinterpret the gesture.

They spoke of Twillig's Gorge and the allies and enemies found there.

Most important, they spoke of the Sandman, the gruesome killing spree the creature had embarked upon, the murder of Oliver's father, and the abduction of Collette. When the Dustman inquired as to why Oliver and his sister had been targeted, silence reigned. They had no answers, only overheard conversations and suspicions.

"The king of Euphrasia has given me a year to prove my worth," Oliver whispered, glancing from time to time at the door, at the sleeping girl, at Kitsune, anything to avoid the narrow eyes of the Dustman. "I hope to convince the king of Yucatazca to do the same. But I can't worry about saving my own life when I don't know what's become of my sister."

Oliver paused. The Dustman stared at him with those eyes, that gray, shifting skin. Perhaps it was the bowler and the coat, or perhaps the mustache gave the disguise its success, but he realized now he had been speaking to the creature as though it were a man, a human being.

The embassy creaked. Radiator pipes ticked. Outside the windows, the Austrian night remained lit with the diffuse color of Christmas lights, but the darkness seemed to gather closer. In the small hours of the night, nothing moved.

He glanced at Kitsune, thinking she would continue, but the fox-woman only watched the Dustman, pulling her fur cloak more tightly around her as though she might at any moment disappear into the copper-red fur and run for the door.

The Dustman shifted again, took two steps toward them. He moved his shoulders and the high collar of his greatcoat seemed to hide much of his face.

"And somehow you believe I will help you?" he rasped, dust swirling around him, scratching the floor. "A human and a trickster, and you would ask me to ally myself with you against the Sandman, a facet of my own legend? My brother? You wish me to destroy my own brother?"

Kitsune sneered, lips curling back to reveal those small, sharp teeth. "He murders children, tears out their eyes. Were he a facet of my legend, it would shame me."

The Dustman shuddered, the grains of sand and grit that made up his form shifting, and he slid his hands from his pockets, pointing at her.

"You dare much, fox."

Oliver's heart thundered in his chest, but on the outside he felt a strange calm settle over him. He stepped between Kitsune and the Dustman.

"The Hunters will come for you soon enough," Oliver said, even as the dust eddied around his shoes, cold and rough as sandpaper. This creature could scour the flesh from his bones, but there was no turning back now. "You're Borderkind. Do you really think they won't come for you? They'll kill you. And your brother is working with them. He's already chosen, and he's sided against you."

The embassy continued to creak, but this time it seemed like more than the ordinary settling of time and weight and temperature and wind. Oliver glanced at Kitsune and saw that she had begun to sniff the air. After a moment, she turned to him, alarm lighting her eyes.

"We should go."

Oliver silently refused. He stared at the Dustman, waiting. The figure regarded him in return, pinpoint-star eyes glittering. Then, with a sound like the hiss of sand through an hourglass, the Dustman smiled and reached up to touch the brim of his bowler, a gesture of courtesy and acceptance.

He strode to the little girl's bed and ducked beneath the floral awning. Dust sifting around his feet, he slid long fingers inside the girl's pillowcase and his hand moved around, searching for something there. In a moment he withdrew a single small white feather, goose down from the pillow.

The Dustman handed the pillow feather to Oliver.

"Hold this and call for me, and I shall come."

Oliver took the feather, staring up at the imposing figure, entranced by the grain of his face, at the apparent reality of the fabric of his hat and coat. He wanted to ask for clarification, to be certain that the creature had truly agreed to help him.

But a strong breeze eddied across the floor again and the Dustman disintegrated before his eyes, slipping away, blowing beneath the bed and through the crack under the door. In seconds, he was gone.

For a moment, Oliver stared at the feather, then he put it into the right-hand pocket of his jeans with the single large seed he still had from his encounter with the gods of the Harvest.

"Oliver," Kitsune whispered.

On the bed, the girl began to stir again.

"We must go."

Gently, Kitsune opened the door and peered out into the hall. She glanced back at him and nodded, then the two of them moved quietly out of the girl's bedroom, leaving the door open.

They had reached the top of the stairs when the girl called out in a sleepy voice for her mother. Oliver froze and looked at Kit, who nodded curtly, urging him to hurry. He started down the stairs, wishing his own tread was as silent as the fox-woman's.

"Martina?" came a voice from the hall above. The ambassador's wife, come to check on their little girl.

Oliver cursed to himself and slid his hand along the banister, stealth now far more important than speed. Kitsune reached the bottom of the stairs ahead of him and vanished.

At the bottom step, Oliver paused. The hair on the back of his neck prickled and he turned to look back up the way they'd come.

A woman in a long cotton nightdress stood at the top of the stairs, staring down at him with her mouth open in shock and fear. She said something in German, a question, then repeated it.

Then she began to shout.

Oliver bolted, no longer taking care to tread lightly. He barreled through the embassy, glancing ahead and over his shoulder with every step, waiting for a guard to appear and put a bullet in his head. The sword banged against his hip as he ran.

In the small office where they had entered the building, Kitsune waited. Voices shouted after him now—male voices—and as he swung himself into the office, holding on to the door frame, a gunshot punctured the air, echoing through the whole building. The sound alone made Oliver feel as though he were a target and he tried to shrink in on himself. Another shot came, and a bullet struck the open door behind him as he ran into the room.

Kitsune dove through the window, heedless of any injury that might await outside. Oliver had only a moment to debate attempting the same, and he knew that the fall was far less likely to kill him than a bullet.

He ran to the window, bent low, and slid his torso over the frame. At the last moment, even as his body careened out the window, he gripped the window frame and flipped forward, so that he did not fall into the alley headfirst. Oliver had gone over chain-link fences the same way as a boy, but boyhood was far behind him now, and the move was far from smooth. He sprawled onto the pavement, skinning his palms and scraping his right knee, the denim tearing. The metal scabbard clattered when it struck the ground, but the sword remained in place.

Adrenaline and terror propelled him forward, staggering to his feet even as he kept up his momentum. His hands were bright with pain, but it felt far away and unimportant.

Kitsune stepped from the shadows and grabbed his wrist. For a moment he'd thought she had left him behind. Now they raced down the alley together, behind the embassy and then between two other buildings. Oliver felt like an idiot. If he'd been running on his own he would have gone back the way they'd come, right past the front doors, and probably been shot dead in the street.

There were shouts and the staccato footfalls of their pursuers, but there were no more gunshots, and soon they had left even that behind in the narrow back alleys of Vienna. The police would be out in force soon, searching for them, but the guards at the British embassy had no jurisdiction to shoot people in the streets of the Austrian capital.

Oliver had long since lost track of their location when Kitsune led him around a corner and he saw the Danube churning by only a hundred yards away.

Slowly, catching her breath, she took his hand again and together they walked to the riverbank. The darkness still clung to the sky, but night would soon be over and Christmas day would dawn. The river raced by, the current powerful, but even so, it was cold enough that ice had formed along its edges, drifting and breaking and spinning on the water.

Kitsune smiled at him, tugging him toward the river.

Then Oliver understood. He stopped, trying to pull her back. "Kit, no. It's freezing."

"Public space, remember?" she said. "Do you know Vienna well enough to find us a place to cross through the Veil before dawn, before the police catch up with us?"

Oliver sighed. "You know I don't."

Kitsune raised her hood, jade eyes gleaming in the dark. "I'll keep you warm," she said.

Together, they leaped into the Danube, and through the Veil.

Oliver lay in a shallow creek, barely more than a trickle, his clothes soaked through from splashing into the Danube. Back on the mundane side of the Veil—the place he thought of less and less as his own world—it had still been dark, the sky that pure indigo of the hour before dawn. But in the realm of the legendary, it was midday and the sun shone, drawing rich colors out of the landscape. Trees seemed remarkably green, the sky extraordinarily blue, and the coppery fur of Kitsune's cloak a brighter red than ever before.

It occurred to Oliver that perhaps this sharpness of color, the vividness of the world around him, might well be an aftereffect of the exultant feeling of escaping with his life. If so, he appreciated that there was at least one benefit to their circumstances.

The air felt cool, the water outright cold, yet he lay there and shivered, feeling the stones beneath him, even through his clothes, and the little rivulets that streamed around him.

Oliver let his head loll to one side and glanced at Kitsune. She shook herself, water spraying from her fur cloak. The absurdity of it and the exultation of their escape must have touched her as well. Giddy, they began to laugh.

"That ... was a close one," Oliver managed.

Kitsune sighed, corners of her lips still turned up in a broad smile. The sun lit her features so that it seemed she had her own internal luminescence.

"Far too close. When you finally get all of your troubles sorted out and go home, you're going to have quite a time explaining yourself."

Oliver's laughter died. Thoughts of home led to thoughts of Julianna, and he stared at Kitsune—her beauty painful to regard—and any trace of humor died.

"What is it?" she asked, still lying there beside him in the small brook.

"I'm not sure what 'home' even is anymore," he said, surprising himself with the honesty of his answer. "After all of this, I don't know what'll be left to go back to. If Julianna's gone ..."

His time with the Borderkind had irrevocably altered him. There was no denying that. And with all that had happened, there were a great many people who had questions for him that he would find impossible to answer. Trouble waited for him back in his world. But his house, his childhood home, that waited as well. And his job. His friends.

But without Julianna, none of that mattered.

Kitsune reached out until her fingertips grazed his, the water rushing over their hands. "Then don't go back."

Oliver stared at her, letting her fingers play against his.

"I love her, you know," he said softly.

Her eyes narrowed and she pulled away. Tendrils of her hair streamed in the brook, and as she lifted her head, water dripped and ran down her cloak, which glistened with droplets.

"Yes," she said. "I know."

"And I'll find her."

Kitsune moved away from the brook a few paces and thrust out her tongue as though using it to test the wind—or taste the wind. Oliver watched the stiffness in her manner, the formality that seemed to have returned to her every gesture, and he rose from the brook in a cascade of water and regret.

He had survived this long partly due to Kitsune's help. Had she not accompanied him, he surely would have been long since dead. But for the first time he began to think that it would be best if he and Kit parted ways. Traveling with her clouded his mind, when he desperately needed focus.

To think he didn't have a home to go back to—that was pure foolishness. When Collette had been in the midst of her divorce and things had gotten ugly, both financially and personally, she'd called the process triage. In catastrophic circumstances, doctors had to make hard decisions, focusing first on the patients who were horribly injured, but not so far gone that they were likely to die even with treatment.

You saved what you could, one problem at a time.

Oliver knew that his homecoming would be problematic when the time came, but between then and now he had to do triage. Save Collette. Save himself. Help the Borderkind if he could. Then get himself home to Julianna and whatever else awaited him.

So, much as he hated the chill that had just descended between himself and Kitsune, Oliver only followed as she walked away.

For nearly an hour they wandered across fields and along cart paths lined with delicate-looking trees and low shrubs with tiny leaves. Kitsune seemed unsure of their direction, but Oliver dared not question. At length they came to a small settlement not large enough even to warrant the word village. Most of the dwellings appeared to be temporary, some no more than tents. Herds of sheep and cows grazed freely on the surrounding hills, not penned but guarded by shepherds with a distinctly eastern aspect. They wore wool vests against the chill, and some had headgear fashioned from fur that reminded Oliver of nothing so much as warriors who would have bowed to the commands of a sultan.

As they made their way into the settlement, men and women alike watched them warily. Oliver saw no weapons, but the Sword of Hunyadi hanging at his hip gave him great comfort.

Kitsune walked ten steps ahead, as though she were his mistress and he some lowly servant. This might have been some affectation for the benefit of their observers, the haughty Borderkind keeping the ordinary man in his place, but Oliver did not think so. The hood of her cloak framed her face, casting her features in shadow so that for once he could not even see the jade gleam of her eyes. He was quite sure this was precisely the effect she desired.

Oliver rested his palm upon the handle of his sword. If she wished for him to appear as though he was some servant or bodyguard, he would. The mid-afternoon shadow stretched before him, making a pantomime of his actions, transforming him into a fierce warrior giant. Yet Oliver knew that shadows were only strange contortions of the truth.

After they had passed through the entire encampment, Kitsune waited on the far side. Oliver thought for a moment she was waiting for him, but then an old woman emerged from one of the large tents and began to shamble toward them, accompanied by a pair of men in horned fur caps. These two carried spears, the first weapons he'd seen.

Kitsune and the old woman greeted one another in a sharp-edged language Oliver did not understand. The nomadic matriarch studied Kit warily as they spoke, and after a few moments, the fox-woman nodded her head in apparent gratitude and then started off again, this time at an angle that would take them past a herd of sheep and into the sunless shade of those delicate, unfamiliar trees.

For a moment, Oliver stared at the nomad woman and her two guards, with their grim eyes and pointed beards.

"Good-bye, Mischief," the old woman said quietly, staring at Kitsune's back as the Borderkind strode away from the encampment.

She'd spoken English. Oliver wanted to know what she'd meant and started to ask, even as the woman turned and made her way back to her tent, the guards at her sides. One of them raised his spear in both hands, hardly paying attention to Oliver and yet menacing him with its point at the same time.

Feeling the fool, he glanced back and forth from one retreating woman to the other, and at last hurried to catch up with Kitsune. As she passed the sheep, the creatures bleated and milled away from her. The sight disconcerted Oliver for a moment, until he realized that of course sheep would shy away from a fox wearing the skin of a woman.

His throat felt dry.

Two wizened old shepherds muttered to themselves as they caught up with their charges. Oliver felt he ought to apologize, but what could he say that they would understand? Instead he hurried on and at last caught up with Kitsune at the top of the slope, just as she stepped into the shade of those strange trees, which looked to him like giant bonsais.

"What did she say?" Oliver asked.

His eyes were still adjusting and in that moment Kitsune existed merely as a hooded outline in the shade. Then Oliver blinked, and the rich color of her fur came into focus. From beneath the hood she gazed at him without malice. A sadness lingered in her features, but otherwise she was only Kitsune, his friend and companion, the only one who had stuck with him.

"The Orient Road is near now. My instincts were correct. We're less than an hour's walk from it. By nightfall, we should reach the stone circle where there is an entrance to the Winding Way."

"But you still don't think I'll be able to walk the Winding Way."

Kitsune cocked her head. "We shall see. Though, yes, to my knowledge, only the legendary can travel that way."

She waited for him to say more, but Oliver feared opening his mouth just then. If he did, he could only say something that would hurt her more. Or, conversely, betray Julianna further than he already had. Neither option appealed to him, so he kept silent.

Kitsune turned and started off through the trees, and soon they found themselves on a narrow trail that led up the hill, across sun-splashed clearings and through copses of trees. On the other side of the hill the land stretched out in a long plain that descended so gradually it could barely be considered a slope.

They walked in silence, so that it seemed to Oliver much more than an hour before they reached the Orient Road. When at last it came into sight, a broad avenue of hard-packed dirt, he saw beyond it a long, rough-hewn post-and-beam fence, and within those confines a handful of tall, proud horses—the largest horses he had ever laid eyes upon.

In the distance, to the east, the road wound toward a mountain range whose snow-capped peaks scraped the heavens. The mountains were far away, but even from here Oliver could make out some kind of long, rambling structure that ran along the edge of a steep cliff. Its isolation and formidable construction made him think it a fortress, but then he thought again, studying its location.

"A monastery?" he asked.

Kitsune glanced at him. "Yes. There are many to the east. It is a quieter life."

She said nothing more, but Oliver felt a great weight lifted from him as they continued on together. Along the way they passed several dwellings and an aged, rickety wagon, with peeling paint and a broken wheel, abandoned on the roadside.

When they came upon a small shrine on the side of the road—really no more than a rabbit hutch full of candles, painted tiles, and small jade figures—Kitsune paused and bowed her head in a silent moment. Respectfully, Oliver did the same. Though he had no idea to what or whom he appealed, he prayed for his sister's life, for the Borderkind's fate, and for his safe return home.

After a moment, Oliver just stood and watched Kitsune.

"The old nomad woman spoke English," he said when she looked up. "Just after you walked off, she said good-bye, but she called you a different name. I can't help thinking if she spoke English, it was for my benefit."

Kitsune gazed at him. "What did she call me?"

"Mischief."

The fox-woman laughed softly, shaking her head. Oliver swallowed, his chest strangely tight.

"Why did she call you that?" he asked.

Kitsune gave him a sidelong glance. "You know my kin and I are called tricksters, Oliver. Mischief is what we are."

"See, that's what I thought, too. But if I think about all of the people I've met since crossing through the Veil, the tricksters are the only ones who really seem to be what they appear to be. No bullshit."

"At the moment, true enough," Kitsune replied. "With all that the Borderkind are suffering of late, there is little call for mischief."

CHAPTER 17

K itsune did not try to take Oliver's hand as they forged ahead along the Orient Road, but she seemed more at ease.

Oliver was grateful. Now that they were on their way again—and with a promise of help from the Dustman—his thoughts were centered on Collette and the monster who had abducted her. His mind worried about the conflict that lay at the end of their travels and its outcome. Finding Collette was only the beginning.

For hours they walked, passing through a small village where the rice harvest was under way and a larger town whose buildings had a distinctly Asian flair. The geography on this side of the Veil might be quite different from that of the other, but clearly this region's Lost Ones and legends corresponded in some way to Asia.

In time, the fields and hills gave way to a tangled forest, and the Orient Road became narrower and more rutted. Several times it snaked to the left or right without any apparent topographical necessity. As the late afternoon shadows grew longer, they saw through the trees a broad expanse of silver lake, its mirror surface reflecting back the beauty of the forest and the sun where it hung low in the sky.

The lake seemed perfectly still, as though it were a sheet of ice. That reminded Oliver of Frost, but he quickly pushed such ruminations away. Questions about the winter man's friendship and loyalty—about his motivations—had plagued him since Twillig's Gorge, but entertaining them now would be a distraction he could ill afford.

The road curved around the lake, and on the far side the giant bonsai forest—as he had begun to think of it—thickened once more. They strode past a knot of thick trees that leaned in over the road, and then came to a clearing.

Since the moment that Kitsune had mentioned the stone circle they were meant to seek, Oliver had held a vague impression of Stonehenge in his mind. But this was no feat of ancient architecture. These stones were as black and smooth as onyx and jutted from the earth as if they had grown there, like the teeth of some giant, burrowing beast attempting to eat its way to the surface.

Each of the black stones had grown tall, but not uniformly so. The largest stood perhaps twenty feet in height, the shortest a dozen. The circle they formed was uneven, yet still undoubtedly a circle, placed that way with some purpose. The gaps between stones were as little as a few inches in some places, and at the widest, no more than two feet.

Flowers grew in clumps amongst the knee-high grass of the clearing, as though the black stones themselves were some sort of shrine or memorial and the flowers had been left by mourners.

Oliver paused at the edge of the road, hesitant to enter the clearing.

"What do you think will happen?" he asked without looking at Kitsune.

"I don't know," the fox-woman replied, her voice soft and, he thought, perhaps even a bit fearful. "But now we find out."

The late afternoon sun still reached fingers of daylight into the clearing, but Oliver shivered as a chill breeze rustled the trees. With a nervous grin he stepped into the clearing, tall grass scritching against the legs of his blue jeans as he walked toward the ebony circle.

Oliver tried to peer between the stones, but there was only shadow there, as though night had already fallen within the circle. He could see that the grass grew in the gaps between the stones, and that heartened him a bit, though he did not know why. What would happen, he wondered, if he was unable to pass through, but Kitsune vanished? Would she be able to come back for him? Would she bother?

Thoughts of Collette steeled him.

Kitsune did not reach out for him, but she took a step past him and cocked her head, looking back curiously. Then she reached up and drew back her hood for the first time since they had come back through the Veil. Despite his fear, he caught his breath just to look at her. Her eyes were kind.

"You must try, Oliver. This will save us days."

He nodded. Collette awaited. The Sandman was also waiting.

Oliver took another step.

As if startled by the motion, a flock of small birds cried out and took off from the tops of several trees at the edge of the clearing, branches waving at the suddenness of their departure.

Something had spooked them.

Oliver glanced at Kitsune and saw that she was sniffing at the air.

"No," he whispered, jaw set tightly. "Not now."

A terrible hiss filled the clearing, resounding off of the stones. Oliver turned, trying to find the source of the echoing sounds, but then he saw that Kitsune's gaze was locked on a spot at the edge of the clearing—at the very same knot of trees that had blocked their view of the stone circle until the last moment.

A creature stood in the shade of those trees, a thing with antlers and green-feathered wings and long, vicious claws. Its features were thin and brutal and its eyes were bright as it stepped into the last of the sunlight and started toward them.

Oliver glanced around. There were others. Of course there were others. Six or seven of the antlered things, each of them terrifying to behold. They carried no weapons, but this troubled Oliver even more than if they had been armed. Their long fingers came to vicious points, and it was clear they needed no other weapon.

Back on the Orient Road, two other figures had appeared from the woods. One was an immense, hunchbacked hag with jaundiced, pustulent skin and a thick mess of gray and black hair. The hag stood at least eight feet high, and she carried a long butcher's knife in each hand, ready to carve.

But she was far from the worst of them. For beside her came the thing responsible for the hissing in the air. It rose and fell, bobbing in the air, and its upper body swayed back and forth. The head was vaguely serpentine, but beneath that it was simply a mass of tentacles that coiled like snakes, turning in upon themselves. Its body was like a tower of vipers, the tentacles lashing out and then curling inward again. It moved across the dusty road without legs, the tentacles dragging and thrusting and dancing it forward.

"Oliver," Kitsune whispered.

From the corner of his eye he saw her raise her hood again. Oliver put his hand on the pommel of his sword, holding his breath.

"You've gone far enough, I think," the hag said.

"Black Annis," Kitsune said, her eyes as cold as her tone. "This is none of your concern. Hunt me another day. We have an errand that will not wait."

The hag crouched lower, the hump on her back more pronounced than ever, and took a step nearer. "*This* errand will not wait."

The tentacled thing roiled toward them, kicking up dust from the road. Oliver stared at it, hating his fear but unable to rise above it. Twisted as she was, the hag at least had human form. The other was unnatural, a nightmare churning forth from his fevered mind.

With a sound like the flap of a flag in high wind, one of the winged Hunters took flight at the edge of the clearing, throwing a dreadful shadow across the grass. The one that had been directly opposite it took flight as well.

"Kit?" Oliver whispered.

The fox-woman did not reply, only stared at Black Annis, then glanced around quickly at the others. He could practically hear her heart pounding, and he saw in her stance that she wanted nothing more than to bolt into the trees and run for her life.

Oliver knew then that they would die here. They stood no chance at all against so many Hunters. Kitsune could drag them across the Veil again, but could she grab him and step through before they attacked? He did not believe so. And from the look of her, she was so frightened that it had not even occurred to her.

I miss you, he thought, images of his sister, and of Julianna, rising in his mind. And he began slowly to draw his sword from its sheath.

He caught his breath. *The Dustman,* he thought. If he could summon the Dustman, at least they would not be alone. The numbers might still be too great, but . . .

And then Oliver realized that there was another alternative.

Leaving his blade sheathed, he reached into his pocket. His fingers pushed aside the feather from the little girl's pillow and he grasped instead the single large seed that the gods of the Harvest had given him what seemed like so very long ago. Promises had been made that day, of help when he needed it.

He could not imagine ever needing it more.

Oliver dropped the seed to the ground. For good measure, he stepped on it, pressing it into the soil.

The ground began to tremble.

The antlered creatures began to close in, but several of them paused and glanced at one another, confused. The two in the air began to swoop downward.

"What have you done?" shrieked the hag.

The hissing of the other Hunter grew so loud it almost drowned out the rumbling of the earth and it darted across the road, propelled by a hundred thick tentacles.

Cornstalks shot up out of the road and wrapped around it, grabbing tentacles one by one and dragging it down. The thing struggled, at war with the cornstalks as they continued to burst up through the hard-packed soil.

Other things grew. Trees and plants came up amongst the grass, only sprouts and saplings one instant and fully grown the next. The Kornbocke himself was there, antlers raised. A low, snarling shape tore itself from a thick crop of cornstalks, and the Kornwolf bounded free.

The appletree man lumbered toward Oliver, taking up a defensive position beside him. Others quickly joined them; elegant women made of bark and thorns; stout little red-faced men who stank of rotting berries; and the king himself, Ahren Konigen, the corn husk man who had given Oliver the seed to begin with. Corn husks lay over the hollows where his eyes ought to be and formed the crown upon his head.

"As good as our word, Oliver Bascombe. These are dark days, and your fight is ours."

The Hunters attacked.

The gods of the Harvest were silent but savage, and blood splattered the grass and the circle of black stones. Oliver drew his sword and raced to stand beside Konigen.

"My sister," Oliver said as one of the antlered things circled above, looking for an angle of attack.

Konigen turned toward him.

"Go, and do what you must," the harvest king said. "It seems to me our troubles are all connected under the surface, roots intertwined."

Oliver nodded. With a single glance around at the furious battle, he spotted Kitsune and raced toward her. Though she surely would have been safer as a fox, she had remained in the shape of a woman, standing and fighting side by side with the gods of the Harvest.

He grabbed her wrist and she spun on him, teeth bared, jaws impossibly wide.

"Kit, stop! Konigen said to go. If they lose, we may not have another chance."

The fox-woman hesitated, jade eyes flashing. Then she shook her wrist loose and ran for the circle of stones. Oliver heard the flap of heavy wings above him, the shadow of a dreadful, antlered thing falling over him, and felt an icy chill grip his heart.

"Fuck that," he snarled, and ran for the circle of onyx stones that thrust up from the clearing, the entrance to the Winding Way, wondering if he would find himself alone amongst the stones, or if their magic would work for him.

"Kill them all, myths and Legend-Born alike!" the hag, Black Annis, screamed nearby.

Oliver glanced back and saw her, slashing at the rotting berry-men as they overwhelmed her. She was splashed with putrid fruit and blood, but they began to draw her down.

"Legend-Born?" he asked, calling after Kitsune as she darted between two towering black stones.

The fox-woman did not look back.

Oliver ran after her and twisted sideways, pushing himself through the narrow gap. He had just a moment to wonder how the battle they had left would end, and to regret abandoning those who had come to his aid, then he plunged into a cloud of thick, gray mist that pulsed and twisted and flowed around him, like something alive.

Ahead, through the mist, he could barely make out Kitsune's presence and, beyond her, a road like a curved ribbon of black glass.

The Winding Way.

Blue Jay's boots squelched in soft, damp earth and water dripped from the feathers tied in his hair as he stepped from the rain forest. The daylight had turned a golden hue, the promise of evening on the horizon. Below, the city of Palenque sprawled across several miles of Yucatazcan valley. He had never been to Palenque. In his mind's eye he had pictured a city that was little more than a series of pyramids like the one where they'd been attacked by Hunters.

He had not expected this.

Already many of the buildings and homes in Palenque had lights burning within, and some of the streets were lined with oil lamps. Towers rose above the skyline, three or four times the height of the average structure. He did not know if they existed for industry or for worship, but they were formidable structures. Homes had been built into the side of a hill at the eastern end of town, rising one upon the other in terraces, each connected by steps and ladders.

The streets were designed in concentric circles, radiating out from the tallest of the towers, which thrust up from the center of Palenque, providing what must have been a breathtaking view of both the city and the hills surrounding it.

The architecture showed myriad influences. Blue Jay had never made a proper study of the subject, but the colors in the stone and the iconic statues that stood as monolithic sentinels at the far edges of the circular city hinted strongly at the Mayan and Aztec past of those who had founded the city and other ancient civilizations. There was a Palenque still in the human world, but Blue Jay felt sure it looked nothing like this.

Leicester Grindylow stepped out of the rain forest and came to stand beside him. The water bogie crossed his long arms and whistled in appreciation.

"She's a beauty," Grin said.

Cheval and Li emerged from the trees as well—each solitary in their grief—with Frost coming along last. The winter man despised the sweltering heat of the rain forest, but at least the moisture helped slow its effects. Now Frost paused on the edge of the hill, not wishing to leave the forest and come into the heat of the waning day. His features were sharp, his body a brittle razor. Blue Jay worried for him, for so many reasons.

Frost started out of the rain forest, beginning the final leg of their journey to Palenque. He moved down the hill toward the outskirts of the city, not even bothering to search the sky for Perytons or glance around for other enemies.

"Watch yourselves," Cheval Bayard said, treading carefully, gliding down the hill, her wary gaze seeking out any sign of trouble.

Grin and Li followed her. The Guardian of Fire had been silent for hours, mourning his dead companion. Whatever physical loss he had suffered because of the tiger's death, it appeared to be permanent. He was pale and thinner, the fire inside him burning through his skin in places, small flames licking across his flesh, unbidden. There was power in him still, but somehow the loss of his tiger had put something off balance inside of him, and the flames seemed to be slowly devouring him from within.

Blue Jay wondered how long it would take for the fire to consume Li completely.

The trickster came last in their procession. Perhaps that was why he was the first to notice the things that flew overhead, slipping out of the rain forest behind them and snaking through the air above them.

"Frost!" Blue Jay shouted.

They all looked up at the alarm in his voice and tracked the progress of the flying things above them. At first, Blue Jay thought the winged serpents were Jaculi, but these creatures were far larger than the one that had spied upon them near Twillig's Gorge.

"Prepare yourselves," Li snapped, opening his arms wide as though to embrace the sky, flickering fire running across his hands and arms all the way to the elbows. It churned in his grasp as though he might sculpt a sword of flame from the air. The patches of burning ember on his skin grew wider, spreading.

Grin took up position beside Li, awaiting an attack. Blue Jay had certainly not been expecting them to be able to enter the city without a fight, but he was tired of fighting, tired of death, tired of the twisted pleasure the Hunters took in their work.

He began to dance, the rhythm of his movements, the precise placement of his feet a gesture of respect to ancient traditions and ancient peoples. As he made his way down the slope, spinning and leaping in that dance, he felt the magic take hold, and the air blurred blue beneath his arms as his mystical wings formed. Whatever these new Hunters were, he would destroy them as quickly as possible, and then move on.

"They are not alone," Cheval Bayard called, her silver hair gleaming in the day's last light. Her eyes were narrow with grim resignation.

Dusk was almost upon them when Blue Jay looked to see what she was talking about. At the base of the hill, just at the outskirts of the city, three large figures slunk catlike along the ground. They raced toward Frost, and the winter man turned to face them.

They rose up on their hind legs twenty feet from where Frost stood. The creatures were jaguars: true jungle cats with black-spotted, golden-brown fur, with white muzzles. Yet they were not jaguars, really, for they stood on their hind legs. They were still built like cats—their faces had not altered and their tails still twitched behind them— but their forelegs were more like arms now, and their claws had lengthened.

"No!" Blue Jay cried.

He took flight, transforming into the bird in a blink. The winged serpents had begun to descend now and were also moving straight toward Frost. These Hunters were here for the winter man. Just as the Borderkind had come to slay Ty'Lis to disrupt their enemies, the Hunters had been sent to murder the leader of the Borderkind.

Li hurled a thin stream of fire into the air and it seared past the serpents. Grin and Cheval raced toward Frost. Blue Jay flew above them all, small wings propelling him forward. He sliced through the air and, just as he was about to reach Frost, prepared himself to change again. In his mind's eye he could see it. Just before he touched ground, the mystical wings that his magic and his legend had given him would appear. He would dance.

He would slay them all.

Whatever Frost's faults, he was a friend and a leader, and Blue Jay would not allow him to be slain so callously.

At the city's edge, where the last of the buildings on its outskirts were capped with tall, ugly-faced stone statues, other creatures began to emerge. Some were troll-like creatures with huge mouths in their bellies. Others were animal-human legends: creatures combining frog and man, or crocodile and woman.

The dusk erupted suddenly with a flash of brilliance, and Blue Jay saw a woman step out from between two buildings and spread glorious wings as she transformed into a bird made of pure golden light.

The winged serpents descended. They were even larger than he'd thought, nearly man-sized, and when they alighted on the hill they held themselves up with their twisting, coiling tails, wings furling behind them, claws outstretched. They had burning red eyes like hot coals, and when they hissed they revealed black mouths full of long fangs.

Somewhere he had heard of these things. The name escaped him, but Blue Jay knew they were a breed of vampire.

He steeled himself for battle, and for death.

Then the jaguar-men bowed to Frost. The vampire serpents did the same, bodies undulating as they lowered themselves into a bow and then lifted their heads again. The rest of the creatures followed suit.

"What the bloody hell is this, then?" Grin barked as he and Li caught up to Cheval.

Blue Jay spun through the air and alighted beside the winter man.

Beneath his arms, mystic wings shimmered, almost invisible. He stared around at all of these creatures who had intercepted them, and who now had made this unexpected gesture of respect.

"Frost, what's going on?" he asked.

The winter man smiled, the ice around his mouth cracking, cold mist streaming off of him.

"You haven't figured it out yet, Jay?" Frost asked, looking at him with mischief in his frozen eyes. "They're not Hunters."

Blue Jay stared at the jaguar-men and the vampire serpents, at the gleaming bird of light and the things with the hideous mouths in their bellies.

"These are Borderkind?"

Frost nodded. "This is Yucatazca, not Euphrasia, my friend. A different kingdom. A different world."

As Blue Jay watched, others streamed out of the city. Humans. Lost Ones, descended from the ancient races that made up this kingdom and the many who had been lost there after its founding.

"What are they doing here?" Cheval asked, stepping up beside Blue Jay in the gathering indigo gloom of dusk. The fires and electrical lights in the city glowed more brightly as darkness fell.

One of the jaguar-men came forward. "They are here to help," he said, his words heavily accented. "Just as we all are."

The Lost Ones and strange Yucatazcan Borderkind gathered more closely around the five who had traveled so far.

"Whispers have come down from the north," the jaguar-man said, cat eyes bright. "The slaughter of our kin has only truly begun in Yucatazca."

"Clever enough," Li said, flames sputtering at the corners of his eyes. The patches of ember on his skin continued to spread like virulent infection. "Ty'Lis wanted the Borderkind here to feel safe, as though it was all happening so far away."

"But we are not fools," the jaguar-man said, grim-faced as he stared at Frost. "This trouble comes to all of us. The whispers from the north have carried stories of your struggles against the Hunters. When word arrived that you were coming to Palenque, we knew there would be Hunters here to greet you."

Frost glanced around. With nightfall, the mist that surrounded him seemed to form a cloud that eddied away on the steady current of the warm night wind.

"But there are no Hunters awaiting us."

If a cat could be said to smile, that is what the jaguar-man did. "Oh, but there *were*. And other enemies will await you in the city."

Once again, the jaguar-man bowed, and the rest of those who had gathered there—human and Borderkind alike—did the same.

"We are here to see that you reach the castle and that you find the answers you seek ... and that whoever is truly the master of the Hunters is punished."

Blue Jay laughed softly to himself, relief washing through him. They were not so alone as they had feared. With all of the setbacks they'd had, he'd expected the worst. It was a pleasure to be wrong for once.

Frost glanced at Cheval, who had been studying the jaguar-man intently. This could be a trap, after all, but she had a sense about things, about creatures and the truth in them. She nodded once. The winter man looked at Li and at Grin and then finally at Blue Jay, his expression clearing.

"What are we waiting for?" Blue Jay said, sliding his hands casually into the pockets of his jeans.

Frost nodded and turned to the jaguar-man. "Lead on."

Collette paced the confines of her prison, trailing her fingers along the hard-packed wall. Her eyes burned with exhaustion and her limbs ached, but she refused to lie down. She would not sleep. The memory of the horror she had witnessed, the Sandman in the bedroom of that little, murdered child, had etched itself in her mind. The only way for her to shake such thoughts was to focus on another memory, the tactile sensation of the sand as it gave way beneath her fingers.

The wall felt hard as concrete, yet it *had* given way. That had been no hallucination. Now as she dragged her fingers across it, the wall was like sandpaper scraping the soft pads of her fingertips, but when she'd heard the sound of that child crying, she found a way to push through and the sand had gone soft.

How ... she wondered. How had she done it?

Without thinking, that was the answer. When the cries of that doomed child had reached her, she had touched the sand and it had changed. When doubt had given way to necessity, something had happened. And, in her very bones, Collette felt sure that the change had not been the Sandman's doing but her own. He had been furious when she had intruded upon his crime.

So now she walked, clearing her mind of anything save exhaustion. Trudging around and around the circumference of that room, she kept contact with the sand wall and she let the rest of her thoughts go.

"There's no place like home," chimed the Vittora. "No place like home."

Her luck, her doom, both were tied into that little sphere of light. But Collette had found a strange peace within herself. The Vittora waned, growing smaller and dimmer, and she knew that the luck of her life was being leeched away. But somehow, the presence of the death spirit had become a comfort to her, an odd companion in her imprisonment. It did nothing but mutter bits of sentences that might mean nothing and lines from her favorite films, snatched from her brain, but it was hers. If this was her luck and her death, she embraced it.

The air stagnated down in that chamber, despite the arched windows high above. It felt warm and close, but from time to time a cool, errant breeze would reach her.

Collette closed her eyes and continued walking. Almost unconsciously she began to press harder against the wall. Her fingers made a rasping noise as she scraped them on the rough surface. Around and around, increasing the pressure so much that her arm shook and her fingertips were scraped raw.

Then the sand gave way, loose grains cascading down the wall with a shushing sound.

Without opening her eyes, Collette froze in place and pushed her fingers further into the wall, digging them into the sand, her heart leaping at the feel of the dry sand spilling around her wrist.

Turning toward the wall, still with her eyes closed, she pushed her other hand into a spot higher on the wall. The sand yielded to her touch, but only as far as she pushed. Where her thumb brushed the wall, it remained intact.

Unable to hold off any longer, she opened her eyes.

The last rays of the day's light streamed into the chamber through those high arched windows, casting odd golden shapes upon the upper walls. Nearby, the Vittora hovered in the air. Collette felt sure it had grown larger and brighter while her eyes were closed. Quietly it hummed a familiar tune, something from a film, she was sure.

A smile touched her lips. It was "In Your Eyes," by Peter Gabriel, from the movie *Say Anything*. God, how she loved that film.

Bracing herself, setting her grip in the handholds she'd made in the wall, she lifted her bare foot and pressed her toes against the wall. It slid through the sand as though the toehold had been there all along, just waiting for her. But that wasn't true. She had investigated every inch of this prison.

Somehow she was doing this herself.

The Vittora hummed more loudly and drifted toward her. Fear tingled at the base of her spine and Collette started to climb as though she might outrun it. Where she thrust her hands and feet at the wall, the sand formed handholds for her to grip. Inch by inch, she scaled the wall as the Vittora danced around her, humming growing louder with each new grip.

It darted across the circular chamber, paused, and then zipped toward her.

Collette tried to cry out, but could not find her voice. The Vittora struck her back and she nearly lost her grip and fell fifteen feet to the bottom of the chamber. But somehow she managed to hold on as the Vittora seared her flesh for a moment . . .

And then was gone. Its light winked out, its voice vanished.

For several seconds she hung there on the wall, and then Collette realized what had happened. The Vittora had not vanished. It had simply returned to the place from which it had come . . . inside of her. Her luck had come back to her, and it seemed her doom was not so imminent as she had believed.

A small voice in the back of her mind wanted to know how any of this was possible, but she existed now in a world of impossible things. Stopping the Sandman, getting out of this hellhole, saving those children and her brother ... those were the things that mattered.

There were secrets here. Secrets that involved her and Oliver. Collette knew that. But secrets could wait.

With the Vittora back inside her, she felt invigorated. Her pajamas were torn and filthy, her hair matted, her skin like leather from the sun, but she climbed swiftly.

When Collette pulled herself through one of those high arched windows, she had a smile on her face. She dragged her belly and breasts on the rough sand of the window ledge and then stood up, turned, and spat down into the chamber that had been her prison.

Then she glanced around. The view from the ledge that surrounded the cell at the level of those windows was a breathtaking panorama, with the soft white sand of a magnificent beach on one side and what seemed like jungle on the other. The building around her was a castle. No other word could have described it.

A sand castle, on the shore of some tropical land. How it was that, throughout her captivity, she had never once heard or caught scent of the ocean, she did not know. Another secret yet to be exposed.

Collette looked around and found a set of stairs that led downward, into the castle. They were the only possible way down. A jump from this height would surely kill her. Exhilaration and fear raged through her, and her skin prickled with anticipation as she started down the stairs.

All the walls of the castle were constructed from the same hard sand as her prison, and she wondered if she could shape them as well. The corridors were dark, save for torches set in sconces on the wall at long intervals, so at times she walked through nearly complete darkness.

There were many doors in the castle. Many stairwells.

On one of the stairwells, the view froze her in place. It revealed a sprawl of sand and a broad, well-traveled road that ran through a lovely landscape of oak and rowan trees, with mountains in the far distance.

Whatever land that was, it existed far from the place she had seen from the castle's pinnacle.

For long minutes, she kept on searching for some way out of this endless labyrinth of halls and stairs, passing through great chambers and eventually through quiet, empty rooms. Only the wind moved here, scouring the sand that created every surface.

At last, when she could stand it not a moment longer, she turned to the nearest wall and began to dig. The sand gave way, spilling all around her, and soon her hands burst through to another chamber beyond the wall. Collette paused and used her fingers to carve into the sand an outline of a door.

She pushed, and all of the sand within that outline collapsed on the floor.

Collette stepped through, into a chamber whose ceiling rose up and up like the greatest of cathedrals. All around the edges of the vast room were doors set into the outer walls. And at one end there stood a pair of enormous, wooden doors, large enough for a parade of elephants.

The doors stood closed, but she felt sure this was the exit and started in that direction.

Elsewhere in the cathedral room she heard a shrill cry, followed by sobbing. The whimpering of a child.

No, she thought. *Not again.*

Escape called to her. But the whimpering continued and she could not simply walk away from that sound.

It took her a minute or two to locate the source of the child's cries. Collette strode toward the door—a real door, it seemed, not something carved of sand—but as she did she glanced around. Her skin itched as though grains of sand were sliding over her flesh. A point at the center of her back felt warm and she searched the shadows all through that huge chamber, certain she was being observed.

"In your eyes," she sang softly, "the light, the heat. In your eyes, I am complete . . ."

It comforted her, like whistling in the dark, though she was hardly aware she was doing it.

Something glittered in the center of the room, in the dark. Careful not to step on it, she bent to pick up a piece of what she thought was broken glass. Yet it didn't seem like ordinary glass. More like crystal. Or diamond.

Another cry came from beyond that door and she tossed the glass down. The child needed her. She rushed now, certain that she had the right door. If she was being observed there was precious little she could do about it.

At the door she paused, hand on the knob, took a deep breath, and then turned, hauling it open.

On the other side stood a little girl with blond hair, hands covering her eyes as she sobbed, muttering words that might have been prayers. The dress she wore seemed familiar, much like something Collette herself had owned as a little girl, with all the bows and trim that her mother had loved.

The girl stood in shadows in a short corridor like the others in the castle, all sand and darkness, all color washed away. Beyond her stood another door, hanging open, the edges of it spilling sand. Through the open door Collette could see a child's bedroom.

Her heart trembled at the scene, so like what she had stumbled upon before. But in this room were bunk beds, and in each bed there slept a small boy, twins from the look of them. Posters covered the walls. Books and video games covered the floor as if a tornado had struck.

The last time she had come upon a scene like this, the child had already been dead, murdered by the Sandman. But these boys still slept, untroubled, unharmed.

The sound of weeping grew louder.

The boys stirred in their bunks.

Collette put her hand against the wall to steady herself, one door behind her and another ahead. If the bedroom belonged to the boys, then who was—

The little girl, crying out in despair, lowered her hands and looked up. Collette gasped and staggered back a step. The girl was herself, a mirror image of Collette at five years old.

But her eyes had been torn out.

The girl's cries turned to laughter as she began to change. Only then, in the shadows, did Collette see that she was not a flesh-and-blood thing but a construct of sand. The sand shifted and twisted and built itself up, a cloak draping around it.

Lemon-yellow eyes peered from beneath the cloak. From the sand.

"Did you think I wouldn't sense your escape, Bascombe?" the Sandman asked.

Collette swore and took a step backward.

The door behind her slammed closed and she jumped at the noise it made. The Sandman blocked her view of the bedroom with the sleeping boys, but she wondered if the sound had woken them.

Slowly, that door closed as well. She whimpered as the light went away, and the blackness closed in around her. She ought to back up, to claw at the walls, to make herself a new door, but the fear gnawed at her heart.

In the darkness, there were only those yellow eyes.

Something brushed her cheek . . . the Sandman's fingers. She batted them away.

There were sounds in the darkness. The swish of his cloak, the rasp of sand against sand. He struck her face, scraping flesh, and she fell to her knees, feeling the sting as blood began to well on her cheek.

Those yellow eyes loomed above her.

"I am not through with you yet," the Sandman whispered.

"Fuck you," she snarled, and pistoned her legs to thrust herself upward and grab hold of the Sandman.

Her fingers closed on his arm, and for just a moment his flesh gave way like sand. With a roar, the monster struck her down again, his strength terrible. Her head rang with the blow, but he did not stop there.

Cloak flapping in the darkness, he fell on top of her. His breath was like the desert, and his yellow eyes like poisoned stars. She felt the tips of his talons press against her cheeks, digging in, drawing blood, scratching furrows in her skin that led to the edges of her eyes.

Collette screamed.

"You tempt me so, Bascombe. I want to taste these eyes. The eyes of the Legend-Born. The wishes of my allies mean little when you tempt me so. I care not about the Legend-Born or the cataclysm you may cause. I merely want to feel your eyes pop in my teeth, to taste the warm fluid as it gushes over my tongue. It isn't very much to ask, after all, is it?"

Those talons pressed harder, drawing tears of blood. Again, Collette cried out.

The Sandman released her. Those yellow eyes floated upward.

"The time has not come. If I were forced to wait much longer, temptation might overwhelm me. But it won't be long now, girl. Word has come to me. No, it won't be long at all now.

"We shall simply sit here in the dark together, and wait."

CHAPTER 18

In the gray mists of the Winding Way, Oliver had never felt so far from home. The world beyond the Veil was a step beyond the reality that he'd known his whole life, but this mystical road clearly represented a further step. No matter how extraordinary and impossible everything felt in the world of the legendary, everything there was tangible. It might be surreal in Oliver's mind, but his senses could react to it.

The Winding Way existed as little more than a dream, yet the most lucid of his life. The mist swirled around him and Kitsune with a pulsing, living rhythm—playful and dancing, and sometimes menacing. In the back of his mind Oliver could not shake the idea that, with its awareness, the mist seemed like a ghost ... or perhaps an entire sea of ghosts, all reacting to their presence.

It ought to have been entirely dark on the twisting road, for there seemed no source of ambient light. Whatever sky might hang above this mystic limbo through which they passed, the mist blotted out any view of it. And no light from stars or moon—if indeed they existed here—came through that gray shroud. Yet enough light filtered through the mist that it seemed, if not dusk, to be perpetually on the verge of full night.

At first Oliver had been cold, but now the mist felt close and warm so that a film of moisture coated his skin. It was not at all pleasant.

Yet simultaneous with this feeling of separation from his past and distance from the familiar there surged up within him a desperate anticipation. When they left this gray road and emerged again into the realm of the legendary, they would be at the castle of the Sandman. If they survived the encounter, he would be reunited with his sister. When he could throw his arms around her and crush her to him, he knew that nothing in his circumstances would seem quite as terrible. Oliver needed that comfort, even if it was fleeting.

If she's still alive . . .

On the Winding Way, doubts seemed to rise like ghosts in the mist and were not easily dispelled. He told himself that Collette was fine, that he would have known somehow if she had died, and that if all of the mysterious things he'd heard were true—or even a fraction of them—the Sandman would have kept her alive as a lure to draw him in.

Which meant that the moment approached where their fates would be decided.

"How much longer?" he whispered. Rather, he'd spoken the words, but something about the Winding Way and its mists turned his voice to a whisper.

Kitsune did not turn. Hidden beneath her hooded cloak, she moved swiftly along the Winding Way, neither walking nor quite running. Oliver hurried to keep up with her, to keep her in sight in the gray mist. The smooth black ribbon of road curved to the left now and he broke into a trot to catch up.

"Kit?" he said, reaching out to touch her.

She slowed and turned toward him even as his fingers grazed her fur cloak. From the abruptness of her reaction he'd thought she might be angry with him, but then he saw the confusion in her eyes. Kitsune blinked several times and shook her head like she was trying to work out some thought that just wouldn't fit in her mind and could not make its way to her lips.

"What . . . Kit, what is it?"

They stood there, though the mist swirling around them seemed to urge them onward, trying to sweep them further along the Winding Way.

"We're here," she said. "Or very nearly, I think."

Oliver peered ahead. The black glass road took one more twist. "How does that work?"

Kitsune pushed back her hood and shook her hair out. She glanced over her shoulder at the mist. "It isn't my magic, but imagine it like a current in an ocean. We step into the Winding Way and we are cast adrift. Except that the magic that created it allows us to alter the current with our desire and our intent, so that we drift to the very shore that is our destination. The road ends for us at the place we wish to go."

"Anywhere in the Two Kingdoms?"

She frowned and he could see she was distracted. "In the eastern region of Euphrasia, almost anywhere. But only within the region. I have heard that there are other places where the Winding Way leads elsewhere—other currents in the ocean—but have never traveled those roads."

Oliver studied her face; her eyes were troubled.

"I don't like it here," he said.

Kitsune shivered. "Neither do I. But I fear we will soon long for the isolation this place provides."

They ought to be going. Oliver glanced toward the final twist in the road and then looked at the fox-woman again. The confusion lingered in her face.

"We should go."

"Yes," Kitsune said.

"My sister—"

"You asked about the Legend-Born . . ."

Oliver stared at Kitsune. "Yeah. One of the Hunters used the term, referring to me. You know what it means?"

Kitsune frowned. "Not precisely. But I have heard the term before. Since we set foot upon this road I have been searching my memory for anything I can remember."

Almost stern, she narrowed her eyes and gazed at him. "You should never have been able to enter the Winding Way, Oliver. I told you—"

"You weren't sure, though. You said yourself, it's not your magic. You said—"

A curtain of gray mist swept between them, momentarily obscuring his view of Kitsune so that she was nothing but a vague outline.

"All of that is true, Oliver," she said, her voice even more of a muffled whisper than it had been before. "I am not like you. I am one of the legendary, a Borderkind. But simply because we're different does not mean I am some omniscient creature. I know only what I have learned. Legends have facets because they change with the telling, and not every aspect is always true. What I had heard about the Winding Way was that only the legendary could travel upon it."

"Yes," Oliver agreed. "And now we've obviously proven that isn't true."

"Have we?"

The words sounded far away and a chill raced through Oliver as he began to unravel precisely what Kitsune was asking.

The mist cleared and they were face-to-face again.

"Kit, I—"

"Oliver, just . . . listen," she said. "When I heard the phrase Legend-Born, I recognized it from bits of folklore I have heard the Lost Ones discuss in the past. And not only Lost Ones, but legends as well. A legend amongst legends. What is most unique about this is that the stories I have heard . . . they're from everywhere. Snatches of conversation in a jungle village in Yucatazca, curses in a pub in Perinthia, prayers in Shangri-La—"

He grinned. "There's a Shangri-La?"

"Of course there is. Have you forgotten where you are? Please, just listen. I do not know the whole story because it is not in my nature to pay attention to such things. I am normally skittish around too many people and prefer my own company. But I have heard enough to understand the gist of the story."

"Which is?"

"In all of the ages since the creation of the Veil, the Borderkind have moved back and forth between worlds, sometimes living amongst humans for long periods. Many of our kind have a fascination for the mundane world, and for humanity. Some even prefer that side to this one. A great many Borderkind chose to keep their tether to your world because they love humans. They watch from the shadows and the forests and from beneath the water. Or they walk amongst you. Borderkind have been known to take human lovers, Oliver. But this is strictly forbidden."

Oliver shook his head. "Why?"

Kitsune frowned. "I'd always thought it superstition. Now I am not sure. There are stories, you see, from centuries past, about children being born from the union between human and Borderkind, and those children being hunted, and captured, and destroyed."

He stared at her. "I don't understand what this—"

"Of all of these stories, there's only one that is recent. It concerns a Borderkind called Melisande, a French legend, a beautiful woman who loved fine dresses and pretty things. She was not simply a woman. She had the wings of a terrible dragon and from the waist down her body was that of a serpent."

Frustrated, Oliver shook his head. "Look, Kit, we're so close now. Collette is so close. We've got to . . . I mean, what does this have to do with anything?"

Her jade eyes flashed with impatience. "Everything! It has everything to do with you and Collette, if I'm right."

Oliver nodded. "All right. Go on."

Kitsune softened. She gnawed her lower lip for a moment and took a breath. "The legend amongst the Lost Ones says that Melisande—a Borderkind, remember—fell in love with an ordinary man and had children by him, and that they still live on the other side of the Veil. Happily ever after."

These last words were laden with spite and irony, but Oliver paid little attention. Thoughts and images clicked through his mind, words overheard and words never understood.

He ran his hands through his hair, clutched the back of his head as if to keep it from breaking open from the pressure within.

"So, you're saying—"

"The conversation I overheard between Frost and Wayland Smith," Kitsune went on. "Frost lied to you, we know that. The Falconer wasn't there hunting him, or not just hunting him. The Falconer was there for you, and Collette as well. I have been so confused by Frost's words, my loyalties torn, but if this is … He really *was* there to protect you, Oliver."

Oliver frowned deeply. "I don't …"

But the words trailed off. He thought of the Hunter calling him Legend-Born, and of the way that the Sandman had murdered his father but abducted Collette in order to lure him in. Why? Why was he so important? And then he remembered—

"The Nagas," Oliver said.

"In Twillig's Gorge? What of them?"

"Don't you remember?" he asked, a sick feeling churning in his stomach. "They called … they called me 'brother.' "

Kitsune stared at him, mouth open in astonishment. She gazed around as though the mist would serve up the rest of the answers they sought. "Melisande was half-serpent, like them."

Oliver sat down hard on the smooth black glass of the road. The mist swirled more tightly around him as though to get a better look, and he was sure he heard soft laughter in the distance. If there were ghosts here, they were amused by his horror.

Revulsion twisted in his gut and he shook his head. "It can't … my mother … she was just my mom, Kit. And she died a long time ago, when I was really young. She was beautiful and kind but just ordinary. Just a woman. And my father … this Melisande could never have fallen in love with him."

Kitsune stared at him. "But she did."

Oliver flinched and stared up at her.

"All of the pieces fit."

"But …" He breathed steadily, trying to catch his breath. "Why didn't Frost tell me?"

"I don't know. He might have thought you would be in more danger if you knew the truth. Oliver, I have told you everything I know of the Legend-Born, but obviously there is more to the story. If the

Hunters want to destroy you and Collette, there must be a reason. We need to know the rest of that legend, to find out what it is about you two that they fear."

The words echoed in his mind. Could it be that the Hunters feared him? No, not the Hunters. Their masters. Whoever had set the Hunters after the Borderkind, and after him and Collette, was the real enemy. If it was all true, it also meant that the quest that Frost and the others had embarked on, the war they were fighting, were Oliver's causes, too. He had planned to stay here as long as it took, help in whatever way he could. But now, if all of this was real, he had little choice.

Kitsune reached down and helped him to his feet. Oliver held on to her hand a moment longer than necessary and a sliver of hurt flashed in her eyes before she pulled away.

They fell into step together, side by side along the twisting black glass road, moving through the mist.

"I've ... I've never been more than ordinary," he said without looking at her. "I always believed in magic. My father tried to grind that out of me, make me more practical, more realistic. But I always believed in my heart that there were magical things in the world. Not in me, though. I never thought there was anything special about me."

"Perhaps your father was simply afraid of what you might become," Kitsune said, as they came around that final curve and saw nothing but mist ahead, thick and impenetrable. "He stifled your imagination, hoping to keep your life from becoming more complicated."

Oliver frowned. "If all of this is true, then what he did was keep secrets. He hid the truth, and he was a callous, hard bastard along the way. Don't make him out to be a hero."

Kitsune did not reply at first. When she did, her voice rasped and the mist muffled it so that it was even less than a whisper.

"For my part, if you and your sister are Legend-Born, I will be relieved."

"What?" Oliver shot her a hard look. "Why?"

She kept walking, and when she answered, she did not look at him.

"I found it ... disconcerting ... to feel what I feel for an ordinary man. If you are half-legend, that would explain a great deal."

Oliver could think of nothing to say to that, and so kept silent as they strode the last few yards into the thickening mist. In moments it grew so dense that Kitsune ceased even to be a shape in the swirling shroud and he reached out to grab a handful of her fur cloak, just to keep her close.

Then he stepped out of the mist and found himself standing beneath a starry night sky, a sliver moon hanging above in a crisp, cool night. He shivered and the clammy film that had built up on his skin during the journey dried in the cold mountain air. For they were, indeed, in the mountains. Oxen grazed nearby on rough grassy land and, around them, Oliver counted three separate mountain peaks. The mountains themselves were steep and the terrain varied from craggy stone to ugly, twisted little trees to a frozen cascade of ice. High up, all three peaks were capped with snow.

"It's beautiful," Kitsune whispered beside him.

Oliver glanced at her and saw behind them the gray mist that had delivered them to this place, evaporating. In moments it had dissipated entirely, leaving no trace of their arrival, save for their actual presence.

Kitsune's admiration had not been for the mountains or the starry sky. Oliver swallowed hard and forced himself to turn his full attention upon the only structure built in the crux of those three mountains. At the base of the nearest there stood a massive pagoda-style palace with its many levels and fluted corners.

Made of sand.

In the eastern region of Euphrasia, this was the Sandman's castle.

The sand that spilled out around the magnificent pagoda reached far enough across the rough land that Oliver and Kitsune were already standing upon it. The oxen grazed on rough grass nearby, but beneath Oliver's feet was only soft, shifting sand.

"Collette's here," he said, more certain than he'd ever been of anything in his life.

Kitsune's jade eyes gleamed in the starlight as she raised her hood, face grim. "Then let us retrieve her."

Oliver slipped a hand into his pocket and clutched between his fingers the pillow feather that the Dustman had given him.

He started toward the pagoda—toward the Sandcastle—and

Kitsune fell in beside him. Together they trudged up toward the tall double doors, the one aspect of the structure's façade that matched the Sandcastle far to the west on the other side of the Atlantic Bridge.

The doors hung slightly open in invitation.

Oliver felt a strange calm descend upon him, settling into his bones with the chill of the night. He could hear his breathing too loud in his head. His hand found its way almost unbidden to the hilt of his sword, and with a bright whisper of metal upon metal, he drew it.

Kitsune slipped through the narrow gap between the doors. Oliver did not have her stealth, but neither was he concerned. The open door told him all that he needed to know about their arrival.

The Sandman expected them. He had been expecting them since the very moment that he had snatched Collette away from the house on Rose Ridge Lane, the Bascombe family home, on its bluff over-looking the ocean. Oliver did not want to think too much about that house and about his parents. If Kitsune's theories about his mother were true, it changed every memory he had.

All that mattered now was Collette.

So if the Sandman knew they were coming, stealth be damned.

He kicked the door and it swung wide. Kitsune twisted to glare at him, surprise in her jade eyes. Oliver ignored the admonition and entered swiftly, investigating the shadows just inside the door, then turning his back to them, gazing into the dark corners he had yet to penetrate. The Sword of Hunyadi felt strangely light in his grasp, and he kept the blade raised, prepared to defend himself. If Rafael, his old fencing instructor, could see him now, the man would likely faint. He'd been taught sport and elegance, balance and dignity. Now he was learning bloodshed and survival.

Oliver recognized the chamber immediately, just as he was sure Kitsune did. They exchanged a glance and she nodded to confirm it, but the gesture was unnecessary. The Sandcastle had aspects in vari-ous regions throughout the Two Kingdoms, and perhaps even in such far-flung lands as Nubia and Atlantis. This was the second they had visited, and they knew of a third in Yucatazca. The exterior of this cas-tle was drastically different.

But inside, it was the same.

In this vast cathedral chamber they had found the dead Red Caps, and the shattered remnants of the Sandman's diamond prison. They had watched La Dormette die and been attacked by the Kirata. On that day, they had barely escaped with their lives, and Frost had been with them. Without him, they would surely have been killed.

Oliver moistened his lips, but his breathing remained steady. Frost wasn't here now; they would have to find a way to survive on their own.

There were no lanterns lit within that massive reception hall. To the right, stairs along one wall led up to a second level, to a door that he presumed would take them deeper into the castle. But there were doors set into the walls on this level as well, all of them tightly closed. Starlight streamed in through the open windows, and a cool breeze whisked along the floor.

At the center of the room remained the shattered remnants of the diamond enclosure where once the Sandman had been imprisoned. Oliver pushed aside some of the broken shards with one boot, then glanced up at Kitsune.

The fox-woman stood twenty feet away, nearly lost in the shadow of a tall, fluted column that rose toward the ceiling high above. A dozen such columns stood in a circle around the hall, supporting the structure.

Cloaked in fur that seemed black, fringed with starlit orange, she caught his eyes and shrugged.

No sign of anyone.

Could it be that the Sandman remained unaware of their arrival? Oliver doubted it. And yet if that was possible, he had to resist the urge to call his sister's name. They would have to start trying doors.

He gestured toward the stairs against the wall. If they were to find Collette, he thought it would be deeper within the castle rather than through any of those doors. He knew from experience that there was no telling where one of them might lead.

As he and Kitsune started to converge upon the stairs, there came the shushing sound of sand being disturbed.

Oliver spun and saw the hard-packed sand floor shifting. Something rose from it, sand cascading off of the figure, and in a moment she stood there, a small female form with wild hair.

"Collette?" he said softly, and took three steps toward her.

Then he slowed. Something was wrong with her. Even in the starlight he could see the utter lack of color in her hair and clothing.

His sword wavered. All of his courage and confidence lapsed in a moment of hesitation.

"Coll, what's wrong?"

The figure turned. Its mouth hung open in a silent scream and where its eyes should have been were only black, empty pits. Oliver would have screamed, but now he was near enough to understand the lack of color.

This thing could not be his sister.

It was made of sand.

Raising his sword, he took the final two steps and brought the blade around in a smooth arc, and sliced the sand creature's head cleanly off. It collapsed into a shapeless pile of dry sand.

In the same moment the floor began to stir and whisper in half a dozen places around the huge chamber.

"Oliver, be careful," Kitsune said.

He nodded. His throat went dry and he could only watch in horror as the sand in the floor resolved itself into six more figures identical to the one he had just destroyed, each one an imitation of Collette, eyeless and silently screaming, desperate, clad only in what might have been ragged pajamas.

Then, in the center of the room—where Oliver himself had stood only moments before—a hissing noise began. A black hole formed and began to widen, sand slipping down into nothing, as though they stood in the upper chamber of an hourglass and the lower atrium beckoned.

A hulking figure rose from that hole, sand slipping around its legs.

It resolved itself in the starlight, becoming not one figure but two. The floor solidified beneath them, but all of the diamond shards had been swallowed by the shifting sand. The ones newly arrived were not like the others, not sculpted effigies of his sister.

Lemon-yellow eyes gleaming in the shadows, the Sandman hunched over Collette Bascombe, clutching her to him, much of her body draped beneath the curtain of his cloak. The starlight blanched his gray flesh to the sickly pallor of a cadaver and his fingers to skeletal bone as he wrapped one hand around her throat and twisted her face round to stare at her brother.

"Collette?" Oliver whispered.

The sand constructs all turned, wretched mouths turning into rictus grins as they started to walk slowly toward him.

His sister flinched at the sound of his voice. He was afraid, for a moment, that the Sandman truly had taken her eyes, but then she leaned away from the monster and he saw her features in the light from the moon and stars that shone through the windows.

"Oliver, you have to run. He'll kill us both. That's all he wants. There's something special about us, something they want to destroy!" she said, voice rising frantically at the last.

The Sandman clapped a hand over her mouth to silence her. The monster, the child-killer, the thing that had murdered Oliver's father and taken his eyes, did not smile or laugh or even speak. This was no storybook villain.

This is death, Oliver thought.

He gripped the sword tightly, raised it, and started toward the Sandman. Kitsune followed, moving around to his right, careful with each step. Her fur rippled with the muscles beneath and she bared her small, sharp teeth in defiance.

With his free hand Oliver reached into his pocket and withdrew the feather that waited for him there. For a moment he was afraid he would have lost it, but it felt almost warm to the touch.

Oliver held the feather before him like some sort of talisman.

"Dustman," he said. "It's time."

The Sandman's yellow eyes narrowed, and he flexed the fingers that covered Collette's mouth. "You confuse me with another legend, foolish Bascombe."

"Not at all," Oliver replied.

A new breeze began swirling across the floor in the vast entrance hall of the Sandman's castle. Dust and grit spun and eddied, and then burst suddenly upward as though something had erupted from within the sand itself.

The breeze died. The dust settled.

Just a few feet away from where Oliver stood, the Dustman brushed sand delicately from the sleeve of his greatcoat. The brim of his bowler obscured his eyes until he glanced up at Oliver.

"I'll take that," he said, retrieving the feather from Oliver's hand. His sand fingers scraped Oliver's skin.

The Dustman slipped the feather in the pocket of his greatcoat, then reached up with one hand and smoothed down his mustache. He turned toward the Sandman.

"Hello, brother."

The Sandman had crouched lower, drawn back a few steps, dragging Collette with him. She struggled and he shushed her, glaring.

"You are not welcome here."

"Nevertheless, here is where I am," the Dustman said. Then his expression changed, and there was venom in his voice and his eyes. "You are the myth that tales have made you—"

"Don't you dare call me that!" the Sandman shrieked, hideous black lips pulled back over needle teeth.

He let his hand come away from Collette's mouth and she cried out Oliver's name. The monster wrapped her hair in his fist and tugged her backward, drove her down, so that she fell to her knees at his side.

Oliver took a step forward, sword at the ready.

Kitsune snapped a cautionary word at him.

"You were never more than a beast," the Dustman said, voice dripping with contempt. "But you've allied yourself with creatures even more monstrous than yourself, and turned your back on all of your kin. There is nothing for you now but death."

The Sandman's lemon eyes went wide and his voice became even more shrill. "My kin? My kin who betrayed me, who allowed me to endure an eternity as captive in my own home? I spurn you all. I spit on you. I shall smear your eyes beneath my heel."

The Dustman nodded. "Come, then."

With a mad roar, mouth stretched impossibly wide, the Sandman burst into a cloud of swirling sand, those sickly lemon eyes floating in its midst, and rushed at this new arrival, this creature who had called him brother.

For a moment, Collette choked on the cloud of him, trying to breathe and getting only sand in her mouth and lungs. Coughing, she bent low, throat and chest burning, eyes tightly closed against the scouring sand.

Then she was alone in the center of the room. Wiping at her eyes, she opened them to see the brothers careening toward one another, the Sandman a dervish of wind and grit and the other—Oliver had called him the Dustman—charging as though he were only a man.

Then the Dustman exploded in a wave of dirt and grit and the two miniature storms lashed at one another in the midst of that vast chamber.

Collette rasped, coughing up the sand that had gotten in her mouth and throat. She bent over, still on her knees, hacking and trying to catch her breath, and when she raised her head, she saw her brother running toward her.

From the moment she had seen Oliver, some dam of emotion had given way inside of her. Now even as she wheezed and coughed, Collette managed a flicker of a smile, relief flooding her.

Oliver ran toward his sister.

"Wait! Watch yourself!" called out his companion.

Collette looked over at the gorgeous Asian woman who had arrived with her brother and saw the alarm in the other woman's face. The cloaked woman pointed and both Oliver and Collette turned to see that the sand-creatures—these horrid constructs that Collette now realized were made in her own image—had begun to close in around them.

The woman wrapped her fur cloak around herself and dropped to all fours. Collette blinked, stunned to see the woman's entire body shrink in upon itself, the fur tightening around her. Instead of a petite, beautiful woman, she hit the ground as a fox.

The fox, a flash of coppery-red fur in the starlight, leaped at the nearest of the sand creatures. It tried to fight her, batting her away. The fox attacked again, driving her snout into the center of the creature. It collapsed, sand spilling down on top of her.

She shook it off.

The wind inside the Sandcastle howled louder and louder. The sand that comprised the floor and walls seemed to erode so that a dust storm whirled through the vast chamber, partially obscuring her vision.

"Oliver!" Collette cried, at last finding her voice.

Not far away she saw the raging twisters separate, and abruptly the Sandman re-formed, standing defiantly in the midst of the driving winds. His cloak whisked around him, but he stood as though entirely untouched. A moment later the Dustman re-formed as well, this so-phisticated, evolved brother to the monstrous thing that had been her captor for so long.

The Sandman glared and whispered something that was lost in the wind and the hiss of sand upon sand.

The constructs moved closer, slow as sleepwalkers, eyeless and silent. Oliver called her name and raced at the nearest of them, squint-ing against the dust storm. Though they had fought as children, she and Oliver had always been close, sharing secrets and troubles and fighting loneliness together in a home with no mother and a distant father. Collette would know her brother anywhere, but looking at him now, she knew that some people would not have recognized him.

Oliver's hair was wild and he sported several weeks' worth of beard. Normally office-pale, his skin had taken on a healthy, ruddy hue. The peacoat and jeans he wore only added to the overall air of roughness that had transformed him, but the sword in his hands provided the finishing touch.

"Keep away from her!" Oliver bellowed as he raced toward Collette, swinging the blade. He hacked one of the sand creatures in half and it collapsed into a small dune on the chamber floor.

In moments, he and the fox had destroyed two others, and the rest of the sand things began to withdraw to a safer distance. Nearby, the Sandman and the Dustman continued tearing at one another. The Dustman thrust his fist through his brother's chest so that when he withdrew it there was a gaping hole left behind, but the sand spilled in to fill the gap instantly.

Over and over, they tore one another apart.

Then Oliver was at her side.

"Collette!" he said, pulling her into an embrace with his free hand.

She fell against him, melting into the pleasure of his company. She was no longer alone in this nightmare place. Her little brother was here with her. Together, everything would be different.

"Hey, little bro," she rasped.

Oliver held her at arm's length and they grinned like fools at one another. His expression wavered first.

"We have a lot to talk about."

Collette nodded. "Oh, yeah. You're pretty much the only thing I'm sure is real in this whole world. I've got a lot of questions. And some things you should know. But can we—"

"Get the hell out of here, first?" her brother said.

The fox trotted up beside him. Though still in motion, her size altered abruptly. Her fur rippled and came loose, hanging down around her, and then as though she were removing her face, the fox drew back her hood to reveal once again the elegant features of the Asian woman who'd arrived with her brother.

"Jesus!" Collette said, flinching and staring at her. "I just . . . I don't think I know what's real!"

Oliver put a comforting hand behind her neck and kissed her forehead. "There's an easy answer to that, sis. Everything. Everything is real. This is Kitsune."

He turned to the fox-woman, whose green eyes were close to the most hypnotic things Collette had ever seen. "And Kit, this is my sister, Collette."

Kitsune inclined her head. "A pleasure to meet you. But we really ought to go, now, while the battle rages." She gestured toward the center of the room where the Sandman and Dustman tore at one another, blasts of grit bursting from their bodies with each blow and re-forming in the swirling, howling wind.

Oliver hesitated. "Shouldn't we help the Dustman?"

Collette had known there was some connection, that somehow they had summoned the creature, but this was confirmation.

"What could we do?" she said. "You haven't seen what he—"

"I know what he does," Oliver said, grief in his eyes. "What he is."

Kitsune nodded. "We should go. If the Dustman cannot destroy the Sandman, there's nothing we can do to help him. He agreed to come, knowing what this war would bring."

"All right," Oliver said. "We go."

Collette kept up with them as best she could. Oliver had his arm around her, helping even as he kept his sword at the ready. Kitsune led the way by a dozen paces and they raced for the door. The sand creatures, those horrible images of her, did not attempt to bar the way.

The door stood open. Fresh air blew in.

When they went out of the Sandcastle, they found an army waiting.

alliwell snapped the reins on his horse and spurred her forward, moving up beside Julianna. The chill night wind raised goosebumps on his flesh but he did not feel cold. In truth, he felt nothing. Exhausted and aching, his butt and thighs pummeled by days on horseback, he felt like a bag of cold and brittle bones.

His frayed nerves felt dulled. The panic that had roiled inside of him for so long had abated with the numb sameness of the hours of their journey. Though they had a clear goal—and Captain Beck's soldiers seemed anxious to reach it—Halliwell felt as though it was all quite pointless. The only things that kept him moving were the horse beneath him and the need to meet Oliver Bascombe face-to-face. Halliwell would ask him the questions he had waited so long to ask, though by now the only one that seemed important was the one he felt sure he already knew the answer to.

Oliver would almost certainly tell them what Hunyadi and Virginia Tsing and Kara had all told them: they were damned to stay in this world, lost forever to the one they had known.

And then Halliwell could die.

Even in the midst of his malaise, he could not have failed to notice the change in Julianna. The journey had been good for her, as though the exposure to the daytime sun and the cold night air had purified her.

Maybe it was the food that King Hunyadi's soldiers had shared with him and Julianna along their journey, or just long-term exposure to the . . . he hated to even think the word, but the magic of this place. From the time they had left Hunyadi's summer residence with Captain Damia Beck and the detachment of soldiers under her command, Julianna had been filled with a sense of purpose. She had a mission now, and with Oliver at the other end of that mission, she had faith that she would have him in her arms again, and that answers would finally be forthcoming.

Halliwell didn't have faith in anything anymore.

"Damia says we're close now," Julianna said.

She gave Halliwell a sidelong glance but he could read nothing in it. The part of her that was a lawyer, a determined professional, had recently returned to the fore. She behaved not like a woman searching for her lost fiancé, but like . . . *well, like a cop,* Halliwell thought.

"Hours?" Halliwell asked.

Julianna had obviously been trained to ride. A young New England girl from a wealthy family, she'd probably been on horseback practically before she could walk. She rode upright in the saddle and had total command of her horse. When her mount moved a few feet further away from his and picked up its pace ever so slightly, Halliwell felt certain it was quite purposeful.

"Minutes," she said.

And turned her face away.

That was when he understood why she'd moved ahead. She did not trust her expression to remain neutral during this exchange. They sought Oliver Bascombe for very different reasons, and Halliwell's were not altogether pleasant. Julianna did not trust him anymore.

"Minutes," he said, tasting the word upon his tongue.

Jaw set, he spurred his horse to move a bit faster, catching up with Julianna though he said nothing further to her. It was not a time for chatter. There had been enough talk about what was to come. Even over the course of this journey they had avoided the subject of its end. Julianna had instead engaged Damia Beck and her soldiers in conversation about the Two Kingdoms and the Lost Ones, and from the fugue of his numbness, Halliwell had listened.

At Twillig's Gorge they had learned a great deal about the legendary and the Borderkind, but by now they realized that ordinary humans—the distant cousins of the people who walked the streets of the world they knew—ruled the Two Kingdoms and most of the rest of the world on this side of the Veil.

In a world of wonders, there was still a place for an ordinary man.

Halliwell should have found some comfort in that. But he could not. If he could never return to his little house in Maine, never see his daughter again, that was the end. There was nothing for him here.

Instead of ruminating on it, he held the reins and he ground his teeth to contend with the pain in his hindquarters from the constant riding. Oliver and this trickster woman, Kitsune, whom he was supposed to be traveling with, had a head start on them, but according to Captain Beck, they hadn't been going directly to the Sandman's castle.

The Sandman's fucking castle. Listen to yourself, he chided. And yet that was only reflex. As absurd as such a thing would once have seemed to him, he knew the truth of it now. Much to his regret.

They rode now, a dozen of Hunyadi's soldiers and a pair of castaways from another world, up a long ridge between two mountain peaks. This part of Euphrasia had a breathtaking beauty and elegance, even in the villages they had passed. The bridges and homes and gardens had all been constructed so as to blend into the landscape.

It had been many hours since they had seen a village, but even here the beauty of the land was staggering. Perhaps here more than anywhere else. The air was crisp and the starlight and the scimitar moon cast a golden light upon the snow-capped peaks. There was such peace here, and perhaps that struck him more than anything else.

Peace.

Somehow, it woke him from the fog he'd traveled in—and woke a rage in him as well.

There could be no peace for him.

At the top of the ridge, a point at which the two mountains met, Captain Beck reined in her mount and peered down into the valley on the other side. She raised a hand, a gesture that Halliwell had quickly learned meant she wanted them all to form on her, and quickly.

He snapped the reins and the horse galloped up the ridge. Julianna raced up beside him, so firm and confident on her horse that she seemed to float along above it instead of bouncing painfully in the saddle like Halliwell.

The detective didn't mind.

They were close.

Fourteen riders gathered at the top of the ridge, in the crux of two mountains. In the starlight they saw a third peak straight ahead. And below, in the cradle formed by the three mountains, a terraced pagoda palace made only of sand.

Halliwell gripped the reins so tightly his knuckles hurt. Answers waited there. One way or another, he would have some answers at last.

"Do you see anything, Damia?" Julianna asked, moving her horse up next to Beck's.

She was the only one who got away with calling the woman by her given name. Everyone else simply called her Captain—even Halliwell. He doubted she would care if he followed Julianna's lead, but he was accustomed to uniforms and protocol and there was a comfort in that.

"No sign of movement," Captain Beck replied. She studied Julianna's face, her own skin shining in the starlight, then looked at Halliwell. "No horses. No indication anyone's there at all."

"The door is open," observed a powerfully built soldier called Tsui.

Halliwell looked down at the Sandcastle, but his eyes were not what they once were and he could not make out from there if the door was, indeed, open.

"We have no way of knowing if Oliver's here or not," Julianna said.

Captain Beck nodded, but her eyes were still on Halliwell. "True. But if he hasn't arrived yet, and what Bascombe has been told is true, his sister is still a prisoner down there."

Halliwell drew his gun. "Why don't we head down, then?"

The captain smiled. "It's what we came for."

She spurred her horse and started down into the cradle of the mountains and her soldiers followed. Halliwell and Julianna kept pace with them as they rode toward the towering pagoda palace. The double doors in front were indeed hanging slightly open.

Captain Beck's horse crossed from rough grass onto shifting sand.

They spread out, taking up position outside the pagoda. Captain Beck raised a hand and Halliwell thought she was about to give the command to dismount, but then the doors were blown wide open from within. The wind howled as a cloud of dust blew out those open doors, originating somehow from within the castle, and three people came out, half stumbling, hurrying as though they feared the place might fall down around them.

Despite her haggard appearance and the dark tan she'd acquired, he recognized Collette Bascombe immediately. The Asian woman in the fur cloak was also familiar, but only vaguely. He'd seen her on Canna Island with Oliver just before they both had disappeared.

And then, of course, there was Oliver himself.

Halliwell held tight to the horse's reins, frozen in the knowledge that the moment had finally arrived. Staring at Oliver Bascombe, he discovered that he felt both hatred and pity for the younger man. If everything he'd learned in his investigation proved true, Oliver was as much a victim as Halliwell himself had become. But if Halliwell had never become involved in Oliver's disappearance and later Max Bascombe's murder case, he would never have had to see the eyeless, mutilated corpse of Alice St. John, or learn about all of the other children who'd been killed the same way. He never would have hunted for the missing man, or for Collette, when she'd gone missing as well.

He wouldn't have been lured here. Trapped here, in this world.

Oliver was not to blame, but Halliwell blamed him anyway. He might be a victim, but the difference, from what he'd heard, was that Oliver could still go home. If nothing else, Halliwell hated him for that.

The panic took him again, mixed with rage and hatred and despair. Just looking at Oliver stoked all of that emotion, and it surged up inside. He felt as though it might erupt from within. He felt his face twist into a sneer.

"Damn you," he whispered. "Damn you for killing me like this."

In his mind, by leading him to this, Oliver Bascombe had destroyed him.

The detective in him wanted answers, wanted to know what had set the Sandman free to slaughter those children and the *why* of it all. But the man, Ted Halliwell, the father ... *he* wanted Oliver to tell him how to get home. And he wanted someone to hold responsible.

Captain Beck shouted something, but Halliwell wasn't listening.

Julianna slipped off of her horse, leaving it to wander, and started running toward the castle.

"Oliver!" she cried, giddy with fear and relief.

Half of the soldiers began to dismount, led by Damia Beck. The other six remained on their horses and spread out, backing away slightly to be prepared for anything.

Halliwell climbed off of the horse, bones and muscles aching from days in the saddle. He clicked the safety on his pistol off and turned toward the front of the castle.

Julianna ran toward her fiancé. Oliver stared at her, then he started to stumble toward her—incredulous, laughing. The Asian woman and Collette followed, glancing anxiously over her shoulder at the wind and sand that continued to blast out of the castle doors.

Limping, cursing his age, Halliwell started across the sand. The gun felt heavy in his grasp.

Julianna and Oliver were still separated by thirty or forty feet when the wall of the Sandcastle exploded. Massive fragments of the wall came down and burst, spilling sand across the ground. Two figures crashed out through the shattered wall, grappling with one another. One of them, cloaked and hooded, with monstrous, hooked talons, had deep yellow eyes that seemed to float in a cloud of shifting sand. The other seemed a figure from Victorian times, in a bowler hat and long, heavy coat—a statue of Dr. Watson carved from granite or sculpted in sand.

They did not crash to the ground.

The two figures burst into twin clouds of sand that spun and slammed together and tore at one another. In a heartbeat they had reformed on the ground twenty yards in front of Halliwell. He stared at these sand creatures as they attacked one another.

He thought of Alice St. John and all of the other children who had shared her fate.

The Sandman.

It was a sick joke.

Suddenly, Halliwell had found another focus for his rage and sorrow and hate. Oliver might have answers, but at last, Ted Halliwell had found someone to blame. Someone to pay for all that he had lost.

He raised his gun and something snapped inside him. He began to scream, but the words were guttural nonsense in his ears, and he ran at the two elemental creatures tearing at one another's limbs and faces.

He pulled the trigger again and again. Gunshots echoed across the crux of those three mountains. Bullets tore through cloak and greatcoat, punched holes in the bodies of the Sandman and the other thing, the other myth.

The monsters did not even notice him. The image of Alice St. John stayed in his mind, and he could not stop. Halliwell would never see his Sara again. The monsters felt like a gift to him. After what they had done to Alice and those other children . . . He marched toward them, finger on the trigger, and knew he had to find a way to get justice for that little girl.

For all of them.

And for himself.

Gunshots echoed off the mountainsides. The wind howled out through the doors of the Sandcastle. The Dustman and the Sandman grappled and tore at one another. Soldiers bearing the crest of King Hunyadi climbed off of their horses and started to spread out, ready to fight if the Sandman should win, but careful to keep their distance.

Oliver barely noticed any of it.

The world seemed to tilt under his feet. Julianna did not belong on this side of the Veil. All that she was and all that she meant to him was so wrapped up in his thoughts of home and Maine that simply seeing her disoriented him. They were supposed to have picnics at the beach and take the catamaran out sailing. In the winter, they'd ski a little, but only to have an excuse to curl up in front of a crackling fire with Irish coffees and blond brownies.

They were not supposed to be here.

Even with Collette standing beside him in her ragged pajamas, skin baked brown from sun exposure, haggard and thin, Oliver had somehow been able to separate himself from the man he had been before Frost and the Myth Hunters had come into his life.

But from the moment he saw Julianna slide from the saddle of that horse and run toward him, something inside of him began to break down. It was as though the Veil had not only separated the ordinary world from the realm of the legendary, but had also split Oliver in two—one the mundane lawyer who'd lived a privileged but plain life, and the other the one who had survived in the wilderness of a world of the fantastic.

Now Julianna stripped that all away.

She raced toward him, calling his name. Oliver sheathed the Sword of Hunyadi. His heart leapt at the sound of her voice and the joy on her face, but with every step she took on the shifting sand, he felt more keenly the horrors that the legendary had inflicted upon his life and his family. His father's murder and Collette's abduction, the utter destruction of his own life and reputation, it all was real. How could he ever try to return to his old life when the friends and colleagues he'd known thought him either a murderer or the accomplice of some child-killer?

Yet here was Julianna.

He started toward her, shaking with a mixture of relief and dread. His elation at seeing her was tempered by the fear that, after all that had happened, things might not be the same between them. The last time they had spoken, on the phone, the pain in her voice had been clear. He had never meant to hurt her, but he knew that he had. He wondered how that might have changed her feelings for him, and how much she understood about what had really happened to him.

Then she was there, and all such thoughts fled. None of it mattered.

An icy wind blew down from the mountains. Her features were

pale in the starlight, her auburn hair almost black in the night. All of his hesitations and second thoughts became damnably insignificant in the face of his love for her. So much could have been avoided if he had only trusted the soul he saw through her eyes, just as he saw it now—this soul that *knew* him, that understood and loved him.

"Oliver," she said, voice barely a whisper, his name quickly stolen away by the wind.

Julianna ran into his arms. He felt her body, so familiar, against his, and pressed his nose into the scent of her hair, holding her tightly.

"I'm sorry," he said, the ache in his heart making it feel as though it weighed a thousand pounds. "Oh, Jules, I'm so sorry."

"You're alive," she said, face pressed to his neck. "Jesus, you're alive. Don't be sorry. None of this was your fault."

"There were ... there were always things I should've said."

Julianna reached up to hold his face steady and stared up at him, gaze sharp with the intelligence that had always challenged and thrilled him.

"Do you love me?" she asked, searching his eyes for the truth.

For a fraction of a moment, he couldn't breathe. Then a pang of remorse went through him, regret for all the time he'd wasted on doubt.

"More than anything."

"Then nothing else matters."

Oliver stared at her, his heart racing. In her eyes, he saw fear and regret and a tiny bit of hope, and he knew that it was all just a reflection of what she must see in him.

He touched her face, then bent and kissed her. The feeling of her lips against his, rough from the wind and the sun, filled his heart with such grateful relief that he wanted to just take her hand and run. Whatever hesitations he'd once felt were gone. They ought to have had a lifetime together.

Oliver pulled back and gazed at her, brushing her hair from her face. If the myth of the Legend-Born was true and if he and Collette really were the children of Melisande, then Julianna was wrong. They might not be to blame for what the Hunters had done, but it was because of them that Julianna had been dragged into it.

Now they were together, here in this impossible place. He wanted to know how she had gotten there, to figure out what it all meant, and where they would go from here.

Behind him, Collette screamed, her voice frantic and her throat raw.

"No, you idiot! Stay away from them!"

Oliver spun, one arm still around Julianna. Collette shouted again. Beyond her, the stranger with the gun—the man Julianna had been traveling with—ran at the two brothers where they were locked in battle. He was an older guy with salt-and-pepper hair and a craggy, Clint Eastwood sort of face, fifty years old if he was a day. But he didn't run like he was fifty. His expression was full of grim rage and he held the gun slightly raised as he hurtled toward the Sandman and the Dustman.

The soldiers called to him. One, a statuesque black woman who was obviously in command, started after him with her sword drawn. The man with the gun appeared not to hear or even remember that the soldiers were with him. He shouted something as he ran at the warring facets of the Sandman, but Oliver couldn't make out the words.

"Hey! Hey, man, don't . . ." He let the words trail off, feeling like an idiot. With the way the man was shouting and the howling wind, there was no way he was going to hear anything.

Then Collette started shouting again, and Oliver pulled away from Julianna. He turned to see his sister running after the man with the gun. Collette, a petite little woman in her torn pajamas, was trying to get in the midst of a fight between myths and one crazy asshole with a gun.

The Sword of Hunyadi felt heavy at his hip.

Whatever truth there might be in the story of the Legend-Born, and no matter how much he wanted to be home, he knew he had become a part of this world. It had changed him. All of the things he had always imagined he might be, had always wished, he was becoming. And there could be no turning back now.

He drew the sword.

In the moment before he ran after his sister, he caught sight of something moving out of the corner of his eye. He glanced over and saw Kitsune by the doors of the Sandman's castle. He'd assumed she had hung back to watch for the sand creatures that had attacked them inside.

Her soft green eyes gleamed in the dark, her fur almost orange in the starlight. The hurt and bitterness on her face was unmistakable. Oliver caught his breath. In the exultation of saving Collette and the shock of seeing Julianna, he'd barely spared a thought for Kitsune.

He forced himself to break the moment, raised his sword, and ran after Collette.

"Wait!" he shouted. "Coll, wait!"

If she heard him, she did not listen. Oliver raced after her. He figured the Sandman was so occupied trying to stay alive that he couldn't control the constructs inside the castle anymore, which helped. But even so, the monster's existence endangered them all. So why weren't these soldiers helping? Even the commander who ran after the man with the gun seemed only to be trying to stop him, to draw him back. Nobody wanted to go anywhere near the Sandman except the nutjob.

That ought to tell you something, he thought.

But fear would not turn Oliver away. Why none of the Myth Hunters had shown up was a mystery, but he figured maybe Frost and the Borderkind were keeping them busy elsewhere, and whoever their hidden enemy really was—Ty'Lis or someone else—they assumed an ordinary brother and sister, soft and pampered humans, shouldn't be much of a challenge for the Sandman.

Under other circumstances, they'd have been right. Oliver would have been dead many times over if not for Kitsune, and they'd both be dead if not for the Dustman. And he knew the Dustman had come at his request, but hadn't been too difficult to persuade. They all faced the same enemy. They were all in danger.

But right now, Oliver wasn't feeling solidarity with anyone. Not Kitsune or the Dustman or the tall woman with the sword or the soldiers who followed her. And sure as hell not the lunatic with the gun. Collette wasn't going to fall into the Sandman's hands again, and now that Julianna was here, he wanted nothing except to get them both away from this place.

"Coll!" he shouted, chasing her.

The sight of the sand-brothers at war sickened him. They tore one another apart, sand swirling and mixing and battering. The Dustman seemed to have weakened, and as he tried to focus himself again, to form the persona he had adopted with his greatcoat and bowler hat and mustache, he faltered. The vague shape remained the same, but the details were a blur, like an old statue with its features eroded by entropy.

After her imprisonment, Collette was in no condition to run. Oliver overtook her easily. He grabbed her arm from behind and pulled her up short. She spun on him, eyes wild.

"Stop!" he shouted. "Stay here. I didn't come to get you just to watch you die!"

"I won't die. We're not helpless here. We can fight! We can hurt him." Collette held up her hands. "I've done it!"

Oliver wanted to ask what she was talking about, but there just wasn't time. A gunshot rang out, the first one in long seconds, and he turned to see the shooter aiming at the Sandman. In the midst of the churning sand, the twist and turmoil of the warring brothers, the monster turned its yellow eyes upon the man with the gun and stared murder at him.

Oliver glanced at Collette, and then they were running together.

"You're sure about this?" he asked

She said nothing, but when he looked down at her, he saw the set of her jaw and the grim knowledge in her eyes, and he knew she had never been so certain of anything in her life.

The tall soldier caught up to the gunman and tried to pull him back. He fought her, trying to get the gun free, to shoot again, no matter how useless his bullets were.

"Who the hell is this guy?" Oliver snapped.

"Halliwell. He's a detective. He was looking for you when you disappeared," Collette said, huffing, trying to keep up with him.

A cold finger of dread went up Oliver's spine. So he was responsible for this Halliwell being here as well.

They were twenty feet from the churning tornado of the screeching battle between the Dustman and the Sandman when the gunman shot an elbow into the tall soldier's abdomen. Cloak billowing out behind her, she staggered back a step and let go of him.

Julianna stared at Halliwell and slowly brought her hands up to cover her mouth. Her fingers splayed across her eyes and she peered between them. Like a marionette whose strings have been cut, all the strength left her muscles and she went down on her knees.

She watched Collette and Oliver run toward Halliwell, but could not rise. A terrible chill enveloped her. She had watched his mood grow darker with each hour that passed, seen his eyes go numb, and his nerves become more brittle. All along, she had wanted nothing more than to keep him going until they could find Oliver, find the answers that they were looking for. Guilt consumed her now as she accepted the selfishness of that. Yet it had not been only for her. She'd wanted to give Halliwell hope, something to hold on to long enough for them to ask Oliver the all-important question: Could they go home again?

Virginia and Ovid Tsing had told them it was impossible, as had the guardians of Twillig's Gorge, and King Hunyadi himself. But Halliwell had never let himself believe it.

Julianna knew that his denial of that fact was the only thing that kept him from falling apart completely. Without hope that he would see his daughter again, he would shatter.

Now it was happening right before her eyes.

Collette and Oliver ran toward Halliwell. Captain Damia Beck tried to get hold of him again, to keep him back. But Julianna could see, even in profile, the expression on his face, and she knew there was no point. Ted had lost all hope, and now all that was left was his anguish.

Halliwell started firing again, and he ran right into the midst of the sandstorm created by the Dustman and Sandman at war.

"No!" Oliver shouted. "What the hell are you doing?"

Too late, Julianna thought. But, in her mind's eye, she could see the way the kindly curmudgeon had changed when they had crossed the Veil into this world, could remember the panic and anger and cynicism that had eaten away at him, and she wondered if it had always been too late.

In the starlight, Julianna could see a difference in the hue of the sand and dust that made up the brothers, one more brown and one more gray. Striations of that sandstorm whipped in a frenzy, twisting in on each other. And when Halliwell stepped into their midst, it whipped at him as well.

He fired his gun one last time. His clothes flapped around him, driven by the force of the wind the two Borderkind were creating. Collette screamed. Oliver shouted at the man to get back, to step away, but it was too late. The sandstorm had him, the war of these two brothers had consumed him.

The churning storm must have been like sandpaper, all of that grit spinning around. It tore Halliwell's clothes from his body and then began to scrape his flesh, stripping the skin and muscle and then scouring every bit of gristle from his bones.

Oliver staggered to a stop in horror. Beside him, Collette also halted.

Where she still sagged on her knees, a hundred feet away, Julianna let her hands slip from her face. Warm tears painted tracks in the dust on her cheeks.

"Ted," she whispered.

As they watched, the storm abated and a figure began to form. With the winds dying, Halliwell's bare bones fell to the ground.

Julianna wept for him, and for his daughter, Sara—a girl she had never met. All Ted Halliwell had wanted was to be with her, to tell her that he loved her and that nothing else mattered. Now he would never have that chance, not until they met again in the afterlife.

As she stared at the place across the sand where his bones lay, a terrible thought occurred to her.

Ted Halliwell had died in the world of the legendary, but his daughter lived on the other side of the Veil. If there truly was a heaven, would they be together there, one day, or separated for all eternity?

Numb, she staggered to her feet and forced the question from her mind. But, deep down, she knew it would haunt her always.

The Sandman stood before them, sickly lemon eyes glaring. His hideous, obscenely long face split in a grin. He spared a single glance for the tall soldier with the night-black skin and then ignored her, turning toward Oliver and Collette.

"Bascombes," the Sandman said.

The soldier raised her sword and barked a command. The men and women in her command began to close in around the Sandman. Oliver knew they stood no chance. The Sandman would slaughter them.

"Come on," he said.

The Bascombes ran toward the monster that had killed their father.

"Back away!" Oliver called to the soldiers. "Leave him to us."

"Oh, yes, by all—" the Sandman began.

His voice cut off. Something shifted in his eyes, in his form. Beneath the cloak he wore, things moved and shifted. Puffs of sand erupted from his back and chest and mouth and he started to twist in upon himself like a dog chasing his tail. For a moment his features blurred, and when the sand stopped swirling enough to make out what they were all seeing, Oliver realized he now wore a bowler hat.

The Dustman and the Sandman had merged and become one, and now the Dustman turned toward Oliver.

"Now, while I am ascendant."

Oliver and Collette raced at him. The Sword of Hunyadi flashed through the night air and cleaved the Dustman's head from his shoulders. It fell to the ground and burst into a cloud of sand that eddied in the mountain breeze. The rest of his body seemed to have frozen, as though sculpted from sand. Collette began to tear at it, and even as she did it crumbled at her touch.

The Dustman collapsed, sand spilling across the ground, half burying the bones of Detective Halliwell, until no form remained at all. Only sand. Only dust.

"How did you . . . ?" one of the soldiers said.

Oliver turned and saw it was the woman who had chased after Halliwell and tried to save him. She wore the insignia of a captain in Hunyadi's service.

"That's just not possible," she said. "They were legends."

Collette leaned against him. Oliver put his arm around her, helping to hold her up with his free hand. In the other, his sword hung low, point digging into the soft sand.

He could not claim to understand exactly what had just happened. Had the Dustman destroyed his brother, or did he and Collette really have some kind of magic in them, some legendary power?

Oliver met the captain's gaze, unflinching. "This world is full of impossible things."

The entire city of Palenque was a maze, a circular labyrinth of dead-end streets and alleys that twisted back upon themselves. The architects who had conceived it were brilliant, and the king who'd ordered its construction ruthless, for the entire city had been created as protection for the palace that lay at its center. Enemies who intended to destroy the palace or usurp the king would become lost in the maze of stone and wood. Each long, curving street of Palenque looked, with its balconies and lanterns and white-washed walls, much like the others.

Ingenious. But it also revealed how little value the king placed upon the lives of his subjects. Instead of building walls to protect his people, the founder of the city had used those very people as his walls.

Tonight, they showed King Mahacuhta the same courtesy.

Night had fallen, and though the city flickered with electric lights and gas lamps alike, Frost felt invigorated by the darkness. The sun and heat had been a constant drain upon his strength and power. Now only clear black velvet hung in the sky, punctured with starry pinpoints and a sliver moon. The heat of the day seeped away quickly, and while the night was still warm, he felt much improved.

"Not exactly the reception we were expecting," Blue Jay whispered beside him.

Frost nodded intently, not returning the trickster's smile. Caution demanded they take care, no matter how cooperative the citizens of Palenque seemed.

"You thought the people would attack us?"

Blue Jay shot him an odd look, punctuated by the rasp of denim on denim and the slap of his boot heels on the street. "Attack? I figured the whole city would be villagers with torches. If Ty'Lis is really the guy behind the Hunters, why would he just let us walk up to his front door?"

The winter man did not reply. This was precisely the question he had been mulling over, and as yet he had not come up with an answer.

The streets of Palenque were alive with life. It was, after all, the capital of Yucatazca, one of the most powerful and most alive cities in all the world. Frost did not eat, but even he marveled at the mélange of aromas that filled the labyrinthine streets: scents of cooking meats and spices and fruits and boiling fish stews. Distant sounds of engines and of the hoofbeats of horses carried to them along the curved alleys and roads of that circular maze city as they made their way toward the palace at its center.

Along the way, as though their route had been announced earlier, hundreds of people gathered to watch them pass. Some of them were grim-faced and anxious, but others cheered and whistled in support as he and Blue Jay, Grin, Li, and Cheval passed by. The strange Borderkind who had met them at the outskirts of the city accompanied them, as did dozens of Lost Ones. Others fell in with the parade as they marched through the streets, all of them headed toward the palace in search of answers.

Music and singing, shouts and laughter came from many of the buildings they passed—inns and drafthouses and restaurants alive with the lives of ordinary people who had toiled all day in the sun.

Some of the people seemed troubled by their passing and strode quickly away, not wishing to be anywhere near the trouble that the Borderkind might cause. Frost felt disgust roil in him. If there was danger to ordinary people in simply being in the presence of Borderkind, the Hunters ought to be accountable, not the Borderkind themselves.

But regardless of who was at fault, just being near Frost and the others could have been fatal.

Yet on this night, when they were so close to their goal, there were no attacks and no resistance. Frost had seen very few of the legendary in the march through Palenque, and those he had seen had been mostly in shadows, standing in arched doorways or watching from windows and quickly disappearing behind curtains when they realized they'd been seen.

The tide had turned.

The Lost Ones had heard rumors that the Legend-Born had been discovered, that they might be within the Two Kingdoms already, and that somehow this was connected to the Myth Hunters' slaughter of the Borderkind.

Frost knew the truth, but he would not speak of it.

Not now.

First, Ty'Lis must be stopped. The Hunters must be recalled and punished for their savagery. Those Borderkind who still lived must be saved. Only then would he answer the Lost Ones' questions about the Legend-Born.

Cheval and Li hung back, both of them grieving, unable to enjoy the camaraderie of the southern Borderkind who had joined them. But Grin caught up to Blue Jay and Frost, took a glance at the winter man, and turned to the trickster instead.

"Right, so what do you think, Blue?" Leicester Grindylow asked. "D'ye think we've killed all the Hunters?"

Blue Jay clapped a hand on Grin's shoulders and tossed back his hair, feathers dancing in the wind. "Not by half, friend. Not by half."

Grin frowned, once again looking from Blue Jay to Frost. "No? Then why do you reckon they're not here trying to kill us? Not like we'd be hard to find, is it?"

"I can think of three reasons," Blue Jay said.

Frost raised an eyebrow, icy mist steaming from his eyes. He said nothing, only continued walking along with his companions, blocking out the sounds of the crowd to listen to the trickster speak.

"First, their master has been moving in secret all of this time, acting without the knowledge of his king or the support of the people, on some kind of personal vendetta against the Borderkind. The people don't like that sort of lying, bullshit politics. If the Hunters tried to attack us here, it'd be wholesale slaughter. Lots of people would die. That would make it even worse. See, if Ty'Lis is behind all of this, you're talking a major diplomatic incident here. Atlantis is neutral, remember? They brokered the truce that created the Two Kingdoms. People might blame Atlantis. Worse yet, they might blame King Mahacuhta, and kings tend to frown on their advisors doing things without permission that could cause their subjects to rise up in anger.

"Second, Mahacuhta may have just killed the bastard already and saved us the trouble. Even if we assume he's been blind and deaf to all that has transpired, kept in the dark by Ty'Lis and his other advisors, by now he's likely to have heard what the Hunters have been up to. If he's traced it back to Ty'Lis ... well, you see where that's going. Also, Ty'Lis might have just run off. The pricks who do this sort of thing, secret genocide orders, conspiracies, that sort of thing ... they're cowards. They're far more likely to run than to fight."

Up ahead, the road narrowed. They had been curving southwest, the palace to their right. There were shops and homes on either side now, but for the most part the whitewashed stone and the gas lamps looked exactly the same as any other part of the city. A butcher's and a small bookshop jutted a bit onto the road and after that it was as though the walls were closing in. In this more residential street, dwarf trees grew in front of the buildings and the windows were mostly dark.

The small army that had gathered around them had to stretch out into a thinner line, only four or five across, to walk this way. Up ahead, the jaguar-men who had been the scouts and guides and vanguard of their march paused and sniffed the air.

They turned north along an alley.

Frost frowned, the ice around his eyes cracking.

How many times would the labyrinth of the city's design turn them away from the direct approach? He could long since have spun himself into a frozen wind, a tiny storm, and gusted toward the palace to find Ty'Lis on his own. That had, in fact, been his plan all along, until they had been met with such a formidable welcome. He'd intended to leave Blue Jay and the others behind to fight whatever enemy tried to block their way, and go up to the palace to face Ty'Lis alone. It would have been best for everyone.

Now the winter man worried that altering his plan might have been an error. The music and the laughter and the spectators had been left behind. Faces watched from windows, but only a few.

"And?" Grin said, staring at Blue Jay. The boggart ambled down the road, long arms nearly dragging on the ground. He seemed entirely caught up in the conversation, and Frost wished he would pay more attention to their surroundings.

Blue Jay paused to touch a damp spot on the road, but then walked on before anyone could collide with him from behind, and before they could lose sight of the jaguar-men as the great cats followed the ever-narrowing alley further northward.

"And what?" the trickster asked, glancing at Frost.

They exchanged a silent but anxious look. The winter man glanced back at Cheval and Li. Cheval Bayard strode along, her silver hair gleaming in the starlight. Several of the Lost Ones walked with her, talking to her quietly, perhaps comforting her. But Li was alone, ignoring the pair of strange vampire serpents that slithered at his side. Much of his clothing had burned away and all over his smooth, ash-gray flesh were large patches of scorched skin, glittering embers. Fully two-thirds of his body seemed to have turned to cinder now, blue-white flames flickering along the surface of his skin. It crackled and flared.

Without the tiger, the Guardian could no longer properly contain the fire within. Even though its strength was diminished, it was consuming him. In time, he would be entirely sculpted of burning embers. What might happen then, Frost did not care to guess.

Li glanced around unhappily, obviously just as concerned about their surroundings as Frost and Blue Jay.

"Three," Grin said, tapping Blue Jay on the shoulder. "You said there was three reasons you could think of why no one's tried to stop us getting to the palace. What's the third?"

Blue Jay moved with a strange grace, there in the narrowing alley, following the jaguar-men. He stepped from side to side, a dark blue blur beneath his arms.

"Hello? What's the matter?" Grin said, noticing at last that they were troubled.

"The third possibility," Frost said, answering for Blue Jay. "It may be that there are no Hunters and no soldiers trying to stop us or attack us because those are their orders. Our arrival may all be a part of the plan."

"Oi, come on, mate," Grin said, turning to the winter man. "You think this is a trap?"

Blue Jay laughed softly, his eyes wild with mischief. "We'll know soon enough."

They followed the jaguar-men until the alley twisted back upon itself once more and they were moving due south, then east, parallel to the center of Palenque again. The alley became so narrow that it was difficult for two of them to walk abreast.

All conversation had ceased. Frost wondered how far back their coterie of Lost Ones and southern Borderkind snaked through the alleys of Palenque, and how vulnerable they all were now.

Then the jaguar-men led them, at last, to a broader avenue. When they stepped out onto the street, they had returned to a city buzzing with nightlife and music. Glasses clinked and laughter came from a nearby bar.

At the far end of the avenue, tall street lamps burned amidst rows of ironwood trees, all of which led to twin sets of high stairs, like those at the pyramid they had passed earlier. At the top of each set of stairs were massive doors, tall enough for gods and monsters.

Mahacuhta's palace.

Frost hesitated. Perhaps it was not a trap after all. Or perhaps the trap lay within.

Now the Lost Ones and Borderkind who had joined with him gathered around, all eyes upon him, waiting. The winter man did not hesitate. He started down the avenue toward the palace stairs with Blue Jay and Grin on either side. As they approached, Li and Cheval joined them so that all five of the Borderkind who had survived the journey south walked together. Others gathered ahead of them and behind, but seemed to keep away from those five out of respect or, perhaps, fear.

As they neared the palace Frost could make out a dozen guards near the top of each staircase, armed with spears and swords. The sentries stood entirely still, but he was not fool enough to think they were there merely for decoration.

"What is that?" Li asked. The Guardian of Fire raised his ember hands, flame dancing on his fingers. His eyes were tiny infernos.

"What do you see?" Cheval asked.

"Beneath the ironwood trees," Blue Jay said. "I see them now. What are they?"

Frost glanced around at the crowd with him, wondering at the best path for them to take cover should an attack come now, wondering how many would die in the process. But then he saw what had caught the attention of his comrades. Near the bottom of the right-hand staircase, outside the dome of light shed by the nearest gas lamp, amidst the trees, three figures stood entirely still as though they were ironwoods themselves.

Leicester Grindylow laughed happily. "Well, they're friends, aren't they, mates? Friends."

The winter man nodded. "Indeed."

The trio of thin, cloaked figures beneath the ironwood trees floated just a bit above the ground, and as the jaguar-men approached they stepped out into the corona of gaslight at the base of the palace steps, the high tower of the king of Yucatazca rising up into the night sky above.

They were Mazikeen.

Cheval quickened her pace. "He called his brothers after all."

The winter man flowed forward, all of his former doubts dispelled. The Mazikeen would keep to themselves as always and so he did not bother to stop and welcome them or thank them, he simply kept going, past the Mazikeen sorcerers, past the jaguar-men, up the stairs toward the palace doors.

A huge cry and furor rose behind him as Borderkind and Lost Ones alike rushed upward in his wake. Frost reached the top of the stairs before any of the others, and as they began to catch up and gather around him, the guards blocked the doors, drawing their swords.

"Turn back, or face the wrath of the king's guard!" shouted one of the sentries.

Frost darted at him, tempted to drive sharp ice fingers through his brain. But this man was not the enemy. He was merely an obstacle. He knocked the guard's sword aside and snatched the man up by the throat, searing his flesh with cold.

"I am Frost of the Borderkind, and on behalf of all my kin, I have come to see the king."

he cold mountain winds blew across the cradle formed by the meeting of those three high peaks. As the sand skittered across the grass and across the bones of Detective Halliwell, it began to snow.

Kitsune raised her hood and from its shadow peered out at the activity around her. The Sandman's pagoda castle—so reminiscent of the styles of old Japan, from which her own legend hailed—remained standing. The doors had been torn away. She kept close to the castle, kept still, and simply watched.

Oliver and his sister celebrated their reunion. He fussed over her, making certain she was not badly injured. The captain of the soldiers had turned out to be Damia Beck, the new advisor to King Hunyadi. After attempting to murder Oliver and Kitsune, the Atlantean advisor to the king of Euphrasia had been removed and executed.

Captain Beck gave Collette Bascombe a change of clothes and her own cloak, so that after a few moments out of sight she had emerged clothed in a dark, heavy tunic and too-long trousers and a black cloak with the crest of Hunyadi upon it. When Collette returned, she thanked Captain Beck profusely, thanked all of Hunyadi's soldiers who had ridden with Julianna and the late detective Halliwell to aid her.

Over the course of these long minutes—slices of eternity—Kitsune had been forced to witness a second reunion. With Collette seen to, Oliver had turned his attentions to Julianna, who though only human was far more beautiful than Kitsune had imagined. Her long auburn hair gleamed darkly in the celestial light. Tall and slender, she had a formidable air about her.

Kitsune could have killed her in seconds, torn out her throat and had Julianna's blood dripping down her chin before any of them could react. She was only human, after all.

But, hidden within her fur cloak, she only watched as Oliver and Julianna held one another close and cooed apologies and promises. Her ears were keen, and she heard most of what they said to one another, heard Oliver's regret and the passionate crack in his voice as he rasped his love to her.

At long last the Bascombes—the Legend-Born—and Julianna said their good-byes to Captain Beck and her soldiers and came back to the massive open doors of the sand castle, where the wind whistled in the vast dark hollow of the place.

"You said we can pass through the Sandman's castle here and come out in any of his other castles, right?" Oliver asked.

His eyes were alight with new passion and hope and courage.

Kitsune bared her sharp little teeth. "That's right."

Oliver looked at his sister and his fiancée, and they nodded their consent before he turned to Kitsune again.

"Then we ought to be going to Yucatazca now, don't you think? Whatever lies Frost may or may not have told, I still believe he is my friend, that he's trying to do his best. And he kept his vow to me, to find Professor Koenig. It's time for me to keep my vow. Captain Beck and her soldiers can't come with us. The treaty between the Two Kingdoms forbids it. But whatever help we can be to the Borderkind, we're going to stand with them."

Kitsune stared at him, eyes narrowed. She smiled, and wondered if he even saw the edge to it. "And while you are in Palenque, if you and Collette can earn a pardon from the king, all the better."

"True enough."

But a look of dark and painful regret passed between Oliver and Julianna then. Collette, looking on, glanced away as though crestfallen.

Kitsune understood. Even if Oliver and Collette could earn the pardon they sought, and were able to travel back to their own world without fear of persecution from beyond the Veil, Julianna would have to remain behind. Unlike the Bascombes, she had not been carried here by a Borderkind. She had touched the Veil.

Julianna would be trapped here forever, one of the Lost Ones.

What would Oliver do now?

The irony was cruel.

Kitsune had the cunning heart of a fox and the mischievous soul of a trickster. Love had touched her for the first time in centuries and now it had curdled into bitterness. She had always hoped and believed that Oliver would come to love her, in time, but Julianna's arrival had ruined any chance of that. Her heart felt dark and heavy now. She saw Julianna's misery and Oliver's pain, and she relished it.

"Let's go, then," the fox-woman said. "Frost and the others need our help."

They all spared a final glance and a wave at Captain Beck and her soldiers, who had mounted their horses and gathered now by the castle doors to see them off. Then Kitsune led the way back into the howling shadows of the Sandcastle, into the darkness, shielding her eyes from the windblown grit, nursing her bitterness at the truth that she had learned.

For she understood now that Oliver could never have been hers, no matter what he may have allowed her to think.

He had hurt the woman in her, quite deeply.

But it was the fox in her that now wished very much to hurt him back.

———————

For a moment, Blue Jay allowed himself to think that it was all going to go smoothly, that Ty'Lis was not prepared for their arrival. Lost Ones and Yucatazcan Borderkind surrounded the palace in the circle at the center of Palenque. In the flickering gas and electric lights they were a sea of curious and angry faces. When Frost gripped the sentry by the throat at the top of the stairs, they were all with him.

The other guards attempted to intervene, but Li snapped at them and sketched a line through the air. Where his hand passed, the air itself lit on fire, a streak of flame suspended above the ground. He held one hand at his side and fire spilled from his palm, forming itself into the shape of an enormous tiger. He staggered with the effort, no longer the legend he had once been. The blazing tiger-thing opened its maw and a gout of flame roared out.

The guards kept still.

Frost released the guard he'd throttled. The man reached up to touch the frozen flesh of his throat where the winter man had clutched him.

"Let them pass," he rasped.

The three Mazikeen were arranged around Frost as though they were his honor guard and several of the sentries stared at them and whispered to one another. One in particular, an imposing soldier whose face was scarred from a lifetime's survival in battles that had claimed others, watched the Mazikeen with cold eyes.

"You must be announced," the scarred sentry said, and it was clear from his tone that he would not be so easily intimidated.

Cheval Bayard threw back her silver hair. "Then announce us."

The grim, scarred man nodded, took one last long look at Frost and the Mazikeen, and then turned to hurry into the palace. The two massive doors had been built large enough for gods and giants to enter the palace, but given the rarity of such occasions—and that the king was a god in name only—there was a pair of smaller doors set into the larger. The scarred sentry disappeared through one of those and it slammed shut behind him.

Cheval seemed pleased with herself, but she had a reckless air about her, as though she no longer cared what fate held for them all. Perhaps, with Chorti dead, that was the truth.

Beside her, and several steps below Frost, Grin smiled. *Soon,* his expression seemed to say, they would have their answers. They weren't alone now. Instead they were surrounded by others demanding the same answers, demanding justice.

Blue Jay remained several steps below the others, watching the crowd, watching the skies, watching the palace itself.

This did not feel right.

Only a fool would have allowed himself to think it would be this simple. He cursed his own momentary lapse.

"Frost," Blue Jay said, moving up the steps past Cheval and Grin, pushing between two of the Mazikeen. The eyes of the sentries watched him carefully. "This isn't going to be—"

The winter man looked at him with a weary, knowing gaze. *Too easy.*

People began to shout at the foot of the stairs. A woman screamed. Blue Jay spun. A sentry reached for him and with a single, solid kick he sent the man tumbling off of the stairs, turning end over end until he struck the cobblestoned street far below.

Soldiers flooded into the plaza around the palace, streaming out of buildings on the main thoroughfare and from every alley. Doors in the base of the palace banged open and hundreds of armed men erupted from the bowels of the massive structure.

"Bloody Hell!" Grin shouted.

The boggart grabbed hold of the nearest sentry, twisted, and hurled the man down the stairs, even as some of their allies raced up after them.

A light, damp snow whistled and eddied around those who had gathered at the top of the palace steps. The winter man ran at the huge doors, sliding through the air, driven by an arctic breeze. A guard grabbed at him and Frost chopped the edge of his hand down— honed to a razor blade—and sheared the man's arm off at the biceps.

Screams and jets of blood gouted as the sentry staggered back. Cheval grabbed the nearest sentry and drew him to her, mouth tight over his. He struggled and kicked as she lifted him off the ground.

When she dropped him, his head tilted to one side and water spilled from his gaping lips. She had drowned him with a kiss.

Two sentries came for Blue Jay. He chanted a few short, guttural syllables deep in his throat, moved his feet in time with a rhythm only he could hear, and as he did he spun, raising his arms. The night blurred with an indigo shimmer beneath his arms, and the magical wings he'd summoned knocked the two men back, cutting them both, nearly slicing the nearest of the two sentries in two.

With an earth-shuddering shriek of metal and wood, the god-doors swung inward, yawning wide, creating an entrance almost forty feet across.

Blue Jay spun and stared past Frost and the Mazikeen at the two towering figures that stood in the open doorway, backlit by torchlight in the palace's entry chamber.

"Oh, shit," he whispered.

The giants were the most hideous things he'd ever seen, their greenish-white flesh marking them instantly as Atlantean. Blue Jay had never heard of Atlantean giants, but that did not seem to matter now. Particularly as the giants were not alone. Dozens of Yucatazcan soldiers charged from the entry chamber onto the stairs, and there were dozens more behind them.

The three Mazikeen surged forward, moving so swiftly they passed Frost, and joined hands. The night blurred around them and a ripple of golden light speared forth, creating a wedge that drove through the midst of the guards, between the two giants, and thrust them all aside. The magic of the Mazikeen had opened an alley amongst their enemies.

Frost glanced back at Blue Jay.

The trickster waved him on. They both knew there was only one way to end all of this, and that was with the death of Ty'Lis or King Mahacuhta, if indeed the Atlantean sorcerer had acted on the king's orders. In the midst of battle, it would be impossible for them all to reach the royal chambers.

But *one* . . . perhaps.

The winter man raced through the alley of shimmering golden light. Sentries tried to attack him, but the magic of the Mazikeen kept them back. In moments, Frost had disappeared within the palace's vast entry chamber. The last glimpse Blue Jay had of the winter man was of him swirling into a storm of wind and sleet.

The heat had drained Frost. In his weakened state, Blue Jay wondered how far he would get.

The winter man was lost in the crush of soldiers coming out of the palace. Down in the plaza there were shouts and cries as the Lost Ones and the Borderkind of Palenque were attacked by the king's guard. A single glance told Blue Jay that his worst fears were being realized. Far too many of those who had followed along in support were being driven out of the plaza, back into the maze of the city's streets, back to their homes.

Even some of the southern Borderkind were fleeing.

Fools. We can win this, he thought. Whoever had sent the Myth Hunters had to be destroyed, but even without that final victory, they could still win. The king's guard were human. The Atlantean giants were the only legendary creatures amongst their enemies. If all of the Borderkind would stand and fight—

"Filthy myth," a voice said.

Blue Jay spun and saw a sword slicing the air toward his neck. He ducked the blade with the quickness and luck of a trickster, grabbed his attacker's wrist, and twisted it, snapping the bone. The soldier screamed and Blue Jay hauled him close.

"Thanks for the warning, friend," he said.

Then he blinked in surprise.

The sentry had greenish-white skin, like the giants. With his colorful leather armor and helmet he had been lost amongst the others— amongst the ordinary human soldiers—but this man was no Lost One. He was Atlantean.

Grimacing in pain, the Atlantean sentry jerked in Blue Jay's grasp. A sliver of pain shot through the trickster's abdomen and raced all through his right side. He glanced down and saw the Atlantean's free hand, and the dagger with which the sentry had stabbed him.

Blue Jay snarled, reached around to grab the back of the Atlantean's helmet, and rammed his forehead into the man's face, crushing his nose and cracking his skull. The trickster's long hair fell across his face. He thrust the dead soldier away, the dagger sliding out of his wound, still clutched in the Atlantean's hand. Warm blood dripped down his hip. Blue Jay shook his hair—and the feathers tied in it—away from his face. One of the feathers was flecked with Atlantean blood.

He spun, hand over his wound, even as other sentries rushed at him.

The three Mazikeen had begun to hum loudly. Golden light pulsed around them. Once again they reached out to join hands. Arcs of light darted out from their aura, striking various guards dead on the spot. The dead men stiffened, a purple-black glow enveloped them for an instant, and then they fell over like abandoned marionettes.

Blue Jay began his dance, swinging his arms, blue light shearing the night around him.

One of the giants bellowed in fury, lifted his leg, and stomped on the nearest Mazikeen. The hum stopped, the golden aura flickered and died. For a moment, Blue Jay stared, sure that a Mazikeen could not be murdered so crudely, but all that came out from beneath the giant's foot was a stream of dark blood that sluiced down over the white palace steps.

The other two Mazikeen were staggered, but quickly stood together and began to chant something. The darkness coalesced around them, blacker than night, and whatever magic they were up to now would be ugly. Of that, Blue Jay was sure.

Li would not wait.

Little more than fire and ash himself, the Guardian of Fire had crafted his massive tiger from flames, a blazing memorial to his fallen comrade. Now the fire-tiger sprang half a dozen steps in a single leap and landed in front of the murderous Atlantean giant.

Fire spilled from Li's eyes. He opened his mouth in a roar like that of his tiger and flames gouted from his throat. The effort rocked him and he seemed to diminish further, his burning cinder body thinning. Before the giant could react, Li shot a stream of fire up at the monster. Its green-white Atlantean skin charred and blackened and the fire spread along its flesh hungrily. In moments, it was engulfed.

The giant beat at its burning flesh wildly, trying to put the flames out. It staggered backward, off the edge of the steps, and plummeted eighty feet to its death. The whole plaza shook with the impact.

The other giant paused and stared in shock as the Guardian of Fire turned on him and began a faltering advance, grinning, liquid fire spilling from his lips and dripping from his hands. Transformed as he was, Li looked more like a demon than a man.

The king's guard—and he wondered how many Atlanteans were hidden amongst them—began to back up.

From the crush of soldiers that had come out of the palace, four new figures stepped forth. Each wore a robe of deep crimson, fringed with black, and had hideously thin features and a familiar greenish-white pallor.

The two surviving Mazikeen ran at them, a wave of black sorcery spilling forward, dark tendrils lashing at the newcomers. The four Atlantean sorcerers raised their hands and silver light sprang from their fingers, erecting magical shields that turned away the Mazikeen attack.

For all of his cunning, Blue Jay had been slow to see the truth in the midst of the chaos. Now he swore and twisted his body. One blurred wing deflected the blade of an attacker even as he leaped up and kicked the other in the head, sending the man tumbling down the stairs. Nearby, Leicester Grindylow and Cheval Bayard were fighting the king's guard. Li faced the surviving giant.

Below in the plaza, at least half the crowd had already been dispersed. The bloody bodies of jaguar-men littered the bottom of the stairs where they had been slaughtered trying to come to the aid of their fellow Borderkind. Other Yucatazcan Borderkind were also dead or had fled. His instinct was to think them cowardly, but now he changed his mind.

"Cheval!" he shouted.

Blue Jay leaped into the air. He did not shift into the shape of a bird, but the spirit-wings beneath his arms let him glide down fifteen stairs to land at her side. He snapped the neck of the guard nearest her and she turned, eyes wild.

"It's Atlantis," he said. "Somehow, it's Atlantis. Either the king's in with them, or they've taken over, or something. We're not prepared for this. It's much bigger than we thought."

Cheval's silver hair framed a blood-spattered face. "But Frost—"

"He's in. And he's our only chance," Blue Jay said. "If he kills Ty'Lis, maybe this is all over. If not, we need help. We need to get word to King Hunyadi."

With a nod, she shouted to Grin. The boggart ran to her as she transformed, growing and stretching, bones popping, until she had taken her equine form again. Grin leaped onto Cheval's back and she started down the steps. Before she reached the phalanx of soldiers coming up at her, a kind of rip appeared in the fabric of the Veil, and Cheval and Grin crossed the border, vanishing from the Two Kingdoms into the world of man.

Blue Jay leaped into the air, spreading his arms, and in a moment he was a bird again, a tiny jay speeding toward Li and the Mazikeen. Seconds later, all four of them did the same, leaving the king's guard and their Atlantean allies behind, leaving the bloody battle on the steps of Mahacuhta's palace, leaving Palenque . . .

Leaving the winter man to his fate.

The Sandman's castle felt hollow, as empty and dead as an ancient ruin. The only sound was the whisper of the wind as it blew scattered grains of sand across floors and walls. Already, the sand had begun to drift and erode, obscuring edges and wearing at corners.

Collette recalled the feeling of the sand falling away at her touch, at the way she had sculpted it and carved a doorway with her hands. She had thought because of that she might feel a kinship with the place. If there was something of the mythic in her heritage, she must certainly have tapped into that.

But now, with only whispers there, she felt no connection to the Sandman's castle except as her prison, and she wanted nothing more than to leave it as quickly as possible. Whatever had allowed her to carve the sand, to manipulate the substance of the place, seemed to be gone.

Kitsune had led them back into the Sandcastle and through that vast entry hall. Collette showed the way to the stairs she had used to escape from her prison and soon they were navigating the seemingly endless corridors and staircases of the castle, whose interior seemed far vaster than its exterior would allow. They took care to keep to the outer walls, never entering a corridor or room that did not have windows.

"I hate to just leave him here. It doesn't seem right," Julianna said. Despite her obvious elation at reuniting with Oliver, the shock and grief of witnessing Halliwell's death was eating at her.

"We have no choice," Collette told her, each time she brought it up. "If it's at all possible, I swear to you we'll come back. We'll bury him."

Such reassurances did not erase the haunted cast of her eyes.

When they had reached the highest point of the castle, they found the tower where Collette had been a captive. She shuddered and hesitated to go any nearer, remaining upon the top step.

Julianna gasped at the sight of the panorama visible from that pinnacle. Her reaction came not only from its beauty, but from the abrupt shift of the view. The landscape was no longer the trio of snow-capped mountains, but instead the ocean on one side and the steaming jungle of Yucatazca on the other.

Oliver came to Collette and held her hand and reluctantly she went with him. Stepping carefully, they moved around the edges of the pit that had been her prison, only darkness visible through the arched windows that looked down into that hole. The Sandman might be dead, but still she did not feel safe here. Her pulse raced and she bit her lip. There were several stairwells leading down from this tower, but they chose the one directly opposite that which they had ascended.

"I don't care if this gets us where we're going," Collette whispered to her brother as they went down again. "I'm not coming back here."

Oliver hugged her gently and kissed her head. Flanking her, Julianna reached down and took her hand. Oliver fell back to make sure they weren't followed, and up ahead, the fox-woman led the way, her harshly beautiful features hidden in the hood of her cloak. At times she turned corners and they lost sight of her for a few seconds, and each time, Collette found herself both anxious at being left alone and relieved to be away from Kitsune.

Their descent proved as uneventful as their climb upward had been, save that through every window now their view was of Yucatazcan jungle or the crashing surf. The air had the salty tang of the ocean, and even in the night they heard the distant cry of sea birds as they passed the windows. There had been no physical awareness of this shift between one kingdom and the other, but at first every time Collette glanced out a window the sense of dislocation rocked her. The Sandman's castle was an extraordinarily powerful bit of magic and she wondered what would happen to it, now that he had been destroyed. Would it collapse or erode, or would it stand open from that moment onward as a portal that travelers might use to move from one place to another?

A mystery for another time.

When at last Kitsune led them back into the vast entry hall, it seemed entirely unchanged, except of course for the view from the windows and the salty tang of the air. Collette remembered all too well the hideous appearance of the sand-creatures that had been summoned by the Sandman and crafted to be her doppelgangers. No trace of such things remained except for the shifting sands of the floor of that great hall.

The doors hung open. The chill of the mountains of eastern Euphrasia was gone, replaced by a thick, humid heat that was uncomfortable at night but would undoubtedly be unbearable come morning.

"Kit, how far from here to Palenque?" Oliver asked.

The fox-woman flinched at the sound of his voice, or perhaps at the familiarity of his tone. Collette watched her as she paused and turned to face them, and something in the Borderkind's bearing troubled her. When Kitsune and Oliver had come to rescue her, Collette had sensed only warmth and courage and nobility in the fox-woman. She did not understand what had changed.

"I am not certain," Kitsune replied, as Oliver, Collette, and Julianna caught up to her, the four of them standing in the midst of that vast hall, whose ceiling was lost in the darkness. "Palenque is a full day's ride on horseback from the ocean, but there is no way to know where along the coast we will emerge."

Julianna slipped her hand into Oliver's. "It's a shame we couldn't have brought horses through."

Kitsune turned away, jade eyes hidden beneath her hood, but before she did Collette saw the venom in her gaze, a hatred directed at Julianna. Only then did she finally understand that the fox-woman had fallen in love with her brother.

This is trouble, she thought.

But then Oliver was talking and Kitsune had started for the door again, back to the rest of them, and Collette became more concerned with their survival and their journey than with inconvenient matters of the heart.

"I know we could probably all use some rest, but—"

Collette shot him a hard look. "I'm not camping here, Ollie."

He nodded. "I know, Coll. I wasn't going to suggest it. But we're all exhausted, and if we've got a long journey ahead of us, we should try to get some rest."

Julianna did look tired, dark circles forming under her eyes, but she stretched and smiled and her eyes were alert. "I could certainly use some sleep. But I'm all for waiting until we've put a lot of distance between us and this place."

A ripple of sadness passed across her face and she glanced at the ground. They all knew she was thinking about Halliwell.

Oliver put his arm around her. "There was nothing you could do, Jules. Nothing anybody could do. He was past listening to anyone—"

"He went a little crazy," Collette said quietly, looking around them at the various doors, remembering the one where she had been trapped with the Sandman with the cries of his victims so close by. "But it's hard not to lose your mind a little in this place."

Julianna shook her head. "He wasn't crazy. He was just ... done. There was so much anger in him, just horror, and frustration over never getting the answers he wanted, and sorrow over things he'd never been able to say or do with people he loved back home. When we found out we were trapped here, he just ..."

She gazed at Oliver, sad and lost. "He thought you could help him find a way to get home."

Kitsune had reached the doors and she stood silhouetted in the moonlight that streamed in from the humid night. She turned toward them, little more than a shape with those gleaming green eyes peering at them.

"You've crossed through the Veil. There is no way home for you."

Cold. Harsh. But as callous as Kitsune's words seemed, no one argued, for they were true. Oliver hugged Julianna close.

Collette shook her head in disgust at the fox-woman's cruelty and turned away. She glanced around again at the many doors in the chamber, studying them in the moonlight. A frown creased her brow. One door in particular drew her attention and she wandered toward it, even though she knew that they had to leave this place.

When she reached the door, she stared a moment. A symbol had been etched upon it, a shield emblazoned with the figure of a winged serpent wrapped around a sword, and spreading out from either side of the shield, the wings of a bat. The shield had been dyed red and white, the serpent green, its eyes gold, and the sword a glittering silver.

"Collette?" Julianna called.

"Wait," she said, almost to herself. Then she blinked and cleared her throat. "Oliver. Come over here."

In moments, all three of the others had joined Collette at the door.

"What is it?" she asked.

Kitsune stepped forward and traced her fingers over the symbol. She turned and studied Oliver's face. "It is the royal emblem of King Mahacuhta of Yucatazca."

Oliver shook his head. "Come on. You've got to be kidding me."

The fox-woman spared not a glance for Collette or Julianna. Her entire focus was on Oliver. "This is a place of doors. The magic of the Sandman brought him almost anyplace he wished, and not merely the bedrooms of small children in the ordinary world. That was his power. If he wanted a door to Palenque—"

"Are you serious?" Collette said. "Isn't this just a little convenient? Like, freakishly convenient?"

But Kitsune was not listening. She slipped her hood back and tilted her head, sniffing the air. Her eyes narrowed and she glanced down, then dropped into a crouch. Her fingers reached out into the shadows just to the right of the door and she plucked something from the ground. Only when she stood and held it up in the moonlight did Collette see what it was.

A green feather.

She shivered with the memory of the Hunters she had seen crouched around the rim of her prison, those scarecrow-thin creatures with their long, black talons, their heavy antlers, and wide, green-feathered wings.

"Perytons," Kitsune said.

"What are they?" Julianna asked.

"Atlantean Hunters," Oliver replied. He glanced at Kitsune. "The Falconer said the Hunters had been sent by Ty'Lis."

"Pretend that some of us don't know who the hell that is," Collette told him.

Oliver ran a hand through his hair, eyes wandering as he sorted out his thoughts. "Atlantean sorcerer. Main advisor to King Mahacuhta. If he sent the Hunters, including the Perytons, then he was also the one who set the Sandman free, sent the fucker after *us*."

Collette stiffened. "The one who gave the order to murder Dad."

"Yeah."

"So it would make sense if the Sandman made a door that would take him right to his new master," Julianna said. She stared expectantly at Kitsune, and a glint in her eye suggested to Collette that the fox-woman's jealousy had not gone unnoticed.

"Yes," Kitsune confirmed. "It does make sense."

"But we have no idea what's on the other side of this door," Oliver warned her.

"Then it's a good thing you have that sword."

Julianna turned, taking her hands from her pockets, and reached for the door. Collette tensed, awaiting some horror. Kitsune snapped that she should wait. But Julianna did not even pause. She swung the door wide.

On the other side was a well-lit, empty corridor of limestone and wood. Shouts and the sound of people running echoed along the walls. Julianna started forward but Kitsune grabbed her arm. The two women stared at one another icily, and then Oliver slipped between them and stepped into the corridor on the other side of the door.

He glanced both ways, then beckoned for them all to follow.

CHAPTER 21

Diminished he might be, but Frost remained the winter man, a legend that stretched from ancient to modern times, the harbinger of the blizzard, the first snow of the season. With one possessed of such power, weakened did not mean weak. If anything, as he rushed through the corridors of the palace of King Mahacuhta, Frost felt reduced not to weakness but to the primal essence of his own legend.

Swift and deadly, he swept around corners and beneath doors, nothing but a frigid wind and a swirl of snow. He manifested a physical form—a jagged, cruel-eyed knife-blade of a creature—only when he encountered a member of the king's guard alone.

When he touched their flesh, freezing bits of them instantly, and bared his icy teeth, they were anxious to answer his question. One single question. Where were the king's personal chambers? Before Frost bothered to visit Ty'Lis, he wanted to know if Mahacuhta was aware of the Atlantean's machinations. He wanted to know if the king was also his enemy.

The deeper he went into the palace, the cooler and drier the air became. Frost whipped along the walls, leaving a rime of ice as he passed, the moisture in the air freezing on every surface. He emerged into a large, open space, lavishly appointed and well lit, with a limestone staircase rising at one end of the room, up and up and up so that it seemed the entire purpose of this enormous palace was to encase those stairs. Twenty armed soldiers guarded them. Frost kept close to the wall, a gust of wind, but as he passed, the glass lamps cracked and burst, bulbs popped, and lights were extinguished.

The soldiers began to shout, drawing their weapons and searching the room for enemies.

By then Frost was halfway up the stairs.

At the top stood the heaviest wooden door he had ever seen, ornately carved with extraordinary figures of legend, birds of light and alligators that walked on two legs. There were images of jungles and temples and human sacrifice. In the midst of it was the royal emblem of King Mahacuhta, the crest of Yucatazca.

The winter man—the first breath of snowfall—blew under the door.

In a single moment, so many of his questions were answered.

This was not the king's bedroom, but a large antechamber where His Majesty might relax or entertain guests. Tonight he had a number of guests, all of them surely unwelcome and uninvited. Three Perytons perched on the far side of the antechamber by a door that must have led into Mahacuhta's bedroom. In a straight-backed, elegant chair with red silk cushions, a man had been bound with chains that shimmered with unnatural light. A black cloth gag had been stuffed into his mouth. Though bald and thin he had powerful features and a rich, dark complexion that made it impossible to discern his age. But the quality of his clothing alone was enough to identify him to Frost.

The Perytons guarded King Mahacuhta closely, green-feathered wings tight against their backs, antlers hanging low as they stood watch. And they were not alone. Seven soldiers were positioned about the antechamber, but Frost saw instantly that despite their Yucatazcan garb, these were Atlanteans.

Another chair, the lavish equal of the one in which Mahacuhta was bound, faced the king's. Upon that seat, hands clasped in his lap,

Ty'Lis sat casually. Frost had never seen the sorcerer before, but he bore the physical signs of Atlantis, the greenish-white skin and narrow features, and his crimson, black-trimmed robes were among the traditional garment choices for sorcerers from his nation.

Ty'Lis had golden hair so thick and wild it resembled a crest or mane, and a twist of braided beard hung from his chin.

The sorcerer glanced at the door even as the gust of cold air Frost had brought reached him. He smiled and his green eyes were lit with hard intellect.

Frost hesitated. Had he taken Ty'Lis unaware, he could easily have slain him. Face-to-face, the contest was in question, and with Perytons there as well ... given an advantage, the savage Hunters would harry him, and the sorcerer destroy him.

Yet he had little choice now.

Ty'Lis did not rise from his chair, but he gestured toward Frost. "You've come alone. A brave myth, aren't you?"

The sorcerer's body began to emanate a strange aura of purple-black light, a glow that surrounded his entire form. He grinned with all the humor of a cadaver.

"You've come all this way, only to die. Before you rush headlong to your own destruction, aren't you at least curious as to *why*?"

Manipulating the air, Frost forged himself anew, there by the door. The winter man stood just inside the king's antechamber, a thin blade of a creature constructed of translucent ice and the very heart of the storm. Frost stared at Ty'Lis, hatred fuming in him, mist rising from his eyes. He tilted his head to one side, staring at his gathered enemies, and the icicles of his hair clinked together, frozen chimes.

"I *know* why."

The Atlantean's eyes widened. He glanced at the Perytons and said something in the lilting tongue of his own nation.

"Do you, really?" Ty'Lis asked. "Tell me of your conjecture, then."

Frost had been formulating a theory of late and with every passing moment he became more certain of its truth. He glanced around at the Perytons and the Atlantean soldiers, set into a combat stance, ready to fight. No one moved. Chained to his chair and bound with magic, King Mahacuhta stared at the winter man with hope in his eyes.

"You want war," Frost said, gathering all of the moisture in the room to him and emanating a frigid power that caused ice to form on the ground beneath him and the door behind him. "You want the Two Kingdoms to break their truce and go to war against one another, to destroy each other so that you can step in and try to rule them both. But the Borderkind presented a threat. My kind are not sworn to serve either government, are not citizens of either kingdom or subjects of any king. You sent the Hunters to slaughter us to prevent us from interfering, or from fleeing to the world beyond the Veil."

Ty'Lis clapped softly. "You have the threads of it. But you miss the largest part. The Veil . . . the hated Veil. With all of you filthy myths destroyed and the enchantments that hold doors open to the world of men undone, the Veil will become an impenetrable border. There will be no more Lost Ones, no more humans to breed here. Atlantis will rule all and, in time, the existence of the human world will become nothing but . . . well, a myth."

Frost glanced around the room, gauging the positions of the soldiers and the Perytons. The temperature in the room continued to drop as he exerted his influence. Ty'Lis had to die first. If any of his allies was able to interfere, Frost wouldn't have a chance.

"And the Legend-Born? You sent Hunters after them as well," he said.

"Naturally," Ty'Lis replied with a dismissive wave of his hand. He still did not rise from his silken chair, as though Frost presented no threat. "They are the most dangerous of all. The Bascombes are the only Legend-Born to appear in the human world for well over a century. Their rare breed have always been eradicated in the past, but it had been so long that the monarchs of our world had become lax, some even doubtful that the Legend-Born were more than myth.

"Of course, I knew better, and took their destruction upon myself. I had hoped they would be dead long before now. Their resilience has forced me to adapt."

The winter man tensed, about to *gust* across the room and freeze the air in the sorcerer's lungs. He would transform in an instant, flowing from solid to storm and then manifesting again as a sheet of ice, shearing the Atlantean's head from his neck.

Ty'Lis stroked his braided beard, the aura of dark light around him pulsing. "Pause a moment, Frost. Your friends are about to join us. The Sandman failed to kill them, but that's all right. It would have been convenient, but I planned well for that possibility."

Frost blocked out the voice, suspecting the sorcerer might use magic to sway him. But there came a blow upon the door behind him that shook its frame, and then a second. With the third the frame splintered and Frost swept aside as the thick wooden door swung open.

Oliver Bascombe stepped into the room, the Sword of Hunyadi brandished before him. Kitsune followed, copper-red fur cloak flowing around her. With them were two women inexpertly wielding swords, one of whom shared enough of his features that she could only be Oliver's sister, Collette.

"Frost," Oliver said, and his tone had no warmth.

Ty'Lis clapped again, yet still he did not rise. "Well timed. I'm rather proud of myself." Then he spread his arms wide, gesturing to the Perytons and the Atlantean soldiers alike.

"Now you may kill them."

Oliver's breath plumed in the frigid chamber. His boots slid on the icy floor but he kept his balance. On the opposite end of the sprawling room he saw the two chairs, the two men . . . and he knew at once that the chained man must be the king. In the other chair, the sorcerer Ty'Lis did not even rise, as though he meant to just sit and watch them die, a spectator at some garish Roman forum.

"Bastard," Oliver hissed.

That was the instant of his entry into the room. From there, the rest unfolded with such speed that he felt lost in a staccato blast of images and strobing motion.

Frost shouted something to him, but the words were lost in the shriek of the Perytons as the creatures spread their massive wings.

They could not fly within the confines of that room, but were no less dangerous. Heads bowed, they seemed to float across the chamber with their antlers down, ready to gore Oliver and Collette and Julianna.

The Atlantean soldiers moved in a sidelong run, trying to surround them, armed with a pair of strangely fashioned daggers, one in each hand.

A gust of icy wind blew past Oliver, so cold that it froze the moisture at the corners of his eyes and seared his left cheek. He stole a glance and saw the two leading Perytons freeze almost solid, ice cracking as they tried to free themselves. The light in their eyes extinguished as they died, and then the third charged through them and their bodies shattered into hideously frozen shards of wing and flesh.

Frost carved himself a shape out of the air. The last Peryton charged at him, antlers down.

The winter man let him come.

The Peryton's antlers punched through the ice of his torso, shattering his body. Frost screamed in pain, and a burst of white, icy mist that might have been the essence of his spirit exploded around him in a cloud. Shuddering and thrashing, his upper body stuck to the Peryton's antlers, Frost gripped the creature's head with one hand and he raised the other. His fingers lengthened to foot-long icicles and he drove them into the side of the Peryton's head with a final cry.

The Hunter fell dead on the floor of the chamber.

Oliver parried the dagger thrust of the nearest soldier, twisted, and drove his elbow into the Atlantean's gut. He spun and swung the Sword of Hunyadi and the magnificently sharp blade separated the man's head from his body with a clean, swift cut, showering greenish-black blood onto the floor, where it froze into a puddle of ice.

Across from him, a streak of copper-red darted through the air and he glimpsed Kitsune, the fox, tearing the throat out of another Atlantean.

Julianna defended herself from a soldier, but only barely. With a cry of anguish, Collette drove her stolen sword through the soldier's back, the point erupting from his chest and spattering Julianna with his blood.

They and Kitsune would have to take care of themselves for the moment.

Ty'Lis sat grinning in his chair.

On the floor, pieces of the winter man had begun to melt, but a cold wind eddied around them and some of the largest shards disintegrated into snow and began to whip up into the air.

The black light that pulsed around the sorcerer flashed once and Ty'Lis stood. He held his hands out, palms down, and like fire the bruise-black light spread, enveloping what remained of Frost. The wind died, the snowflakes frozen in place, neither falling nor drifting.

Frost might not be dead yet, but Ty'Lis was about to put an end to his legend forever.

Oliver raised the Sword of Hunyadi. Questions of his own heritage raced through his mind as he ran toward the sorcerer. He screamed as he lunged and thrust the blade at the Atlantean's chest. It shook in his grip as it pierced muscle and flesh and cracked bone.

Ty'Lis screamed and staggered back with the force of the attack. Oliver lifted his boot and kicked the sorcerer's body off of his blade, then raised the Sword of Hunyadi again. Ty'Lis fell to his knees and Oliver brought the blade down with a strength and savagery he would never have guessed he possessed. As though it were an axe, he hacked downward with it and cleaved the sorcerer's skull in two. It wedged in bone, and this time, as the corpse fell, he let the grip of the sword slip from his hands, lodged in the dead man's head.

"Oliver!" Kitsune screamed. She had taken the form of a woman again. "What have you done?"

He blinked and stepped back.

The first thing he noticed was that the black aura still surrounded the shattered fragments of the winter man. The gusting wind and the snow and the broken pieces of Frost's head were still suspended there as though frozen in time.

But the black umbilical of that sorcery did not stretch to the corpse that lay before Oliver.

It was attached to the man in the other chair, to the fingers of King Mahacuhta.

Yet even as Oliver saw this, the image of the man shimmered and the chains that had pulsed with magic vanished as though they had never been there. Instead, those same chains gleamed around the corpse that lay at Oliver's feet. Now they too faded, even as the body seemed to shift, the flesh running like hot wax.

His sword, the Sword of Hunyadi, was lodged in the cloven skull of the king.

Ty'Lis sat in the king's chair in his lush crimson robes, grinning and unharmed.

"No," Oliver whispered.

"I do so love my puppets," Ty'Lis murmured, as if to himself.

The door to the king's bedroom crashed open and more Atlantean soldiers thundered into the antechamber. Shouts came from out in the corridor and more soldiers—the king's own guard—appeared, herding into the room, angry and brutal.

Collette had already been caught, held by a pair of Atlanteans. Julianna stood in a corner, sword raised, but she had no hope as they gathered round her.

"Murder!" Ty'Lis cried, voice shrill as he leaped to his feet. "They've slain the king! Arrest them!"

Kitsune and Oliver stared at one another across the room. For a moment her eyes were full of love and sadness and regret. He saw it all, just as he saw all of those emotions drain from her. The fox-woman reached out and touched the fabric of the Veil, the air at her fingertips shimmered and opened, and she went to step through.

"Wait!" Julianna shouted. "You can't leave without us!"

Oliver called to her to stop, but Julianna clashed swords with the guard in front of her, then kept going forward. She knocked him down and let go of her blade, skirting around the fallen man even as he tried to grab her long legs. Julianna dodged the hands of two other guards and reached for Kitsune.

She could not pass through the Veil. Julianna was one of the Lost Ones. With her in tow, Kitsune would never have been able to escape.

Even so, Oliver flinched as Kitsune struck her with the back of her hand, splitting Julianna's lip and staining her own knuckles with blood.

Oliver called her name.

Julianna's name.

Kitsune sneered at him, eyes cold. She stepped through the Veil, the air shimmered and closed, and she was gone.

Oliver stood staring mutely at the place where she had been as the king's guard surrounded him. His hands flexed instinctively, but fighting now would be suicide and mean death for Collette and Julianna. They were all disarmed.

They were prisoners.

Ty'Lis strode toward Oliver, picking his way delicately around the dead guards and shattered fragments of frozen Perytons. The aura no longer surrounded him, but it pulsed now around what remained of Frost, and Oliver did not know if that sorcery was his prison or his final destruction.

"Bascombe," Ty'Lis said, glancing from Oliver to Collette, ignoring Julianna completely. He leaned in toward Oliver and his voice lowered to a whisper. "Legend-Born."

Oliver gritted his teeth and shook his head. "I don't even know what that means."

Ty'Lis blinked and glanced at him. "No? Truly? None of your myth friends ever told you?"

Unwilling to play along, Oliver looked away, staring instead at Julianna and then at Collette, trying to assure them that everything would be all right. Somehow.

"You and your sister, boy, you're half of this world and half of that. An uncommon breed, and an unwelcome one."

Collette screamed at him, "You hideous freak! What the fuck are you *talking* about?"

Ty'Lis ran his fingers over the braids of his beard. "Idiot girl. You haven't an inkling, have you?" And now he whispered so that only Oliver could hear, so that none of the soldiers, Atlantean or Yucatazcan, could make out a word.

"We made the Veil to separate the ordinary from the legendary. From time to time, couplings between Borderkind and humans have produced creatures that are *both*. You are the opposite of the Veil in every way, anathema to the magic used to create it. The stories the

Lost Ones tell say that one day a Legend-Born will tear the Veil down, reuniting the two worlds, so that at last they can all go home again."

Ty'Lis pressed his forehead to Oliver's, heat pulsing on the sorcerer's clammy skin, and stared into his eyes.

"That is why you must die. To take away any such false hope. But first, I have need of you . . ."

Again the sorcerer stepped back and gestured broadly to the king's guards.

"Put them all in chains," Ty'Lis commanded. "And I shall attend to the Borderkind. They are under arrest on charges of conspiracy and regicide. You are all witnesses to the crime. You see the Sword of Hunyadi, which was wielded by the hand of this Intruder from beyond the Veil. No other evidence is necessary. He and his companions are assassins, sent by Hunyadi himself.

"The king of Euphrasia has shattered the truce between the Two Kingdoms, and in the name of Mahacuhta, my robes stained with his blood, I swear that Yucatazca shall have her vengeance, that there will be justice.

"That there will be war."

EPILOGUE

he day after Christmas, Sara Halliwell rode up to Kitteridge with Sheriff Norris. The twenty-sixth of December had always seemed a strange day to her, simmering with the surreal. Many shops remained closed in the morning, so that a drive through Kitteridge gave the impression that the night before had brought some silent apocalypse. People slept in, recovered from the holiday, enjoyed their gifts in quiet solitude as they finished digesting the Christmas feast. Yet the holiday lights were still lit, decorations still hung. No one dared drag their tree to the curb on the day after Christmas. Not yet.

After a day of such passionate celebration, the twenty-sixth of December felt like a national day of mourning.

Fly the flags at half-mast, Sara thought as she gazed out the window of the sheriff's car at the stillness of the day. *Santa's dead and gone.*

By the time Sheriff Norris turned the car onto Rose Ridge Lane, tears made thin tracks down her cheeks. She wiped them away as he pulled into the long driveway of the Bascombe house. This was Sara's first glimpse of the place and it astonished her. They passed a carriage house, a lovely little cottage larger than the house she'd grown up in, and then the car rolled to a halt in the shadow of what could only be called a mansion. The house itself was painted a light rose and it would have been a thing of beauty if not for the sheer emptiness of it. Like the twenty-sixth of December, the Bascombe house was a monument to what it had lost.

"I shouldn't be doing this," Jackson Norris said.

Again, Sara wiped her eyes. "I really appreciate it."

"It's just—" he began, but faltered when he turned to her and saw that she'd been crying.

The sheriff hesitated, then he killed the engine and plucked his keys from the ignition, choosing not to comment on her tears. Sara felt absurdly grateful.

"I don't know what you expect to find here," he said.

Sara tucked her hair behind her ears as she bent to look out through the windshield at the magnificent façade of the house. The place looked almost magical, like something out of a storybook.

"I just need to see it."

Jackson Norris stared at her for another long moment, then nodded and climbed out of the car. Sara got out and closed her door with a soft click, staring at the house even as she followed the sheriff up the walk to the front door.

"The caretaker, or whatever he is, has gone to visit relatives over the holiday," the sheriff said as he fished out the key he had acquired as part of his investigation. "The guy said he'd be back, but I doubt it. After a little time away, he's gonna realize he's got nothing to come back to."

He unlocked the door and swung it open, then stepped in and glanced around as though worried there might be someone there after all. Or maybe that was just what you did in a house where people had vanished without a trace, and where an unsolved murder had taken place.

Sheriff Norris did not wipe his boots on the mat. He stepped inside and out of the way to let Sara enter. She paused inside the grand foyer to wipe her shoes. As she did, the grandfather clock against the wall to her left began to chime twelve. It was exactly noon.

The sheriff watched her curiously as she started to move through the house. She had promised she would not touch anything, so she kept her hands in her pockets. Though what more the police could learn here, she had no idea. The investigation was not closed, but surely they had finished in the house.

Then again, she was no cop. What did she know?

From room to room she moved, examining the furniture and the paintings on the walls as though she were a thief in the night, or visiting a museum.

How could Jackson Norris possibly understand? Her father had been investigating a mystery and now had become a part of that mystery. She had lost him, somehow, and even more than the fear that they would never talk again, that she would never be able to relinquish all of the love and anger and hurt in her, and never get the embrace that she had always wanted and never dared to hope for . . . more than that was the fear that she would never know the truth of what had happened to him.

Sara Halliwell was no detective. She could not even begin to imagine what had become of her father, or to hunt for him. Lots of people were already busy doing just that.

But she had to see this place, because this was where it had all begun.

The Bascombe house was the heart of this mystery.

Now, as she walked from room to room, she could almost feel it. There was an elegance to the rooms, but they also had an ethereal quality to them. Something terrible had happened here, but something incredible as well. How did people simply vanish?

As she passed through a sitting room with a fireplace, she saw several framed photographs on the mantel. They were old pictures, including a wedding portrait and several of the family together. Though he was much younger in the photos, she recognized the late Max Bascombe in the wedding photograph right away.

His wife had been beautiful in her white dress, like the snow queen in a fairy tale.

The other photographs were of Mrs. Bascombe with her children, laughing and innocent. They had grown up, those children. Their mother had died when they were young and now their father had been taken from them as well. But what had become of Oliver and Collette Bascombe?

Where are you? Sara thought, staring at the photograph of the two children with their mother.

Fingers on the mantel to steady herself, she closed her eyes. *Where are you, Daddy?*

In the eastern region of Euphrasia, in the crèche created by the meeting of three mountains, near the entrance to a sprawling pagoda sculpted entirely of sand, a light breeze rose. It stirred and eddied, entirely independent of the winds that swept down from the mountain peaks.

The breeze spun in circles, a small dust devil centered around the scoured bones of Ted Halliwell and the sand and grit that had once constituted two distinct figures, brothers, facets of the same legend. The sand shifted, sculpted now by the wind, and identity became blurred. What had once been the Sandman and what had once been the Dustman could no longer be separated. The sand rose, a little whirlwind, and merged.

Then the bones began to rise as well.

Slowly, grain by grain, the sand and dust and grit touched bone and stuck, gathering gradually around the skeleton. A new figure began to take shape, neither Dustman nor Sandman. It looked a great deal like a dead man named Ted Halliwell and contained within it his thoughts and emotions, his very spirit. But it was only sand, and there were other spirits contained there as well.

One of them a monster.

ABOUT THE AUTHOR

CHRISTOPHER GOLDEN is the award-winning, bestselling author of such novels as *The Myth Hunters, Wildwood Road, The Boys Are Back in Town, The Ferryman, Strangewood, Of Saints and Shadows,* and the *Body of Evidence* series of teen thrillers. Working with actress/writer/director Amber Benson, he co-created and co-wrote *Ghosts of Albion,* an animated supernatural drama for BBC online, from which they created the book series of the same name (www.ghostsofalbion.net).

With Thomas E. Sniegoski, he is the co-author of the dark fantasy series *The Menagerie* as well as the young-readers' fantasy series *Out-Cast* and the comic book miniseries *Talent,* both of which were recently acquired by Universal Pictures.

Golden was born and raised in Massachusetts, where he still lives with his family. He graduated from Tufts University. He has recently completed a lavishly illustrated gothic novel entitled *Baltimore, or, the Steadfast Tin Soldier and the Vampire,* a collaboration with Hellboy creator Mike Mignola. There are more than eight million copies of his books in print. Please visit him at www.christophergolden.com.

And be sure not to miss one of the season's most special titles:

BALTIMORE
or, The Steadfast Tin Soldier and the Vampire

by

Mike Mignola and Christopher Golden

Featuring 150 black-and-white illustrations by Mike Mignola

Renowned comic artist and *Hellboy* creator Mike Mignola teams up with Bram Stoker Award–winning author Christopher Golden in this illustrated novel that is a feast for the eyes and the imagination.

"On a cold autumn night, under a black sky leached of starlight and absent the moon, Captain Henry Baltimore clutches his rifle and stares across the dark abyss of the battlefield, and knows in his heart that these are the torture fields of Hell, and damnation awaits mere steps ahead. . . ."

Rich in haunting prose and lush with fantastical drawings, this stunning collaboration pushes the boundaries of contemporary fiction to carve its own niche. Gorgeously produced in an oversize keepsake edition, it is a dazzling visual and literary experience, perfect as a gift or a collectible for fans of fantasy and graphic novels alike.

"The lush, labyrinthine *Baltimore* evokes the best from two of our most gifted artists. Christopher Golden and Mike Mignola have created a book that will be enjoyed and admired for decades to come." —Peter Straub

On sale August 28, 2007